IN THE
SHADOW OF
SHERLOCK
HOLMES

In the Shadow of Sherlock Holmes

CLASSIC DETECTIVE FICTION 1862–1910

Edited with Introductions and Notes by

LESLIE S. KLINGER

Illustrated by

MICHAEL MANOMIVIBUL

SAN DIEGO
2011

To Sir Arthur Conan Doyle:

Steel true, blade straight.

Book Design by Jeff Conner • Assistant Design by Robbie Robbins • Text Font: Adobe Caslon

Thanks to Sharon, who will always be "the woman." – Leslie S. Klinger

ISBN: 978-1-61377-113-6   14 13 12 11   1 2 3 4

Ted Adams, CEO & Publisher
Greg Goldstein, Chief Operating Officer
Robbie Robbins, EVP/Sr. Graphic Artist
Chris Ryall, Chief Creative Officer/Editor-in-Chief
Matthew Ruzicka, CPA, Chief Financial Officer
Alan Payne, VP of Sales

Become our fan on Facebook **facebook.com/idwpublishing**
Follow us on Twitter **@idwpublishing**
Check us out on YouTube **youtube.com/idwpublishing**
www.IDWPUBLISHING.com

"The mystery is still a mystery…"

Dick Donovan,
"The Problem of Deadwood Hall"

CONTENTS

ILLUSTRATIONS

INTRODUCTION

Leslie S. Klinger

D R. JOHN H. WATSON remarked about Sherlock Holmes's fascination with the adventuress Irene Adler, "In his eyes she eclipses and predominates the whole of her sex." Of course the same might be said of Holmes and the public's view of him relative to the other detectives of the era.

In the second half of the nineteenth century, the period from which many of the stories in this volume are drawn, the very concept of the detective was new to the reading public. Short for "detective-police," a phrase appearing in *Chambers' Journal* in 1843, the detective force was a special branch of the police, "intelligent men," in the words of the *Journal*, who attired themselves in the dress of ordinary men. Of course, the police themselves were also a relatively new force, having sprung into being in 1829 under the direction of Sir Robert Peel. Not surprisingly, stories of detection did not flourish until the nineteenth century, with the rise of the professional criminal investigator. The first great writer of tales of criminal detection was the Frenchman Eugène Vidocq (1775–1857), whose memoirs and novels found a ready audience. Vidocq, a reformed criminal, was appointed in 1813 to be the first head of the Sûreté Nationale, the outgrowth of an informal detective force created by Vidocq and adopted by Napoleon as a supplement to the police. His memoirs recounted his adventures in the detection and capture of criminals, often involving disguises and wild flights. Later books told of his criminal career, and sensational novels published under his name (probably written by others) capitalized on his reputation as a bold detective.

While Vidocq's stories captivated the public, they were hardly original tales of detective fiction. The first great purveyor of fictional stories about a detective was Edgar Allan Poe (1809–1849), whose Chevalier Auguste Dupin set the standard for a generation to come. The cerebral Dupin first appeared in Poe's short story "Murders in the Rue Morgue" (1841). At the same time, Poe introduced another staple of detective fiction, the partner and chronicler (nameless in Poe's tales) who is less intelligent than the detective but serves as a sounding-board for the detective's brilliant deductions. In each of the three Dupin stories (the other two are "The Mystery of Marie Rogêt" [1842] and "The Purloined Letter" [1844]), the detective outwits the police and shows them to be ineffective crime-fighters and problem-solvers. Yet Poe apparently lost interest in the notion, and his detective "series" ended in 1844.

Another Frenchman, Emile Gaboriau, created the detective known as Monsieur Lecoq, drawing heavily on Vidocq as his model. First appearing in *L'Affaire Lerouge* (1866), Lecoq was a minor police detective who rose to fame in six cases, appearing between 1866 and 1880. Although Sherlock Holmes describes Lecoq as a "miserable bungler," Gaboriau's works were immensely popular, and Fergus Hume, English author of the best-selling detective novel of the nineteenth century, *The Mystery of a Hansom Cab* (1886), which sold over 500,000 copies worldwide, explained that Gaboriau's financial success inspired his own work.

In England, criminals and detectives peopled Charles Dickens's tales as well. While not widely regarded as an author of detective fiction, Dickens created Inspector Bucket, the first significant detective in English literature. When Bucket appeared in *Bleak House* (1852–1853), he became the prototype of the official representative of the police department: honest, diligent, stolid, and confident, albeit not very colorful, dramatic, or exciting. Wilkie Collins, author of two of the greatest novels of suspense of the nineteenth century, *The Woman in White* (1860) and *The Moonstone* (1868), contributed a similar character, Sergeant Cuff, who appears in *The Moonstone*. Cuff is known as the finest police detective in England, who solves his cases with perseverance and energy, rather than genius. Sadly, after *The Moonstone*, he is not heard from again. In each case, however, the detective is too late to help any of the affected persons.

Another important but often overlooked part of the stream of detective fiction is the dime novel or "penny dreadful," as it was known in England. These serials started in the 1830s, originally as a cheaper alternative to mainstream fictional part-works, such as those by Charles Dickens (which cost a shilling), for working-class adults. By the 1850s the serial stories were aimed exclusively at teenagers. Although many of the stories were reprints or rewrites of Gothic thrillers, some were stories about famous criminals, such as Sweeney Todd and Spring-Heeled Jack, or had lurid titles like "The boy detective; or, The crimes of London" (1866), "The dance of death; or, The hangman's plot. A thrilling romance of two cities." (1866; written by Brownlow, "Detective," and Tuevoleur, "Sergeant of the French Police"), or a series like "Lives of the most notorious highwaymen, footpads and murderers" (1836–1837). Highwaymen were popular heroes. *Black Bess or the Knight of the Road*, outlining the largely imaginary exploits of real-life highwayman Dick Turpin, continued for 254 episodes. As crime literature became popular, so did the detective story. Early popular American titles include *The*

Old Sleuth and *Butts the Boy Detective*, and of course countless Sexton Blake and Nick Carter stories.

Despite the rise of science and invention in the first three-quarters of the nineteenth century, they had little role to play in the detection or prevention of crime. In 1860, the press was filled with reports of the so-called Rode Hill House murder, and the English reading public was electrified by the efforts of the "detectives." However, as the reports make clear, the detective force of Scotland Yard relied largely on the practical training of detectives in criminal methods and techniques, personal recognition of criminals, and apprehension of criminals in the act of committing the crime. "Bertillonage," the French system of anthropometry, which would later prove so useful in bringing criminals to justice, was not adopted in England until 1883; and although Francis Galton and others had recognized the usefulness of fingerprinting much earlier, it was not a serious aid in the apprehension of criminals until the twentieth century, primarily because of the lack of a central database of criminals' prints.

It was in this context, then, that Arthur Conan Doyle formed his belief in his own ability.

> I felt now that I was capable of something fresher and crisper and more workmanlike. Gaboriau had rather attracted me by the neat dovetailing of his plots, and Poe's masterful detective, M. Dupin, had from boyhood been one of my heroes. But could I bring an addition of my own? I thought of my old teacher Joe Bell, of his eagle face, of his curious ways, of his eerie trick of spotting details. If he were a detective he would surely reduce this fascinating but unorganized business to something nearer to an exact science.

Conan Doyle's timing was excellent. Although his first two Holmes efforts, the short novels *A Study in Scarlet* (1887) and *The Sign of Four* (1889), later proved popular, it was the *magazine* readership of England that provided his ticket to success. In the late spring of 1891, he submitted "over the transom" of the newly formed *Strand Magazine* the first two of some short stories he had conceived about Holmes and Watson. Greenough Smith, the editor of the *Strand*, recollected the day some forty years later: "I at once realized that here was the greatest short-story writer since Edgar Allan Poe. I remember rushing into [the publisher] Mr. Newnes's room and thrusting the stories before his eyes.... Here was a new and gifted story-writer; there was no mistaking the ingenuity of the plot, the limpid clearness of the style, the perfect art of telling a story." The stories, "A Scandal in Bohemia" and "The Red-Headed League," appeared in the July and August issues, respectively, and the success of both Conan Doyle and the *Strand Magazine* was made. Over the succeeding thirty-six years, fifty-six more stories and novellas would appear, including what is regarded by many as the greatest mystery tale of the twentieth century—*The Hound of the Baskervilles*. But in 1893, Conan Doyle abruptly ceased penning tales of Sherlock Holmes and announced to the world that Holmes had died, at the hands of his archenemy Professor James Moriarty.

The success of the Holmes stories and the intense demand of the reading public for detectives and detective fiction was the result of several factors. By the time of Queen Victoria, the tradition of English roguery, which populated the drama in the early seventeenth century, turned into new forms. Frank W. Chandler, in his sweeping study *The Literature of Roguery* (1907), viewed the tradition as cooperating to create the novel in the eighteenth century and the detective story in the nineteenth century. This literature served as a vehicle for satire, revealed the manners and life of the underworld, contributed to an understanding of character, and furthered a study of social conditions with a view toward social improvement. Above all, it entertained.

The time of Sherlock Holmes was a time of great change in the world. As Victoria's reign ended and Edward's began, the world stood poised on the brink of war, and industrial and social revolutions altered Western society irrevocably. By the late nineteenth century, thirty percent of the population of London lived in poverty. Though recorded crime diminished and the prison population was proportionally much smaller than in mid-century, the first ten years of the twentieth century had the highest murder rate of any decade before 1970. Disturbance was persistent, in the form of nationalism, anarchism, feminism, and labor agitation.

Detective fiction offered palliative stories of the triumph of reason and order. As Joseph A. Kestner pointed out (in *The Edwardian Detective, 1901–1915*), detective literature "deals with disturbance and destabilization as much as crime *per se*." Ernst Kaemmel (1983) argued that Holmes was "a representative of law, justice, and capitalist order." His readers were interested because they identified themselves with Holmes and "expect[ed] the violated order to be reconstituted in a suspenseful story." The detective narrative reasserted stability through closure—a satisfying ending in which the criminal is caught and justice is served.

Between 1893 and 1901, when *The Hound of the Baskervilles*, a reminiscence of the departed Holmes, appeared, the hunger for new tales of Holmes grew. In the words of Conan Doyle's brother-in-law, E. W. Hornung (himself the author of the brilliant tales of gentleman-thief Raffles), they mourned, "There's no p'lice like Holmes." New writers and detectives rose to the challenge. They found an audience, and while none achieved the popularity of the Great Detective, detection by gaslight was evidently in good hands. Holmes himself returned in a series of short stories beginning in 1903 (some readers grumbled that Holmes wasn't the man he was before he met his nemesis), but by then, the publishers were happy to serve up a broad menu of detective fiction, as is illustrated in this volume. At last, those who had been in the shadow of Sherlock Holmes stepped into the spotlight. While many are forgotten today, their stories are as fresh, interesting, and evocative as the enduring tales recorded by John H. Watson. Come—the game is afoot!

❧

In the Shadow of Sherlock Holmes

Thomas Bailey Aldrich

THOMAS BAILEY ALDRICH (1836-1907) was an American poet, travel writer, editor, and novelist; he was born in New Hampshire but raised in New Orleans. Upon the death of his father when Aldrich was sixteen, he took up journalism. In 1865, he returned to New England and served as the editor of several important magazines, including the *Atlantic Monthly* for nine years. His poetry was well known, and he also wrote numerous short stories and novels.

The following is an excerpt from his *avant garde* novel titled *Out of His Head* (1862). Ellery Queen, in his *Queen's Quorum*, pointed out that while the story revealed Aldrich's debt to Edgar Allan Poe, here he created the first American variation of Poe's *locked room*, first depicted in *The Murders in the Rue Morgue*. Not only is Aldrich's detective eccentric, he is mad; furthermore, the central rôle of the narrator anticipates the startling device used by Agatha Christie in *The Murder of Roger Ackroyd* (1926).

THE DANSEUSE

THOMAS BAILEY ALDRICH

CHAPTER XI
The Danseuse

THE ENSUING SUMMER I returned North depressed by the result of my sojourn in New Orleans. It was only by devoting myself, body and soul, to some intricate pursuit that I could dispel the gloom which threatened to seriously affect my health.

The MOON-APPARATUS[1] was insufficient to distract me. I turned my attention to mechanism, and was successful in producing several wonderful pieces of work, among which may be mentioned a brass butterfly, made to flit so naturally in the air as to deceive the most acute observers. The motion of the toy, the soft down and gorgeous damask-stains on the pinions, were declared quite perfect. The thing is rusty and won't work now; I tried to set it going for Dr. Pendegrast, the other day.

A manikin musician, playing a few exquisite airs on a miniature piano, likewise excited much admiration. This figure bore such an absurd, unintentional resemblance to a gentleman who has since distinguished himself as a pianist, that I presented the trifle to a lady admirer of Gottschalk.[2]

I also became a taxidermist, and stuffed a pet bird with springs and diminutive flutes, causing it to hop and carol, in its cage, with great glee. But my master-piece was a nimble white mouse, with pink eyes, that could scamper up the walls, and masticate bits of cheese in an extraordinary style. My chamber-maid shrieked, and jumped up on a chair, whenever I let the little fellow loose in her presence. One day, unhappily, the mouse, while nosing around after its favorite aliment,[3] got snapt in a rat-trap that yawned in the closet, and I was never able to readjust the machinery.

Engaged in these useful inventions—

---

[1] A strange device mentioned earlier in the novel, irrelevant to this episode.
[2] Louis Moreau Gottschalk (1829-1869) was a celebrated American composer-pianist of the day.
[3] Food, sustenance.

useful, because no exercise of the human mind is ever in vain—my existence for two or three years was so placid and uneventful, I began to hope that the shadows which had followed on my path from childhood, making me unlike other men, had returned to that unknown world where they properly belong; but the Fates were only taking breath to work out more surely the problem of my destiny. I must keep nothing back. I must extenuate nothing.

I am about to lift the veil of mystery which, for nearly seven years, has shrouded the story of Mary Ware; and though I lay bare my own weakness, or folly, or what you will, I do not shrink from the unveiling. No hand but mine can now perform the task. There was, indeed, a man who might have done this better than I. But he went his way in silence. I like a man who can hold his tongue.

On the corner of Clarke and Crandall streets, in New York, stands a dingy brown frame-house. It is a very old house, as its obsolete style of structure would tell you. It has a morose, unhappy look, though once it must have been a blithe mansion. I think that houses, like human beings, ultimately become dejected or cheerful, according to their experience. The very air of some front-doors tells their history.

This house, I repeat, has a morose, unhappy look, at present, and is tenanted by an incalculable number of Irish families, while a picturesque junk-shop is in full blast in the basement; but at the time of which I write, it was a second-rate boarding-place, of the more respectable sort, and rather largely patronized by poor, but honest, literary men, tragic-actors, members of the chorus, and such like gilt people.[4]

My apartments on Crandall Street were opposite this building, to which my attention was directed soon after taking possession of the rooms, by the discovery of the following facts:

First, that a charming lady lodged on the second-floor front, and sang like a canary every morning.

Second, that her name was Mary Ware.

Third, that Mary Ware was a danseuse,[5] and had two lovers—only two.

Fourth, that Mary Ware and the page, who, years before, had drawn Howland and myself into that fatal masquerade, were the same person.

This last discovery moved me strangely, aside from the fact that her presence opened an old wound. The power which guides all the actions of my life constrained me to watch this woman.

Mary Ware was the leading-lady at The Olympic.[6] Night after night found me in the parquette.[7] I can think of nothing with which to compare the airiness and utter abandon of her dancing. She seemed a part of the music. She was one of beauty's best thoughts, then. Her glossy gold hair reached down to her waist, shading one of those mobile faces which remind you of Guido's picture of Beatrix Cenci[8]—there was something so fresh and enchanting in the mouth. Her luminous,

---

[4] Perhaps this means superficially attractive or glamorous people (as in "covered in gilt").

[5] A female ballet dancer.

[6] The Olympic Theatre, at 622 Broadway, was torn down in 1880.

[7] Seating on the main floor of the theater, farther from the stage than the orchestra section.

[8] Beatrice Cenci (1577-1599) was an Italian noblewoman; her portrait is attributed to Guido Reni (1575-1642), an Italian painter of the Mannerist school.

almond eyes, looking out winningly from under their drooping fringes, were at once the delight and misery of young men.

Ah! You were distracting in your nights of triumph, when the bouquets nestled about your elastic ankles, and the kissing of your castanets made the pulses leap; but I remember when you lay on your cheerless bed, in the blank daylight, with the glory faded from your brow, and "none so poor as to do you reverence."[9]

Then I stooped down and kissed you—but not till then.

Mary Ware was to me a finer study than her lovers. She had two, as I have said. One of them was commonplace enough—well-made, well-dressed, shallow, flaccid. Nature, when she gets out of patience with her best works, throws off such things by the gross, instead of swearing. He was a lieutenant, in the navy I think. The gilt button has charms to soothe the savage breast.

The other was a man of different mold, and interested me in a manner for which I could not then account. The first time I saw him did not seem like the first time. But this, perhaps, is an after-impression.

Every line of his countenance denoted character; a certain capability, I mean, but whether for good or evil was not so plain. I should have called him handsome, but for a noticeable scar which ran at right angles across his mouth, giving him a sardonic expression when he smiled.

His frame might have set an anatomist wild with delight—six feet two, deep-chested, knitted with tendons of steel. Not at all a fellow to amble on plush carpets.

"Some day," thought I, as I saw him stride by the house, "he will throw the little Lieutenant out of that second-story window."

I cannot tell, to this hour, which of those two men Mary Ware loved most—for I think she loved them both. A woman's heart was the insolvable charade with which the Sphinx nipped the Egyptians. I was never good at puzzles.

The flirtation, however, was food enough for the whole neighborhood. But faintly did the gossips dream of the strange drama that was being shaped out, as compactly as a tragedy of Sophocles, under their noses.

They were very industrious in tearing Mary Ware's good name to pieces. Some laughed at the gay Lieutenant, and some at Julius Kenneth; but they all amiably united in condemning Mary Ware.

This, possibly, was strictly proper, for Mary Ware was a woman: the woman is always to blame in such cases; the man is hereditarily and constitutionally in the right; the woman is born in the wrong. That is the world's verdict, that is what Justice says; but we should weigh the opinion of Justice with care, since she is represented, by poets and sculptors, not satirically, I trust, as a blind Woman.

It was so from the beginning. Was not the first lady of the world[10] the cause of all our woe? I feel safe in leaving it to a jury of gentle dames. But from all such judges, had I a sister on trial good Lord deliver her.

This state of affairs had continued for five or six months, when it was reported that Julius Kenneth and Mary Ware were affianced. The Lieutenant was less frequently

---

[9] A paraphrase of a remark by Antony about Caesar in Shakespeare's *Julius Caesar*, Act III, Sc. 2, line 1663 ("and none so poor to do him reverence").

[10] Eve, that is.

seen in Crandall Street, and Julius waited upon Mary's footsteps with the fidelity of a shadow.

Mrs. Grundy[11] was somewhat appeased.

Yet—though Mary went to the Sunday concerts with Julius Kenneth, she still wore the Lieutenant's roses in her bosom.

Mrs. Grundy said that.

CHAPTER XII
A Mystery

ONE DRIZZLY NOVEMBER morning—how well I remember it!—I was awakened by a series of nervous raps on my bedroom door. The noise startled me from an unpleasant dream.

"O, sir!" cried the chamber-maid on the landing, "There's been a dreadful time across the street. They've gone and killed Mary Ware!"

"Ah!"

That was all I could say. Cold drops of perspiration stood on my forehead.

I looked at my watch; it was eleven o'clock; I had over-slept myself, having sat up late the previous night.

I dressed hastily, and, without waiting for breakfast, pushed my way through the murky crowd that had collected in front of the house opposite, and passed up stairs, unquestioned.

When I entered the room, there were six people present: a thick-set gentleman, in black, with a bland professional air, a physician; two policemen; Adelaide Woods, an actress; Mrs. Marston, the landlady; and Julius Kenneth.

In the center of the chamber, on the bed, lay the body of Mary Ware—as pale as Seneca's wife.[12]

I shall never forget it. The corse[13] haunted me for years afterwards, the dark streaks under the eyes, and the wavy hair streaming over the pillow—the dead gold hair. I stood by her for a moment, and turned down the counterpane, which was drawn up closely to the chin.

> "There was that across her throat
> Which you had hardly cared to see."[14]

At the head of the bed sat Julius Kenneth, bending over the icy hand which he held in his own. He was kissing it.

The gentleman in black was conversing in undertones with Mrs. Marston, who every now and then glanced furtively toward Mary Ware. The two policemen were examining the doors, closets and windows of the apartment with, obviously, little success.

There was no fire in the air-tight stove, but the place was suffocatingly close. I opened a window, and leaned against the casement to get a breath of fresh air.

The physician approached me. I muttered something to him indistinctly, for I was partly sick with the peculiar moldy smell that pervaded the room.

---

[11] Figuratively, a very conventional person, who first appeared in Thomas Morton's 1798 play "Speed the Plough."

[12] Seneca, a Roman philosopher and orator, was forced to commit suicide to escape the tyranny of Nero. Seneca's wife, Pompeia Paulina, attempted to do the same, but in order to save his reputation, Nero forced her to survive. Legend has it that she had a very pale face after the suicide attempt (having slit her wrists), and her demeanor became proverbial.

[13] Corpse.

[14] A paraphrase of Alfred Tennyson's "Lady Clara Vere de Vere" (1842), "There was that across his throat, which you had hardly cared to see."

"Yes," he began, scrutinizing me, "the affair looks very perplexing, as you remark. Professional man, sir? No? Bless me!—beg pardon. Never in my life saw anything that looked so exceedingly like nothing. Thought, at first, 'twas a clear case of suicide—door locked, key on the inside, place undisturbed; but then we find no instrument with which the subject could have inflicted that wound on the neck. Queer. Party must have escaped up chimney. But how? Don't know. The windows are at least thirty feet from the ground. It would be impossible for a person to jump that far, even if he could clear the iron railing below. Which he couldn't. Disagreeable things to jump on, those spikes, sir. Must have been done with a sharp knife. Queer, very. Party meant to make sure work of it. The carotid neatly severed, upon my word."

The medical gentleman went on in this monologic style for fifteen minutes, during which time Kenneth did not raise his lips from Mary's fingers.

Approaching the bed, I spoke to him; but he only shook his head in reply.

I understood his grief.

After regaining my chamber, I sat listlessly for three or four hours, gazing into the grate. The twilight flitted in from the street; but I did not heed it. A face among the coals fascinated me. It came and went and came. Now I saw a cavern hung with lurid stalactites; now a small Vesuvius vomiting smoke and flame; now a bridge spanning some tar - tarean gulf; then these crumbled, each in its turn, and from out the heated fragments peered the one inevitable face.

THE *EVENING MIRROR*, of that day, gave the following detailed report of the inquest:

"This morning, at eight o'clock, Mary Ware, the celebrated danseuse, was found dead in her chamber, at her late residence on the corner of Clarke and Crandall streets. The perfect order of the room, and the fact that the door was locked on the inside, have induced many to believe that the poor girl was the victim of her own rashness. But we cannot think so. That the door was fastened on the inner side, proves nothing except, indeed, that the murderer was hidden in the apartment. That the room gave no evidence of a struggle having taken place, is also an insignificant point. Two men, or even one, grappling suddenly with the deceased, who was a slight woman, would have prevented any great resistance. The deceased was dressed in a ballet-costume, and was, as we conjecture, murdered directly after her return from the theatre. On a chair near the bed, lay several fresh bouquets, and a water-proof cloak which she was in the habit of wearing over her dancing-dress, on coming home from the theatre at night. No weapon whatever was found on the premises. We give below all the material testimony elicited by the coroner. It explains little.

"*Josephine Marston* deposes: I keep a boarding house at No. 131 Crandall Street. Miss Ware has boarded with me for the past two years. Has always borne a good character as far as I know. I do not think she had many visitors; certainly no male visitors, excepting a Lieutenant King, and Mr. Kenneth to whom she was engaged. I do not know when King was last at the house; not within three days, I am confident. Deceased told me that he had gone away. I did not see her last night when she came home. The hall-door is never locked; each of the boarders has a latchkey. The last time I saw Miss Ware was just before she went to the theatre, when she asked me to call her at eight o'clock (this morning) as she had promised to walk with 'Jules,' meaning Mr. Kenneth. I knocked at the door nine or ten times, but received no answer. Then I grew frightened and called one of the lady boarders, Miss Woods, who helped me to force the lock. The key fell on the floor inside as we pushed against the door. Mary Ware was lying on the bed, dressed. Some matches were scattered under the gas-burner by the bureau. The room presented the same appearance it does now.

"*Adelaide Woods* deposes: I am an actress by profession. I occupy the room next to that of the deceased. Have known her twelve months. It was half-past eleven when she came home; she stopped in my chamber for perhaps three-quarters of an hour. The call-boy[15] of The Olympic usually accompanies her home from the theatre when she is alone. I let her in. Deceased had misplaced her night-key. The partition between our rooms is of brick; but I do not sleep soundly, and should have heard any unusual noise. Two weeks ago, Miss Ware told me she was to be married to Mr. Kenneth in January next. The last time I saw them together was the day before yesterday. I assisted Mrs. Marston in breaking open the door. [Describes the position of the body, etc., etc.]

"Here the call-boy was summoned, and testified to accompanying the deceased home the night before. He came as far as the steps with her. The door was opened by a woman; could not swear it was Miss Woods, though he knows her by sight. The night was dark, and there was no lamp burning in the entry .

"*Julius Kenneth* deposes: I am a master-machinist. Reside at No.— Forsythe Street.

Miss Ware was my cousin. We were engaged to be married next— [Here the witness' voice failed him.] The last time I saw her was on Wednesday morning, on which occasion we walked out together. I did not leave my room last evening: was confined by a severe cold. A Lieutenant King used to visit my cousin frequently; it created considerable talk in the neighborhood: I did not like it, and requested her to break the acquaintance. She informed me, Wednesday, that King had been ordered to some foreign station, and would trouble me no more. Was excited at the time, hinted at being tired of living; then laughed, and was gayer than she had been for weeks. Deceased was subject to fits of depression. She had engaged to walk with me this morning at eight. When I reached Clark Street I learned that she— [Here the witness, overcome by emotion, was allowed to retire.]

"*Dr. Wren* deposes: [This gentleman was very learned and voluble, and had to be suppressed several times by the coroner. We furnish a brief synopsis of his testimony.] I was called in to view the body of the deceased. A deep incision on the throat, two inches below the left ear, severing the left common carotid and the internal jugular vein, had been inflicted with some sharp instrument. Such a wound would, in my opinion, produce death almost instantaneously. The body bore no other signs of violence. A slight mark, almost indistinguishable, in fact, extended from the upper lip toward the right nostril—some hurt, I suppose, received in infancy. Deceased must have been dead a number of hours, the rigor mortis having already supervened, etc., etc.

"*Dr. Ceccarini* corroborated the above testimony.

---

[15] A boy who summons the actors when their presence on stage is called for.

"The night-watchman and seven other persons were then placed on the stand; but their statements threw no fresh light on the case.

"The situation of Julius Kenneth, the lover of the ill-fated girl, draws forth the deepest commiseration. Miss Ware was twenty-four years of age.

"Who the criminal is, and what could have led to the perpetration of the cruel act, are questions which, at present, threaten to baffle the sagacity of the police. If such deeds can be committed with impunity in a crowded city, like this, who is safe from the assassin's steel?"

CHAPTER XIII
Thou Art The Man

I COULD BUT smile on reading all this serious nonsense.

After breakfast, the next morning, I made my toilet with extreme care and presented myself at the sheriff's office.

Two gentlemen who were sitting at a table, busy with papers, started nervously to their feet, as I announced myself. I bowed very calmly to the sheriff, and said,

"I am the person who murdered Mary Ware!"

Of course I was instantly arrested; and that Evening, in jail, I had the equivocal pleasure of reading these paragraphs among the police items of the *Mirror*:

"The individual who murdered the ballet-girl, in the night of the third inst., in a house on Crandall Street, surrendered himself to the sheriff this forenoon.

"He gave his name as Paul Lynde, and resides opposite the place where the tragedy was enacted. He is a man of medium stature, has restless gray eyes, chestnut hair, and a supernaturally pale countenance. He seems a person of excellent address, is said to be wealthy, and nearly connected with an influential New England family. Notwithstanding his gentlemanly manner, there is that about him which would lead one to select him from out a thousand, as a man of cool and desperate character.

"Mr. Lynde's voluntary surrender is not the least astonishing feature of this affair; for, had he preserved silence he would, beyond a doubt, have escaped even suspicion. The murder was planned and executed with such deliberate skill, that there is little or no evidence to complicate him. In truth, there is *no* evidence against him, excepting his own confession, which is meager and confusing enough. He freely acknowledges the crime, but stubbornly refuses to enter into any details. He expresses a desire to be hanged immediately!!

"How Mr. Lynde entered the chamber, and by what means he left it, after committing the deed, and why he cruelly killed a lady with whom he had had (as we gather from the testimony,) no previous acquaintance—are enigmas which still perplex the public mind, and will not let curiosity sleep. These facts, however, will probably be brought to light during the impending trial. In the meantime, we await the denouement with interest."

CHAPTER XIV
Paul's Confession

ON THE AFTERNOON following this disclosure, the door of my cell turned on its hinges, and Julius Kenneth entered.

In *his* presence I ought to have trembled;

but I was calm and collected. He, feverish and dangerous.

"You received my note?"

"Yes; and have come here, as you requested."

I waved him to a chair, which he refused to take. Stood leaning on the back of it.

"You of course know, Mr. Kenneth, that I have refused to reveal the circumstances connected with the death of Mary Ware? I wished to make the confession to you alone."

He regarded me for a moment from beneath his shaggy eyebrows.

"Well?"

"But even to you I will assign no reason for the course I pursued. It was necessary that Mary Ware should die."

"Well?"

"I decided that she should die in her chamber, and to that end I purloined her night-key." Julius Kenneth looked through and through me, as I spoke.

"On Friday night after she had gone to the theatre, I entered the hall-door by means of the key, and stole unobserved to her room, where I secreted myself under the bed, or, in that small clothes-press near the stove—I forget which. Sometime between eleven and twelve o'clock, Mary Ware returned. While she was in the act of lighting the gas, I pressed a handkerchief, saturated with chloroform, over her mouth. You know the effect of chloroform? I will, at this point spare you further detail, merely remarking that I threw my gloves and the handkerchief in the stove; but I'm afraid there was not fire enough to consume them."

Kenneth walked up and down the cell greatly agitated; then seated himself on the foot of the bed

"Curse you!"

"Are you listening to me, Mr. Kenneth?"

"Yes!"

"I extinguished the light, and proceeded to make my escape from the room, which I did in a manner so simple that the detectives, through their desire to ferret out wonderful things, will never discover it, unless, indeed, *you* betray me. The night, you will recollect, was foggy; it was impossible to discern an object at four yards distance—this was fortunate for me. I raised the window-sash and let myself out cautiously, holding on by the sill, until my feet touched on the molding which caps the window below. I then drew down the sash. By standing on the extreme left of the cornice, I was able to reach the tin water-spout of the adjacent building, and by that I descended to the sidewalk."

The man glowered at me like a tiger, his eyes green and golden with excitement. I have since wondered that he did not tear me to pieces.

"On gaining the street," I continued coolly, "I found that I had brought the knife with me. It should have been left in the chamber—it would have given the whole thing the aspect of suicide. It was too late to repair the blunder, so I threw the knife—"

"Into the river!" exclaimed Kenneth, involuntarily.

And then I smiled.

"How did you know it was I!" he shrieked.

"Hush! They will overhear you in the corridor. It was as plain as day. I knew it before I had been five minutes in the room. First, because you shrank instinctively from the corpse, though you seemed to be caressing it. Secondly, when I looked into the stove, I saw a glove and handkerchief, partly consumed; and then I instantly accounted for the faint close smell which had affected me before the room was ventilated. It was chloroform. Thirdly, when I went to open the window, I noticed that the paint was scraped off the brackets which held the spout to the next house. This conduit had been newly painted two days previously—I watched the man at work; the paint on the brackets was thicker than anywhere else, and had not dried. On looking at your feet, which I did critically, while speaking to you, I saw that the leather on the inner side of each boot was slightly chafed, paint-marked. It is a way of mine to put this and that together!"

"If you intend to betray me—"

"O, no, but I don't, or I should not be here—alone with you. I am, as you may allow, not quite a fool."

"Indeed, sir, you are as subtle as—"

"Yes, I wouldn't mention him."

"Who?"

"The devil."

Kenneth mused.

"May I ask, Mr. Lynde, what you intend to do?"

"Certainly—remain here."

"I don't understand you," said Kenneth with an air of perplexity.

"If you will listen patiently, you shall learn why *I* have acknowledged this deed, why *I* would bear the penalty. I believe there are vast, intense sensations from which we are excluded, by the conventional fear of a certain kind of death. Now, this pleasure, this ecstasy, this something, I don't know what, which I have striven for all my days, is known only to a privileged few—innocent men, who, through some oversight of the law, are *hanged by the neck!* How rich is Nature in compensations! Some men are born to be hung, some have hanging thrust upon them, and some (as I

hope to do,) achieve hanging. It appears ages since I commenced watching for an opportunity like this. Worlds could not tempt me to divulge your guilt, nor could worlds have tempted me to commit your crime, for a man's conscience should be at ease to enjoy, to the utmost, this delicious death! Our interview is at an end, Mr. Kenneth. I held it my duty to say this much to you."

And I turned my back on him.

"One word, Mr. Lynde."

Kenneth came to my side, and laid a heavy hand on my shoulder, that red right hand, which all the tears of the angels cannot make white again.

As he stood there, his face suddenly grew so familiar to me—yet so vaguely familiar—that I started. It seemed as if I had seen such a face, somewhere, in my dreams, hundreds of years ago. The face in the grate.

"Did you send this to me last month?" asked Kenneth, holding up a slip of paper on which was scrawled, *Watch them*—in my handwriting.

"Yes," I answered.

Then it struck me that these few thoughtless words, which some sinister spirit had impelled me to write, were the indirect cause of the whole catastrophe.

"Thank you," he said hurriedly. "I watched them!" Then, after a pause, "I shall go far from here. I can not, I *will* not die yet. Mary was to have been my wife, so she would have hidden her shame—O cruel! She, my own cousin, and we the last two of our race! Life is not sweet to me, it is bitter, bitter; but I shall live until I stand front to front with *him*. And you? They will not harm you—*you* are a madman!"

Julius Kenneth was gone before I could reply. The cell door shut him out forever—

shut him out in the flesh. His spirit was not so easily exorcised.

AFTER ALL, IT was a wretched fiasco. Two officious friends of mine, who had played chess with me, at my lodgings, on the night of the 3rd, proved an alibi; and I was literally turned out of the Tombs;[16] for I insisted on being executed.

Then it was maddening to have the newspapers call me a monomaniac.

I a monomaniac?

What was Pythagoras, Newton, Fulton? Have not the great original lights of every age, been regarded as madmen? Science, like religion, has its martyrs.

Recent surgical discoveries have, I believe, sustained me in my theory; or, if not, they ought to have done so. There is said to be a pleasure in drowning. Why not in strangulation?

In another field of science, I shall probably have full justice awarded me—I now allude to the MOON-APPARATUS, which is still in an unfinished state, but progressing.

❧

---

[16] The New York Halls of Justice and House of Detention, demolished in 1902 and subsequently replaced several times, each bearing the same nickname.

Emile Gaboriau

EMILE GABORIAU (1832-1873) was a pioneering figure in the history of the mystery, along with Eugène François Vidocq (1775-1857), whose writing influenced a century of detective fiction. A journalist and prolific writer of novels and short stories, Gaboriau's first detective novel, *L'Affaire Lerouge* (1866) introduced a young police detective called Monsieur Lecoq. Lecoq was likely based on Vidocq, who was a thief turned police officer whose immensely popular memoirs mixed fiction and fact. Although Sherlock Holmes dismissed Lecoq scornfully as "a miserable bungler," Arthur Conan Doyle himself was more generous, saying, "Gaboriau had rather attracted me by the neat dovetailing of his plots…"

The Lecoq character was immensely popular and was featured in three later novels by Gaboriau. The following tale, however, published posthumously in 1876, is an account of *another* detective, Monsieur Méchinet, a consultant to the police, and appears to be the first of an intended series of tales, never written.

THE LITTLE OLD MAN OF BATIGNOLLES

EMILE GABORIAU

SOME THREE OR four months ago, a man in his early forties, correctly dressed in black, called at the offices of the editor of *Le Petit Journal*. He brought with him a handwritten manuscript of such exquisite penmanship that it would have inspired the jealousy of even a professional calligrapher.

"I will call again in a fortnight," he said, "to find out what you think of my work."

Since no one was curious enough to un - tie the ribbon holding it together, the manuscript was stored away as usual in the box labeled: "MSS to be read."

And time went by…

I ought to add that a great many manuscripts are offered to *Le Petit Journal*, and that the reader's job is no sinecure.

The author, however, failed to return, and everyone had forgotten him when, one morning, the head reader arrived tremendously excited.

" 'Pon my word," he exclaimed as he came in, "I have just read something extraordinary."

"Well, what is it?" we asked him.

"The manuscript of the gentleman, you remember, dressed all in black… I make no reservations, I was gripped by it."

And as we made fun of his enthusiasm—for he was, as a rule, very rarely enthusiastic—he threw the manuscript on the table, saying, "Read it for yourselves."

This was enough to intrigue us seriously. One of us picked up the manuscript, and by the end of the week it had made the round of all the editorial staff. The verdict was unanimous: *Le Petit Journal* must publish the story.

But now an unforeseen difficulty arose: the manuscript did not bear the name of its author. Only a visiting-card, inscribed "J. B. Casimir Godeuil," was attached to it. There was no address.

What was to be done? Publish the manuscript anonymously? That was hardly possible at a time when the French press laws required someone to accept responsibility for every printed line.

It was agreed, therefore, that the only course was to search for this more than modest author, and for several days the management of *Le Petit Journal* instituted inquiries in all directions.

But without result. No one had ever heard of J. B. Casimir Godeuil.

At this point, as a last resort, the streets were placarded with the mysterious posters which so intrigued Paris and also, to some extent, the provinces.

"Who can this man Godeuil possibly be," people wondered, "that he is advertised for like this?"

Some took him for a prodigal son fled from under the parental roof, others for a missing heir, but most for an absconded cashier.

This time we were successful.

Scarcely were the first bills posted, when J. B. Casimir Godeuil hastened to our offices and *Le Petit Journal* contracted to publish his narrative, *The Little Old Man of Batignolles*, which constituted the first part of his memoirs.[1]

Having said this, we leave the rest to the words of J. B. Casimir Godeuil. The following short preface—which we have decided to retain because of the light it throws on the author's character and the worthy objective he pursued in writing his memoirs—precedes his narrative.

PREFACE

A PRISONER WHO was brought before the magistrates was convicted of both forgery and aggravated theft, despite all his tricks and denials and an alleged alibi.

Overwhelmed by the evidence I had collected against him, he confessed his crime and exclaimed:

"Ah! If I had only known the methods used by the police, and how impossible it is to escape from them, I would have remained an honest man."

It was these words which inspired me to write my memoirs. "If I had only known..."

And I publish my recollections today in the hope, no, I will go further, in the firm conviction that I have accomplished a highly moral task and one of exceptional value.

Is it not desirable to strip crime of her sinister poetry, to show her as she really is: cowardly, ignoble, abject and repulsive?

Is it not desirable to prove that the most wretched beings in the world are those madmen who have declared war on society?

This is what I claim to do.

I shall establish beyond all doubt that it is to everyone's advantage to remain honest—an advantage which is immediate, positive, mathematical. You can depend on it!

I will demonstrate so that it is as clear as daylight that with our present social organization, with the railways and the electric telegraph, impunity is impossible.

Punishment may be deferred, but it is not to be escaped.

And without doubt there will be many misguided beings who will profit from my words by reflecting before they abandon themselves to crime.

And many who were not held back by the weak murmurings of their consciences will be arrested by the voice of fear...

Do I need to explain the nature of these memoirs any further?

---

[1] Unfortunately, J. B. Casimir Godeuil, who promised us the conclusion of his manuscript, has completely disappeared, and all efforts made to find him have been unsuccessful. The following narrative (complete in itself), which constitutes an extremely moving drama, is therefore his only published work. (*Editor's note.*)

I attempt to describe the struggles, the successes and the defeats of a handful of loyal men to whom the security of Paris is entrusted.

How many are they to hold in check all the criminals of a capital which, with her suburbs, counts more than three million inhabitants?

They number two hundred.

It is to them that I dedicate this book.

I.

WHILST I WAS pursing my studies to become a doctor—I was but twenty-three at the time—I lived in the Rue Monsieur-le-Prince, almost at the corner of the Rue Racine.

For thirty francs a month, service included, I rented a furnished room there which would easily cost a hundred today; a room which was large enough to allow me to stretch out my arms without having to open the windows when I put on my overcoat.

Leaving very early in the mornings to make my rounds at the hospital, and returning as late at night due to the irresistible attraction that the Café Leroy held for me, it happened that I hardly knew my neighbors—who were for the most part quiet people living either by their trade or off their incomes—even by sight.

There was one, however, with whom I gained, little by little, acquaintance.

He was a man of medium height, with unexceptional features, always clean shaven, and called, respectfully, Monsieur Méchinet.

The doorkeeper treated him with a special consideration, and never missed the courtesy of taking off his cap when he passed in front of his lodge. M. Méchinet's apartment opened on to the same landing as my own, in fact his door was exactly opposite mine, and from time to time we would pass each other on the stairs. On these occasions we were in the habit of saluting each other.

One night he would knock on my door to ask me to oblige him with some lucifers;[2] another night, I would borrow some tobacco from him; and one morning we chanced to leave the building at the same time and walked together to the end of the road, talking…

Such were our first points of contact.

Without being either curious or suspicious—one is not at the age I was then—I was eager to discover with what sort of person I was forming an acquaintance. Naturally, I did not start to spy on my neighbor's life, but I did take note of his movements and behavior.

He was married, and Madam Caroline Méchinet—a small, fair-haired, plump, jovial woman—appeared to worship her husband. He, however, seemed to be a man of most irregular habits. Frequently, he left home before daybreak and I often heard him coming in after being out all night. Occasionally, he would disappear for whole weeks at a time…

Intrigued, I thought that our doorkeeper, usually a most garrulous fellow, would provide me with some information.

Error…! Scarcely had I mentioned the name Méchinet before he sent me about my business, rolling his great eyes and saying at the same time that he was not accustomed to spying on the tenants.

This reception so fanned my curiosity that, oblivious to all restraint, I applied myself to watching my neighbor.

I soon made certain discoveries which seemed most ominous. One day, I saw him

[2] Matches.

come home dressed in the latest fashion, the ribbons of five or six medals displayed in his button-hole; the next day, I glimpsed him on the staircase wearing a dirty blouse and a ragged cap which lent him a sinister appearance.

And this was not all. One afternoon, just as he was going out, I saw his wife taking leave of him on the landing; she hugged him fondly and said: "Be careful, Méchinet, I beg of you. Think of your poor little wife."

Be careful…! Why…? With regard to what danger? What did this mean…? Was his wife his accomplice then?

I was fairly astonished, yet there was more to come.

I was soundly asleep one night when there was an urgent knocking at my door. I rose and opened it. M. Méchinet came in, or rather, burst in, his clothes disheveled and torn, his cravat and the front of his shirt ripped open, his head bare, and his face covered with blood.

"What has happened?" I exclaimed, terrified.

"Speak lower!" he said. "You might be heard… It's probably only a scratch but it hurts like the devil… I thought that as you are a medical student you might have a look at it for me."

Without saying a word, I made him sit down and examined his wound.

Although it had bled profusely, the wound was not deep. To tell the truth, it was only a graze, running from his left ear to the corner of his mouth.

"Well, I've managed to escape safe and sound this time," said M. Méchinet to me when I had finished dressing his wound. "Many thanks, my dear M. Godeuil. Above all, though, I'd be grateful if you didn't breathe a word of my little accident to anyone and… well, good night."

Good night! As if I would be able to sleep after that!

When I think of the absurd theories and the flights of fancy which passed through my head that night, I can hardly prevent myself from laughing.

In my imagination, M. Méchinet began to take on fantastic proportions.

He, however, called quietly on me the next day to thank me once again and invite me to dinner.

As you might have supposed, on entering my neighbor's rooms, I was all eyes and ears, but despite my closest attentions I discovered nothing to dispel the mystery which I found so absorbing.

Still, from the time of this dinner, our acquaintanceship flourished. M. Méchinet definitely seemed to regard me with favor. Hardly a week went by without him inviting me to take "pot-luck," as he called it, at his table; and practically every day he would come to join me towards four o'clock at the Café Leroy for the customary vermouth, and we would play a hand of dominoes.

It was in this way that one afternoon in July, a Friday, at the stroke of five, when he was on the brink of catching me with the double-six in my hand,[3] that a shifty-looking, badly dressed character came brusquely in and whispered into his ear a few words that I didn't catch.

M. Méchinet's face suddenly became animated, and he sprang from his chair.

"I'm coming," he said. "Run and tell them that I'm coming."

---

[3] Tiles left in the loser's hand count against him in most forms of dominoes.

The man made off in a hurry, and M. Méchinet held out his hand.

"You must excuse me, but business before pleasure, you know…we can resume tomorrow."

Consumed with curiosity as I was, I dare say I showed a good deal of ill-humor; in any case I said that I regretted that I could not accompany him now.

"Indeed," he muttered, "why not? Would you care to come? You might find it not without interest…"

My only reply was to pick up my hat and leave with him.

II.

CERTAINLY I WAS far from thinking, at that moment, that such an apparently insignificant exercise as this would have a profound effect on my whole life.

And as I trotted along beside M. Méchinet I was full of stupid, puerile satisfaction. "This time," I thought, "I will know everything."

I use the word "trotted" advisedly, for I had great difficulty in keeping up with my companion. Pushing through the passersby, he rushed on all the way down the Rue Racine as if his life depended on it.

In the Place de l'Odeon, a cab luckily drove by.

M. Méchinet stopped it and, opening the door for me, shouted up imperatively to the coachman:

"Thirty-nine Rue Lécluse, at Batignolles…and don't spare the horses."

The distance of the fare produced a string of oaths from the driver. All the same, he whipped up the horses and we lurched off.

"So we are going to Batignolles?" I asked with the false smile of a courtesan on my face.

But M. Méchinet did not reply; I doubt if he even heard me.

A complete transformation had come over him. He did not appear excited exactly, but his pursed lips and the manner with which his bushy eyebrows were drawn together in a frown betrayed his preoccupation. His gaze, staring into space, seemed to indicate that he was studying some mysterious unfathomable problem. He had taken out his snuff-box, and he incessantly extracted enormous pinches which, after rolling between his forefinger and his thumb, he held up to his nose without, however, inhaling.

I had observed this little idiosyncrasy before and it greatly amused me. The worthy man had a horror of snuff, yet he always went out equipped with this snuff-box in the manner of a musical-hall villain. Whenever anything unforeseen occurred, whether it pleased or irritated him, he invariably drew it from his pocket and pretended to provide himself with pinch after pinch. He made the same gestures even when the box was empty.

Later, I learnt that it was part of an act he had deliberately created to divert the attention of those around him, and so conceal his reactions.

Meanwhile, we were making progress.

The cab labored up the Rue de Clichy, crossed the outer boulevard and drew up in the Rue Lécluse, a little way from the address that had been tended. It was not possible to go further as the street was obstructed by a large crowd.

In front of No. 39, some two or three hundred people were standing, craning their necks, breathless with excitement. Half a dozen policemen vainly tried to contain them, shouting, "Move on, please. Move on!"

Alighting from the carriage, we elbowed our way through the bystanders. Just as we reached the doorway of the house, a sergeant pushed us back roughly.

My companion looked him up and down critically, then, drawing himself up to his full height, said:

"Don't you know me? I am Méchinet. And this young man is with me."

"Please excuse me, sir," stammered the sergeant, saluting us, "I didn't recognize you. This way, sir."

In the hall, a stout, middle-aged woman with a red face, obviously the concierge, was holding forth with much gesticulation amidst a group of tenants.

"Where is he?" asked M. Méchinet abruptly.

"On the third floor, sir," she replied. "Third floor, door on the right. Lord God! What a tragedy…in a house like ours! And such a decent man!"

I did not hear any more. M. Méchinet was bounding up the stairs, with me on his heels, four at a time, my heart beating as if it would burst.

On the third floor, the door was already open.

We went in, crossed an ante-room, a dining-room, and a parlor, and finally reached the bedroom.

If I were to live a thousand years, I would not forget the sight which met my eyes. Even as I write about it now, after a good many years, I can still see it down to the last detail.

Two men were leaning against the mantelpiece in front of the door: the Police Inspector, wearing his sash of office, and the investigating magistrate. On the right hand side, a young man, the latter's clerk, was seated writing at a table.

On the floor, in the middle of the room, lay the corpse of an old man surrounded by a pool of dark, coagulating blood. He was stretched out on his back with his arms extended.

Terrified, I stood rooted to the threshold, so overwhelmed that, in order to avoid falling, I was obliged to support myself against the frame of the door.

My profession had familiarized me with death. I had conquered my repugnance of the operating-theatre a long time ago, but this was the first occasion on which I found myself at the actual scene of a crime.

Because it was obvious that some abominable crime had been committed here.

Less impressed than myself, my companion entered the room with a firm step.

"Ah! It's you, Méchinet," said the Inspector. "I'm sorry to have troubled you now."

"Why is that?"

"Because we no longer have need of your special talents… We know the culprit and I have already given the order for his arrest which should have been carried out by now."

How strange! From the look of M. Méchinet, I would have said that this news failed to please him. He took out his snuff-box, and pretended to take two or three pinches.

"So you know the culprit?"

"Yes, M. Méchinet," replied the investigating magistrate, "and our information is quite beyond question. After committing the crime, the murderer fled, believing his victim to be dead. He was mistaken. Providence was watching…this poor old man was barely breathing but, summoning up all his strength, he dipped one of his fingers into the blood which was streaming from his wound, and there, on the floor, wrote the name of his assassin in his own blood, thereby handing him over to earthly justice… However, look for yourselves."

On the floor, in large, badly formed, though quite legible letters, was written in blood: MONIS…

"Well?" asked M. Méchinet.

"They are the first five letters of the name of the deceased's nephew," replied the Inspector. "A nephew of whom he was very fond, and whose name is Monistrol.

"By the devil!" exclaimed M. Méchinet.

"I fancy," resumed the investigating magistrate, "that the wretch won't try to deny his guilt. Those five letters are an overwhelming proof against him. And besides, who else could profit from this cowardly crime? He alone, the sole heir of the old man, who leaves him, it is said, a considerable fortune… Furthermore, the crime was committed last night, and the only person to visit him last night was this nephew. The concierge saw him arrive at about nine o'clock and leave a little before midnight."

"It's clear then," confirmed M. Méchinet, "quite clear. This fellow Monistrol is a perfect fool." He shrugged his shoulders. "Did he steal anything? Did he disturb any of the furniture to put us on the wrong track?"

"Until now nothing has appeared out of order to us," replied the Inspector. "As you say, the wretch is not very adept. He will confess as soon as he is arrested."

On that note, the Inspector and M. Méchinet withdrew into the recess of the window and spoke together in low voices while the investigating magistrate dictated some instructions to his clerk.

III.

As FAR AS M. Méchinet was concerned, I was satisfied.

The profession which my enigmatic neighbor exercised was no longer a mystery to me. His irregular life-style—his absences, his late homecoming, his sudden disappearances, the fears and the complicity of his young wife, the wound which I had dressed for him—was completely accounted for.

What did it matter to me now?

I had gradually recovered my capacity for logical thought, and I examined everything around me with keen interest. From where I was, propped up against the door jamb, I could take in the whole room at a glance. There was nothing to betray it as the scene of a murder. On the contrary, everything tended to show the easy circumstances and the neat, parsimonious even, habits of the victim.

Everything was as it should be. There was not even a fold out of place in the curtains, and the woodwork of the furniture was bright with polish, indicating the daily attention it received.

It seemed evident, besides, that the theories of the investigating magistrate and the Inspector of Police were correct, and that the unfortunate old man had been assassinated the night before just as he was about to go to bed.

In fact the bed was turned down, and night-shirt and night-cap were laid out on the coverlet. On the bedside table, I saw a glass of water, a box of lucifers, and an evening paper.

On the corner of the mantelpiece, a large, heavy copper candlestick shone. But the murderer had fled without blowing it out, for the candle which had lit the crime had burnt away, blackening the alabaster save-all in which it had been fixed.

I noticed these details in a moment, without a conscious act of will. My eyes became the lens of a camera, and the scene of the murder impressed itself on my mind, as if on a photographic plate, so precisely that even today I could draw the apartment of "the little old man of Batignolles" from memory without forgetting anything, not even the cork with the green wax seal which I still seem to see lying on the floor beneath the chair of the magistrate's clerk.

I was unaware that I possessed this extraordinary faculty, revealed so suddenly in me, for I had previously never had cause to use it, and, too greatly excited, I neglected to analyze my observations.

I had only one desire, obstinate and irresistible: to approach the corpse stretched out two yards away from me.

At first, I fought against this obsessive impulse, but it was stronger than me, and I drew near. My presence had not, I think, been remarked. In any case, no one paid any attention to me now.

M. Méchinet and the Inspector of Police were still talking over by the window, and the clerk was reading back some report to the investigating magistrate in an undertone.

Moreover, I must admit it, I was seized by a sort of fever which rendered me absolutely insensible to what was happening around me, isolating me utterly.

This feeling was so profound that I dared to kneel beside the body, the better to see and examine it. Indeed, I was so far removed from imagining that someone would ask me, "What are you up to?" that I acted with complete composure.

It seemed to me that this poor old man had seen some seventy or seventy-five winters; he was thin and wiry, but hale all the same, and built, I would have said, to withstand another twenty-five.

He still possessed a good head of yellowish, curly hair. The grey bristles covering his face gave him the appearance of having gone unshaven for five or six days, but they had grown since his death, a phenomenon I had often noted in the hospital mortuary and so was not surprised by.

What did surprise me was the expression on the old man's face. It was calm and, I might say, welcoming. The lips were slightly apart, as if he had been greeting a friend when death had overtaken him so quickly that he still retained his kind demeanor. This was the first thought which came to my mind.

But how could these incongruous circumstances be reconciled? Sudden death and those five letters which I had seen traced on the floor: M O N I S. To write them would have required an enormous effort of a dying man. Only the wish to be avenged could have imparted him such energy. And what rage he must have felt to know that death was cheating him of his life before he had completed the name of his murderer...

And yet his face seemed to smile.

The poor old man had been struck in the throat, the weapon had slightly severed his neck.

The instrument of the crime could only have been a dagger, or perhaps one of those formidable Catalan knives with blades as large as a man's hand, yet sharp as a razor.

In all my life, I had never been prey to such strange emotions. My temples throbbed with unbelievable violence and my heart swelled as if it would burst.

Was I about to discover something…?

Driven on by this same mysterious and irresistible impulse which annihilated my will, I took the rigid, frozen hands of the corpse between my own.

The right hand was quite clean…it was with one of the fingers of the left, the index finger, that he had written, for it was stained with blood.

What! The old man had written with the left hand! Then…

Gripped as if by vertigo, with haggard eyes and bristling scalp, and certainly as pale as the dead man stretched out in front of me, I struggled to my feet and let out a terrible cry.

"God Almighty!"

The others rushed to my side.

"What is it? What is it?" they insisted, with great excitement.

I tried to answer but the words stuck in my throat. I could only point to the hands of the deceased and stammer:

"There! Look, the hands!"

In an instant, M. Méchinet was on one knee beside the body. He saw immediately what I had seen because he was amazed by it as I had been. He rose to his feet in a movement.

"It was not the old man who wrote those letters," he announced.

And as the investigating magistrate and the Inspector of Police were looking at him with open mouths, he explained to them that the left hand alone was stained with blood.

"And to think I didn't even notice it," said the Inspector forlornly.

"It is often like that," said M. Méchinet, energetically helping himself to imaginary pinches of snuff. "We often don't see the things right in front of our eyes. No matter.

The situation is completely changed now, however. Since they were not written by the old man, they must have been written by the murderer…"

"Evidently," concurred the Inspector.

"Well," continued my neighbor, "is it possible to imagine a murderer so maladroit as to denounce himself straight off by signing his name beside the corpse of his victim? No, it is not. Hence, we must conclude…"

The investigating magistrate had become thoughtful.

"It is clear," he said. "We have been misled by appearances… Monistrol is not culpable… But, then, who is? It is up to you, Méchinet, to uncover him."

He paused as a policeman entered the room.

"Monistrol has been arrested, sir, and is in custody at the Dépôt," he said. "He has confessed everything."

IV.

THE SHOCK WAS all the greater because it was unexpected. Imagine our amazement in the face of the impossible! What—whilst we had been making every effort to establish Monistrol's innocence, he had formally admitted his guilt!

M. Méchinet was the first to recover himself. He abruptly raised his hand from his snuff-box to his nose five or six times. Then, turning towards the agent, he said:—

"Either you've been deceived or you're trying deliberately to mislead us. There is no other alternative."

"I swear to you, M. Méchinet…"

"Hold your tongue, man! Either you have misunderstood what Monistrol has said or else you have been carried away by your desire to surprise us with the announcement that the affair is concluded."

The policeman, who had been polite and respectful until this point, now protested:

"Excuse me, but I am neither a fool nor a liar. I know what I say."

It seemed so likely that the discussion would turn into an argument that the magistrate thought it advisable to intervene.

"Calm yourself, M. Méchinet," he said. "Listen to all the evidence before pronouncing judgment."

Then, turning to the agent, he continued:

"Now, my good fellow, tell us everything you know and explain why you are so confident about what you have just said."

Encouraged by the magistrate, the policeman directed a look of withering irony towards M. Méchinet, and, with an appreciable note of self-importance in his voice, began to speak:

"According to your instructions, sir, and those of the Inspector here, Sergeant Goulard, my colleague Poltin and myself were to proceed to 75 Rue Vivienne, the residence of the party Monistrol, a dealer in imitation jewelry, and effect the arrest of the aforementioned Monistrol and charge him with the murder of his uncle."

"Quite correct," approved the Inspector gently.

"Acting on these instructions," continued the man, "we hailed a cab and proceeded to the same address. Upon arrival, we found M. Monistrol in a small room at the rear of his shop. He was about to sit down to dinner with his wife, a woman of no small beauty, twenty-five to thirty years of age.

"Perceiving the three of us lined up, the accused jumped to his feet and asked us what we wanted, whereupon Sergeant Goulard

drew the warrant from his pocket and said. 'In the name of the Law, I arrest you.'"

"Come to the point, can't you," interrupted M. Méchinet impatiently.

But the policeman continued in the same level voice as if he had not heard.

"I have arrested a good many people in my time, but I've never seen one take it like him. 'You must be joking,' he said, 'or else you are making a mistake.' 'No,' said Goulard, 'there is no mistake.' 'Well what are you arresting me for?' said Monistrol. 'Don't come the child with us. What about your uncle? His body has been found and there is compelling evidence against you.' That finished the rogue, eh? He staggered to a chair, crying and stammering I don't know what, half of which was unintelligible anyway.

"On seeing this, Goulard seized him by the collar of his coat and said to him: 'If you take my advice, you'll confess. It'll go easier for you if you do.'

"He looked at us with bewildered eyes and murmured: 'Oh, well, yes. I admit it all.'"

"Well done, Goulard," noted the Inspector with approval.

The policeman enjoyed the moment of triumph and resumed his story:

"We were best getting it over and done with, sir, as we'd been instructed to avoid drawing attention to ourselves. A group of idlers had already begun to gather outside. So Goulard grabbed the accused by the arm and ordered us back to the Préfecture. Monistrol rose to his feet, as best he was able, for both his legs were shaking with fear, and, summoning up his courage like a man, said, 'Yes, let's be on our way.'

"We thought that the worst was over, but we hadn't reckoned with his wife.

"Until then she had been sitting in her armchair as if she had fainted, not saying a word, not even looking as if she understood what was going on.

"But when she saw that we really intended to carry off her husband, she sprang forward like a lioness and blocked the door. 'You shan't pass,' she cried. My word, she was good, but Goulard has had plenty of experience. 'Come along now, my good woman,' said he, 'don't get in our way. We'll bring back your husband.'

"However, instead of making way for us, she clung even more resolutely to the doorpost, swearing her husband was innocent, and declaring that if we took him off to prison, she would follow him there; one minute threatening and hurling insults at us, the next imploring us in her most beguiling tones.

"Really, it moved us all, but he was an insensitive devil. He even had the barbarity to push his poor wife so roughly that she fell to the ground in the corner of the room…

"And that was that, fortunately.

"His wife really had fainted, and we took the opportunity to pack him off in the cab which had brought us there.

"Pack him off is the right word, too! He had become totally listless, he couldn't even stand up, and we had to carry him… And not to omit anything, I ought to add that his dog, some kind of black mongrel, tried to jump into the carriage, and we had the devil of a job to get rid of it.

"On the way, as is only right, Goulard tried to chat with the prisoner, take his mind off it… But we couldn't get a word out of him. He seemed to come round only when we reached the Préfecture. When he had been securely stowed away in one of the cells put aside for solitary confinement, he threw himself on the bed, repeating, 'What have I done? My God, what have I done?'

"At this moment, Goulard went up to him and asked for the second time, 'Do you admit it?'

"Monistrol nodded his head and said in a hoarse voice, 'Please, leave me alone.'

"Then we arranged for a guard to watch him through the grille in case he should try to take his own life.

"Goulard and Poltin stayed where they were, and I came here to report the arrest."

"Precise," murmured the Inspector, "very precise indeed."

The magistrate was of the same opinion: "After all that, how can you still have doubts as to his guilt?"

As for me, I was surprised, but my convictions were firm. I was about to say something by way of an objection when M. Méchinet forestalled me.

"That's all very well," he exclaimed, "except that if we admit that Monistrol is the murderer, we are also bound to admit that he himself wrote his own name there, on the floor… And, well… Damn it all! It's a bit thick."

"Phooey!" interrupted the Inspector. "Since the accused has admitted it, what's the point of worrying about a circumstance that will certainly be explained at the trial?"

But my neighbor's remark had reawakened all the perplexities of the magistrate, who said, without specifically mentioning them: "I shall pay a visit to the Préfecture and interrogate Monistrol myself this very night."

After requesting the Inspector to proceed with the formalities and to attend the pathologists who would conduct the autopsy, he took his leave, followed by his clerk and the policeman who had announced Monistrol's arrest.

"I only hope these doctors won't keep me too long," grumbled the Inspector, who was thinking of his dinner.

Neither M. Méchinet nor myself answered him. Standing face to face, we were both evidently obsessed by the same idea.

"After all," murmured my neighbor, "perhaps it could have been the old man who wrote…"

"With his left hand? Is it likely? And how do you account for the fact that his death must have been instantaneous?"

"Are you sure of it?"

"Judging by his injuries, I'd swear to it… In any case, the pathologists will be here soon. They will say whether I'm right or wrong."

M. Méchinet was toying with his nose in a veritable frenzy.

"Perhaps there is a crime to be solved after all. We must wait and see. But let us start the inquiry on a new tack. Shall we have a word or two with the concierge?"

He hurried out to the landing and, leaning over the banister, shouted:

"Down there! The concierge, please. Would you mind stepping up here a moment?"

V.

WAITING FOR THE concierge to appear, M. Méchinet conducted a rapid but thorough examination of the scene of the crime.

The lock on the exterior door of the apartment particularly engaged his attention. The mechanism had not been forced and the key turned easily. This absolutely ruled out any idea of a stranger penetrating the apartment at night by means of some device.

I, for my part, without thinking, or rather, inspired by that amazing instinct which had revealed itself in me so suddenly, returned to the bedroom and picked up the cork with the green wax seal which I had already noticed lying on the floor.

On one side, that of the seal, there was the puncture mark made by the cork-screw; but, on the other side, there was a deep impression obviously caused by a sharp, pointed instrument.

Realizing the importance of my discovery, I showed it immediately to M. Méchinet, who could not prevent an exclamation of delight from escaping him.

"At last," he chuckled, "we have a clue! It was the murderer who dropped this cork here… He used it to protect the fragile point of the murder weapon. Conclusion: the crime was committed with a fix-blade dagger and not one which closes. With this cork, nothing can prevent me from tracing the murderer."

The Inspector of Police was in the bedroom completing whatever formalities remained. M. Méchinet and myself were talking alone in the parlor when we were interrupted by the sound of someone on the stairs catching their breath.

A moment later, the portly little gossip arrived whom I had seen lecturing to the tenants in the hall. The concierge was even redder in the face, if that was possible, than when we had arrived.

"What can I do for you, sir?" she asked M. Méchinet.

"Take a seat, please," he replied.

"But I have such a lot of people downstairs…"

"They can wait. Sit down."

Taken aback by the tone of his voice, she

obeyed. M. Méchinet stared at her with his penetrating little grey eyes and said:—

"I am making some inquiries, and I would like to ask you some questions. I advise you that it is in your own interest to answer them frankly. First, what is the name of this poor old gentleman?"

"He was called Pigoreau, sir, but he was better known as 'Anténor,' a name he went by formerly as better suited to his business."

"How long has he lived here?"

"At least eight years."

"Where did he live before that?"

"In the Rue Richelieu. He had his shop there, the one which made him his fortune. He was a hairdresser by profession."

"He was thought to be rich?"

"I have heard his niece say that she wouldn't let his throat be cut for a million francs."

This could be verified, since an inventory of all the deceased's papers had been carried out.

"Now," continued M. Méchinet, "what kind of man was this M. Pigoreau or Anténor?"

"Oh! One of the best, sir," replied the concierge, "though you can't imagine a man more obstinate or eccentric than he was. But he wasn't proud. And he could be entertaining when he chose to be. You could spend hours listening to his stories when the mood took him. He knew no end of stories about different people, as you can guess. Being a hairdresser he had had, as he often said, the prettiest women in Paris sitting in his chair."

"What was his life-style?"

"No different from anyone else. Just like anyone living off their savings, he was not inclined to be extravagant."

"Can you give me some details?"

"Oh, I should think so, sir, seeing that I did his cleaning for him…not that there was much for me to do, him doing most of it himself, sweeping, dusting, polishing. It was one of his fads, you know… Anyway, I would bring him up a cup of hot chocolate every day at twelve o'clock. After drinking it, he would swallow a tumbler of water, and that was his breakfast. Then he would get dressed, and that took him until two o'clock for he was very particular about his appearance, he always looked as if he was on his way to a wedding. When he was dressed, he would go out and stroll about Paris until six o'clock when he would eat dinner at a family boarding-house kept by the Mlles Gomet in the Rue de la Paix. After dinner, he would walk to the Café Guerbois, where he took his coffee, and would play cards. He was usually back by eleven o'clock and ready for bed. Really, if he had a fault, it was that he was a bit too fond of women for my liking. Often I used to say to him, "Aren't you ashamed of yourself at your age?" But then, none of us is perfect, and it's understandable coming from an old hairdresser; after all, he'd had his fair share of luck in his time…" An obsequious smile strayed across the lips of the corpulent concierge, but M. Méchinet remained as grave as ever.

"Did M. Pigoreau receive many visitors?"

"Very few. I saw hardly anyone come here except his nephew, M. Monistrol, whom he used to invite to dinner every Sunday at the restaurant Père Lathuile."

"And how did they get on together, the uncle and his nephew?"

"They were thick as thieves, sir."

"They never had any arguments?"

"Never…excepting that they were always quarrelling about Madam Clara."

"Who is Madam Clara?"

"Why, M. Monistrol's wife. A beautiful

woman, but old M. Anténor couldn't stand the sight of her and was for ever telling his nephew that he was too much in love with his wife and that, as a result, she was leading him up the garden path. M. Anténor claimed that she didn't care for her husband, that she acted above her station, and that she would end up by doing something foolish. In fact, Madam Clara and the uncle had quite a tiff only last year. She wanted the old man to lend her husband a hundred thousand francs to buy a jeweler's business in the Palais-Royale. But he refused, saying that he didn't mind what they did with his fortune after he was dead, but, until then, having earned it himself, he'd do with it exactly as he pleased."

I hoped M. Méchinet would pursue this highly suggestive point but, despite the signs I made to him, he continued:

"Who discovered the crime?"

"I did, sir. I discovered the crime," bewailed the concierge. "It was frightful! You can't imagine! This morning, as twelve o'clock was striking, I brought up M. Anténor his cup of chocolate as usual. I have my own key to his rooms as I do his cleaning for him. I opened the door and went in… And what did I see? Oh my God…!"

She started weeping in her shrill voice.

"Your grief shows the goodness of your soul, madam," observed M. Méchinet earnestly, "only, as I am very pressed for time, I beg of you to control yourself. What was your first thought when you saw your tenant lying there, murdered?"

"I said to myself that this rogue of a nephew was at the bottom of it, for the inheritance. And I don't mind who hears me say it."

"Why are you so sure? After all, to accuse

a man of such a serious crime is tantamount to sending him to the scaffold."

"But who else could it be? M. Monistrol came to see his uncle yesterday evening, and left when it was nearly midnight. He always exchanges a greeting with me, but last night he didn't say a word either on arrival or when he departed. And I am sure that no one else went to see M. Anténor before I found him in the morning."

I must admit that this testimony confounded me.

Uninstructed as I was in the art of interviewing witnesses, I thought it useless to continue. Fortunately, M. Méchinet's experience was more extensive. Moreover, he knew the knack of drawing precise information from those whom he questioned.

"You are quite certain, then," he insisted, "that Monistrol came last night?"

"Quite certain."

"Then you saw him, recognized him…?"

"Ah, allow me! I didn't see his face. He passed by very quickly, trying to hide himself, the villain that he is, and the stairs are badly lit…" When I heard this statement of incalculable significance, I jumped up and advanced towards the concierge. "How dare you state that you recognized Monistrol!" I exclaimed.

She weighed me up, and replied with an ironical smile, "If I didn't see the face of the master, at least I saw the muzzle of his dog. I'm always kind to the animal, and he came into my room. I was just about to give him a bone of mutton when his master whistled." I looked anxiously at M. Méchinet to see what he thought of this reply, but he, impassively, simply asked:

"What breed of dog is M. Monistrol's?"

"A Pomeranian, the sort that used to be

trained as guide dogs. Black all over except for a white patch under one ear. His master calls him Pluto."

M. Méchinet rose. "Thank you," he said. "That is all. You may go now."

When she was gone, he said to me:

"His nephew must be guilty—I don't see any other solution."

However, the police surgeon had arrived during this long conversation, and he told us his conclusions.

"M. Pigoreau's death was definitely instantaneous. Consequently, it could not have been he who wrote the five letters—MONIS—on the floor, by the body."

I had not been mistaken.

"If it was not him," pondered M. Méchinet, "then who was it? Monistrol? What on earth could have put it into his head to do such a thing!"

However, the Inspector, delighted to be able to go to his dinner, mocked the difficulties raised by M. Méchinet. They seemed ridiculous to him since Monistrol had admitted it all.

"Perhaps I am only an old fool," said M. Méchinet. "We shall see... Meanwhile, my dear M. Godeuil, shall we pay a visit to the Préfecture?"

VI.

WE ENGAGED THE same hansom to take us to the Préfecture.

M. Méchinet was tremendously preoccupied, his fingers never ceasing to travel from his empty snuff-box to his nose, and I heard him mumble to himself, "I'll get to the bottom of it yet."

Then, taking the cork from his pocket, he turned it over and over again, like a mon-key inspecting a nut, and muttered, "A valuable clue. Ah! If only this sealing-wax could speak!"

Ensconced in my corner, I did not say a word. In truth, my situation was rather peculiar, but I did not dwell on it. My mind was completely absorbed in the case. I tried to bring some order to the incongruous elements which I possessed, until the point where I despaired of finding any solution to the problem. When we arrived it was dark.

The Quai des Orfèvres was silent and deserted: not a sound, not a passer-by. The few shops of the neighborhood were closed. The only sign of life came from the little restaurant near the corner of the Rue de Jérusalem, and I could see the shadows of the customers against the red curtains of the front window.

"Will they let you see the accused?" I asked M. Méchinet.

"Certainly," he replied. "I've been entrusted with the affair, haven't I? Then I must have the right to see the prisoner at any time of the day or night as new evidence comes to light."

And as he disappeared under the arch with rapid footsteps, he added, "Come along now, we've no time to lose."

I had no need of encouragement. As I hurried after him, I was filled with many indefinable emotions and, above all, an uneasy curiosity.

This was the first time in my life that I had crossed the threshold of the Préfecture of Police. And, no doubt, I shared the same prejudices against it as most other Parisians.

"Here," he whispered, not without a slight shudder, "here is the secret of Paris." I was so lost in my reflections that, forgetting to watch my feet, I almost fell.

This jolt brought my thoughts back to the present.

We walked down a long passage with damp walls and uneven flagstones. Then my companion went into a little room where two men were playing cards while three or four more smoked their pipes stretched out on camp-beds. The words he exchanged with them did not reach me outside. He came out and we set off again.

We crossed a courtyard and hurried down another corridor, and came to a halt in front of an iron gate secured by heavy bolts and a formidable lock.

At a word from M. Méchinet, a guard opened the gate. We passed a vast guardroom, on our right, where there seemed to be a great number of town sergeants and guards, and climbed a steep flight of stairs.

On the landing above, at the entry to a narrow passage lined with little doors, sat a fat, jovial man, who had nothing of the public's conception of the gaoler about him.

"Why, if it isn't M. Méchinet!" he exclaimed when he saw my companion. "To tell you the truth, I was rather expecting you. I bet you've come to see the man who has been arrested for the murder at Batignolles."

"Precisely. Is there anything new?"

"No."

"But the investigating magistrate has been here?"

"Yes, he has only just left."

"Did he say anything?"

"He only stopped two or three minutes with the accused, but he looked pretty satisfied when he came out. He met the Governor at the bottom of the stairs and I heard him say, 'It's in the bag, he made no attempt to deny it…'"

M. Méchinet gave a start. The gaoler did not notice it since he continued:

"I can't say I was surprised. As soon as I set eyes on him I said to myself: 'Here's a fellow who doesn't know what he's about.'"

"What is he doing now?"

"Whining to himself in his cell. I was instructed to watch him in case he tried to kill himself. Well, I do keep an eye on him, but, between ourselves, there's not much point… his sort are more worried by how to save their necks."

"I should like to see him," interrupted M. Méchinet, "without him knowing." We crept, the three of us, as far as the thick oak door with its tiny observation grille at eye-level. Through the aperture, you could see everything that happened in the cell, badly lit as it was by a single gas jet. First of all, the guard peered through the wire mesh, followed by M. Méchinet, then I took my turn.

On a narrow iron bed, covered by a grey blanket with yellow stripes, I could dimly see a man lying on his stomach, his head half-obscured by his arms.

He was weeping: I could hear his sobs. From time to time, a convulsive spasm shook him from head to toe.

"You may open the door now," said M. Méchinet.

The gaoler did as he was bid, and we went in.

At the sound of the key grating in the lock, the prisoner sat up on his pallet, with drooping arms and legs and his head leaning on his chest, and looked blankly at us.

He was a man of between thirty-five and thirty-eight years of age, of slightly more than average height, broad-chested, with a short apoplectic neck sunk between his powerful shoulders. He was not handsome, his face having been disfigured by smallpox, and his long straight nose and reclining forehead gave him the truly stupid aspect of a sheep. However, his eyes were blue and clear and his teeth exceptionally white.

"Come, come, M. Monistrol," began M. Méchinet, "worrying won't do you any good."

And since the unfortunate man did not reply, he continued, "I agree, the situation is not very brilliant. But, if I were in your place, I would be keen to show myself as a man. I would use my intelligence and set about proving my innocence."

"I am not innocent."

There was no room for ambiguity; this dreadful confession, coming from the very mouth of the accused, was not the garbled report of some dull sergeant.

"What!" exclaimed M. Méchinet. "It really was you?"

"Yes, it really was me!" shouted the prisoner angrily.

He staggered to his feet. His eyes were blood-shot and his mouth palpitated.

"Me. Alone. How many more times must I repeat it? I signed my confession in front of the judge only five minutes ago. What more do you want? Yes, I know what will happen to me. I'm not afraid. I killed a man and now it's my turn to be killed. Go on, cut off my head! The sooner the better as far as I'm concerned."

Though at first disconcerted by this, M. Méchinet quickly recovered himself.

"Wait a minute, for God's sake," he said. "We don't guillotine people just like that. First, you must be proved guilty. And then the courts will take into consideration your sanity, whether you were provoked, and so on; in fact, all the 'extenuating circumstances,' as they are called."

Monistrol gave a groan of anguish.

"You really hated your uncle as much as that?"

"No, not at all."

"Then, why…?"

"For the inheritance. I was ruined. Your inquiries will tell you that. I needed money and my uncle, who was very rich, refused to help me."

"I see. And you thought that you wouldn't be found out?"

"I hoped so."

I was surprised at the desultory manner in which M. Méchinet conducted the interrogation. Now I saw the trap he was laying for the prisoner.

"By the way," he said in an off-hand fashion, "where did you come by the revolver with which you killed him?"

Monistrol showed no surprise at the question.

"Oh, I've had it for some years," he replied.

"What did you do with it after the crime?"

"I threw it away outside, in the street."

"Very good. I will institute a search and we shall find it."

After a moment of silence, M. Méchinet added:

"What I cannot understand is why you took your dog with you."

"What! My dog?"

"Yes, your dog, Pluto. The concierge recognized him."

Monistrol clenched his fists. He opened his mouth as if he was about to say something, but a new thought crossed his mind, and he flung himself on the bed, saying in a tone of unshakeable resolution:

"That's enough torture. You won't wring another word out of me."

Clearly, no further progress could be made.

We withdrew. When we were outside on the quay, I took M. Méchinet by the arm. "You heard him as well as I did. He doesn't even know how his uncle died. How can his innocence still be in doubt?"

But this old detective was a great skeptic.

"Perhaps so," he replied. "I've seen so many great actors in my time... But that's enough for today. I must sleep on it... Come home and have a bite to eat with my wife and me."

VII.

IT WAS NEARLY ten o'clock when M. Méch - inet, still accompanied by myself, rang at the door of his apartment.

"I never carry a key," he told me. "In this wretched business you never know what is going to befall you next... There are plenty of rogues itching to get even with me, and if I am not always so careful about myself, I have to think of my wife."

It was the pretty Madam Méchinet herself who opened the door.

With a quick, feline grace she slipped her arms around her husband's neck.

"Back at last, then... I was beginning to get worried..."

But she stopped short when she saw me. Her bright smile faded from her lips and she took a pace backwards.

"What! It's ten o'clock and you've only just left the café? Haven't the pair of you any sense?" she said, directing her remarks to me as much as to her husband.

M. Méchinet had the indulgent smile on his face of the man who is confident of his wife's affection and knows he can make peace with a single word.

"Don't be angry with us, Caroline," he replied, implicating me in his affairs, "we left the café hours ago and haven't been wasting our time. I was called out on some business at Batignolles—a murder."

His wife looked from one to the other of us suspiciously. When she was convinced that she was not being deceived, she said:

"Ah...!"

The exclamation was brief enough, yet charged with meaning.

Delivered to her husband, it seemed to say:

"What! Have you confided your profession to this young man? Revealed our secrets to him? How dare you!"

At least, that was how I interpreted the eloquent exclamation, and my neighbor construed it similarly because he replied:

"Well, yes. I didn't see any harm in it. Even if I have to fear the scoundrels I've handed over to the courts, I do not see why I should be afraid of honest folk. I'm not going to lock myself away, and I'm certainly not ashamed of my profession..."

"You misunderstand me, my dear," objected Madam Méchinet.

M. Méchinet did not even hear her.

He had mounted his favorite hobby-horse—I was to find that out later—and there is no disputing against hobby-horses.

"Really, my love, you have the most ridiculous ideas. Here I am, one of the sentries at an outpost of civilization. I lose my sleep and risk my life to ensure the safety of society—and you think I should blush for my profession. It's too comical for words... I know as well as you do the foolish prejudices which are held against the police. But that's all history now. Do you think it makes any difference to me? Yes, even if those simpletons look down their noses at us! I would like to see the looks on their faces if we went on strike tomorrow, leaving Paris in the hands of all those rogues we try to keep off the streets!"

No doubt accustomed to displays of this kind, Madam Méchinet wisely did not utter a word, and M. Méchinet, realizing there was no prospect of being contradicted, calmed down as if by magic.

"That's enough for the time being," he said. "Just now we have a more important matter: we have not yet eaten. Is there any supper for us?"

Obviously, Madam Méchinet had been taken by surprise in this way too often in the past to be caught out again.

"I'll have something ready in five minutes," she replied with her pleasant smile.

And, in fact, the next minute there was a succulent joint of cold beef on the table in front of us. Madam Méchinet served us and at the same time kept our glasses filled with an excellent Mâcon wine.

While M. Méchinet plied his knife and fork with determination, I glanced around his peaceful apartment, saw his plump, kindly wife, and I asked myself: "Is he really one of those violent detectives of the Sûreté that you read about in so many implausible novels?"

However, when we had finished eating, M. Méchinet told his wife of our expedition.

He spoke precisely, entering into the most minute details.

She sat beside him, listening intently, clearly no novice to these revelations, interrupting every now and again to clarify some obscure point: a middle-class, French, Delphic oracle, not accustomed merely to be consulted but also prone to expect her advice to be followed.

In fact, as soon as M. Méchinet finished his narrative, she said:

"You have made a great error, one you may not be able to remedy…"

"What was that?"

"When you left Batignolles, it was not to the Préfecture that you should have gone."

"But Monistrol…"

"Yes, I know. You wanted to interrogate him. But what good has it done you?"

"Well, my dear, it brought to my attention…"

"Nothing. You should have gone to the Rue Vivienne and spoken with his wife. You would have caught her while she was still upset about her husband's arrest, and if she is mixed up in this affair, as must be supposed, you might easily have procured her confession."

I sat up at these words.

"What? Do you really think that Monistrol is guilty, madam?"

She hesitated for a moment.

"Yes," she said. Then she quickly resumed, "But I'm certain that it was her idea. Of every twenty crimes committed by men, fifteen are conceived, counseled and procured by their wives. Ask M. Méchinet here. You should have seen the light after what you were told by the concierge. Who is this Madam Monistrol? A great beauty, you were told; flirtatious, ambitious, hankering after wealth, leading her husband by the nose. What is her present situation? Shabby, straitened and precarious. She had had enough of it—and the proof of this is that she asked her husband's uncle to lend him a hundred thousand francs. The old man refused to do so, and all her hopes were destroyed. She must have hated him to death after that. And I bet she used to say to herself, 'If only that old miser would die, my husband and I would be rich!' And when she saw him, fit as a fiddle, she said to herself: 'He'll live to be a hundred… We won't have any teeth in our heads by the time we get our hands on his inheritance… Who knows, he might even outlive us.' From there, it is not very far to the conception of the crime. Once the idea had taken root, she slowly started to work on her husband: she familiarized him with the idea of being an assassin, virtually put the knife into his hands… Until, one day, menaced by bankruptcy and maddened by his wife's complainings, he strikes the fatal blow."

"All that is logical enough," concurred M. Méchinet.

Very logical, no doubt, but did it fit the facts?

"Do you think, madam," I said, "that Monistrol would have been fool enough to denounce himself by signing his name…"

"Fool enough?" she asked with a slight shrug of her shoulders. "No, I don't think so, since it is the strongest point that you can adduce in favor of his innocence."

This reasoning was so specious that, for a moment, I was at a loss.

"But he confesses his guilt," I urged, as soon as I recovered myself.

"An excellent means of inducing the police to establish his innocence."

"Oh, madam!"

"You, yourself, are the living proof of it, my dear M. Godeuil."

"But, madam, the poor fellow doesn't even know how his uncle was killed."

"Excuse me, he *appears* not to know… that's not altogether the same thing."

The discussion was becoming animated, and would have lasted some little while longer if M. Méchinet had not drawn it to a close at that point.

"I think you are rather too romantic tonight, Caroline," he said.

Then, turning to me, he added:

"Well, I must bid you good night, I'm half-asleep already. Tomorrow morning I will give you a knock and we can go to see Madam Monistrol together… Good night."

He might be able to sleep, but not I. I could not shut my eyes.

A mysterious voice, calling out from the depths of my soul, cried, "Monistrol is innocent!"

In my imagination, I could picture the sufferings of this unfortunate man, alone in his cell at the Dépôt.

But why had he confessed…?

VIII.

I LACKED EXPERIENCE in those days—I have had occasion to remark it a hundred times since—professional experience; above all, I lacked the exact knowledge of the manner in which the police conduct their investigations.

I vaguely realized that this inquiry had been conducted improperly, negligently even, but I would have been extremely embarrassed if I had been called on to explain where the mistakes had been made or to say what ought to have been done.

All the same, I was as passionately involved as Monistrol.

It seemed to me that his cause was mine. This was not surprising: I had my young vanity at stake! Wasn't it one of my observations which had raised the first doubts as to his guilt?

"For my own sake I must prove him innocent," I said to myself.

The arguments expressed by Madam Méchinet had so confused me though that I was no longer certain of which fact I should select as the foundation of my defense.

As always happens when the mind is applied too long to the solution of a problem, my ideas at last became a tangled skein[4] and I could see nothing clearly.

At nine o'clock the next morning, when M. Méchinet came to collect me as he had promised, I was as perplexed as before.

"Come along now," he said, "we must be off."

As we hurried down the stairs, I noticed that my worthy neighbor was dressed rather more carefully than usual. He had succeeded in giving himself that prosperous, good-natured appearance which Parisian shopkeepers are so pleased to see in their customers.

He had the high spirits of a man marching off to certain victory.

"Well" said he as soon as we were in the street, "what do you think of my wife? They take me for a wise-blood at the Préfecture, yet, you see, I consult my wife, and she's often right. I believe it was Moliere who was in the habit of consulting his servant, wasn't it? Her one failing is that she attributes every miscreant with powers of diabolical cunning; for her, there are no crimes committed as a result of stupidity… My failing is just the opposite, I look no further than the facts. Between us, we rarely fall far short of the truth."

"What!" I exclaimed. "Have you penetrated the mystery surrounding this Monistrol affair?"

He stopped, took out his snuff-box, and helped himself to three or four imaginary pinches.

"At least I am convinced as to the strategy I must pursue to penetrate it," he replied in a modest but satisfied voice.

We arrived shortly at the Rue Vivienne, not far from Monistrol's shop.

"Look here," said M. Méchinet. "Follow me, but whatever happens don't let on that you are surprised by anything I do."

He did well to warn me otherwise I would not have been able to hide my astonishment at seeing him abruptly enter a shop selling umbrellas.

As stiff and serious as an Englishman, he examined almost every umbrella in the establishment without, however, finding one which suited him for he finished by asking if it was possible to have an umbrella made to specification.

It seemed there was nothing simpler, and he left promising to call again the next day.

The half-hour he had spent in the shop had not been wasted. Even as he studied the wares which the shopkeeper had displayed to him, he had skillfully learnt from them everything that they knew about Monistrol and his wife.

It was no difficult matter. The murder of "the little old man of Batignolles" and the arrest of the imitation jeweler had caused a sensation in the district and was the primary topic of conversation.

"There we are!" he sighed when we were on the pavement once again. "That's the way to gather information which is reliable… Why, if they so much as guessed who I was, they would embroider the truth out of all recognition."

---

[4] "A Tangled Skien" was the initial title of Arthur Conan Doyle first Sherlock Holmes adventure, *A Study in Scarlet* (1887). While a *skien* is a length of thread wound onto a reel, in literature the term is commonly associated with narrative, such as a story's "plot thread" being a *skein of events.*

My companion repeated this little comedy in seven or eight other shops in the neighborhood.

In one of them, where the tradesman was short-tempered and not inclined to talk, he even spent twenty francs.

To my amazement, we spent two hours in this singular fashion, at the end of which time we knew exactly the climate of opinion about M. Monistrol and his wife in the quarter where they had been living since their marriage four years ago.

Opinion was unanimous as to the husband.

He enjoyed a good reputation: he was thought to be good-natured, obliging, honest, intelligent and hard-working. It was through no fault of his that business had not prospered. Fortune does not always smile on those who are most deserving of her favors. He had been unwise enough to take a shop doomed to failure; in fifteen years, four traders had ruined themselves in it.

He was very fond of his wife, everyone was aware of it and talked about it, but he had not displayed his affections ostentatiously, had done nothing to make himself appear ridiculous…

No one believed him to be guilty.

"The police must have made some mistake," they said.

Opinion was divided about Madam Monistrol.

Some found her tastes too elegant for her station; others thought that a jeweler's wife was obliged in the interests of the business to be fashionably dressed.

There was general agreement, however, that she was very attached to her husband.

And everyone wished to praise her modesty, a modesty all the more essential in a woman of remarkable beauty, a woman to whom a man might offer his attentions. But her reputation was uncompromised by even the slightest shadow of a suspicion.

This information clearly troubled M. Méchinet.

"It's unbelievable," he said. "No slander, no lies, no backbiting…! Caroline has got it wrong this time. According to her, we should find one of those flighty shopkeeper's wives who flaunt themselves more than their husband's merchandise. They rule the household, their husbands being too weak or too blind to raise a hand to them."

I was as confused as he was and I made no reply.

You would hardly think that these honest traders and the concierge at the Rue Lécluse were describing the same person. In Paris, attitudes vary from quarter to quarter. What is taken as shocking in Batignolles is an exigency in the Bourse.

We had already spent too much time on the inquiry to think of pausing and exchanging impressions and conjectures.

"We had better have a good look at it from the outside before going in," said M. Méchinet.

Adroit in the art of observing without being observed even in the bustling streets of Paris, he led me under a covered passageway situated opposite Monistrol's shop.

It was a modest-looking establishment, poor in comparison with those around it. The shop-front was in need of a fresh coat of paint. Above the door, in faded gilt letters blackened and dingy, was the name, "MONISTROL." Across the windows I read, "*Gold and imitation.*"

There was little besides "imitation" which glittered in the window display. Steel-gilt chains, jet[5] ornaments, tiaras decorated with clusters of rhinestones, imitation coral necklaces and brooches, rings and cuff-links bright with false stones of every color.

A glance was all that was necessary to see that there was nothing in this poor cabinet to tempt the poorest window thief.

"Shall we go in?" I said to M. Méchinet.

He had not my impatience, or concealed it better for catching me by the arm, he said:

"One moment… I should like a glimpse of Madam Monistrol before we go in."

We waited another twenty minutes at our observation-post, in vain; the shop remained empty and Madam Monistrol did not appear.

"Well, that's enough hanging around," remarked M. Méchinet at last. "Come along, M. Godeuil, let us chance it."

IX.

WE HAD ONLY to cross the street to reach Monistrol's shop.

At the sound of the opening of the door, a little servant girl, fifteen or sixteen years old, came out of the small room at the back of the shop.

"Can I be of assistance, gentlemen?"

"Is Madam Monistrol here?"

"Yes, sir, I'll run and fetch her, she is…"

M. Méchinet did not allow the girl to finish. He pushed her roughly aside. "It's all right, as she's here, I'll speak to her myself, he said as he strode through into the back room.

I followed hard on his heels, convinced that I would not leave the premises without the solution of the enigma.

The backroom was a cheerless little abode, serving at the same time as parlor, dining-room and bedroom.

It was in a state of considerable confusion and had the incongruous aspect you find in the homes of poor people who pretend to be rich.

The bed, draped with curtains of blue damask, stood at the farthest end, the pillow cases trimmed with lace, whilst on the table in front of the chimney remained the scraps of a most unappetizing meal.

Sitting, or rather, reclining, in an armchair beside the table was a young woman with fair hair. She was holding in her hands some kind of official document.

This was Madam Monistrol. The neighbors had certainly not exaggerated when they spoke of her beauty. I was stunned.

Only the quality of her grief caused me any displeasure: she was dressed in a low-necked, black silk gown, which looked very becoming on her…

It showed too much presence of mind in one genuinely afflicted. At that moment, she resembled to me a scheming actress rehearsing the role she intended to play.

She sprang to her feet like a startled doe when she saw us, and asked in a tearful voice:

"What do you want, gentlemen?"

I realized that M. Méchinet had drawn the same conclusions as I had.

"Madam," he replied, "I am here by the authority of the court; I am a detective of the Sûreté."

At this declaration, she fell back into her chair with a dreadful groan.

Then, as if gripped by a fever, with shining eyes and trembling lips, she climbed to her feet again.

---

[5] Coal that is cut, polished, and set in jewelry and from which the term jet-black is derived.

"Have you come to arrest me? Bless you, I'm ready, lead me away… Lead me to the honest man you arrested last night… I will share the same fate as him, whatever it might be… He is as innocent as I am. No matter, if he is to be the victim of another of the police's mistakes, I prefer to die alongside him."

She was interrupted by a protracted growl coming from one of the corners of the room.

I saw a black dog, with bristling fur, bloodshot eyes and bared teeth, ready to attack us.

"Stay, Pluto, stay. Lie down. These gentlemen don't wish me any harm."

The dog slowly crawled backwards under the bed, still fixing us with his furious eyes.

"You were quite correct in saying that we don't wish you any harm, madam," said M. Méchinet, "nor have we come to arrest you."

She did not appear to be listening.

"I have already received this summons this morning. It requires me to be at the chambers of the investigating magistrate at three o'clock this afternoon. What does he want me for? My God, what does he want?"

"He wants information. Information which I hope will prove your husband's innocence. You mustn't think of me as your enemy. My only interest is in finding out the truth."

He drew out his snuff-box and hastily helped himself to several pinches.

"That is to say, madam," he continued in a solemn tone which I had not heard him employ before, "that the replies you give to the following questions are of the utmost importance. Do you think you can answer me frankly?"

Her blue eyes gazed at my neighbor through her tears. For a long time she made no reply. At last, she said with resignation:—

"Ask me what you like, monsieur."

As I have said before, I was completely without experience in these matters, and yet I was dissatisfied with the manner in which M. Méchinet had commenced the interrogation.

It seemed to me that his own perplexities were too much in evidence and that, rather than pursuing some fixed object, he wandered haphazardly from point to point.

How well I would have conducted it myself—if I had only dared to interrupt!

M. Méchinet sat imperturbably in front of Madam Monistrol.

"You are of course aware of the fact that the night before last, M. Pigoreau, better known as Anténor, your husband's uncle, was murdered at about eleven o'clock."

"Yes."

"Where was M. Monistrol at this time?"

"It's no good."

M. Méchinet did not flinch.

"I repeat. Where was your husband the night before last?"

She choked on her sobs, and M. Méchinet allowed her to reply when she was composed.

"The day before yesterday, my husband was away from home all evening."

"Do you know where he was?"

"Yes, I can tell you that. One of our suppliers who lives in Montrouge was supposed to deliver us a set of false pearls. He hadn't shown up. We were afraid that the person who had ordered them would leave us with them on our hands. We couldn't afford that—business is bad enough as it is. So, while we were having dinner, my husband said to me: 'I'd better go and have a word with that fine fellow out in Montrouge.' And, sure enough, at nine o'clock, out he went. I walked as far as the corner of the Rue Richelieu with him, where I saw him get on the bus myself."

I began to breathe again. This could provide the alibi he needed.

M. Méchinet had the same idea.

"If that is so," he said gently, "your supplier will certainly confirm that he was with M. Monistrol at eleven o'clock."

"Unfortunately not."

"What? Why not?"

"Because he was out. My husband did not see him."

"This is a catastrophe. Perhaps the con-cierge will remember M. Monistrol?"

"Our supplier lives in a house which does not have a concierge."

That might well be true. But as far as the unfortunate prisoner was concerned, it was the end of his last hope.

"And what time did your husband come home?" continued M. Méchinet.

"A little after midnight."

"Didn't you think that he'd been a long time?"

"Oh, yes. I even reproached him about it. He apologized and said that he had decided to walk back, stopping at a café for a glass of beer on the way."

"What was he like when he came in?"

"He looked rather annoyed, but that's only natural."

"What clothes was he wearing?"

"The same as when he was arrested."

"You didn't notice anything extraordinary about him?"

"No, nothing."

X.

STANDING A LITTLE behind M. Méchinet, I was able to study Madam Monistrol's features at my leisure and note each fleeting expression as it crossed her face.

She seemed to be overwhelmed by a boundless grief, large tears streamed down her pale cheeks, and yet, at times, I fancied I could discern a gleam of joy in the depths of her big, blue eyes.

"Is she really guilty?" I wondered.

The idea had occurred to me before, now it returned with greater persistency. I stepped forward.

"But what about you, madam?" I asked gruffly. "Where were you on that fatal evening, while your husband was wasting his time trotting off to Montrouge to see this supplier?"

She paused and looked at me with a good deal of surprise.

"I was here, monsieur," she answered softly, "and I have witnesses who will bear me out."

"Witnesses!"

"Yes, monsieur. It was very warm that evening and I felt like having an ice-cream. But ice-cream is so tedious when you are on your own that I sent my servant to invite two of my neighbors to join me, Madam Dor-strich, the wife of the shoe-maker who lives next door, and Madam Rivaille, who keeps the glove shop across the road. They both accepted and stayed here until half-past eleven. Go and ask them if you like. With all these other cruel circumstances against us, this accident is a real blessing…"

Was it really so accidental? M. Méchinet and I asked ourselves this question as we exchanged quick, doubtful glances.

When chance acts to resolve such an issue so dexterously, it is not easy but to suspect that she has been given some assistance.

Unfortunately, it was hardly a suitable moment to pursue this thought.

"You have never been suspected, madam," replied M. Méchinet shamelessly. "The worst that has been supposed was that your husband might have said something to you before committing the crime."

"Monsieur…if you only knew us."

"Let me finish. We have been told that your business was floundering, that you were hard up…"

"Just lately, yes, that's true."

"Your husband must have been very worried about his precarious situation. He must have suffered, above all, on account of you, the wife he adored, young and beautiful… For you far more than for himself, he must have longed for the life of ease and respect which money buys."

"Monsieur, I can only repeat again, my husband is innocent."

With a pensive air, M. Méchinet pretended to fill his nose with snuff before unexpectedly asking:

"For God's sake, then, how do you account for his confession? For an innocent man to admit his guilt as soon as the crime of which he is suspected is mentioned is more than unusual, madam. It is prodigious!"

A blush briefly touched the young woman's cheeks.

Her regard, straight and clear until then, vacillated for the first time.

"I suppose," she replied in a voice muffled with tears and barely audible, "I suppose that my husband lost his head after finding himself accused of such a dreadful crime."

M. Méchinet shook his head.

"At the very most we might entertain the idea of a passing delirium…but after reflecting all night, M. Monistrol persists this morning in his original confession."

Was this true? Did my worthy neighbor say that on his own initiative or had he actually been to the Préfecture before calling on me?

However that may be, the young woman nearly fainted and, hiding her head between her hands, murmured:

"God Almighty! My poor husband has taken leave of his senses."

That was certainly not my opinion. In fact, I was convinced that Madam Monistrol's grief was nothing more than an act and I asked myself whether, for reasons which escaped me, she herself had not chosen the terrible role that her husband should play and, if he was innocent, whether she did not know the identity of the real murderer.

If these opinions were also shared by M. Méchinet, he gave no indication of it.

After addressing the common expressions of consolation to the young woman, without revealing any of his own thoughts, he gave her to understand that she might silence a great many suspicions by allowing him to make a thorough search of her establishment.

She accepted this suggestion with unfeigned enthusiasm.

"Search as much as you like, gentlemen. I shall be most obliged to you. It won't take you very long. We rent only this shop, this room where we are now, a room on the top floor for the servant, and a small cellar. Here are the keys to everything."

To my great astonishment, M. Méchinet readily accepted the offer and seemed to devote himself to a most meticulous investigation.

What was his objective? Surely he must have some secret purpose because this step would obviously lead nowhere.

When he had the appearance of having finished, he said:

"There just remains the cellar."

"I'll show you the way, monsieur," said Madam Monistrol.

On these words, she picked up a lighted candle and conducted us across a courtyard on which the back room had issue and down a flight of slippery steps to a door which she opened herself.

"Here it is…go in, gentlemen."

I began to understand.

M. Méchinet scanned the cellar with a quick, appraising glance. It was ill-kept and untidy. A small barrel of beer was set up in one corner and, just in front, resting on some logs, was a cask of wine. Both were on draught since they were fitted with small wooden taps. On the right, ranged on a metal rack, were four dozen or so bottles of wine.

M. Méchinet took down these bottles one by one, examining them carefully.

He noted, like myself, that not a single bottle was sealed with green wax.

The cork which I had discovered, used by the murderer to protect the point of his dagger, had not come from Monistrol's cellar.

"There's nothing here," said M. Méchinet, assuming a look of disappointment, "we may as well go upstairs."

We did not climb the stairs in the same order as we had descended them. I went first this time, and so it happened that I reached the back room of the shop before the others. As soon as I opened the door that wretched dog sprang from under the bed and set up such a tremendous barking that I took a step backwards.

"That dog of yours has a bad temper," said M. Méchinet to the young woman.

"Not at all," she replied, calming the animal with a wave of her hand, "he's very good. And he's an excellent watch-dog. Jewelers are more vulnerable to burglars than most people so we trained him well."

When one has been threatened by a dog, the instinctive response is to call it by name, which I proceeded to do.

"Pluto, here boy!"

But instead of coming forward he backed away from me, growling and showing his teeth.

"Oh! It's no use you calling him," remarked Madam Monistrol carelessly, "he won't obey you."

"Really. Why not?"

"This breed of dog is famous for its loyalty. He knows only his master and me."

This response did not seem to have any particular bearing on the crime we were investigating, but to me it flashed a sudden light on the mystery.

Without thinking—I would hardly do the same today—I asked:

"And where was your dog which is so faithful on the night of the crime?"

This question put point-blank caused her so great a surprise that she almost dropped the candlestick which she still held in her hand.

"I've no idea," she stammered, "I can't remember."

"Perhaps he went with your husband?"

"Yes. I believe he did, come to think of it."

"Is he trained to follow buses, then? You've already told us that you saw your husband get on the bus."

She made no reply. I was about to continue when I was interrupted by M. Méchinet. Far from trying to take advantage of Madam Monistrol's confusion, he did everything possible to reassure her and, after strongly advising her not to ignore the magistrate's subpoena, he took his leave.

When we were outside he said to me:

"Have you taken leave of your senses?"

The remark stung me.

"If I have taken leave of my senses, it was because I have found the solution to the problem… The dog is the key to the affair, he will lead us to the truth."

My outburst brought a smile to my neighbor's face.

"You are quite correct," he said paternally, "I saw the point you were trying to establish… Only, if Madam Monistrol guessed your suspicions as easily as I did, the dog either will be dead or have disappeared before the day is over."

XI.

I HAD COMMITTED an enormous indiscretion, certainly.

On the other hand, at least I had discovered the weak point in their armor—a chink which could be used to penetrate the strongest defenses.

I, a volunteer, had kept my bearings while the old campaigner of the Sûreté had lost his way.

Another man might have been jealous of my success but not him.

His one thought was how to turn my discovery to best account, which should not prove very difficult now we had a positive point of departure.

Accordingly, we went to a nearby restaurant to hold a counsel of war.

Where was the problem which, an hour ago, had seemed so unlikely of solution?

Even the evidence proclaimed Monistrol's innocence. And although we could only guess as to his reasons for pleading guilty, for the time being the question was a mere detail.

We were equally certain that Madam Monistrol had not left home on the night of the murder, though all the indications pointed to her moral complicity. Even if she had not counseled and procured the crime, she had been fully acquainted with it and consequently knew the murderer well.

But who was the murderer?

Someone whom Monistrol's dog obeyed as he would his master. Had he not followed him all the way to Batignolles?

Consequently, he must be on intimate terms with the Monistrol household.

And he must have a profound hatred of the husband to contrive such an infamous scheme to throw the blame on him.

On the other hand, he must be close to Madam Monistrol's heart; she knew his name but, preferring to sacrifice her husband, refused to denounce him.

There could only be one conclusion. The murderer was some despicable dissembler who had abused the confidences of the husband to seduce his wife.

In short, notwithstanding her reputation, Madam Monistrol had, without doubt, a lover; and this lover, inevitably, was the murderer.

Convinced of this, I racked my brains to devise some infallible scheme to lead us to the wretch.

"It seems to me," I said to M. Méchinet, "that the way we should proceed is this. Madam Monistrol and the murderer must have agreed not to see each other for the time being, just after the crime. It would be a most elementary precaution. She will be becoming impatient to see her accomplice again though. If you order one of your men to follow her night and day, we will have him before half a week is out."

M. Méchinet played implacably with his empty snuff-box, muttering unintelligibly to himself between his teeth, without replying. He turned towards me suddenly:

"That won't do. You have a genius for the profession, I am sure of it, but you are deficient in the practical aspects. Fortunately, I am here. A chance remark put you on the right track and now you don't want to follow it any further…"

"How do you mean?"

"We must make use of the dog."

"I still don't understand you."

"Well, wait and see. Madam Monistrol will have to leave the shop at two o'clock to be at the Palais-de-Justice for three. The little servant girl will be on her own in the shop. And now not a word more…"

Of course, I implored him to explain himself, but he would not be drawn, taking a mischievous pleasure in paying me back for his own failures.

I had no choice but to accompany him to the nearest café where he forced me to play dominoes.

My mind was not on the game, and he took advantage of my distraction to beat me unmercifully until, at last, two o'clock sounded.

"Once more into the breach," said he, abandoning the hand.

We paid and left the café, and a moment later we were once more standing in the covered passageway from where we had surveyed Monistrol's shop previously.

Ten minutes later Madam Monistrol appeared in the doorway opposite. She had added a black crêpe veil to complete the same black silk dress she had been wearing earlier. She looked like a widow.

"Dressed to kill, I see! I hope the magistrate likes it," grumbled M. Méchinet.

She gave some last instructions to the servant and hurried off.

My companion waited five long minutes before he was satisfied that she was not coming back.

"It is time," he said. And for the second time that day we entered the jeweler's shop.

The girl was sitting alone behind the counter, absent-mindedly sucking lumps of sugar stolen from the bowl of her employer.

She recognized us immediately and stood up, flushed and a little frightened.

"Where is Madam Monistrol?" asked M. Méchinet before she had had chance to utter a word.

"She has gone out, monsieur."

"Gone out? Impossible! She's there, in the back room."

"Gentlemen, I swear to you…but, please, see for yourselves."

M. Méchinet tapped his forehead as if greatly inconvenienced.

"How annoying! Poor Madam Monistrol will be most upset about it."

The girl stared at him with wide eyes and open mouth.

"But perhaps you can help me out," he continued. "I've only come back because I've lost the address of the gentleman whom madam asked me to visit on her behalf."

"Which gentleman would that be?"

"You know, Monsieur… Confound it! I've even forgotten his name now! Monsieur… Monsieur… You know, the gentleman that dog of yours obeys so readily."

"Ah! Monsieur Victor."

"That's the name! Do you know what he does?"

"He's a jewelry worker, a great friend of Monsieur Monistrol. They used to work together before Monsieur set up his own business. That's why he can do what he likes with Pluto."

"Then you must know where M. Victor lives?"

"Of course, he lives at 23 Rue du Roi-Doré."

The poor girl was so pleased to be so helpful that I could not help regretting the unsuspecting manner in which she betrayed her mistress.

Such scruples did not appear to trouble M. Méchinet's more hardened nature.

As I opened the door, our business concluded, he even launched a grim jest over his shoulder:

"Thank you. You have been most helpful. You have just rendered your mistress a great service. She will be most satisfied with you."

XII.

I HAD ONLY ONE thought in my head when we were outside on the pavement.

M. Méchinet and I should unite our forces on the spot and hasten to the Rue du Roi-Doré to arrest this Monsieur Victor who was clearly the real murderer.

But M. Méchinet immediately threw cold water on my enthusiasm.

"There are formalities, you know," he said. "I can do nothing without a warrant of arrest. It is to the Palais-de-Justice that we must go."

"And if Madam Monistrol sees us there? She will warn her accomplice and…"

"Perhaps so," replied M. Méchinet with undisguised bitterness, "perhaps we shall observe the formalities only to see our quarry disappear… Well, I might be able to do something about that. But we must make haste."

Hurrying, we arrived at the Palais-de-Justice and mounted four at a time the steep flight of steps leading to the chambers of the investigating magistrate, stopping only to ask the chief usher if the magistrate charged with the affair of "the little old man of Batignolles" was in his office.

"Yes, he is," replied the attendant, "but he has a witness with him at the moment—a young woman in black."

"That must be Madam Monistrol," whispered my companion to me; then he turned to the man again, "You know who I am, don't you? Quickly, give me something on which to write him a brief note. You can take it in for me."

The usher departed, dragging his feet along the dusty flagstones of the gallery, returning shortly to say that the magistrate would see us in an adjoining room, No. 9.

The magistrate, leaving Madam Monistrol under the watchful eye of his clerk, received us in the room of a colleague.

"What is it?" he asked in a tone which did nothing to disguise the distance which separates a judge from a humble detective.

M. Méchinet gave a brief but clear account of our achievements, hopes and disappointments.

Needless to say, the magistrate hardly seemed inclined to share our views.

"But he admits it!" he repeated, with a persistency which exasperated me.

However, after a series of protracted explanations, he consented:

"Oh, very well. I'll sign this warrant for you."

As soon as he was in possession of this indispensable document, M. Méchinet rushed from the building so precipitously that I almost fell down the stairs following him.

Outside, there was not a cab to be seen; nonetheless we covered the distance to the Rue du Roi-Doré in less than a quarter of an hour.

"Take care now," he said to me. And he himself was completely composed as we turned into the narrow alley of the house bearing the number 23.

"Where will I find M. Victor, please?" he asked the concierge.

"Fourth floor, door on the right."

"Is he in?"

"Yes."

M. Méchinet took a step in the direction of the staircase, then seemed to change his mind.

"I must treat my old friend to a good bottle of wine," he observed to the concierge. "Which is the nearest wine shop that he patronizes?"

"The one over the way."

To reach it we had only to cross the street.

"A bottle of wine, please, a good one… The one with the green seal," he said, as if he were an habitué.

I must admit that this simple idea had not occurred to me.

As soon as the bottle was brought, my companion produced the cork which I had found in the bedroom at Batignolles. The seals were undoubtedly identical.

It was not with moral certitude alone that M. Méchinet knocked firmly at M. Victor's door—now we had material proof.

"Come in, it's open," replied a voice with a pleasant ring to it.

The door was on the latch and we went in. The room was clean and tidy, and a pale, slightly-built man of thirty was bent over a workbench. Our visit did not seem to trouble him.

"What can I do for you?" he asked politely.

M. Méchinet strode forward and caught him by the arm.

"In the name of the Law, I arrest you."

The man blanched but did not lower his eyes.

"You've a damned cheek!" he said insolently. "What am I supposed to have done?"

M. Méchinet shrugged his shoulders.

"Don't come the child with me," he replied. "Your account is settled. You were seen leaving the house at Batignolles and in my pocket I have the cork which you used to protect the point of your dagger."

These words were a crushing blow for the wretch. He collapsed into a chair.

"I didn't do it," he stammered.

"You can tell that to the judge," said M. Méchinet without emotion, "but I fear he won't believe you. Your accomplice, Monistrol's wife, has confessed everything."

Victor sprang resiliently to his feet.

"Impossible! She knew nothing about it."

"So you delivered the blow on your own? Very well… That will do for a confession."

M. Méchinet turned to me and continued confidently:

"My dear M. Godeuil, if you would be good enough to look in the drawers I think you will probably find the dagger belonging to this fine fellow; in any case, you'll come across his mistress's portrait and her love letters."

The murderer clenched his teeth and I could read the rage in his eyes, but the relentless iron grip of M. Méchinet extinguished all hope of resistance in him.

In a chest of drawers I found the items my companion had mentioned.

And twenty minutes later, M. Victor was securely stowed away between M. Méchinet and myself in a cab rolling towards the Préfecture of Police.

I was amazed by how simple it had been. Was there no more than this to arresting a man destined for the scaffold?

Later I learnt to my cost that there are more dangerous criminals.

This one, however, gave himself up for lost as soon as he saw his cell at the Dépôt. In despair, he recounted the details of his crime to us.

He had known old M. Pigoreau a good many years, he explained. His single objective for murdering him, though, had been to compromise Monistrol in the crime—for whom he had reserved the full penalty of the Law. That was the reason he had dressed as Monistrol and taken Pluto with him. And once he had killed the old man, he dipped one of the fingers of the cadaver into the pool of blood and wrote those five letters which so nearly cost an innocent man his life.

"Oh, it was a clever scheme all right," he added with cynical effrontery. "If it had only succeeded, I would have killed two birds with one stone: I would have got rid of that fool whom I hated, and profited by winning the woman I love."

"Unfortunately," interposed M. Méch - inet, "you lost your head at the last minute. It always happens like that. Your mistake was to pick on the left hand of the body…"

Victor sprang to his feet.

"What!" he exclaimed. "That's what gave me away?"

"Exactly."

With the typical gesture of the misunderstood genius, he shook his fists at the heavens.

"God! What it is like to be an artist!" he shouted.

And looking at us with pity, he added:

"Didn't you know? M. Pigoreau was left-handed!"

And so an error in the investigation led to the discovery of the murderer.

The lesson was not lost on me, as I will prove at a later date by narrating some circumstances happily rather less dramatic than these.

Monistrol was released the next day.

The judge severely rebuked him at the same time for placing the outcome of justice in jeopardy with his persistent lies. He simply replied: "I love my wife. I thought she was guilty. I chose to sacrifice myself for her…"

Was she guilty? I would swear to it.

She was arrested; but was acquitted by the same judge who condemned Victor to life imprisonment with hard labor.

Today, the Monistrols keep a wine shop of ill repute on the Cours de Vincennes. Their uncle's inheritance is long spent and they live in fearful poverty.

James M'Govan

WILLIAM C. HONEYMAN (1845-?) wrote a series of what we would now term "police procedurals" under the pen name James M'Govan. According to Ellery Queen, "M'Govan" was a little, bandy-legged man, with a black spade beard; he invariably wore a velvet jacket; his chief interest in life was playing the violin and he was rarely seen without his violin case. He wrote a number of important books about the violin and violin-playing, including drawings probably depicting himself playing the violin.

Honeyman was the fiction editor of the *People's Journal* and wrote short stories, serials, and novels. Among his seventeen published books of fiction, *Brought to Bay; or, Experience of a City Detective* (1878), *Strange Clues; or Chronicles of a City Detective* (1881), and *Traced and Tracked; or Memoirs of a City Detective* (1884) were hugely popular, relating crime stories from the perspective of a street detective in Edinburgh. The books are incredibly rare today; the following excerpt is from *Traced and Tracked*.

THE MURDERED TAILOR'S WATCH
(A Curiosity in Circumstantial Evidence)

JAMES M'GOVAN

THE CASE OF the tailor, Peter Anderson, who was beaten to death near the Royal Terrace, on the Calton Hill, may not yet be quite forgotten by some, but, as the after-results are not so well known, it will bear repeating.

Some working men, hurrying along a little before six in the morning, found Anderson's body in a very steep path on the hill, and in a short time a stretcher was got and it was conveyed to the Head Office. The first thing I noticed when I saw the body was that one of the trousers' pockets was half-turned out, as if with a violent wrench, or a hand too full of money to get easily out again; and from this sprang another discovery—that the waistcoat button-hole in which the link of his albert[1] had evidently been constantly worn was wrenched clean through. There was no watch or chain visible, and the trousers' pockets were empty, so the first deduction was clear—the man had been robbed.

Robbery, indeed, appeared to me, at this stage of the case, to have been the prime cause of the outrage, and an examination of the body confirmed the idea. The neck was not broken, but there were marks of a strangulating arm about the neck, and the injuries about the head were quite sufficient to cause death. These seemed to indicate that two persons had been engaged in the crime, as is common in garroting cases—one to strangle and the other to rob and beat—and made me more hopeful of tracking the doers. On examining the spot at which the body had been found, I found traces of a violent struggle, and also a couple of folded papers, which proved to be unreceipted accounts headed "Peter Anderson, tailor and clothier," with the address of his place of business. These might have given us a clue to his identity had such been needed, but his wife had been at the Office reporting his absence only an hour before his body was brought in, and we had only to turn to her description of his person and clothing to confirm our suspicion.

Anderson, on the fatal night on which he

[1] A gold chain, worn in the fashion of Prince Albert, the consort of Queen Victoria.

disappeared, had unexpectedly drawn an account of some £10 or £12 from a customer, and in the joy of receiving the money had invited the man to an adjoining public-house to drink "a jorum,"[2] and one round followed another until poor Peter Anderson's head was fitter for his pillow than for guiding his feet. On entering the public-house—which was a very busy one, not far from the Calton Hill—Anderson, I found, had gone up to the bar, and before all the loungers or hangers-on pulled a handful of notes, and silver, and gold from his trousers' pocket, saying to his companion:—

"What will you have?"

Afterwards, when they got into talk, they adjourned to a private box at the back; but it was there I thought that the mischief had been done. Anderson had a gold albert across his breast, and might be believed to have a watch at the end of it; but the chain, after all, might have been only plated, and the watch a pinchbeck[3] thing, to a thief not worth taking; but the reckless display of a handful of notes, gold, and silver; if genuine criminals chanced to see it, was a temptation and revelation too powerful to be resisted. The man who carried money in that fashion was likely to have more in his pockets, and a gold watch at least. If he got drunk, or was likely to get drunk, he would be worth waiting and watching for; so, at least, I thought the intending criminals would reason; never dreaming of course of the plan ending in determined resistance and red-handed murder. Your garroter is generally a big coward, and will never

risk his skin or his liberty with a sober man if he can get one comfortably muddled with drink.

There was no time to elaborate theories or schemes of capture. A gold watch and chain valued at about £30, and £14 in money, were gone.[4] A rare prize was afloat among the sharks, and I surmised that the circumstance would be difficult to hide. The thief and the honest man are alike in one failing—they find it difficult to conceal success. It prints itself in their faces; in the quantity of drink they consume; in the tread of their feet; the triumphant leer at the baffled or sniffing detective, and in their reckless indulgence in gaudy articles of flash dress. I went down to the Cowgate[5] and Canongate[6] at once, strolling into every likely place, and nipping up quite a host of my "bairns." I thought I had got the right men indeed when I found two known as "The Crab Apple" and "Coskey" flush of money and muddled with drink, but a day's investigation proved that they owed their good fortune to a stupid swell who had got into their clutches over in the New Town.[7] Coskey, indeed, strongly declared that he did not believe the Anderson affair had been managed by a professional criminal at all.

"If it had been done by any of us I'd have heard on it," was his frank remark to me.

I was pretty sure that Coskey spoke the truth, for in his nervous anxiety to escape Calcraft's toilet he had actually confessed to me all the particulars of the New Town robbery by which his own pockets had been filled, and

---

[2] A large drinking vessel—figuratively, that is.

[3] Imitation gold.

[4] £44 in 1884 is the modern equivalent of almost £24,000 in equivalent earnings, a substantial sum for a working-class thief.

[5] A district in Edinburgh named after its former use for herding cows, then known as "Little Ireland."

[6] A poor district in the center of Edinburgh, named for the canons of Holyrood Abbey, located there.

[7] Built in the mid- to late 18th century, this carefully planned area was a response to overcrowding in the "Old Town" of Edinburgh.

which afterwards led to a seven years' retirement from the scene of his labors.

The hint thus received prepared me for making the worst slip of all I had made in the case. I went to Anderson's widow to get the number of the watch, and some description by which it might be identified. She could not tell me the number or the maker's name; she could only say that it had a white dial and black figures, but declared that she would know it out of a thousand by a deep "clour" or indentation on the back of the case.

"I was there when it got the mark," she said, "and I could never be mistaken if the watch was put before me. A thief might alter the number, but nobody could take out that mark, for we tried it, and the watchmaker could do nothing for it. My man was working hard one day with the watch on, when a customer called to be measured. The waistcoat he wore wasn't a very bonny one, and he whipped it off in a hurry, forgetting about the watch, which was tugged out, and came bang against the handle of one of his irons. The watch was never a bit the worse, but the case had aye the mark on it—just there," and the widow, to illustrate her statement, showed me a spot on the back of my own watch, and then so minutely explained the line of the indentation, its length and its depth, that I felt sure that if it came in my way I should be able to identify it as readily as by a number.

This would have been all very well if her information had there ended, but it didn't.

"You are hunting away among thieves and jail birds for the man that did it," she bitterly remarked, "but I think I could put my hand on him without any detective to help me."

"You suspect some one, then?" I exclaimed, with a new interest.

"Suspect? I wish I was as sure of any-

thing," she answered, with great emphasis. "The brute threatened to do it."

"What brute?"

"Just John Burge, the man who was work-ing to him as journeyman two months ago."

"Indeed. Did they quarrel?"

"A drunken passionate wretch that no-body would have any thing to do wi'," vehemently continued the widow, waxing hotter in her words with every word she had uttered, "but just because they had been apprentices together Peter took pity on him and gave him work. They were aye quarrelling, but one day it got worse than usual, and I thought my man would have killed him. It was quite a simple thing began it—an argument as to which is the first day in summer—but in the end they were near fighting, and after Peter had near choked him, Burge swore that he would have his life for it—that he would watch him night and day, and then knock the 'sowl oot o' him in some dark corner, before he knew where he was.' That was after the master and the laddies had thrown him out at the door and down the stair; and for some days I wouldn't let Peter cross the door. But he only laughed at me after a bit, and said that Burge's 'bark was waur than his bite,' and went about just as usual. And all the time the wicked, ungrateful wretch was watching for a chance to take his life."

"Why did you not tell us of this quarrel at first?" I asked, after a pause.

"Because I thought you detectives were so sharp and clever that you would have Burge in your grips before night, without a word from me; but you're not nearly so clever as you're called."

"But he never actually attacked your hus-band?" I quietly interposed, knowing that wives are apt to take exceedingly exaggerated views of their husband's wrongs or rights.

"Oh, but he did, though. He came up once, not long after the quarrel, and said he had not got all the money due to him, and tried to murder Peter with the cutting shears."

"Murder him? How could he murder him with shears?" I asked, with marked skepticism.

"Well, I didn't wait to see; but ran in and gripped him by the arms till my man took the shears from him. The creatur' had no more strength than a sparry, though he's as tall as you."

"No more strength than a sparrow?" That incidental revelation staggered me. It seemed to me quite impossible that a weak man could have been the murderer of Anderson, unless, indeed, he had had an accomplice, and that was unlikely with a man seeking mere revenge. For a moment I was inclined to think it possible that Burge might have tracked his victim to the hill and accomplished the revenge, and that afterwards, when he had fled the spot, some of the "ghosts" haunting the hill might have stripped the dead or dying man of his valuables; but several circumstances led me to reject the supposition—wisely, too, as it appeared in the end. Burge, the widow told me, was a tall man, with a white, "potty" face, and a little, red, snub-nose, and always wore a black frock coat and dress hat. I took down the name of the street in which he lived—for I could get no number—and turned in that direction. In about fifteen minutes I had reached, not the street, but the crossing leading to it, when I met full in the face a man answering his description, and having the unmistakable tailor's "nick" in his back.

"That should be Burge," was my mental conclusion, though I had never seen him before. "If he's not, he is at least a tailor, and may know him," and then I stopped him with the words:—

"Do you know a tailor called John Burge who lives hereabout?"

"That's me," he said, with sudden animation, taking the pipe from his mouth, and evidently expecting a call at his trade, "who wants me?"

"I do."

"Oh," and he looked me all over, evidently wondering how I looked so unlike the trade.

There was a queer pause, and then I said:

"My name's M'Govan, and I want you to go with me as far as the Police Office, about that affair on the Calton Hill."

A wonderful change took place in his face the moment I uttered the words—a change which, but for the grave nature of the case, would have been actually comical; his "potty" white cheeks became red, and his red snub-nose as suddenly became white.

"Well, do you know, that's curious!" he at length gasped; "but I was just coming up to the Office now, in case I should be suspected of having a hand in it. I had a quarrel with Anderson, and said some strong things, I've no doubt, in my passion, but of course I never meant them."

I listened in silence; but my mental comment, I remember, was, "A very likely story!"

"I was coming up to say what I can prove—that I was at the other end of the town that night, and home and in my bed by a quarter to eleven," he desperately added, rightly interpreting my silence.

I became more interested at the mention of the exact hour; for I had ascertained beyond doubt that Anderson had not left the public-house and parted with his friend till eleven o'clock struck. He had, in fact, been "warned out," along with a number of bar-loafers, at shutting-up time.

"Did anyone see you at home at that hour?" I asked, after cautioning him.

"Yes, the wife and bairns."

"Imphm."

"You think that's not good evidence; but I have more; I was in a public-house with some friends till half-past ten; they can swear to that; and they went nearly all the road home with me," he continued with growing excitement. "Do I look like a murderer? My God! I could swear on a Bible that such a thing was never in my mind. Don't look so horrible and solemn, man, but say you believe me!"

I couldn't say that, for I believed the whole a fabrication got up in a moment of desperation; and little more was spoken on either side till we reached the Head Office, where he repeated the same story to the Fiscal,[8] and was locked up. I fully expected that I should easily tear his story to pieces by taking his so-called witnesses one by one, but I was mistaken. His wife and children, for example, the least reliable of his witnesses in the eyes of the law, became the strongest, for when I called and saw them they were in perfect ignorance both of Burge's arrest and the fact that he expected to be suspected.

They distinctly remembered their father being home "earlier" on that Friday night, and the wife added that it was more than she had expected, for by being in bed so early Burge had been able to rise early on the following morning and finish some work on the Saturday which she had fully expected would be "disappointed." Then the men with whom he had been drinking and playing dominoes up to half-past ten were emphatic in their statements, which tallied almost to a minute with those of Burge. Burge had not been particularly flush of money after that date, but, on the contrary, had pleaded so hard for payment of the work done on the Saturday that the man was glad to compromise matters and get rid of him by part payment in shape of half-a-crown. The evidence, as was afterwards remarked, was not the best—a few drinkers in a public-house, whose ideas of time and place might be readily believed to be hazy, and the interested wife and children of the suspected man; but in the absence of condemning facts it sufficed, and after a brief detention Burge was set at liberty.

About that time, among the batch of suspected persons in our keeping was a man named Daniel O'Doyle. How he came to be suspected I forget, but I believe it was through having a deal of silver and some sovereigns in the pockets of his ragged trousers when he was brought to the Office as a "drunk and disorderly." O'Doyle gave a false name, too, when he came to his senses; but then it was too late, for a badly-written letter from some one in Ireland had been found in his pocket when he was brought in. He was a powerfully-built man, and in his infuriated state it took four men to get him to the Office. He could give no very satisfactory account of how he came by the money in his possession. He had been harvesting, he said, but did not know the name of the place or its geographical position, except that it was east of Edinburgh "a long way," and he was going back to Ireland with his earnings, but chanced to take a drop too much and half-murder a man in Leith Walk, and so got into our hands. On the day after his capture and that of his remand O'Doyle was "in the horrors," and at night

---

[8] The Crown Office and Procurator Fiscal Service is responsible for the prosecution of crime in Scotland, the investigation of sudden or suspicious deaths, and the investigation of complaints against the police. The procurators fiscal are the public prosecutors.

during a troubled sleep was heard by a man in the same cell to mutter something about "Starr Road," and having "hidden it safe there." This brief and unintelligible snatch was repeated to me next morning, but, stupid as it now appears to me, I could make nothing of it. I knew that there was no such place as "Starr Road" in Edinburgh, and said so; and as for him having hidden something, that was nothing for a wandering shearer, and might, after all, be only his reaping hook or bundle of lively linen.[9] O'Doyle was accordingly tried for assault, and sentenced to thirty days' imprisonment, at the expiry of which he was set at liberty and at once disappeared. My impression now is that O'Doyle was never seriously suspected of having had a hand in the Calton Hill affair, but that, being in our keeping about the time, he came in for his share of suspicion among dozens more perfectly innocent. If he had had bank-notes about him it might have been different, for I have found that there is a strong feeling against these and in favor of gold among the untutored Irish, which induces them to get rid of them almost as soon as they chance to receive them.

So the months passed away and no discovery was made; we got our due share of abuse from the public; and the affair promised to remain as dark and mysterious as the Slater murder in the Queen's Park. But for the incident I am now coming to, I believe the crime would have been still unsolved.

About two years after, I chanced to be among a crowd at a political hustings in Parliament Square, at which I remember Adam Black came in for a great deal of howling and abuse. I was there, of course, on business, fully expecting to nip up some of my diligent "family" at work among the pockets of the excited voters; but no game could have been further from my thoughts than that which I had the good fortune to bag. I was moving about on the outskirts of the crowd, when a face came within the line of my vision which was familiar yet puzzling. The man had a healthy prosperous look, and nodded smilingly to me, more as a superior than an inferior in position.

"Don't you remember me?—John Burge; I was in the Anderson murder, you mind; the Calton Hill affair;" and then I smiled too and shook the proffered hand.

"How are you getting on now?"

"Oh, first rate—doing well for myself," was the bright and pleased-looking answer. "Yon affair was a lesson to me; turned teetot.[10] when I came out, and have never broke it since. It's the best way."

It seemed so, to look at him. The "potty" look was gone from his face; his cheeks had a healthy color, and his nose had lost its rosiness. His dress too was better. The glossy, well-ironed dress hat was replaced by one shining as if fresh from the maker, and the threadbare frock coat by one of smooth, firm broadcloth. He was getting stouter, too, and his broad, white waistcoat showed a pretentious expanse of gold chain. He chatted away for some time, evidently a little vain of the change in his circumstances, and at length drew out a handsome gold watch, making, as his excuse for referring to it, the remark:

"Ah, it's getting late; I can't stay any longer."

My eye fell upon the watch, as it had evidently been intended that it should, and

---

[9]   Meaning, his extra clothing.

[10] Teetotaler—one who abstains from drinking alcohol. The etymology of the term is obscure.

almost with the first glance I noticed a deep nick in the edge of the case, at the back. Possibly the man's own words had taken my mind back to the lost watch of the murdered tailor and its description, but certainly the moment I saw the mark on the case I put out my hand with affected carelessness, as he was slipping it back to his pocket, saying:—

"That's a nice watch; let's have a look at it."

It was tendered at once, and I found it to have a white china dial and black figures. At last I came back to the nick and scrutinized it closely.

"You've given it a bash there," I remarked, after a pause.

"No, that was done when I got it."

"Bought it lately?"

"Oh, no; a long time ago."

"Who from?"

"From one of the men working under me; I got it a great bargain," he answered with animation. "It's a chronometer, and belonged to an uncle of his, but it was out of order— had lain in the bottom of a sea chest till some of the works were rusty—and so I got it cheap."

"Imphm. There has been some lying in the bargain anyhow," I said, after another look at the watch, "for it is an ordinary English lever, not a chronometer. Is the man with you yet?"

"No; but, good gracious! You don't mean to say that there's anything wrong about the watch? It's not—not a stolen one?"

"I don't know, but there was one exactly like this stolen that time that Anderson was killed."

In one swift flash of alarm, his face, before so rosy, became as white as the waistcoat covering his breast. Then he slowly examined the watch with a trembling hand, and finally stammered out:—

"I remember it, and this is not unlike it. But that's nothing—hundreds of watches are as like as peas."

I differed with him there, and finally got him to go with me to the Office, at which he was detained, while I went in search of Anderson's widow to see what she would say about the watch.

If I had an opinion at all about the case at this stage, it was that the watch taken was not that of the murdered man. I could scarcely otherwise account for Burge's demeanor. He appeared so surprised and innocent, whereas a man thus detected in the act of wearing such a thing, knowing its terrible history, could scarcely have helped betraying his guilt.

My fear, then, as I made my way to the house of Anderson's widow, was that she, woman like, would no sooner see the mark on the case than she would hastily declare it to be the missing watch. To avoid as far as possible a miscarriage of justice, I left the watch at the Office, carefully mixed up with a dozen or two more then in our keeping, one or two of which resembled it in appearance. I found the widow easily enough, and took her to the Office with me, saying simply that we had a number of watches which she might look at, with the possibility of finding that of her husband. The watches were laid out before her in a row, faces upward, and she slowly went over them with her eye, touching none till she came to that taken from Burge. Then she paused, and there was a moment's breathless stillness in the room.

"This ane's awfu' like it," she said, and, lifting the watch, she turned it, and beamed out in delight as she recognized the sharp nick on the back of the case. "Yes, it's it! Look at the mark I told you about."

She pointed out other trifling particulars

confirming the identity, but practically the whole depended on exactly what had first drawn my attention to the watch—the nick on the case. Now dozens of watches might have such a mark upon them, and it was necessary to have a much more reliable proof before we could hope for a conviction against Burge on such a charge.

I had thought of this all the way to and from the widow's house. She knew neither the number of the watch nor the maker's name, but with something like hopefulness I found that she knew the name of the watchmaker in Glasgow who had sold it to her husband, and another in Edinburgh who had cleaned it. I went through to Glasgow the same day with the watch in my pocket, found the seller, and by referring to his books discovered the number of the watch sold to Anderson, which, I was electrified to find, was identical with that on the gold lever[11] I carried. The name of the maker and description of the watch also tallied perfectly; and the dealer emphatically announced himself ready to swear to the identity in any court of justice. My next business was to visit the man who had cleaned the watch for Anderson in Edinburgh. I was less hopeful of him, and hence had left him to the last, and therefore was not disappointed to find that he had no record of the number or maker's name. On examining the watch through his working glass, however, he declared that he recognized it perfectly as that which he had cleaned for Anderson by one of the screws, which had half of its head broken off, and thus had caused him more trouble than usual in fitting up the watch after cleaning.

"I would have put a new one in rather than bother with it," he said, "but I had not one beside me that would fit it, and as I was pressed for time, I made the old one do. It was my own doing, too, for I broke the top in taking the watch down."

I was now convinced, almost against my will, that the watch was really that taken from Anderson; my next step was to test Burge's statement as to how it came into his possession. If that broke down, his fate was sealed.

When I again appeared before Burge he was eager to learn what had transpired, and appeared unable to understand why he should still be detained; all which I now set down as accomplished hypocrisy. It seemed to me that he had lied from the first, and I was almost angry with myself for having given so much weight to his innocent looks and apparent surprise.

Cutting short his questions with no very amiable answers, I asked the name and address of the man from whom he alleged he had bought the watch. Then he looked grave, and admitted that the man, whose name was Chisholm, might be difficult to find, as he was a kind of "orra"[12] hand, oftener out of work than not. I received the information in silence, and went on the hunt for Chisholm, whom I had no difficulty whatever in finding at the house of a married daughter with whom he lodged. He was at home when I called—at his dinner or tea—and stared at me blankly when I was introduced, being probably acquainted with my face, like many more whom I have never spoken to or noticed.

"I have called about a watch that you sold to Burge the tailor, whom you were working with some six months ago," I said quietly.

---

[11] A style of pocket watch with a lever escapement mechanism to drive the hands.
[12] Scottish slang: irregular, "odd" as in odd jobs.

The man, who had been drinking tea or coffee out of a basin, put down the dish in evident concern, and stared at me more stupidly than before.

"A watch!—what kin' o' a watch?" he huskily exclaimed. "I haena had a watch for mair nor ten years."

"The watch is a gold lever, but he says you sold it to him as a chronometer which had belonged to your uncle, a seaman."

Chisholm's face was now pale to the very point of his nose, but that did not necessarily imply guilt on his part. I have noticed the look far oftener on the faces of witnesses than prisoners.

"What? An uncle! A seaman!" he cried with great energy, turning an amazed look on his daughter. "I havena an uncle leeving—no ane. The man must be mad," and this statement the daughter promptly supported.

"Do you mean to say—can you swear that you never sold him a watch of any kind—which was rusty in the works through lying in a sea-chest?"

"Certainly, sir—certainly, I can swear that. I never had a watch to sell, and I'll tell him that to his face," volubly answered Chisholm, whose brow now was as thick with perspiration as if he had been doing a hard day's work since I entered. "Onybody that kens me can tell ye I've never had a watch, or worn ane, for ten year and mair. I wad be only owre glad if I had."

I questioned him closely and minutely, but he declared most distinctly and emphatically that the whole story of Burge was an invention. I ought to have been satisfied with this declaration—it was voluble and decided, and earnest as any statement could be—but I was not.

The man's manner displeased me. It was too noisy and hurried, and his looks of astonishment and innocence were, if anything, too marked. I left the house in a puzzled state.

"What if I should have to deal with *two* liars?" was my reflection. "How could I pit them against each other?"

Back I trudged to the Office, and saw Burge at once.

"I have seen the man Chisholm, and he declares that he not only did not sell you a watch of any kind, but that he has not had one in his possession for upwards of ten years."

Burge paled to a deathly hue, and I saw the cold sweat break out in beads on his temples.

"I was just afraid of that," he huskily whispered, after a horrible pause. "Chisholm's an awful liar, and will say that now to save his own skin. There must have been something wrong about the way he got it. I was a fool to believe his story. I remember now he made me promise not to say that I had bought the watch from him, or how I got it, in case the other relatives should find out that he had taken it."

"Indeed! Then you have no witness what ever to produce as to the purchase?" I cried, after a long whistle.

"None."

"Did you not speak of it to anybody?"

"Not a soul but yourself that I mind of."

"Well, all I can say is that your case looks a bad one," I said at last, as I turned to leave him. "By the by, though, what about the chain? Did you buy that from him too?"

My reason for asking was, that the chain was a neck one, not an albert,[13] and, of course, had not been identified by the widow of Anderson.

"No, I had the chain; I had taken it in

[13] An albert chain had a swivel hook at the end; evidently, a "neck" chain attached in a different manner.

payment of an account; but he wanted me to buy a chain, too, now that I remember."

"What kind of a chain? Did you see it?"

"No; I said I did not need it; but I would look at the watch. He wanted a pound for the chain, and eight for the watch. I got it for £5, 10s., and then he went on the spree for a fortnight."

"A whole fortnight? Surely some one will be able to recall that," I quickly interposed, half inclined to believe that Burge was not at least the greater liar of the two. "His daughter will surely remember it?"

"I don't know about that," groaned Burge, in despairing tones. "That man takes so many sprees that it's difficult to mind ane frae anither."

I resolved to try the daughter, nevertheless, and after getting from Burge, as near as he could remember, the date of the bargain, I left him and began to ponder how I could best get an unvarnished tale from this prospective witness. While I pondered, a new link in this most mysterious case was thrown into my hands.

We had been particularly careful after the arrest of Burge to keep the affair secret, but in spite of the precaution, an account of the arrest, altogether garbled and erroneous, appeared in the next day's papers. From this account it appeared that we were confident of Burge's guilt, and were only troubled because we could not discover his accomplices in the crime, and on that account "were not disposed to be communicative," as the penny-a-liner grandly expressed himself. The immediate result of this stupid paragraph, which seemed to book Burge for the gallows beyond redemption, was a letter from the West, bearing neither name nor address, it is true, but still written with such decision and vigor that I

could not but give it some weight in my feeble gropings at the truth. This letter was placed in my hands, though not addressed to me particularly, just as I was wondering how to best question Chisholm's daughter about her father's big spree. The letter was short, and well-written and spelled, and began by saying that Burge, whom we had in custody on suspicion of being concerned in the robbery and murder of Anderson, was perfectly innocent; that the whole of the facts were known to the writer, whose lips were sealed as to who the criminal really was, and who only wrote that he might save an innocent man from a shameful death. The post-mark on the letter was that of a considerable town on the Clyde, or my thoughts would inevitably have reverted to Chisholm as the author or prompter. With the suspicion of this man had come at last an idea that he was in some way mixed up in the crime; yet he did not look either strong enough or courageous enough to be the murderer. Quite uncertain how to act, I left the Office, and wandered down in the direction of Chisholm's home. It was quite dark, I remember, and I was ascending the narrow stair in hope that Chisholm might by that time be out of the house, when a man stumbled down on me in the dark, cursing me sharply for not calling out that I was there. The man was Chisholm, as I knew at once by the tone of the voice, and how I did not let him pass on, and make my inquiries at the daughter, is more than I can tell to this day. I merely allowed him to reach the bottom of the stair, and then turned and followed him. At the bottom I watched his figure slowly descending the close towards the Back Canongate till he reached the bottom, when he paused and peered cautiously forth before venturing out. The stealthy walk and that cunning look forth

I believe decided me, coupled with the decided change in the tone in which he cursed me in the dark from the smooth and oily manner in which he had answered my questions during the day. I would follow him, though wherefore or why I did not trouble to ask. About half-way down the South Back Canongate, where the Public Washing House now stands, there was at that time an open drain which ran with a strong current in the direction of the Queen's Park. As it left the green for the Park, this drain emptied itself down an iron-barred opening in the ground, and made a sudden dip downwards of twenty or thirty feet on smooth flag-stones, which carried the water away into the darkness with a tremendous rush and noise. So steep was the gradient at this covered part of the drain, and so smooth the bottom, that miserable cats and dogs, doomed to die, had merely to be put within the grating, when down they shot, and were seen or heard no more.

I followed Chisholm as far as this green, which he entered, and then wondered what his object could be. That it was not quite a lawful one I could guess from the fact that he so often paused and looked about him that I had the greatest difficulty in keeping him in sight without myself being seen. At length he came to the opening in the wall where the open drain ceased and dipped into the iron bars with a roar audible even to me, and then with another furtive look around, and before I had the slightest idea of what he was intending to do, he put his hand in his pocket, drew something forth, and threw it sharply into the roaring, scurrying water. A moment more and my hand was on his arm. He started round with a scared cry, and recognized and named me.

"What's that you threw down the drain?" I sternly demanded, without giving him time

to recover, and tightening my grip on his arm.

"Oh, naething, naething, sir—only an auld pipe that's nae mair use," he confusedly stammered.

"A pipe!" I scornfully echoed. "Man, what do you think my head's made of? You didn't come so far to throw away a pipe. Were you afraid that, like some of the cats the laddies put down there, it would escape and come back again?"

He tried to grin, cringingly, but the effect was ghastly in the extreme.

"No, no, Maister M'Govan; I was just walking this way ony way, and thought I wad get rid o' my auld pipe."

"More like, it was a gold albert," I sharply said, getting out the handcuffs. "If I had only guessed what you were after I might have been nearer, and prevented the extravagance. You're unlike every one else in the world, throwing away good gold while others are breaking their hearts to get it. Come, now, try your hand in these; and then I'll have to see if the burn will give up your offering."

He was utterly and abjectly silenced, and accepted the bracelets without demur, which led me to believe that my surmise was a hit. The tailor's gold albert, supposing Burge's story to be true, was all that remained unaccounted for, and its possession now was frightfully dangerous. What more natural, then, that Chisholm should take alarm at my visit, and hasten to dispose of it in the most effectual manner within his reach? If he had put it through the melting pot, and I had arrived only in time to see the shapeless nugget tossed out of the crucible, he could not have given me a greater pang; but of course I did not tell him that. I expected never to see it again, and I was right, for the chain has never been seen or heard of since. My thoughts on the way to the Office were not pleasant; afterthoughts with an "if" are always tormenting; and mine was "If I had only seized him before he reached the drain, and had him searched." Then he was so secretive and cunning that I had no hope whatever of him committing himself to a confession. In this I made the error of supposing him entirely guilty. I forgot the case of "Cosky" and "The Crab Apple," who were only too glad to save their necks at the expense of their liberty. Chisholm, though cunning as a fox, was a terrible coward, and as we neared the Office he tremblingly said:—

"Will I be long, think ye, o' getting oot again?"

I stared at him in surprise, and then, with some impatience, said:—

"About three weeks after the trial probably."

"What? How? Will three weeks be the sentence?" he stammered in confusion.

"No; but that is the interval generally allowed between sentence and hanging."

"Good God, man! They canna hang me!" he exclaimed, nearly dropping on the street with terror.

"Wait. If I get that chain out of the drain it will hang you as sure as fate;" I grimly replied. I was rather pleased at being able to say it, for I was snappish and out of temper.

"But I never killed the tailor; never saw the man," he exclaimed, evidently fearfully in earnest.

"I've nothing to do with that; it all depends on what the jury think," I shortly answered, and then we got to the Office, and he made a rambling statement about being taken up innocently, and was then locked up.

My immediate task was to have the drain explored, but that was all labor thrown away. The rush of water had been too strong, and the chain was gone, buried in mud and slime, or carried away to sea. I soon had abundant evidence that Chisholm had been on the spree for a fortnight about the time stated by Burge, but my intention of weaving a complete web round him was stayed by a message from himself, asking to see me that he might tell all he knew of the watch and chain. He did not know that I had failed to get the chain, or he might have risked absolute silence.

"Ye ken, I'm a bit of a fancier of birds," he said, in beginning his story.

"Including watches and chains," I interposed.

"I was oot very early ae Sunday morning, for however late I'm up on a Saturday, I can never sleep on Sunday morning," he continued, with a dutiful grin at my remark. "I gaed doon by the Abbey Hill to the Easter Road, and when I was hauf way to Leith I saw a yellow finch flee oot at a dyke where its nest was, and begin flichering along on the grund to draw me away frae the place. Cunnin' brutes them birds, but I was fly for it, and instead o' following it, and believing it couldna flee, I stoppit and begoud to look for the nest in the dyke. But before I got forrit I had kind o' lost the exact place. I searched aboot, wi' the bird watchin' me geyan feared—like a wee bit off, and at last I found a hole half filled up wi' a loose stane. Oot cam' the stane, and in gaed my haund; but instead o' a nest I fund a gold watch and chain; and that's the God's truth, though I should dee this meenit."

"Did you mention the finding to anyone?"

"No me; I didna even tell my daughter, for I kent if it was fund oot I might get thirty days for keeping it up. I had an idea that the watch had been stolen and planted there, or I might have gaen to a pawnshop wi' it. It was kind o' damaged wi' lying in the dyke, so at last I made up a story and sent it to Maister Burge."

"You are good at making up stories, I think?" I reflectively observed.

"I'm thinkin' there's a pair of us, Maister M'Govan," he readily returned, with a pawky dab at my ribs.

But for his coolness and evident relief at getting the thing off his mind, I should have set down the whole as another fabrication. But when a man begins to smile and joke, it may be taken for granted that he does not think himself in immediate danger of being hanged. His story, however, might have availed him but little had I not chanced to turn up my notes on the case at its earlier stages, and found there the hitherto meaningless words muttered by Daniel O'Doyle. "Starr Road" muttered in sleep might be but a contraction of Easter Road, or be those actual words imperfectly overheard. Then there were the words about something being "hidden safely" there, and the whole tallied so closely that I was at last sure that I was on the right track. These additional gleanings made me revert to my anonymous correspondent in the west. It was scarcely likely that I should be able to trace him; but he spoke in his note of the guilty one being a person or persons outside of himself—known to him. This lessened my interest in him personally, but made me think that if I visited the town I might get hold of O'Doyle himself, which would be quite as good, if not better. I accordingly went to the place, in which there is a public prison, and as a first step called on the police superintendent. An examination of the books at length sent me in the direction of the prison, in which a man answering the description, and having O'Doyle for one of his names, had

been confined on a nine months' sentence for robbery. I was now in high spirits, and quite sure that in the prisoner I should recognize the O'Doyle I wanted; but on reaching the place I found that a more imperative and inexorable officer had been there before me in shape of death. Immediately on getting the answer I made the inquiry, "Did he make any statement or confession before he died?" This was not easily answered, and before it could be, with satisfaction, a number of the officials had to be questioned, and then I found that O'Doyle had been attended, as is usual, in his last moments by a Catholic priest.

This gentleman was still in the town, though not stationed in the Prison, and knowing something of the vows of a priest, I despaired at once of extracting anything from him, but became possessed of a desire to have a look at his handwriting. Accordingly I sent him a polite note requesting him to send me word when he would be at liberty to see me for a few minutes' conversation. I fully expected to get a written note in reply, however short, but instead I got a message delivered by the servant girl, to the effect that her master was at home, and would see me now. I grinned and bore it, though it is not pleasant to feel eclipsed in cunning by anyone. I went with the girl, and found the priest, a pale, hardworked looking man, leaning back in his chair exhausted and silent, and certainly looking as if he at least did not eat the bread of idleness. I felt rather small as I introduced myself and ran over the case that had brought me there, he listening to the whole with closed eyes, and a face as immovable as that of a statue. When I had finished there was an awkward pause. I had not exactly asked anything, but it was implied in my sudden pull up, but for a full minute there was no response.

At last he opened his eyes—and very keen, penetrating eyes they were—and, fixing me sternly with his gaze, he said:—

"Did you ever come in contact with a Catholic priest before, Mr. M'Govan?"

"Frequently."

"Did you ever know one to break his vows and reveal the secrets of heaven?"

"Never."

"Do you think one of them would do it if you asked him?"

"I think not."

"Do you think he would do it if you threatened him with prison?"

"Scarcely."

"Or with death—say if you had power to tear him limb from limb, or torture every drop of blood from his body?"

"I don't know—I shouldn't like to try."

"Then what do you come to me for?" he sharply continued, with a slight tinge of red in his pale cheeks. "Am I, think you, more unworthy than any other that has yet lived?"

"No, I should hope not," I stammered; "and I did not come expecting you to reveal what was told you in confession—"

"What then—you wish to know if I wrote that letter maybe?"

"Yes."

"And you'll be satisfied that I speak the truth when I answer?"

"Yes."

"And you'll ask no more?"

"I'll ask no more."

"Then I didn't. Bridget, show the gentleman out." I was so staggered and nonplussed that I was in the street before I had time to ponder his reply. I was convinced then, as I am now, that the priest spoke the literal truth; how then had the letter been written? Certainly not by O'Doyle himself. Was it possible that a third person could have got at the information?

Back I went to the jail, and by rigid questioning discovered that at the time of O'Doyle's death there was one other person, a delicate man of some education, in the hospital, who complained of pains in the head, and of having grown stone deaf since his incarceration. This man had been set at liberty shortly after, and made no secret of having malingered so successfully as to get all the luxuries of the hospital instead of the hard labor of the other prisoners. There was then an excited and prolonged conversation between this man and the priest I had visited; and as they were of the same faith I have little doubt but the father had bound him down in some way to keep secret what he had chanced to overhear of O'Doyle's confession. This at least was my theory, and a peculiar flash of the priest's eyes when I afterwards hinted at the discovery convinced me that I was not far off the truth.

Chisholm, for his bird-nesting experiment, got thirty days' imprisonment, and Burge, after about a month's detention, was discharged.

C. L. Pirkis

CATHERINE LOUISA PIRKIS (1841-1910) was an English writer of fourteen novels, published between 1877 and 1894, and numerous short stories. With her husband, she founded the National Canine Defence League. The following story was first published in *The Ludgate Monthly* in 1893 and collected in *The Experiences of Loveday Brooke, Lady Detective* (1894).

Loveday Brooke was not the first female detective in print (that honor goes to Mrs. Paschal's *The Experiences of a Lady Detective* [1861], by "Anonym"), but she had "the faculty—so rare among women—of carrying out orders to the very letter." A lady in her early thirties, always found primly dressed in black, Brooke was a popular character of the day.

THE REDHILL SISTERHOOD

C. L. PIRKIS

THEY WANT YOU at Redhill, now," said Mr. Dyer, taking a packet of papers from one of his pigeon-holes. "The idea seems gaining ground in many quarters that in cases of mere suspicion, women detectives are more satisfactory than men, for they are less likely to attract attention. And this Redhill affair, so far as I can make out, is one of suspicion only."

It was a dreary November morning; every gas jet in the Lynch Court office was alight, and a yellow curtain of outside fog draped its narrow windows.

"Nevertheless, I suppose one can't afford to leave it uninvestigated at this season of the year, with country-house robberies beginning in so many quarters," said Miss Brooke.

"No; and the circumstances in this case certainly seem to point in the direction of the country-house burglar. Two days ago a somewhat curious application was made privately, by a man giving the name of John Murray, to Inspector Gunning, of the Reigate police—Redhill, I must tell you, is in the Reigate po-

lice district. Murray stated that he had been a greengrocer in South London, had sold his business there, and had, with the proceeds of the sale, bought two small houses in Redhill, intending to let the one and live in the other. These houses are situated in a blind alley, known as Paved Court, a narrow turning leading off the London and Brighton coach road. Paved Court has been known to the sanitary authorities for the past ten years as a regular fever nest, and as the houses which Murray bought—numbers 7 and 8—stand at the very end of the blind alley, with no chance of thorough ventilation, I dare say the man got them for next to nothing. He told the Inspector that he had had great difficulty in procuring a tenant for the house he wished to let, number 8, and that consequently when, about three weeks back, a lady, dressed as a nun, made him an offer for it, he immediately closed with her. The lady gave her name simply as 'Sister Monica,' and stated that she was a member of an undenominational Sisterhood that had recently been founded by a wealthy lady, who wished her name kept a secret. Sister Monica gave no references, but, instead, paid a quarter's rent in advance, saying that she wished to take possession of the house immediately, and open it as a home for crippled orphans."

"Gave no references—home for cripples," murmured Loveday, scribbling hard and fast in her note-book.

"Murray made no objection to this," continued Mr. Dyer, "and, accordingly, the next day, Sister Monica, accompanied by three other Sisters and some sickly children, took possession of the house, which they furnished with the barest possible necessaries from cheap shops in the neighborhood. For a time, Murray said, he thought he had secured most desirable tenants, but during the last ten days suspicions as to their real character have entered his mind, and these suspicions he thought it his duty to communicate to the police. Among their possessions, it seems, these Sisters number an old donkey and a tiny cart, and this they start daily on a sort of begging tour through the adjoining villages, bringing back every evening a perfect hoard of broken victuals and bundles of old garments. Now comes the extraordinary fact on which Murray bases his suspicions. He says, and Gunning verifies his statement, that in whatever direction those Sisters turn the wheels of their donkey-cart, burglaries, or attempts at burglaries, are sure to follow. A week ago they went along towards Horely, where, at an outlying house, they received such kindness from a wealthy gentleman. That very night an attempt was made to break into that gentleman's house—an attempt, however, that was happily frustrated by the barking of the house-dog. And so on in other instances that I need not go into. Murray suggests that it might be as well to have the daily move-

ments of these Sisters closely watched, and that extra vigilance should be exercised by the police in the districts that have had the honor of a morning call from them. Gunning coincides with this idea, and so has sent to me to secure your services."

Loveday closed her note-book. "I suppose Gunning will meet me somewhere and tell me where I'm to take up my quarters?" she said.

"Yes; he will get into your carriage at Merstham—the station before Redhill—if you will put your hand out of the window, with the morning paper in it. By the way, he takes it for granted that you will take the 11:05 train from Victoria. Murray, it seems, has been good enough to place his little house at the disposal of the police, but Gunning does not think espionage could be so well carried on there as from other quarters. The presence of a stranger in an alley of that sort is bound to attract attention. So he has hired a room for you in a draper's shop that immediately faces the head of the court. There is a private door to this shop of which you will have the key, and can let yourself in and out as you please. You are supposed to be a nursery governess on the lookout for a situation, and Gunning will keep you supplied with letters to give color to the idea. He suggests that you need only occupy the room during the day, at night you will find far more comfortable quarters at Laker's Hotel, just outside the town."

This was about the sum total of the instructions that Mr. Dyer had to give.

The 11:05 train from Victoria, that carried Loveday to her work among the Surrey Hills, did not get clear of the London fog till well away on the other side of Purley. When the train halted at Merstham, in response to her signal, a tall, soldier-like individual made for her carriage, and, jumping in, took the seat facing her. He introduced himself to her as Inspector Gunning, recalled to her memory a former occasion on which they had met, and then, naturally enough, turned the talk upon the present suspicious circumstances they were bent upon investigating.

"It won't do for you and me to be seen together," he said; "of course I am known for miles round, and any one seen in my company will be at once set down as my coadjutor, and spied upon accordingly. I walked from Redhill to Merstham on purpose to avoid recognition on the platform at Redhill, and half-way here, to my great annoyance, found that I was being followed by a man in a workman's dress and carrying a basket of tools. I doubled, however, and gave him the slip, taking a short cut down a lane which, if he had been living in the place, he would have known as well as I did. By Jove!" this was added with a sudden start, "there is the fellow, I declare; he has weathered me after all, and has no doubt taken good stock of us both, with the train going at this snail's pace. It was unfortunate that your face should have been turned towards that window, Miss Brooke."

"My veil is something of a disguise, and I will put on another cloak before he has a chance of seeing me again," said Loveday.

All she had seen in the brief glimpse that the train had allowed, was a tall, powerfully-built man walking along the siding of the line. His cap was drawn low over his eyes, and in his hand he carried a workman's basket.

Gunning seemed much annoyed at the circumstance. "Instead of landing at Redhill," he said, "we'll go on to Three Bridges, and wait there for a Brighton train to bring us back, that will enable you to get to your room somewhere between the lights; I don't want

to have you spotted before you've so much as started your work."

Then they went back to their discussion of the Redhill Sisterhood.

"They call themselves 'undenominational,' whatever that means," said Gunning, "they say they are connected with no religious sect whatever, they attend sometimes one place of worship, sometimes another, sometimes none at all. They refuse to give up the name of the founder of their order, and really no one has any right to demand it of them, for, as no doubt you see, up to the present moment the case is one of mere suspicion, and it may be a pure coincidence that attempts at burglary have followed their footsteps in this neighborhood. By the way, I have heard of a man's face being enough to hang him, but until I saw Sister Monica's, I never saw a woman's face that could perform the same kind of office for her. Of all the lowest criminal types of faces I have ever seen, I think hers is about the lowest and most repulsive."

After the Sisters, they passed in review the chief families resident in the neighborhood.

"This," said Gunning, unfolding a paper, "is a map I have specially drawn up for you— it takes in the district for ten miles round Redhill, and every country house of any importance is marked on it in red ink. Here, in addition, is an index of those houses, with special notes of my own to every house."

Loveday studied the map for a minute or so, then turned her attention to the index.

"Those four houses you've marked, I see, are those that have been already attempted. I don't think I'll run them through, but I'll mark them 'doubtful'; you see the gang—for, of course, it is a gang—might follow our reasoning on the matter, and look upon those houses as our weak point. Here's one I'll run through, 'house empty during winter months,'—that means plate and jewelry sent to the bankers. Oh! And this one may as well be crossed off, 'father and four sons all athletes and sportsmen,' that means fire-arms always handy—I don't think burglars will be likely to trouble them. Ah! Now we come to something! Here's a house to be marked 'tempting' in a burglar's list. 'Wootton Hall, lately changed hands and rebuilt, with complicated passages and corridors. Splendid family plate in daily use and left entirely in the care of the butler.' I wonder does the master of that house trust to his 'complicated passages' to preserve his plate for him? A dismissed dishonest servant would supply a dozen maps of the place for half a sovereign. What do these initials, 'E. L.' against the next house in the list, North Cape, stand for?"

"Electric lighted. I think you might almost cross that house off also. I consider electric lighting one of the greatest safeguards against burglars that a man can give his house."

"Yes, if he doesn't rely exclusively upon it; it might be a nasty trap under certain circumstances. I see this gentleman also has magnificent presentation and other plate."

"Yes…Mr. Jameson is a wealthy man and very popular in the neighborhood; his cups and epergnes[1] are worth looking at."

"Is it the only house in the district that is lighted with electricity?"

"Yes; and, begging your pardon, Miss Brooke, I only wish it were not so. If electric lighting were generally in vogue it would save the police a lot of trouble on these dark winter nights."

"The burglars would find some way of meeting such a condition of things, depend upon it; they have reached a very high development in these days. They no longer stalk about as they did fifty years ago with blunderbuss and bludgeon; they plot, plan, contrive, and bring imagination and artistic resource to their aid. By the way, it often occurs to me that the popular detective stories, for which there seems so large a demand at the present day, must be, at times, uncommonly useful to the criminal classes."

At Three Bridges they had to wait so long for a return train that it was nearly dark when Loveday got back to Redhill. Mr. Gunning did not accompany her thither, having alighted at a previous station. Loveday had directed her portmanteau to be sent direct to Laker's Hotel, where she had engaged a room by telegram from Victoria Station. So, enburthened by luggage, she slipped quietly out of the Redhill Station and made her way straight for the draper's shop in the London Road. She had no difficulty in finding it, thanks to the minute directions given her by the Inspector.

Street lamps were being lighted in the sleepy little town as she went along, and as she turned into the London Road, shopkeepers were lighting up their windows on both sides of the way. A few yards down this road, a dark patch between the lighted shops showed her where Paved Court led off from the thoroughfare. A side door of one of the shops that stood at the corner of the court seemed to offer a post of observation whence she could see without being seen, and here Loveday, shrinking into the shadows, ensconced herself in order to take stock of the little alley and its

[1] A table centerpiece, usually silver and many-branched.

inhabitants. She found it much as it had been described to her—a collection of four-roomed houses of which more than half were unlet. Numbers 7 and 8 at the head of the court presented a slightly less neglected appearance than the other tenements. Number 7 stood in total darkness, but in the upper window of number 8 there showed what seemed to be a night-light burning, so Loveday conjectured that this possibly was the room set apart as a dormitory for the little cripples.

While she stood thus surveying the home of the suspected Sisterhood, the Sisters themselves—two, at least, of them—came into view, with their donkey-cart and their cripples, in the main road. It was an odd little cortege. One Sister habited in a nun's dress of dark blue serge, led the donkey by the bridle; another Sister, similarly attired, walked alongside the low cart, in which were seated two sickly-looking children. They were evidently returning from one of their long country circuits, and, unless they had lost their way and been belated, it certainly seemed a late hour for the sickly little cripples to be abroad.

As they passed under the gas lamp at the corner of the court, Loveday caught a glimpse of the faces of the Sisters. It was easy, with Inspector Gunning's description before her mind, to identify the older and taller woman as Sister Monica, and a more coarse-featured and generally repellent face Loveday admitted to herself she had never before seen. In strik - ing contrast to this forbidding countenance was that of the younger Sister. Loveday could only catch a brief passing view of it, but that one brief view was enough to impress it on her memory as of unusual sadness and beauty. As the donkey stopped at the corner of the court, Loveday heard this sad-looking young woman addressed as "Sister Anna" by one of

the cripples, who asked plaintively when they were going to have something to eat.

"Now, at once," said Sister Anna, lifting the little one, as it seemed to Loveday, tenderly out of the cart, and carrying him on her shoulder down the court to the door of number 8, which opened to them at their approach. The other Sister did the same with the other child; then both Sisters returned, unloaded the cart of sundry bundles and baskets, and, this done, led off the old donkey and trap down the road, possibly to a neighboring costermonger's stables.

A man, coming along on a bicycle, exchanged a word of greeting with the Sisters as they passed, then swung himself off his machine at the corner of the court, and walked it along the paved way to the door of number 7. This he opened with a key, and then, pushing the machine before him, entered the house.

Loveday took it for granted that this man must be the John Murray of whom she had heard. She had closely scrutinized him as he had passed her, and had seen that he was a dark, well-featured man of about fifty years of age.

She congratulated herself on her good fortune in having seen so much in such a brief space of time, and, coming forth from her sheltered corner, turned her steps in the direction of the draper's shop on the other side of the road.

It was easy to find. "Golightly" was the singular name that figured above the shop-front, in which were displayed a variety of goods calculated to meet the wants of servants and the poorer classes generally. A tall, powerfully-built man appeared to be looking in at the window. Loveday's boot was on the doorstep of the draper's private entrance, her hand on the door-knocker, when this individual, suddenly turning, convinced her of his identity with the journeyman workman who had so disturbed Mr. Gunning's equanimity. It was true he wore a bowler instead of a journeyman's cap, and he no longer carried a basket of tools, but there was no possibility for any one, with so good an eye for an outline as Loveday possessed, not to recognize the carriage of the head and shoulders as that of the man she had seen walking along the railway siding. He gave her no time to make minute observation of his appearance, but turned quickly away, and disappeared down a by-street.

Loveday's work seemed to bristle with difficulties now. Here was she, as it were, unearthed in her own ambush; for there could be but little doubt that during the whole time she had stood watching those Sisters, that man, from a safe vantage-point, had been watching her.

She found Mrs. Golightly a civil and obliging person. She showed Loveday to her room above the shop, brought her the letters which Inspector Gunning had been careful to have posted to her during the day. Then she supplied her with pen and ink and, in response to Loveday's request, with some strong coffee that she said, with a little attempt at a joke, would "keep a dormouse awake all through the winter without winking."[2]

While the obliging landlady busied herself about the room, Loveday had a few questions to ask about the Sisterhood who lived down the court opposite. On this head, how - ever, Mrs. Golightly could tell her no more

than she already knew, beyond the fact that they started every morning on their rounds at eleven o'clock punctually, and that before that hour they were never to be seen outside their door.

Loveday's watch that night was to be a fruitless one. Although she sat, with her lamp turned out and safely screened from observation, until close upon midnight, with eyes fixed upon numbers 7 and 8, Paved Court, not so much as a door opening or shutting at either house rewarded her vigil. The lights flitted from the lower to the upper floors in both houses, and then disappeared, somewhere between nine and ten in the evening; and after that, not a sign of life did either tenement show.

And all through the long hours of that watch, again and again there seemed to flit before her mind's eye, as if in some sort it were fixed upon its retina, the sweet, sad face of Sister Anna.

Why it was this face should so haunt her, she found it hard to say.

"It has a mournful past and a mournful future written upon it as a hopeless whole," she said to herself. "It is the face of an Andromeda![3] 'Here am I,' it seems to say, 'tied to my stake, helpless and hopeless.'"

The church clocks were sounding the midnight hour as Loveday made her way through the dark streets to her hotel outside the town. As she passed under the railway arch that ended in the open country road, the echo of not very distant footsteps caught her ear. When she stopped they stopped, when she went on they went on, and she knew that

---

[2] A dormouse is an English species of rodent known for its long period of hibernation. A dormouse figures in Chapter VII of *Alice's Adventures in Wonderland* by Lewis Caroll.

[3] Andromeda, a Greek princess of legend, was chained to a rock as a sacrifice to a sea-monster, as a punishment for her mother Cassiopeia's boasting. Andromeda was rescued by her husband-to-be Perseus.

once more she was being followed and watched, although the darkness of the arch prevented her seeing even the shadow of the man who was thus dogging her steps.

The next morning broke keen and frosty. Loveday studied her map and her country-house index over a seven o'clock breakfast, and then set off for a brisk walk along the country road. No doubt in London the streets were walled in and roofed with yellow fog; here, however, bright sunshine playing in and out of the bare tree-boughs and leafless hedges on to a thousand frost spangles, turned the prosaic macadamized road into a gangway fit for Queen Titania herself[4] and her fairy train.

Loveday turned her back on the town and set herself to follow the road as it wound away over the hill in the direction of a village called Northfield. Early as she was, she was not to have that road to herself. A team of strong horses trudged by on their way to their work in the fuller's-earth[5] pits. A young fellow on a bicycle flashed past at a tremendous pace, considering the upward slant of the road. He looked hard at her as he passed, then slackened speed, dismounted, and awaited her coming on the brow of the hill.

"Good-morning, Miss Brooke," he said, lifting his cap as she came alongside of him. "May I have five minutes' talk with you?"

The young man who thus accosted her had not the appearance of a gentleman. He was a handsome, bright-faced young fellow of about two-and-twenty, and was dressed in ordinary cyclist's dress; his cap was pushed back from his brow over thick, curly, fair hair, and Loveday, as she looked at him, could not repress the thought how well he would look at

the head of a troop of cavalry, giving the order to charge the enemy.

He led his machine to the side of the footpath.

"You have the advantage of me," said Loveday; "I haven't the remotest notion who you are."

"No," he said; "although I know you, you cannot possibly know me. I am a north-country man, and I was present, about a month ago, at the trial of old Mr. Craven, of Troyte's Hill—in fact, I acted as reporter for one of the local papers. I watched your face so closely as you gave your evidence that I should know it anywhere, among a thousand."

"And your name is…?"

"George White, of Grenfell. My father is part proprietor of one of the Newcastle papers. I am a bit of a literary man myself, and sometimes figure as a reporter, sometimes as reader-writer, to that paper." Here he gave a glance toward his side pocket, from which protruded a small volume of Tennyson's poems.

The facts he had stated did not seem to invite comment, and Loveday ejaculated merely: "Indeed!"

The young man went back to the subject that was evidently filling his thoughts. "I have special reasons for being glad to have met you this morning, Miss Brooke," he went on, making his footsteps keep pace with hers. "I am in great trouble, and I believe you are the only person in the whole world who can help me out of that trouble."

"I am rather doubtful as to my power of helping any one out of trouble," said Loveday; "so far as my experience goes, our troubles are

---

[4] The legendary queen of the faerie-folk, who figures prominently in Shakespeare's *A Mid-Summer Night's Dream*.
[5] A clay used in various Victorian industrial processes.

as much a part of ourselves as our skins are of our bodies."

"Ah, but not such trouble as mine," said White eagerly. He broke off for a moment, then, with a sudden rush of words told her what that trouble was. For the past year he had been engaged to be married to a young girl, who, until quite recently, had been fulfilling the duties of a nursery governess in a large house in the neighborhood of Redhill.

"Will you kindly give me the name of that house?" interrupted Loveday.

"Certainly; Wootton Hall, the place is called, and Annie Lee is my sweetheart's name. I don't care who knows it!" He threw his head back as he said this, as if he would be delighted to announce the fact to the whole world. "Annie's mother," he went on, "died when she was a baby, and we both thought her father was dead also, when suddenly, about a fortnight ago, it came to her knowledge that, instead of being dead, he was serving his time at Portland for some offense committed years ago."

"Do you know how this came to Annie's knowledge?"

"Not the least in the world; I only know that I suddenly got a letter from her announcing the fact, and, at the same time, breaking off her engagement with me. I tore the letter into a thousand pieces, and wrote back saying I would not allow the engagement to be broken off, but would marry her if she would have me. To this letter she did not reply; there came instead a few lines from Mrs. Copeland, the lady at Wootton Hall, saying that Annie had thrown up her engagement, and joined some Sisterhood, and that she, Mrs. Copeland, had pledged her word to Annie to reveal to no one the name and whereabouts of that Sisterhood."

"And I suppose you imagine I am able to do what Mrs. Copeland is pledged not to do?"

"That's just it, Miss Brooke!" cried the young man enthusiastically. "You do such wonderful things; everyone knows you do. It seems as if, when anything is wanting to be found out, you just walk into a place, look round you, and, in a moment, everything becomes clear as noonday."

"I can't quite lay claim to such wonderful powers as that. As it happens, however, in the present instance, no particular skill is needed to find out what you wish to know, for I fancy I have already come upon the traces of Miss Annie Lee."

"Miss Brooke!"

"Of course, I cannot say for certain, but it is a matter you can easily settle for yourself—settle, too, in a way that will confer a great obligation on me."

"I shall be only too delighted to be of any, the slightest, service to you!" cried White, enthusiastically as before.

"Thank you. I will explain. I came down here specially to watch the movements of a certain Sisterhood who have somehow aroused the suspicions of the police. Well, I find that instead of being able to do this, I am myself so closely watched—possibly by confederates of these Sisters—that unless I can do my work by deputy I may as well go back to town at once."

"Ah! I see—you want me to be that deputy."

"Precisely. I want you to go to the room in Redhill that I have hired, take your place at the window—screened, of course, from observation—at which I ought to be seated—watch as closely as possible the movements of these Sisters, and report them to me at the hotel, where I shall remain shut in from morning till night—it is the only way in which I can throw my persistent spies off the scent. Now, in doing this for me, you will be doing yourself a good turn, for I have little doubt but what under the blue serge hood of one of the Sisters you will discover the pretty face of Miss Annie Lee."

As they talked they had walked, and now stood on the top of the hill at the head of the one little street that constituted the whole of the village of Northfield.

On their left hand stood the village school and the master's house; nearly facing these, on the opposite side of the road, beneath a clump of elms, stood the village pound. Beyond this pound, on either side of the way, were two rows of small cottages with tiny squares of garden in front, and in the midst of these small cottages a swinging sign beneath a lamp announced a "Postal and Telegraph Office."

"Now that we have come into the land of habitations again," said Loveday, "it will be best for us to part. It will not do for you and me to be seen together, or my spies will be transferring their attentions from me to you, and I shall have to find another deputy. You had better start on your bicycle for Redhill at once, and I will walk back at leisurely speed. Come to me at my hotel without fail at one o'clock and report proceedings. I do not say anything definite about remuneration, but I assure you, if you carry out my instructions to the letter, your services will be amply rewarded by me and by my employers."

There were yet a few more details to arrange. White had been, he said, only a day and night in the neighborhood, and special directions as to the locality had to be given to him. Loveday advised him not to attract attention by going to the draper's private door,

but to enter the shop as if he were a customer, and then explain matters to Mrs. Golightly, who, no doubt, would be in her place behind the counter; tell her he was the brother of the Miss Smith who had hired her room, and ask permission to go through the shop to that room, as he had been commissioned by his sister to read and answer any letters that might have arrived there for her.

"Show her the key of the side door—here it is," said Loveday; "it will be your credentials, and tell her you did not like to make use of it without acquainting her with the fact."

The young man took the key, endeavoring to put it in his waistcoat pocket, found the space there occupied, and so transferred it to the keeping of a side pocket in his tunic.

All this time Loveday stood watching him.

"You have a capital machine there," she said, as the young man mounted his bicycle once more, "and I hope you will turn it to account in following the movements of these Sisters about the neighborhood. I feel confident you will have something definite to tell me when you bring me your first report at one o'clock."

White once more broke into a profusion of thanks, and then, lifting his cap to the lady, started his machine at a fairly good pace.

Loveday watched him out of sight down the slope of the hill, then, instead of following him as she had said she would "at a leisurely pace," she turned her steps in the opposite direction along the village street.

It was an altogether ideal country village. Neatly-dressed, chubby-faced children, now on their way to the school, dropped quaint little curtseys, or tugged at curly locks as Loveday passed; every cottage looked the picture of cleanliness and trimness, and, although so late in the year, the gardens were full of late flowering chrysanthemums and early flowering Christmas roses.

At the end of the village, Loveday came suddenly into view of a large, handsome, red-brick mansion. It presented a wide frontage to the road, from which it lay back amid extensive pleasure grounds. On the right hand, and a little on the rear of the house, stood what seemed to be large and commodious stables, and immediately adjoining these stables was a low-built, red-brick shed, that had evidently been recently erected.

That low-built, red-brick shed excited Loveday's curiosity.

"Is this house called North Cape?" she asked of a man, who chanced at that moment to be passing with a pickaxe and shovel.

The man answered in the affirmative, and Loveday then asked another question: Could he tell her what was that small shed so close to the house—it looked like a glorified cow-house—now what could be its use?

The man's face lighted up as if it were a subject on which he liked to be questioned. He explained that that small shed was the engine-house where the electricity that lighted North Cape was made and stored. Then he dwelt with pride upon the fact, as if he held a personal interest in it, that North Cape was the only house, far or near, that was thus lighted.

"I suppose the wires are carried underground to the house," said Loveday, looking in vain for signs of them anywhere.

The man was delighted to go into details on the matter. He had helped to lay those wires, he said: they were two in number, one for supply and one for return, and were laid three feet below ground, in boxes filled with pitch. They were switched on to jars[6] in the engine-house, where the electricity was stored,

and, after passing underground, entered the family mansion under the flooring at its western end.

Loveday listened attentively to these details, and then took a minute and leisurely survey of the house and its surroundings. This done, she retraced her steps through the village, pausing, however, at the "Postal and Telegraph Office" to dispatch a telegram to Inspector Gunning.

It was one to send the Inspector to his cipher-book. It ran as follows:

Rely solely on chemist and
coal-merchant throughout the day. L.B.

After this, she quickened her pace, and in something over three-quarters of an hour was back again at her hotel.

There she found more of life stirring than when she had quitted it in the early morning. There was to be a meeting of the "Surrey Stags" about a couple of miles off, and a good many hunting men were hanging about the entrance of the house, discussing the chances of sport after last night's frost. Loveday made her way through the throng in leisurely fashion, and not a man but what had keen scrutiny from her sharp eyes. No, there was no cause for suspicion there; they were evidently one and all just what they seemed to be loud-voiced, hard-riding men, bent on a day's sport; but and here Loveday's eyes traveled beyond the hotel courtyard to the other side of the road—who was that man with a bill-hook hacking at the hedge there—a thin-featured, round-shouldered old fellow, with a bent-about hat? It might be as well not to take it too rashly for granted that her spies had withdrawn, and had left her free to do her work in her own fashion.

---

[6] Leyden jars were an early form of capacitor.

She went upstairs to her room. It was situated on the first floor in the front of the house, and consequently commanded a good view of the high road. She stood well back from the window, and at an angle whence she could see and not be seen, took a long, steady survey of the hedger. And the longer she looked the more convinced she was that the man's real work was something other than the bill-hook seemed to imply. He worked, so to speak, with his head over his shoulder, and when Loveday supplemented her eyesight with a strong field-glass, she could see more than one stealthy glance shot from beneath his bent-about hat in the direction of her window.

There could be little doubt about it: her movements were to be as closely watched today as they had been yesterday. Now it was of first importance that she should communicate with Inspector Gunning in the course of the afternoon: the question to solve was how it was to be done?

To all appearance Loveday answered the question in extraordinary fashion. She pulled up her blind, she drew back her curtain, and seated herself, in full view, at a small table in the window recess. Then she took a pocket inkstand from her pocket, a packet of correspondence cards from her letter-case, and with rapid pen set to work on them.

About an hour and a half afterwards, White, coming in, according to his promise, to report proceedings, found her still seated at the window, not, however, with writing materials before her, but with needle and thread in her hand, with which she was mending her gloves.

"I return to town by the first train tomorrow morning," she said as he entered, "and I find these wretched things want no end of stitches. Now for your report."

White appeared to be in an elated frame of mind. "I've seen her!" he cried, "my Annie—they've got her, those confounded Sisters; but they sha'n't keep her—no, not if I have to pull the house down about their ears to get her out!"

"Well, now you know where she is, you can take your time about getting her out," said Loveday. "I hope, however, you haven't broken faith with me, and betrayed yourself by trying to speak with her, because, if so, I shall have to look for another deputy."

"Honor, Miss Brooke!" answered White indignantly. "I stuck to my duty, though it cost me something to see her hanging over those kids and tucking them into the cart, and never say a word to her, never so much as wave my hand."

"Did she go out with the donkey-cart today?"

"No, she only tucked the kids into the cart with a blanket, and then went back to the house. Two old Sisters, ugly as sin, went out with them. I watched them from the window, jolt, jolt, jolt, round the corner, out of sight, and then I whipped down the stairs, and on to my machine, and was after them in a trice, and managed to keep them well in sight for over an hour and a half."

"And their destination today was?"

"Wootton Hall."

"Ah, just as I expected."

"Just as you expected?" echoed White.

"I forgot. You do not know the nature of the suspicions that are attached to this Sisterhood, and the reasons I have for thinking that Wootton Hall, at this season of the year, might have an especial attraction for them."

White continued staring at her. "Miss Brooke," he said presently, in an altered tone, "whatever suspicions may attach to the Sisterhood, I'll stake my life on it, my Annie has had no share in any wickedness of any sort."

"Oh, quite so; it is most likely that your Annie has, in some way, been inveigled into joining these Sisters—has been taken possession of by them, in fact, just as they have taken possession of the little cripples."

"That's it! That's it!" he cried excitedly; "that was the idea that occurred to me when you spoke to me on the hill about them, otherwise you may be sure…"

"Did they get relief of any sort at the Hall?" interrupted Loveday.

"Yes; one of the two ugly old women stopped outside the lodge gates with the donkey-cart, and the other beauty went up to the house alone. She stayed there, I should think, about a quarter of an hour, and when she came back was followed by a servant, carrying a bundle and a basket."

"Ah! I've no doubt they brought away with them something else beside old garments and broken victuals."

White stood in front of her, fixing a hard, steady gaze upon her.

"Miss Brooke," he said presently, in a voice that matched the look on his face, "what do you suppose was the real object of these women in going to Wootton Hall this morning?"

"Mr. White, if I wished to help a gang of thieves break into Wootton Hall tonight, don't you think I should be greatly interested in procuring for them the information that the master of the house was away from home; that two of the menservants, who slept in the house, had recently been dismissed and their places had not yet been filled; also that the dogs were never unchained at night, and that their kennels were at the side of the house at which the butler's pantry is not situated?

These are particulars I have gathered in this house without stirring from my chair, and I am satisfied that they are likely to be true. At the same time, if I were a professional burglar, I should not be content with information that was likely to be true, but would be careful to procure such that was certain to be true, and so would set accomplices to work at the fountain head. Now do you understand?"

White folded his arms and looked down on her.

"What are you going to do?" he asked, in short, brusque tones.

Loveday looked him full in the face. "Communicate with the police immediately," she answered; "and I should feel greatly obliged if you would at once take a note from me to Inspector Gunning at Reigate."

"And what becomes of Annie?"

"I don't think you need have any anxiety on that head. I have no doubt that when the circumstances of her admission to the Sisterhood are investigated, it will be proved that she has been as much deceived and imposed upon as the man, John Murray, who so foolishly let his house to these women. Remember, Annie has Mrs. Copeland's good word to support her integrity."

White stood silent for awhile.

"What sort of a note do you wish me to take to the Inspector?" he presently asked.

"You shall read it as I write it, if you like," answered Loveday. She took a correspondence card from her lettercase, and, with an indelible pencil, wrote as follows:

Wootton Hall is threatened tonight— concentrate attention there. L.B.

White read the words as she wrote them with a curious expression passing over his handsome features.

"Yes," he said, curtly as before; "I'll deliver that, I give you my word, but I'll bring back no answer to you. I'll do no more spying for you—it's a trade that doesn't suit me. There's a straightforward way of doing straightforward work, and I'll take that way—no other—to get my Annie out of that den."

He took the note, which she sealed and handed to him, and strode out of the room.

Loveday, from the window, watched him mount his bicycle. Was it her fancy, or did there pass a swift, furtive glance of recognition between him and the hedger on the other side of the way as he rode out of the courtyard?

She seemed determined to make that hedger's work easy for him. The short winter's day was closing in now, and her room must consequently have been growing dim to outside observation. She lighted the gas chandelier which hung from the ceiling, and, still with blinds and curtains undrawn, took her old place at the window, spread writing materials before her, and commenced a long and elaborate report to her chief at Lynch Court.

About half an hour afterwards, she threw a casual glance across the road, and saw that the hedger had disappeared, but that two ill-looking tramps sat munching bread and cheese under the hedge to which his bill-hook had done so little service. Evidently the intention was, one way or another, not to lose sight of her so long as she remained in Redhill.

Meantime, White had delivered Loveday's note to the Inspector at Reigate, and had disappeared on his bicycle once more.

Gunning read it without a change of expression. Then he crossed the room to the fireplace and held the card as close to the bars as he could without scorching it.

"I had a telegram from her this morning," he explained to his confidential man, "telling me to rely upon chemicals and coals throughout the day, and that, of course, meant that she would write to me in invisible ink. No doubt this message about Wootton Hall means nothing…"

He broke off abruptly, exclaiming: "Eh! What's this!" as, having withdrawn the card from the fire, Loveday's real message stood out in bold, clear characters between the lines of the false one.

Thus it ran:

North Cape will be attacked tonight—a desperate gang—be prepared for a struggle. Above all, guard the electrical engine-house. On no account attempt to communicate with me—I am so closely watched that any endeavor to do so may frustrate your chance of trapping the scoundrels. L.B.

That night when the moon went down behind Reigate Hill an exciting scene was enacted at North Cape. The *Surrey Gazette*, in its issue the following day, gave the subjoined account of it under the heading:

DESPERATE ENCOUNTER WITH BURGLARS

Last night, "North Cape," the residence of Mr. Jameson, was the scene of an affray between the police and a desperate gang of burglars. "North Cape" is lighted throughout by electricity, and the burglars, four in number, divided in half—two being told off to enter and rob the house, and two to remain at the engine-shed, where the electricity is stored, so that, at a given signal, should need arise, the wires might be un-switched, the inmates of the house thrown into sudden darkness and confusion, and the escape of the marauders thereby facilitated. Mr. Jameson, however, had received timely warning from the police of the intended attack, and he, with his two sons, all well-armed, sat in darkness in the inner hall awaiting the coming of the thieves. The police were stationed, some in the stables, some in out-buildings nearer to the house, and others in more distant parts of the grounds. The burglars effected their entrance by means of a ladder placed to a window of the servants' staircase, which leads straight down to the butler's pantry and to the safe where the silver is kept. The fellows, however, had no sooner got into the house than two policemen, issuing from their hiding-place outside, mounted the ladder after them and thus cut off their retreat. Mr. Jameson and his two sons, at the same moment, attacked them in front, and thus overwhelmed by numbers the scoundrels were easily secured. It was at the engine-house outside that the sharpest struggle took place. The thieves had forced open the door of this engine-shed with their jemmies immediately on their arrival, under the very eyes of the police, who lay in ambush in the stables, and when one of the men, captured in the house, contrived to sound an alarm on his whistle, these outside watchers made a rush for the electrical jars, in order to unswitch the wires. Upon this the police closed upon them, and a hand-to-hand struggle followed, and if it had not been for the timely assistance of Mr. Jameson and his sons, who had fortunately conjectured that their presence here might be useful, it is more than likely that one of the burglars, a powerfully-built man, would have escaped.

The names of the captured men are John Murray, Arthur and George Lee (father and son), and a man with so many aliases that it is difficult to know which is his real name. The whole thing had been most cunningly and carefully planned. The elder Lee, lately released from penal servitude for a similar offense, appears to have been prime mover in the affair. This man had, it seems, a son and a daughter, who, through the kindness of friends, had been fairly well placed in life; the son at an electrical engineer's in London, the daughter as nursery governess at Wootton Hall. Directly this man was released from Portland, he seems to have found out his children and done his best to ruin them both. He was constantly at Wootton Hall endeavoring to induce his daughter to act as an accomplice to a robbery of the house. This so worried the girl that she threw up her situation and joined a Sisterhood that had recently been established in the neighborhood. Upon this, Lee's thoughts turned in another direction. He induced his son, who had saved a little money, to throw up his work in London, and join him in his disreputable career. The boy is a handsome young fellow, but appears to have in him the makings of a first-class criminal. In his work as an electrical engineer he had made the acquaintance of the man John Murray, who, it is said, has been rapidly going downhill of late. Murray was the owner of the house rented by the Sisterhood that Miss Lee had joined, and the idea evidently struck the brains of these three scoundrels that this Sisterhood, whose antecedents were not generally known, might be utilized to draw off the attention of the police from themselves and—from the especial house in the neighborhood that they had planned to attack. With this end in view, Murray made an application to the police to have the Sisters watched, and still further to give color to the suspicions he had endeavored to set afloat concerning them, he and his confederates made feeble attempts at burglary upon the houses at which the Sisters had called, begging for scraps. It is a matter for congratulation that the plot, from beginning to end, has been thus successfully unearthed, and it is felt on all sides that great credit is due to Inspector Gunning and his skilled coadjutors for the vigilance and promptitude they have displayed throughout the affair.

Loveday read aloud this report, with her feet on the fender of the Lynch Court office.

"Accurate, so far as it goes," she said, as she laid down the paper.

"But we want to know a little more," said Mr. Dyer. "In the first place, I would like to know what it was that diverted your suspicions from the unfortunate Sisters?"

"The way in which they handled the children," answered Loveday promptly. "I have seen female criminals of all kinds handling children, and I have noticed that although they may occasionally—even this is rare—treat them with a certain rough sort of kindness, of tenderness they are utterly incapable. Now Sister Monica, I must admit, is not pleasant to look at; at the same time, there was something absolutely beautiful in the way in which she lifted the little cripple out of the cart, put his tiny thin hand round her neck, and carried him into the house. By the way, I would like to ask some rabid physiognomist how he would account for Sister Monica's repulsiveness of features as contrasted with young Lee's undoubted good looks—heredity, in this case, throws no light on the matter."

"Another question," said Mr. Dyer, not paying heed to Loveday's digression; "how was it you transferred your suspicions to John Murray?"

"I did not do so immediately, although at the very first it had struck me as odd that he should be so anxious to do the work of the police for them. The chief thing I noticed concerning Murray, on the first and only occasion on which I saw him, was that he had had an accident with his bicycle, for in the right-hand corner of his lamp-glass there was a tiny star, and the lamp itself had a dent on the same side had also lost its hook, and was fastened to the machine by bit of electric fuse. The next morning, as I was walking the hill towards Northfield, I was accosted by a young

man mounted on that selfsame bicycle—not a doubt of it—star in glass, dent, fuse, all there."

"Ah, that sounded an important keynote, and led you to connect Murray and the younger Lee immediately."

"It did, and, of course, also at once gave the lie to his statement that he was a stranger in the place, and confirmed my opinion that there was nothing of the north-countryman in his accent. Other details in his manner and appearance gave rise to other suspicions. For instance, he called himself a press reporter by profession, and his hands were coarse and grimy, as only a mechanic's could be. He said he was a bit of a literary man, but the Tennyson that showed so obtrusively from his pocket was new, and in parts uncut, and totally unlike the well-thumbed volume of the literary student. Finally, when he tried and failed to put my latchkey into his waistcoat pocket, I saw the reason lay in the fact that the pocket was already occupied by a soft coil of electric fuse, the end of which protruded. Now, an electric fuse is what an electrical engineer might almost unconsciously carry about with him, it is so essential a part of his working tools, but it is a thing that a literary man or a press reporter could have no possible use for."

"Exactly, exactly. And it was, no doubt, that bit of electric fuse that turned your thoughts to the one house in the neighborhood lighted by electricity, and suggested to your mind the possibility of electrical engineers turning their talents to account in that direction. Now, will you tell me what, at that stage of your day's work, induced you to wire to Gunning that you would bring your invisible ink bottle into use?"

"That was simply a matter of precaution;

it did not compel me to the use of invisible ink, if I saw other safe methods of communication. I felt myself being hemmed in on all sides with spies, and I could not tell what emergency might arise. I don't think I have ever had a more difficult game to play. As I walked and talked with the young fellow up the hill, it became clear to me that if I wished to do my work I must lull the suspicions of the gang, and seem to walk into their trap. I saw by the persistent way in which Wootton Hall was forced on my notice that it was wished to fix my suspicions there. I accordingly, to all appearance, did so, and allowed the fellows to think they were making a fool of me."

"Ha! Ha! Capital, that—the biter bit[7], with a vengeance! Splendid idea to make that young rascal himself deliver the letter that was to land him and his pals in jail. And he all the time laughing in his sleeve and thinking what a fool he was making of you! Ha, ha, ha!" And Mr. Dyer made the office ring again with his merriment.

"The only person one is at all sorry for in this affair is poor little Sister Anna," said Loveday pityingly; "and yet, perhaps, all things considered, after her sorry experience of life, she may not be so badly placed in a Sisterhood where practical Christianity—not religious hysterics—is the one and only rule of the order."

❧

---

[7] In this context, a "biter" is a cheater or swindler.

L.T. Meade & Clifford Halifax, M.D.

IN THE MID-1890S, medical mysteries became popular, and the first prominent collection was *Stories from the Diary of a Doctor* (1894), all of which appeared in the *Strand Magazine*, simultaneously with the second collection of Holmes adventures (collected as *The Memoirs*). Elizabeth Thomasina Meade Smith (1854-1914) was a prolific Irish writer, with more than 300 books to her credit, including numerous mystery novels and stories. Her *Sorceress of the Strand* stories, co-written with her frequent collaborator Robert Eustace (the pen-name of Dr. Eustace Robert Barton, 1854-1943), feature a memorable female villain, Madame Sara.

Mrs. Meade was also the author of numerous children's books, including her well-known *A World of Girls* (1886), and was the editor of the popular girls' magazine *Atalanta*. Halifax was the pseudonym of Dr. Edgar Beaumont (1860-1921), a general practitioner who supplied plots to Mrs. Meade. The following story appeared in the March 1894 issue of the *Strand Magazine*.

AN OAK COFFIN

L. T. MEADE & CLIFFORD HALIFAX, M.D.

ON A CERTAIN cold morning in early spring, I was visited by two ladies, mother and daughter. The mother was dressed as a widow. She was a tall, striking-looking woman, with full, wide-open dark eyes, and a mass of rich hair turned back from a white and noble brow. Her lips were firm, her features well formed. She seemed to have plenty of character, but the deep lines of sadness under her eyes and round her lips were very remarkable. The daughter was a girl of fourteen, slim to weediness. Her eyes were dark, like her mother's, and she had an abundance of tawny brown and very handsome hair. It hung down her back, below her waist, and floated over her shoulders. She was dressed, like her mother, in heavy mourning, and round her young mouth and dark, deep eyes there lingered the same inexpressible sadness.

I motioned my visitors to chairs, and waited as usual to learn the reason of their favoring me with a call.

"Name is Heathcote," said the elder lady.

"I have lately lost my husband. I have come to you on account of my daughter—she is not well."

I glanced again more attentively at the young girl. I saw that she looked over-strained and nervous. Her restlessness, too, was so apparent that she could scarcely sit still, and catching up a paper-knife which stood on the table near, she began twirling it rapidly between her finger and thumb.

"It does me good to fidget with something," she said, glancing apologetically at her mother.

"What are your daughter's symptoms?" I asked. Mrs. Heathcote began to describe them in the vague way which characterizes a certain class of patient. I gathered at last from her word that Gabrielle would not eat—she slept badly—she was weak and depressed—she took no interest in anything.

"How old is Miss Gabrielle?" I asked.

"She will be fifteen her next birthday," replied her mother.

All the while Mrs. Heathcote was

speaking, the young daughter kept her eyes fixed on the carpet—she still twirled the paper-knife, and once or twice she yawned profoundly.

I asked her to prepare for the usual medical examination. She complied without any alacrity, and with a look on her face which said plainly, "Young as I am, I know how useless all this fuss is—I only submit because I must."

I felt her pulse and sounded her heart and lungs. The action of the heart was a little weak, but the lungs were perfectly healthy. In short, beyond a general physical and mental debility, I could find nothing whatever the matter with the girl.

After a time, I rang the bell to desire my servant to take Miss Heathcote into another room, in order that I might speak to her mother alone.

The young lady went away very unwillingly. The skeptical expression on her face was more apparent than ever.

"You will be sure to tell me the exact truth?" said Mrs. Heathcote, as soon as we were alone.

"I have very little to tell," I replied. "I have examined your daughter carefully. She is suffering from no disease to which a name can be attached. She is below par, certainly; there is weakness and general depression, but a tonic ought to set all these matters right."

"I have tried tonics without avail," said Mrs. Heathcote.

"Has not your family physician seen Miss Heathcote?"

"Not lately." The widow's manner became decidedly hesitating. "The fact is, we have not consulted him since—since Mr. Heathcote's death," she said.

"When did that take place?"

"Six months ago."

Here she spoke with infinite sadness, and her face, already very pale, turned perceptibly paler.

"Is there nothing you can tell me to give me a clue to your daughter's condition? Is there anything, for instance, preying on her mind?"

"Nothing whatever."

"The expression of her face is very sad for so young a girl."

"You must remember," said Mrs. Heathcote, "that she has lately lost her father."

"Even so," I replied; "that would scarcely account for her nervous condition. A healthy-minded child will not be overcome with grief to the serious detriment of health after an interval of six months. At least," I added, "that is my experience in ordinary cases."

"I am grieved to hear it," said Mrs. Heathcote.

She looked very much troubled. Her agitation was apparent in her trembling hands and quivering lips.

"Your daughter is in a nervous condition," I said, rising. "She has no disease at present, but a little extra strain might develop real disease, or might affect her nerves, already overstrung, to a dangerous degree. I should recommend complete change of air and scene immediately."

Mrs. Heathcote sighed heavily.

"You don't look very well yourself," I said, giving her a keen glance.

She flushed crimson.

"I have felt my sorrow acutely," she replied. I made a few more general remarks, wrote a prescription for the daughter, and bade Mrs. Heathcote good-bye. About the same hour on the following morning I was astonished when my servant brought me a card on which was scribbled in pencil the name *Gabrielle Heathcote*, and underneath, in the same upright, but unformed hand, the words, "I want to see you most urgently."

A few moments later, Miss Gabrielle was standing in my consulting-room. Her appearance was much the same as yesterday, except that now her face was eager, watchful, and all awake.

"How do you do?" she said, holding out her hand, and blushing.

"I have ventured to come alone, and I haven't brought a fee. Does that matter?"

"Not in the least," I replied. "Pray sit down and tell me what you want."

"I would rather stand," she answered; "I feel too restless and excited to sit still. I stole away from home without letting mother know. I liked your look yesterday and determined to see you again. Now, may I confide in you?"

"You certainly may," I replied.

My interest in this queer child was a good deal aroused. I felt certain that I was right in my conjectures of yesterday, and that this young creature was really burdened with some secret which was gravely undermining her health.

"I am willing to listen to you," I continued. "You must be brief, of course, for I am a very busy man, but anything you can say which will throw light on your own condition and so help me to cure you, will, of course, be welcome."

"You think me very nervous?" said Miss Gabrielle.

"Your nerves are out of order," I replied.

"You know that I don't sleep at night?"

"Yes."

Gabrielle looked towards the door.

"Is it shut?" she asked, excitedly.

"Of course it is."

She came close to me, her voice dropped to a hoarse whisper, her face turned not only white but grey.

"I can stand it no longer," she said. "I'll tell you the truth. You wouldn't sleep either if you were me. *My father isn't dead!*"

"Nonsense," I replied. "You must control such imaginings, Miss Gabrielle, or you will really get into a very unhealthy condition of mind."

"That's what mother says when I speak to her," replied the child. "But I tell you, this thing is true. My father is not dead. I know it."

"How can you possibly know it?" I asked.

"I have seen him—there!"

"You have seen your father!—but he died six months ago?"

"Yes. He died—and was buried, and I went to his funeral. But all the same he is not dead now."

"My dear young lady," I said, in as soothing a tone as I could assume, "you are the victim of what is called a hallucination. You have felt your father's death very acutely."

"I have. I loved him beyond words. He was so kind, so affectionate, so good to me. It almost broke my heart when he died. I thought I could never be happy again. Mother was as wretched as myself. There weren't two more miserable people in the wide world. It seemed impossible to either of us to smile or be cheerful again. I began to sleep badly, for I cried so much, and my eyes ached, and I did not care for lessons any more."

"All these feelings will pass," I replied; "they are natural, but time will abate their violence."

"You think so?" said the girl, with a strange smile. "Now let me go on with my story: It was at Christmas time I first saw my father. We live in an old house at Brixton. It has a walled-in garden. I was standing by my window about midnight. I had been in bed for an hour or more, but I could not sleep. The house was perfectly quiet. I got out of bed and went to the window and drew up the blind. I stood by the window and looked out into the garden, which was covered with snow. There, standing under the window, with his arms folded, was father. He stood perfectly still, and turned his head slowly, first in the direction of my room and then in that of mother's. He stood there for quite five minutes, and then walked across the grass into the shelter of the shrubbery. I put a cloak on and rushed downstairs. I unbolted the front door and went into the garden. I shouted my father's name and ran into the shrubbery to look for him, but he wasn't there, and I—I think I fainted. When I came to myself I was in bed and mother was bending over me. Her face was all blistered as if she had been crying terribly. I told her that I had just seen father, and she said it was a dream."

"So it was," I replied.

Miss Gabrielle's dark brows were knit in some pain.

"I did not think you would take that commonplace view," she responded.

"I am sorry I have offended you," I answered. "Girls like you do have bad dreams when they are in trouble, and those dreams are often so vivid, that they mistake them for realities."

"Very well, then, I have had more of those vivid dreams. I have seen my father again. The last time I saw him he was in the house. It was about a month ago. As usual, I could not sleep, and I went downstairs quite late to get the second volume of a novel which interested me. There was father walking across the passage. His back was to me. He opened the study door and went in. He shut it behind him. I rushed to it in order to open it and follow him. It was locked, and though I screamed through the key-hole, no one replied to me. Mother found me kneeling by the study door and shouting through the key-hole to father. She was up and dressed, which seemed strange at so late an hour. She took me upstairs and put me to bed, and pretended to be angry with me, but when I told her that I had seen father she burst into the most awful bitter tears and said:—

"'Oh, Gabrielle, he is dead—dead—quite dead!'

"'Then he comes here from the dead,' I said. 'No, he is not dead. I have just seen him.'

"'My poor child,' said mother, 'I must take you to a good doctor without delay. You must not get this thing on your brain.'

"'Very well,' I replied; 'I am quite willing to see Dr. Mackenzie.'"

I interrupted the narrative to inquire who Dr. Mackenzie was.

"He is our family physician," replied the young lady. "He has attended us for years."

"And what did your mother say when you proposed to see him?"

"She shivered violently, and said: 'No, I won't have him in the house.' After a time she decided to bring me to you."

"And have you had that hallucination again?" I inquired.

"It was not a hallucination," she answered, pouting her lips.

"I will humor you," I answered. "Have you seen your father again?"

"No, and I am not likely to."

"Why do you think that?"

"I cannot quite tell you—I think mother is in it. Mother is very unhappy about something, and she looks at me at times as if she were afraid of me." Here Miss Heathcote rose. "You said I was not to stay long," she remarked. "Now I have told you everything. You see that it is absolutely impossible for ordinary medicines to cure me, any more than ordinary medicines can cure mother of her awful dreams."

"I did not know that your mother dreamt badly," I said.

"She does—but she doesn't wish it spoken of. She dreams so badly, she cries out so terribly in her sleep, that she has moved from her old bedroom next to mine, to one in a distant wing of the house. Poor mother, I am sorry for her, but I am glad at least that I have had courage to tell you what I have seen. You will make it your business to find out the truth now, won't you?"

"What do you mean?" I asked.

"Why, of course, my father is alive," she retorted. "You have got to prove that he is, and to give him back to me again. I leave the matter in your hands. I know you are wise and very clever. Good-bye, good-bye!"

The queer girl left me, tears rolling down her cheeks. I was obliged to attend to other patients, but it was impossible for me to get Miss Heathcote's story out of my head. There was no doubt whatever that she was telling me what she firmly believed to be the truth. She had either seen her father once more in the flesh, or she was the victim of a very strong hallucination. In all probability

the latter supposition was the correct one. A man could not die and have a funeral and yet still be alive: but, then, on the other hand, when Mrs. Heathcote brought Gabrielle to see me yesterday, why had she not mentioned this central and principal feature of her malady? Mrs. Heathcote had said nothing whatever with regard to Gabrielle's delusions. Then why was the mother so nervous? Why did she say nothing about her own bad dreams, dreams so disturbing, that she was obliged to change her bedroom in order that her daughter should not hear her scream?

"I leave the matter in your hands!" Miss Heathcote had said. Poor child, she had done so with a vengeance. I could not get the story out of my thoughts, and so uncomfortable did the whole thing make me that I determined to pay Dr. Mackenzie a visit.

Mackenzie was a physician in very large practice at Brixton. His name was already familiar to me—on one or two occasions I had met him in consultation. I looked up his address in the Medical Directory, and that very evening took a hansom to his house. He happened to be at home. I sent in my card and was admitted at once.

Mackenzie received me in his consulting-room, and I was not long in explaining the motive of my visit. After a few preliminary remarks, I said that I would be glad if he would favor me with full particulars with Heathcote's death.

"I can easily do so," said Mackenzie. "The case was a perfectly straightforward one—my patient was consumptive, had been so for years, and died at last of hemoptysis."[1]

---

[1] Not a cause of death, but a symptom—the coughing-up of blood. It is common in severe cases of tuberculosis (consumption).

"What aged man was he?" I asked.

"Not old—a little past forty—a tall, slight, good-looking man, with a somewhat emaciated face. In short, his was an ordinary case of consumption."

I told Mackenzie all about the visit which I had received from Mrs. Heathcote, and gave him a faithful version of the strange story which Miss Gabrielle Heathcote had told me that day.

"Miss Gabrielle is an excitable girl," replied the doctor. "I have had a good deal to do with her for many years, and thought her nerves highly strung. She is evidently the victim of a delusion, caused by the effect of grief on a somewhat delicate organism. She probably inherits her father's disease. Mrs. Heathcote should take her from home immediately."

"Mrs. Heathcote looks as if she needed change almost as badly as her daughter," I answered; "but now you will forgive me if I ask you a few questions. Will you oblige me by describing Heathcote's death as faithfully as you can?"

"Certainly," replied the physician.

He sank down into a chair at the opposite side of the hearth as he spoke.

"The death, when it came," he continued, "was, I must confess, unexpected. I had sounded Heathcote's lungs about three months previous to the time of his death seizure. Phthisis[2] was present, but not to an advanced degree. I recommended his wintering abroad. He was a solicitor by profession, and had a good practice. I remember his asking me, with a comical rise of his brows, how he was to carry on his profession so many miles from Chancery Lane. But to come to his death. It took place

six months ago, in the beginning of September. It had been a hot season, and I had just returned from my holiday. My portmanteau and Gladstone bag had been placed in the hall, and I was paying the cabman his fare, when a servant from the Heathcotes arrived, and begged of me to go immediately to her master, who was, she said, dying.

"I hurried off to the house without a moment's delay. It is a stone's throw from here. In fact, you can see the walls of the garden from the windows of this room in the daytime. I reached the house. Gabrielle was standing in the hall. I am an old friend of hers. Her face was quite white and had a stunned expression. When she saw me she rushed to me, clasped one of my hands in both of hers, and burst into tears.

" 'Go and save him!' she gasped, her voice choking with sobs, which were almost hysterical.

"A lady who happened to be staying in the house came and drew the girl away into one of the sitting-rooms, and I went upstairs. I found Heathcote in his own room. He was lying on the bed—he was a ghastly sight. His face wore the sick hue of death itself; the sheet, his hair, and even his face were all covered with blood. His wife was standing over him, wiping away the blood, which oozed from his lips. I saw, of course, immediately what was the matter. Hemoptysis had set in, and I felt that his hours were numbered.

" 'He has broken a blood vessel,' exclaimed Mrs. Heathcote. 'He was standing here, preparing to go down to dinner, when he coughed violently—the blood began to pour from his mouth; I got him on the bed and sent for you. The hemorrhage seems to be a little less violent now.'

"I examined my patient carefully, feeling

---

[2] Another, now obsolete, name for tuberculosis.

his pulse, which was very weak and low; I cautioned him not to speak a single word, and asked Mrs. Heathcote to send for some ice immediately. She did so. I packed him in ice and gave him a dose of ergotine.[3] He seemed easier, and I left him, promising to return again in an hour or two. Miss Gabrielle met me in the hall as I went out.

" 'Is he any better? Is there any hope at all?' she asked, as I left the house.

" 'Your father is easier now,' I replied; 'the hemorrhage has been arrested. I am coming back soon. You must be a good girl and try to comfort your mother in every way in your power.'

" 'Then there is no hope?' she answered, looking me full in the face.

"I could not truthfully say that there was. I knew poor Heathcote's days were numbered, although I scarcely thought the end would come so quickly."

"What do you mean?" I inquired.

"Why this," he replied. "Less than an hour after I got home, I received a brief note from Mrs. Heathcote. In it she stated that fresh and very violent hemorrhage had set in almost immediately after I left, and that her husband was dead."

"And—" I continued.

"Well, that is the story. Poor Heathcote had died of hemoptysis."

"Did you see the body after death?" I inquired, after a pause.

"No—it was absolutely unnecessary—the cause of death was so evident. I attended the funeral, though. Heathcote was buried at Kensal Green."

I made no comment for a moment or two.

"I am sorry you did not see the body after death," I said, after a pause.

My remark seemed to irritate Mackenzie. He looked at me with raised brows.

"Would you have thought it necessary to do so?" he asked. "A man known to be consumptive dies of violent hemorrhage of the lungs. The family is in great trouble—there is much besides to think of. Would you under the circumstances have considered it necessary to refuse to give a certificate without seeing the body?"

I thought for a moment.

"I make a rule of always seeing the body," I replied; "but, of course, you were justified, as the law stands. Well, then, there is no doubt Heathcote is really dead?"

"Really dead?" retorted Mackenzie. "Don't you understand that he has been in his grave for six months?—That I practically saw him die?—That I attended his funeral? By what possible chance can the man be alive?"

"None," I replied. "He is dead, of course. I am sorry for the poor girl. She ought to leave home immediately."

"Girls of her age often have delusions," said Mackenzie. "I doubt not this will pass in time. I am surprised, however, that the Heathcotes allowed the thing to go on so long. I remember now that I have never been near the house since the funeral. I cannot understand their not calling me in."

"That fact puzzles me also," I said. "They came to me, a total stranger, instead of consulting their family physician, and Mrs. Heathcote carefully concealed the most important part of her daughter's malady. It is strange altogether; and, although I can give

---

[3] An alkaloid extracted from ergot, a fungus, then used to treat various diseases and symptoms. Studies in 1881 showed that it had a powerful contracting effect on blood vessels—hence its use here.

no explanation whatever, I am convinced there is one if we could only get at it. One more question before I go, Mackenzie. You spoke of Heathcote as a solicitor: has he left his family well off?"

"They are not rich," replied Mackenzie; "but as far as I can tell, they don't seem to want for money. I believe their house, Ivy Hall is its name, belongs to them. They live there very quietly, with a couple of maid-servants. I should say they belonged to the well-to-do middle classes."

"Then money troubles cannot explain the mystery?" I replied.

"Believe me, there is no mystery," answered Mackenzie, in an annoyed voice.

I held out my hand to wish him good-bye, when a loud peal at the front door startled us both. If ever there was frantic haste in anything, there was in that ringing peal.

"Someone wants you in a hurry," I said to the doctor.

He was about to reply, when the door to the consulting-room was flung wide open, and Gabrielle Heathcote rushed into the room.

"Mother is very ill," she exclaimed. "I think she is out of her mind. Come to her at once."

She took Mackenzie's hand in hers.

"There isn't a minute to lose," she said, "she may kill herself. She came to me with a carving knife in her hand; I rushed away at once for you. The two servants are with her now, and they are doing all they can; but, oh! pray do be quick."

At this moment Gabrielle's eyes rested on me. A look of relief and almost ecstasy passed over her poor, thin little face.

"You are here!" she exclaimed. "You will come, too? Oh, how glad I am."

"If Dr. Mackenzie will permit me," I replied. "I shall be only too pleased to accompany him."

"By all means come, you may be of the greatest use," he answered.

We started at once. As soon as we left the house Gabrielle rushed from us.

"I am going to have the front door open for you both when you arrive," she exclaimed. She disappeared as if on the wings of the wind.

"That is a good girl," I said, turning to the other doctor.

"She has always been deeply attached to both her parents," he answered.

We did not either of us say another word until we got to Ivy Hall. It was a rambling old house, with numerous low rooms and a big entrance-hall. I could fancy that in the summer it was cheerful enough, with its large, walled-in garden. The night was a dark one, but there would be a moon presently.

Gabrielle was waiting in the hall to receive us.

"I will take you to the door of mother's room," she exclaimed.

Her words came out tremblingly, her face was like death. She was shaking all over. She ran up the stairs before us, and then down a long passage which led to a room a little apart from the rest of the house.

"I told you mother wished to sleep in a room as far away from me as possible," she said, flashing a glance into my face as she spoke.

I nodded in reply. We opened the door and went in. The sight which met our eyes was one with which most medical men are familiar.

The patient was lying on the bed in a state of violent delirium. Two maid-servants were bending over her, and evidently much exciting her feelings in their efforts to hold her down. I spoke at once with authority.

"You can leave the room now," I said— "only remain within call in case you are wanted." They obeyed instantly, looking at me with surprised glances, and at Mackenzie with manifest relief.

I shut the door after them and approached the bed. One glance showed that Mrs. Heathcote was not mad in the ordinary sense, but that she was suffering at the moment from acute delirium. I put my hand on her forehead: it burned with fever. Her pulse was rapid and uneven. Mackenzie took her temperature, which was very nearly a hundred and four degrees. While we were examining her she remained quiet, but presently, as we stood together and watched her, she began to rave again.

"What is it, Gabrielle? No, no, he is quite dead, child. I tell you I saw the men screw his coffin down. He's dead—quite dead. Oh, God! Oh, God! Yes, dead, dead!"

She sat up in bed and stared straight before her.

"You mustn't come here so often," she said, looking past us into the center of the room, and addressing someone whom she seemed to see with distinctness, "I tell you it isn't safe. Gabrielle suspects. Don't come so often—I'll manage some other way. Trust me. Do trust me. You know I won't let you starve. Oh, go away, go away."

She flung herself back on the bed and pressed her hands frantically to her burning eyes.

"Your father has been dead six months now, Gabrielle," she said, presently, in a changed voice.

"No one was ever more dead. I tell you I saw him die; he was buried, and you went to his funeral." Here again her voice altered. She sat upright and motioned with her hand. "Will you bring the coffin in here, please, into this room? Yes; it seems a nice coffin—well finished. The coffin is made of oak. That is right. Oak lasts. I can't bear coffins that crumble away very quickly. This is a good one— you have taken pains with it—I am pleased. Lay him in gently. He is not very heavy, is he? You see how worn he is. Consumption!—yes, consumption. He had been a long time dying, but at the end it was sudden. Hemorrhage of the lungs. We did it to save Gabrielle, and to keep away—what, what, *what* did we want to keep away?—Oh, yes, dishonor! The— the—" Here she burst into a loud laugh.

"You don't suppose, you undertaker's men, that I'm going to tell you what we did it for? Dr. Mackenzie was there—he saw him just at the end. Now you have placed him nicely in his coffin, and you can go. Thank you, you can go now. I don't want you to see his face. A dead face is too sacred. You must not look on it. He is peaceful, only pale, very pale. All dead people look pale. Is he as pale as most dead people? Oh, I forgot—you can't see him. And as cold? Oh, yes, I think so, quite. You want to screw the coffin down, of course, of course—I was forgetting. Now, be quick about it. Why, do you know, I was very nearly having him buried with the coffin open! Screw away now, screw away. Ah, how that noise grates on my nerves. I shall go mad if you are not quick. Do be quick—be *quick*, and leave me alone with my dead. Oh, God, with my dead, my dead!"

The wretched woman's voice sank to a hoarse whisper. She struggled on to her knees, and folding her hands, began to pray.

"God in Heaven have mercy upon me and upon my dead," she moaned. "Now, now, now! Where's the screwdriver? Oh, *heavens*, it's lost, it's lost! We are undone! My God, what is the matter with me? My brain reels. Oh, my God, my God!"

She moaned fearfully. We laid her back on the bed. Her mutterings became more rapid and indistinct. Presently she slept.

"She must not be left in this condition," said Mackenzie to me. "It would be very bad for Gabrielle to be with her mother now. And those young servants are not to be trusted. I will go and send in a nurse as soon as possible. Can you do me the inestimable favor of remaining here until a nurse arrives?"

"I was going to propose that I should, in any case, spend the night here," I replied.

"That is more than good of you," said the doctor.

"Not at all," I answered; "the case interests me extremely."

A moment or two later Mackenzie left the house. During his absence Mrs. Heathcote slept, and I sat and watched her. The fever raged very high—she muttered constantly in her terrible dreams, but said nothing coherent. I felt very anxious about her. She had evidently been subjected to a most frightful strain and now all her nature was giving way. I dared not think what her words implied. My mission was at present to do what I could for her relief.

The nurse arrived about midnight. She was a sensible, middle-aged woman, very strong too, and evidently accustomed to fever patients. I gave her some directions, desired her to ring a certain bell if she required my assistance, and left the room. As I went slowly downstairs I noticed the moon had risen. The house was perfectly still—the sick woman's

moans could not be heard beyond the distant wing of the house where she slept. As I went downstairs I remembered Gabrielle's story about the moonlit garden and her father's figure standing there. I felt a momentary curiosity to see what the garden was like, and, moving aside a blind, which concealed one of the lobby windows, looked out. I gave one hurried glance and started back. Was I, too, the victim of illusion? Standing in the garden was the tall figure of a man with folded arms. He was looking away from me, but the light fell on his face; it was cadaverous and ghastly white; his hat was off; he moved into a deep shadow. It was all done in an instant—he came and went like a flash.

I pursued my way softly downstairs. This man's appearance seemed exactly to coincide with Mackenzie's description of Heathcote; but was it possible, in any of the wonderful possibilities of this earth, that a man could rise from his coffin and walk the earth again?

Gabrielle was waiting for me in the cheerful drawing-room. A bright fire burned in the grate, there were candles on brackets, and one or two shaded lamps placed on small tables. On one table, a little larger than the rest, a white cloth was spread. It also contained a tray with glasses, some claret and sherry in decanters, and a plate of sandwiches.

"You must be tired," said Gabrielle. "Please have a glass of wine, and please eat something. I know those sandwiches are good—I made them myself."

She pressed me to eat and drink. In truth, I needed refreshment. The scene in the sick room had told even on my iron nerves, and the sight from the lobby window had almost taken my breath away.

Gabrielle attended on me as if she were

my daughter. I was touched by her solicitude, and by the really noble way in which she tried to put self out of sight. At last she said, in a voice which shook with emotion:—

"I know, Dr. Halifax, that you think badly of mother."

"Your mother is very ill indeed," I answered.

"It is good of you to come and help her. You are a great doctor, are you not?"

I smiled at the child's question.

"I want you to tell me something about the beginning of your mother's illness," I said, after a pause. "When I saw her two days ago, she scarcely considered herself ill at all—in fact, you were supposed to be the patient."

Gabrielle dropped into the nearest chair.

"There is a mystery somewhere," she said, "but I cannot make it out. When I came back, after seeing you today, mother seemed very restless and troubled. I thought she would have questioned me about being so long away, and ask me at least what I had done with myself. Instead of that, she asked me to tread softly. She said she had such an intolerable headache that she could not endure the least sound. I saw she had been out, for she had her walking boots on, and they were covered with mud. I tried to coax her to eat something, but she would not, and as I saw she really wished to be alone, I left her.

"At tea time, our parlor-maid, Peters, told me that mother had gone to bed and had given directions that she was on no account to be disturbed. I had tea alone, and then came in here and made the place as bright and comfortable as I could. Once or twice before, since my father's death, mother has suffered from acute headaches, and has gone to bed; but when they got better, she has dressed and come downstairs again. I thought she might

like to do so tonight, and that she would be pleased to see a bright room and everything cheerful about her.

"I got a story-book and tried to read, but my thoughts were with mother, and I felt dreadfully puzzled and anxious. The time seemed very long too, and I heartily wished that the night were over. I went upstairs about eight o'clock, and listened outside mother's door. She was moaning and talking to herself. It seemed to me that she was saying dreadful things. I quite shuddered as I listened. I knocked at the door, but there was no answer. Then I turned the handle and tried to enter, but the door was locked. I went downstairs again, and Peters came to ask me if I would like supper. She was still in the room, and I had not made up my mind whether I could eat anything or not, when I heard her give a short scream, and turning round, I saw mother standing in the room in her nightdress. She had the carving-knife in her hand.

" 'Gabrielle,' she said, in a quiet voice, but with an awful look in her eyes, 'I want you to tell me the truth. Is there any blood on my hands?'

" 'No, no, mother,' I answered.

"She gave a deep sigh, and looked at them as if she were Lady Macbeth.

" 'Gabrielle,' she said again, 'I can't live any longer without your father. I have made this knife sharp, and it won't take long.'

"Then she turned and left the room. Peters ran for cook, and they went upstairs after her, and I rushed for Dr. Mackenzie."

"It was a fearful ordeal for you," I said, "and you behaved very bravely; but you must not think too much about your mother's condition, nor about any words which she happened to say. She is highly feverish at present, and is not accountable for her actions. Sit down now, please, and take a glass of wine yourself."

"No, thank you—I never take wine."

"I'm glad to hear you say so, for in that case a glass of this good claret will do wonders for you. Here, I'm going to pour one out—now drink it off at once."

She obeyed me with a patient sort of smile. She was very pale, but the wine brought some color into her cheeks.

"I am interested in your story," I said after a pause. "Particularly in what you told me about your poor father. He must have been an interesting man, for you to treasure his memory so deeply. Do you mind describing him to me?"

She flushed up when I spoke. I saw that tears were very near her eyes and she bit her lips to keep back emotion.

"My father was like no one else," she said. "It is impossible for me to make a picture of him for one who has not seen him.

"But you can at least tell me if he were tall or short, dark or fair, old or young?"

"No, I can't," she said, after another pause. "He was just father. When you love your father, he has a kind of eternal youth to you, and you don't discriminate his features. If you are his only child, his is just the one face in all the world to you. I find it impossible to describe the face, although it fills my mind's eye, waking and sleeping. But, stay, I have a picture of him. I don't show it to many, but you shall see it."

She rushed out of the room, returning in a moment with a morocco case. She opened it, and brought over a candle at the same time so that the light should fall on the picture within. It represented a tall, slight man with deep-set eyes and a very thin face. The eyes were somewhat piercing in their glance; the lips were closely set and firm; the chin was cleft. The face showed determination. I gave it a quick glance, and, closing the case, returned it to Gabrielle.

The face was the face of the man I had seen in the garden.

MY PATIENT PASSED a dreadful night. She was no better the next morning. Her temperature was rather higher, her pulse quicker, her respiration more hurried. Her ravings had now become almost incoherent. Mackenzie and I had an anxious consultation over her. When he left the house I accompanied him.

"I am going to make a strange request of you," I said. "I wish for your assistance, and am sure you will not refuse to give it to me. In short, I want to take immediate steps to have Heathcote's coffin opened."

I am quite sure Mackenzie thought that I was mad. He looked at me, opened his lips as if to speak, but then waited to hear my next words.

"I want to have Heathcote's body exhumed," I said. "If you will listen to me, I will tell you why."

I then gave him a graphic account of the man I had seen in the garden.

"There is foul play somewhere," I said, in conclusion. "I have been dragged into this thing almost against my will, and now I am determined to see it through."

Mackenzie flung up his hands.

"I don't pretend to doubt your wisdom," he said; "but to ask me gravely to assist you to exhume the body of a man who died of consumption six months ago, is enough to take my breath away. What reason can you possibly give to the authorities for such an action?"

"That I have strong grounds for believ-ing that the death never took place at all," I replied. "Now, will you co-operate with me in this matter, or not?"

"Oh, of course, I'll co-operate with you," he answered. "But I don't pretend to say that I like the business."

We walked together to his house, talking over the necessary steps which must be taken to get an order for exhumation. Mackenzie promised to telegraph to me as soon as ever this was obtained, and I was obliged to hurry off to attend to my own duties. As I was step-ping into my hansom I turned to ask the doc-tor one more question.

"Have you any reason to suppose that Heathcote was heavily insured?" I asked.

"No; I don't know anything about it," he answered.

"You are quite sure there were no money troubles anywhere?"

"I do not know of any; but that fact amounts to nothing, for I was not really inti-mate with the family, and, as I said yesterday evening, never entered the house until last night from the day of the funeral. I have never *heard* of money troubles; but, of course, they might have existed."

"As soon as ever I hear from you, I will make an arrangement to meet you at Kensal Green," I replied, and then I jumped into the hansom and drove away.

In the course of the day I got a telegram acquainting me with Mrs. Heathcote's con-dition. It still remained absolutely unchanged, and there was, in Mackenzie's opinion, no necessity for me to pay her another visit. Early the next morning, the required order came from the coroner. Mackenzie wired to apprise me of the fact, and I telegraphed back, making an appointment to meet him at

Kensal Green on the following morning.

I shall not soon forget that day. It was one of those blustering and intensely cold days which come oftener in March than any other time of the year. The cemetery looked as dismal as such a place would on the occa-sion. The few wreaths of flowers which were scattered here and there on newly-made graves were sodden and deprived of all their frail beauty. The wind blew in great gusts, which were about every ten minutes accom-panied by showers of sleet. There was a hol-low moaning noise distinctly audible in the intervals of the storm.

I found, on my arrival, that Mackenzie was there before me. He was accompanied by one of the coroner's men and a police-constable. Two men who worked in the ceme-tery also came forward to assist. No one expressed the least surprise at our strange errand. Around Mackenzie's lips, alone, I read an expression of disapproval.

Kensal Green is one of the oldest ceme-teries which surround our vast Metropolis, and the Heathcotes' burying-place was quite in the oldest portion of this God's acre. It was one of the hideous, ancient, rapidly-going-out-of-date vaults. A huge brick erection was placed over it, at one side of which was the door of entrance.

The earth was removed, the door of the vault opened, and some of the men went down the steps, one of them holding a torch, in order to identify the coffin. In a couple of minutes' time it was borne into the light of day. When I saw it I remembered poor Mrs. Heathcote's wild ravings.

"A good, strong oak coffin, which wears well," she had exclaimed.

Mackenzie and I, accompanied by the police-constable and the coroner's man, followed the bearers of the coffin to the mortuary.

As we were going there, I turned to ask Mackenzie how his patient was.

He shook his head as he answered me.

"I fear the worst," he replied. "Mrs. Heathcote is very ill indeed. The fever rages high and is like a consuming fire. Her temperature was a hundred and five this morning."

"I should recommend packing her in sheets wrung out of cold water," I answered. "Poor woman!—how do you account for this sudden illness, Mackenzie?"

He shrugged his shoulders.

"Shock of some sort," he answered. Then he continued: "If she really knew of this day's work, it would kill her off pretty quickly. Poor soul," he added, "I hope it may never reach her ears."

We had now reached the mortuary. The men who had borne the coffin on their shoulders lowered it on to a pair of trestles. They then took turn-screws out of their pockets, and in a business-like and callous manner unscrewed the lid. After doing this they left the mortuary, closing the door behind them.

The moment we found ourselves alone, I said a word to the police-constable, and then going quickly up to the coffin, lifted the lid. Under ordinary circumstances, such a proceeding would be followed by appalling results, which need not here be described. Mackenzie, whose face was very white, stood near me. I looked at him for a moment, and then flung aside the pall which was meant to conceal the face of the dead.

The dead truly! Here was death, which had never, in any sense, known life like ours. Mackenzie uttered a loud exclamation. The constable and the coroner's man came close. I lifted a bag of flour out of the coffin!

There were many similar bags there. It had been closely packed, and evidently with a view to counterfeit the exact weight of the dead man.

Poor Mackenzie was absolutely speechless. The coroner's man began to take copious notes; the police-constable gravely did the same.

Mackenzie at last found his tongue.

"I never felt more stunned in my life," he said. "In very truth, I all but saw the man die. Where is he? In the name of Heaven, what has become of him? This is the most monstrous thing I have ever heard of in the whole course of my life, and—and I attended the funeral of those *bags of flour!* No wonder that woman never cared to see me inside the house again. But what puzzles me," he continued, "is the motive—what *can* the motive be?"

"Perhaps one of the insurance companies can tell us that," said the police-officer. "It is my duty to report this thing, sir," he continued, turning to me. "I have not the least doubt that the Crown will prosecute."

"I cannot at all prevent your taking what steps you think proper," I replied, "only pray understand that the poor lady who is the principal perpetrator in this fraud lies at the present moment at death's door."

"We must get the man himself," murmured the police-officer. "If he is alive we shall soon find him."

Half an hour later, Mackenzie and I had left the dismal cemetery.

I had to hurry back to Harley Street to attend to some important duties, but I arranged to meet Mackenzie that evening at the Heathcotes' house. I need not say that my thoughts were much occupied with Mrs. Heathcote and her miserable story. What a life that wretched Heathcote must have led during the last six months. No wonder he looked cadaverous as the moonlight fell over his gaunt figure. No ghost truly was he, but a man of like flesh and blood to ourselves—a man who was supposed to be buried in Kensal Green, but who yet walked the earth.

It was about eight o'clock when I reached the Heathcotes' house. Mackenzie had already arrived—he came into the hall to meet me.

"Where is Miss Gabrielle?" I asked at once.

"Poor child," he replied; "I have begged her to stay in her room. She knows nothing of what took place this morning, but is in a terrible state of grief about her mother. That unfortunate woman's hours are numbered. She is sinking fast. Will you come to her at once, Halifax—she has asked for you several times."

Accompanied by Mackenzie, I mounted the stairs and entered the sick room. One glance at the patient's face showed me all too plainly that I was in the chamber of death. Mrs. Heathcote lay perfectly motionless. Her bright hair, still the hair of quite a young woman, was flung back over the pillow. Her pale face was wet with perspiration. Her eyes, solemn, dark, and awful in expression, turned and fixed themselves on me as I approached the bedside. Something like the ghost of a smile quivered round her lips. She made an effort to stretch out a shadowy hand to grasp mine.

"Don't stir," I said to her. "Perhaps you want to say something? I will stoop down to listen to you. I have very good hearing, so you can speak as low as you please."

She smiled again with a sort of pleasure at my understanding her.

"I have something to confess," she said, in a hollow whisper. "Send the nurse and—and Dr. Mackenzie out of the room."

I was obliged to explain the dying woman's wishes to my brother physician. He called to the nurse to follow him, and they immediately left the room.

As soon as they had done so, I bent my head and took one of Mrs. Heathcote's hands in mine.

"Now," I said, "take comfort—God can forgive sin. You have sinned?"

"Oh, yes, yes; but how can you possibly know?"

"Never mind. I am a good judge of character. If telling me will relieve your conscience, speak."

"My husband is alive," she murmured.

"Yes," I said, "I guessed as much."

"He had insured his life," she continued, "for—for about fifteen thousand pounds. The money was wanted to—to save us from dishonor. We managed to counterfeit—death."

She stopped, as if unable to proceed any further. "A week ago," she continued, "I—I saw the man who is supposed to be dead. He is really dying now. The strain of knowing that I could do nothing for him—nothing to comfort his last moments—was too horrible. I felt that I could not live without him. On the day of my illness I took—poison, a preparation of Indian hemp. I meant to kill myself. I did not know that my object would be effected in so terrible a manner."

Here she looked towards the door. A great change came over her face. Her eyes shone with sudden brightness. A look of awful joy filled them. She made a frantic effort to raise herself in bed.

I followed the direction of her eyes, and then, indeed, a startled exclamation passed my lips.

Gabrielle, with her cheeks crimson, her lips tremulous, her hair tossed wildly about her head and shoulders, was advancing into the room, leading a cadaverous, ghastly-looking man by the hand. In other words, Heathcote himself in the flesh had come into his wife's dying chamber.

"Oh, Horace!" she exclaimed; "Horace—to die in your arms—to know that you will soon join me. This is too much bliss—this is too great joy!"

The man knelt by her, put his dying arms round her, and she laid her head on his worn breast.

"We will leave them together," I said to Gabrielle.

I took the poor little girl's hand and led her from the room.

She was in a frantic state of excitement.

"I said he was not dead," she repeated—"I always said it. I was sitting by my window a few minutes ago, and I saw him in the garden. This time I was determined that he should not escape me. I rushed downstairs. He knew nothing until he saw me at his side. I caught his hand in mine. It was hot and thin. It was like a skeleton's hand—only it burned with living fire. 'Mother is dying—come to her at once,' I said to him, and then I brought him into the house."

"You did well—you acted very bravely," I replied to her.

I took her away to a distant part of the house.

An hour later, Mrs. Heathcote died. I was not with her when she breathed her last. My one object now was to do what I could for poor little Gabrielle. In consequence, therefore, I made arrangements to have an interview with Heathcote. It was no longer possible for the wretched man to remain in hiding. His own hours were plainly numbered, and it was more than evident that he had only anticipated his real death by some months.

I saw him the next day, and he told me in a few brief words the story of his supposed death and burial.

"I am being severely punished now," he said, "for the one great sin of my life. I am a solicitor by profession, and when a young man was tempted to appropriate some trust funds—hoping, like many another has done before me, to replace the money before the loss was discovered. I married, and had a happy home. My wife and I were devotedly attached to each other. I was not strong and more than one physician told me that I was threatened with a serious pulmonary affection. About eight months ago, the blow which I never looked for fell. I need not enter into particulars. Suffice it to say that I was expected to deliver over twelve thousand pounds, the amount of certain trusts committed to me, to their rightful owners within three months' time. If I failed to realize this money, imprisonment, dishonor, ruin, would be mine. My wife and child would also be reduced to beggary. I had effected an insurance on my life for fifteen thousand pounds. If this sum could be realized, it would cover the deficit in the trust, and also leave a small overplus for the use of my wife and daughter. I knew that my days were practically numbered, and it did not strike me as a particularly heinous crime to forestall my death by a few months. I talked the matter over with my wife, and at last got her to consent to help me. We managed everything cleverly, and not a soul suspected the fraud which was practiced on the world. Our old servants, who had lived with us for years, were sent away on a holiday. We had no servant in the house except a char-woman, who came in for a certain number of hours daily."

"You managed your supposed dying con-dition with great skill," I answered. "That hemorrhage, the ghastly expression of your face, were sufficiently real to deceive even a keen and clever man like Mackenzie."

Heathcote smiled grimly.

"After all," he said, "the fraud was simple enough. I took an emetic, which I knew would produce the cadaverous hue of approaching death, and the supposed hemorrhage was managed with some bullock's blood. I got it from a distant butcher, telling him that I wanted it to mix with meal to feed my dogs with."

"And how did you deceive the under-taker's men?" I asked.

"My wife insisted on keeping my face covered, and I managed to simulate rigidity. As to the necessary coldness, I was cold enough lying with only a sheet over me. After I was placed in the coffin my wife would not allow anyone to enter the room but herself: she brought me food, of course. We bored holes, too, in the coffin lid. Still, I shall never forget the awful five minutes during which I was screwed down.

"It was all managed with great expedi-tion. As soon as ever the undertaker's men could be got out of the way, my wife un-screwed the coffin and released me. We then filled it with bags of flour, which we had al-ready secured and hidden for the purpose. My supposed funeral took place with due honors. I left the house that night, intending to ship to America. Had I done this, the appalling consequences which have now ended in the death of my wife might never have taken place, but, at the eleventh hour, my courage failed me. I could do much to shield my child, but I could not endure the thought of never seeing them again. Contrary to all my wife's entreaties, I insisted on coming into the gar-den, for the selfish pleasure of catching even a glimpse of Gabrielle's little figure, as she moved about her bedroom. She saw me once, but I escaped through the shrubbery and by a door which we kept on purpose unlocked, before she reached me. I thought I would never again transgress, but once more the temptation assailed me, and I was not proof against it. My health failed rapidly. I was really dying, and on the morning when my wife's illness began, had suffered from a genuine and very sharp attack of hemorrhage. She found me in the wretched lodging where I was hid-ing in a state of complete misery, and almost destitution. Something in my appearance seemed suddenly to make her lose all self-control.

" 'Horace,' she exclaimed, 'I cannot stand this. When you die, I will die. We will carry our shame and our sorrow and our unhappy love into the grave, where no man can follow us. When you die, I will die. Oh, to see you like this drives me mad!'

"She left me. She told me when I saw her during those last few moments yesterday, that she had hastened her end by a powerful dose of Indian hemp. That is the story. I know that I have laid myself open to criminal pros-ecution of the gravest character, but I do not think I shall live to go through it."

Heathcote was right. He passed away

that evening quite quietly in his sleep. Poor little Gabrielle! I saw her once since her parents' death, but it is now a couple of years since I have heard anything about her. Will she ever get over the severe shock to which she was subjected? What does the future hold in store for her? I cannot answer these questions. Time alone can do that.

Arthur Morrison

ARTHUR GEORGE MORRISON (1863-1945) wrote a number of novels and short stories about the East End of London, Essex, and his remarkable detective Martin Hewitt, whose tales appeared in three collections. The Hewitt stories began to appear in the *Strand Magazine* hot on the tail of Sherlock Holmes. "The Final Problem," the tale of Holmes's demise, appeared in December 1893; "The Lenton Croft Robberies," the first of the Hewitt adventures, was published in March 1894.

Hewitt was in some ways the anti-Holmes: He was short, ordinary, mild-mannered, and freely cooperated with the police; however, he often played the law against the criminal for his own profit. The following story appeared in *Windsor Magazine*, a rival of the *Strand*, in May 1895 and was published in book form in *The Chronicles of Martin Hewitt* (1895).

THE CASE OF LAKER, ABSCONDED

ARTHUR MORRISON

THERE WERE SEVERAL of the larger London banks and insurance offices from which Hewitt held a sort of general retainer as detective adviser, in fulfillment of which he was regularly consulted as to the measures to be taken in different cases of fraud, forgery, theft, and so forth, which it might be the misfortune of the particular firms to encounter. The more important and intricate of these cases were placed in his hands entirely, with separate commissions, in the usual way. One of the most important companies of the sort was the General Guarantee Society, an insurance corporation which, among other risks, took those of the integrity of secretaries, clerks, and cashiers. In the case of a cash-box elopement on the part of any person guaranteed by the society, the directors were naturally anxious for a speedy capture of the culprit, and more especially of the booty, before too much of it was spent, in order to lighten the claim

upon their funds, and in work of this sort Hewitt was at times engaged, either in general advice and direction or in the actual pursuit of the plunder and the plunderer.

Arriving at his office a little later than usual one morning, Hewitt found an urgent message awaiting him from the General Guarantee Society, requesting his attention to a robbery which had taken place on the previous day. He had gleaned some hint of the case from the morning paper, wherein appeared a short paragraph, which ran thus:

SERIOUS BANK ROBBERY.—In the course of yesterday a clerk employed by Messrs Liddle, Neal & Liddle, the well-known bankers, disappeared, having in his possession a large sum of money, the property of his employers—a sum reported to be rather over £15,000. It would seem that he had been entrusted to collect the money in his capacity of "walk-clerk"[1] from various

---

[1] The "walk-clerk" was a courier employed by the bank or other institution who carried funds (typically in a portfolio locked to his wrist) from the institution to the clearing-house or vice versa. Typically young men starting in the banking industry, these clerkships required a certain physical prowess, for there were many incidents of robberies of the walk-clerks.

other banks and trading concerns during the morning, but failed to return at the usual time. A large number of the notes which he received had been cashed at the Bank of England before suspicion was aroused. We understand that Detective-Inspector Plummer, of Scotland Yard, has the case in hand.

The clerk, whose name was Charles William Laker, had, it appeared from the message, been guaranteed in the usual way by the General Guarantee Society, and Hewitt's presence at the office was at once desired in order that steps might quickly be taken for the man's apprehension and in the recovery, at any rate, of as much of the booty as possible.

A smart hansom brought Hewitt to Threadneedle Street in a bare quarter of an hour, and there a few minutes' talk with the manager, Mr. Lyster, put him in possession of the main facts of the case, which appeared to be simple. Charles William Laker was twenty-five years of age, and had been in the employ of Messrs Liddle, Neal & Liddle for something more than seven years—since he left school, in fact—and until the previous day there had been nothing in his conduct to complain of. His duties as walk-clerk consisted in making a certain round, beginning at about half-past ten each morning. There were a certain number of the more important banks between which and Messrs Liddle, Neal & Liddle there were daily transactions, and a few smaller semi-private banks and merchant firms acting as financial agents with whom there was business intercourse of less importance and regularity; and each of these, as necessary, he visited in turn, collecting cash due on bills and other instruments of a like nature. He carried a wallet, fastened securely to his person by a chain, and this wallet contained the bills and the cash. Usually at the end of his round, when all his bills had been converted into cash, the wallet held very large sums. His work and responsibilities, in fine, were those common to walk-clerks in all banks.

On the day of the robbery he had started out as usual—possibly a little earlier than was customary—and the bills and other securities in his possession represented considerably more than £15,000. It had been ascertained that he had called in the usual way at each establishment on the round, and had transacted his business at the last place by about a quarter-past one, being then, without doubt, in possession of cash to the full value of the bills negotiated. After that, Mr. Lyster said, yesterday's report was that nothing more had been heard of him. But this morning there had been a message to the effect that he had been traced out of the country—to Calais, at least, it was thought. The directors of the society wished Hewitt to take the case in hand personally and at once, with a view of recovering what was possible from the plunder by way of salvage; also, of course, of finding Laker, for it is an important moral gain to guarantee societies, as an example, if a thief is caught and punished. Therefore Hewitt and Mr. Lyster, as soon as might be, made for Messrs Liddle, Neal & Liddle's, that the investigation might be begun.

The bank premises were quite near—in Leadenhall Street. Having arrived there, Hewitt and Mr. Lyster made their way to the firm's private rooms. As they were passing an outer waiting-room, Hewitt noticed two women. One, the elder, in widow's weeds, was sitting with her head bowed in her hand over a small writing-table. Her face was not visible, but her whole attitude was that of a person overcome with unbearable grief; and she sobbed quietly. The other was a young woman of twenty-two or twenty-three. Her thick black veil revealed no more than that her features were small and regular and that her face was pale and drawn. She stood with a hand on the elder woman's shoulder, and she quickly turned her head away as the two men entered.

Mr. Neal, one of the partners, received them in his own room. "Good-morning, Mr. Hewitt," he said, when Mr. Lyster had introduced the detective. "This is a serious business—very. I think I am sorrier for Laker himself than for anybody else, ourselves included—or, at any rate, I am sorrier for his mother. She is waiting now to see Mr. Liddle, as soon as he arrives—Mr. Liddle has known the family for a long time. Miss Shaw is with her, too, poor girl. She is a governess, or something of that sort, and I believe she and Laker were engaged to be married. It's all very sad."

"Inspector Plummer, I understand," Hewitt remarked, "has the affair in hand, on behalf of the police?"

"Yes," Mr. Neal replied; "in fact, he's here now, going through the contents of Laker's desk, and so forth; he thinks it possible Laker may have had accomplices. Will you see him?"

"Presently. Inspector Plummer and I are old friends. We met last, I think, in the case of the Stanway cameo, some months ago. But, first, will you tell me how long Laker has been a walk-clerk?"

"Barely four months, although he has been with us altogether seven years. He was promoted to the walk soon after the beginning of the year."

"Do you know anything of his habits—what he used to do in his spare time, and so forth?"

"Not a great deal. He went in for boating, I believe, though I have heard it whispered that he had one or two more expensive tastes—expensive, that is, for a young man in his position," Mr. Neal explained, with a dignified wave of the hand that he peculiarly affected. He was a stout old gentleman, and the gesture suited him.

"You have had no reason to suspect him of dishonesty before, I take it?"

"Oh, no. He made a wrong return once, I believe, that went for some time undetected, but it turned out, after all, to be a clerical error—a mere clerical error."

"Do you know anything of his associates out of the office?"

"No, how should I? I believe Inspector Plummer has been making inquiries as to that, however, of the other clerks. Here he is, by the bye, I expect. Come in!"

It was Plummer who had knocked, and he came in at Mr. Neal's call. He was a middle-sized, small-eyed, impenetrable-looking man, as yet of no great reputation in the force. Some of my readers may remember his connection with that case, so long a public mystery, that I have elsewhere fully set forth and explained under the title of "The Stanway Cameo Mystery." Plummer carried his billycock hat[2] in one hand and a few papers in the other. He gave Hewitt good-morning, placed his hat on a chair, and spread the papers on the table.

"There's not a great deal here," he said, "but one thing's plain—Laker had been betting. See here, and here, and here"—he took a few letters from the bundle in his hand—"two letters from a bookmaker about settling—wonder he trusted a clerk—several

[2] A derby or bowler hat.

telegrams from tipsters, and a letter from some friend—only signed by initials—asking Laker to put a sovereign on a horse for the friend 'with his own.' I'll keep these, I think. It may be worth while to see that friend, if we can find him. Ah, we often find it's betting, don't we, Mr. Hewitt? Meanwhile, there's no news from France yet."

"You are sure that is where he is gone?" asked Hewitt.

"Well, I'll tell you what we've done as yet. First, of course, I went round to all the banks. There was nothing to be got from that. The cashiers all knew him by sight, and one was a personal friend of his. He had called as usual, said nothing in particular, cashed his bills in the ordinary way, and finished up at the Eastern Consolidated Bank at about a quarter-past one. So far there was nothing whatever. But I had started two or three men meanwhile making inquiries at the railway stations, and so on. I had scarcely left the Eastern Consolidated when one of them came after me with news. He had tried Palmer's Tourist Office, although that seemed an unlikely place, and there struck the track."

"Had he been there?"

"Not only had he been there, but he had taken a tourist ticket for France. It was quite a smart move, in a way. You see it was the sort of ticket that lets you do pretty well what you like; you have the choice of two or three different routes to begin with, and you can break your journey where you please, and make all sorts of variations. So that a man with a ticket like that, and a few hours' start, could twist about on some remote branch route, and strike off in another direction altogether, with a new ticket, from some out-of-the-way place, while we were carefully sorting out and inquiring along the different routes he *might*

have taken. Not half a bad move for a new hand; but he made one bad mistake, as new hands always do—as old hands do, in fact, very often. He was fool enough to give his own name, C. Laker! Although that didn't matter much, as the description was enough to fix him. There he was, wallet and all, just as he had come from the Eastern Consolidated Bank. He went straight from there to Palmer's, by the bye, and probably in a cab. We judge that by the time. He left the Eastern Consolidated at a quarter-past one, and was at Palmer's by twenty-five-past—ten minutes. The clerk at Palmer's remembered the time because he was anxious to get out to his lunch, and kept looking at the clock, expecting another clerk in to relieve him. Laker didn't take much in the way of luggage, I fancy. We inquired carefully at the stations, and got the porters to remember the passengers for whom they had been carrying luggage, but none appeared to have had any dealings with our man. That, of course, is as one would expect. He'd take as little as possible with him, and buy what he wanted on the way, or when he'd reached his hiding-place. Of course, I wired to Calais (it was a Dover to Calais route ticket) and sent a couple of smart men off by the 8.15 mail from Charing Cross. I expect we shall hear from them in the course of the day. I am being kept in London in view of something expected at headquarters, or I should have been off myself."

"That is all, then, up to the present? Have you anything else in view?"

"That's all I've absolutely ascertained at present. As for what I'm going to do"—a slight smile curled Plummer's lip—"well, I shall see. I've a thing or two in my mind."

Hewitt smiled slightly himself; he recognized Plummer's touch of professional jealousy. "Very well," he said, rising, "I'll make an inquiry or two for myself at once. Perhaps, Mr. Neal, you'll allow one of your clerks to show me the banks, in their regular order, at which Laker called yesterday. I think I'll begin at the beginning."

Mr. Neal offered to place at Hewitt's disposal anything or anybody the bank contained, and the conference broke up. As Hewitt, with the clerk, came through the rooms separating Mr. Neal's sanctum from the outer office, he fancied he saw the two veiled women leaving by a side door.

The first bank was quite close to Liddle, Neal & Liddle's. There the cashier who had dealt with Laker the day before remembered nothing in particular about the interview. Many other walk-clerks had called during the morning, as they did every morning, and the only circumstances of the visit that he could say anything definite about were those recorded in figures in the books. He did not know Laker's name till Plummer had mentioned it in making inquiries on the previous afternoon. As far as he could remember, Laker behaved much as usual, though really he did not notice much; he looked chiefly at the bills. He described Laker in a way that corresponded with the photograph that Hewitt had borrowed from the bank; a young man with a brown moustache and ordinary-looking fairly regular face, dressing much as other clerks dressed—tall hat, black cutaway coat, and so on. The numbers of the notes handed over had already been given to Inspector Plummer, and these Hewitt did not trouble about.

The next bank was in Cornhill, and here the cashier was a personal friend of Laker's—at any rate, an acquaintance—and he remembered a little more. Laker's manner had been quite as usual, he said; certainly he did not seem preoccupied or excited in his manner. He spoke for a moment or two—of being on the river on Sunday, and so on—and left in his usual way.

"Can you remember *everything* he said?" Hewitt asked. "If you can tell me, I should like to know exactly what he did and said to the smallest particular."

"Well, he saw me a little distance off—I was behind there, at one of the desks—and raised his hand to me, and said, 'How d'ye do?' I came across and took his bills, and dealt with them in the usual way. He had a new umbrella lying on the counter—rather a handsome umbrella—and I made a remark about the handle. He took it up to show me, and told me it was a present he had just received from a friend. It was a gorse-root handle, with two silver bands, one with his monogram, C.W.L. I said it was a very nice handle, and asked him whether it was fine in his district on Sunday. He said he had been up the river, and it was very fine there. And I think that was all."

"Thank you. Now about this umbrella. Did he carry it rolled? Can you describe it in detail?"

"Well, I've told you about the handle, and the rest was much as usual, I think; it wasn't rolled—just napping loosely, you know. It was rather an odd-shaped handle, though. I'll try and sketch it, if you like, as well as I can remember." He did so, and Hewitt saw in the result rough indications of a gnarled crook, with one silver band near the end, and another, with the monogram, a few inches down the handle. Hewitt put the sketch in his pocket, and bade the cashier good-day.

At the next bank the story was the same as at the first—there was nothing remembered but the usual routine. Hewitt and the clerk turned down a narrow paved court, and through into Lombard Street for the next visit. The bank—that of Buller, Clayton, Ladds & Co.—was just at the corner at the end of the court, and the imposing stone entrance-porch was being made larger and more imposing still, the way being almost blocked by ladders and scaffold-poles. Here there was only the usual tale, and so on through the whole walk. The cashiers knew Laker only by sight, and that not always very distinctly. The calls of walk-clerks were such matters of routine that little note was taken of the persons of the clerks themselves, who were called by the names of their firms, if they were called by any names at all. Laker had behaved much as usual, so far as the cashiers could remember, and when finally the Eastern Consolidated was left behind, nothing more had been learnt than the chat about Laker's new umbrella.

Hewitt had taken leave of Mr. Neal's clerk, and was stepping into a hansom, when he noticed a veiled woman in widow's weeds hailing another hansom a little way behind. He recognized the figure again, and said to the driver: "Drive fast to Palmer's Tourist Office, but keep your eye on that cab behind, and tell me presently if it is following us."

The cabman drove off, and after passing one or two turnings, opened the lid above Hewitt's head, and said: "That there other keb *is* a-follerin' us, sir, an' keepin' about even distance all along."

"All right; that's what I wanted to know. Palmer's now." At Palmer's the clerk who had attended to Laker remembered him very well and described him. He also remembered the wallet, and *thought* he remembered the umbrella—was practically sure of it, in fact, upon reflection. He had no record of the name

given, but remembered it distinctly to be Laker. As a matter of fact, names were never asked in such a transaction, but in this case Laker appeared to be ignorant of the usual procedure, as well as in a great hurry, and asked for the ticket and gave his name all in one breath, probably assuming that the name would be required.

Hewitt got back to his cab, and started for Charing Cross. The cabman once more lifted the lid and informed him that the hansom with the veiled woman in it was again following, having waited while Hewitt had visited Palmer's. At Charing Cross Hewitt discharged his cab and walked straight to the lost property office. The man in charge knew him very well, for his business had carried him there frequently before.

"I fancy an umbrella was lost in the station yesterday," Hewitt said. "It was a new umbrella, silk, with a gnarled gorse-root handle and two silver bands, something like this sketch. There was a monogram on the lower band—'C.W.L.' were the letters. Has it been brought here?"

"There was two or three yesterday," the man said; "let's see." He took the sketch and retired to a corner of his room. "Oh, yes—here it is, I think; isn't this it? Do you claim it?"

"Well, not exactly that, but I think I'll take a look at it, if you'll let me. By the way, I see it's rolled up. Was it found like that?"

"No; the chap rolled it up what found it—porter he was. It's a fad of his, rolling up umbrellas close and neat, and he's rather proud of it. He often looks as though he'd like to take a man's umbrella away and roll it up for him when it's a bit clumsy done. Rum fad, eh?"

"Yes; everybody has his little fad, though. Where was this found—close by here?"

"Yes, sir; just there, almost opposite this window, in the little corner."

"About two o'clock?"

"Ah, about that time, more or less."

Hewitt took the umbrella up, unfastened the band, and shook the silk out loose. Then he opened it, and as he did so a small scrap of paper fell from inside it. Hewitt pounced on it like lightning. Then, after examining the umbrella thoroughly, inside and out, he handed it back to the man, who had not observed the incident of the scrap of paper.

"That will do, thanks," he said. "I only wanted to take a peep at it—just a small matter connected with a little case of mine. Good morning."

He turned suddenly and saw, gazing at him with a terrified expression from a door behind, the face of the woman who had followed him in the cab. The veil was lifted, and he caught but a mere glance of the face ere it was suddenly withdrawn. He stood for a moment to allow the woman time to retreat, and then left the station and walked toward his office, close by.

Scarcely thirty yards along the Strand he met Plummer.

"I'm going to make some much closer inquiries all down the line as far as Dover," Plummer said. "They wire from Calais that they have no clue as yet, and I mean to make quite sure, if I can, that Laker hasn't quietly slipped off the line somewhere between here and Dover. There's one very peculiar thing," Plummer added confidentially. "Did you see the two women who were waiting to see a member of the firm at Liddle, Neal & Liddle's?"

"Yes. Laker's mother and his *fiancée*, I was told."

"That's right. Well, do you know that girl—Shaw her name is—has been shadowing me ever since I left the Bank. Of course I spotted it from the beginning—these amateurs don't know how to follow anybody—and, as a matter of fact, she's just inside that jeweler's shop door behind me now, pretending to look at the things in the window. But it's odd, isn't it?"

"Well," Hewitt replied, "of course it's not a thing to be neglected. If you'll look very carefully at the corner of Villiers Street, without appearing to stare, I think you will possibly observe some signs of Laker's mother. She's shadowing *me*."

Plummer looked casually in the direction indicated, and then immediately turned his eyes in another direction.

"I see her," he said; "she's just taking a look round the corner. That's a thing not to be ignored. Of course, the Lakers' house is being watched—we set a man on it at once, yesterday. But I'll put some one on now to watch Miss Shaw's place too. I'll telephone through to Liddle's—probably they'll be able to say where it is. And the women themselves must be watched, too. As a matter of fact, I had a notion that Laker wasn't alone in it. And it's just possible, you know, that he has sent an accomplice off with his tourist ticket to lead us a dance while he looks after himself in another direction. Have you done anything?"

"Well," Hewitt replied, with a faint reproduction of the secretive smile with which Plummer had met an inquiry of his earlier in the morning, "I've been to the station here, and I've found Laker's umbrella in the lost property office."

"Oh! Then probably he *has* gone. I'll bear that in mind, and perhaps have a word with the lost property man."

Plummer made for the station and Hewitt for his office. He mounted the stairs and reached his door just as I myself, who had been disappointed in not finding him in, was leaving. I had called with the idea of taking Hewitt to lunch with me at my club, but he declined lunch. "I have an important case in hand," he said. "Look here, Brett. See this scrap of paper. You know the types of the different newspapers[3]—which is this?"

He handed me a small piece of paper. It was part of a cutting containing an advertisement, which had been torn in half.

> oast. You 1st. Then to–
> 3rd L. No.197 red bl. straight
> time.

"I *think*," I said, "this is from the *Daily Chronicle*, judging by the paper. It is plainly from the 'agony column,' but all the papers use pretty much the same type for these advertisements, except the *Times*. If it were not torn I could tell you at once, because the *Chronicle* columns are rather narrow."

"Never mind—I'll send for them all." He rang, and sent Kerrett for a copy of each morning paper of the previous day. Then he took from a large wardrobe cupboard a decent but well-worn and rather roughened tall hat. Also a coat a little worn and shiny on the collar. He exchanged these for his own hat and coat, and then substituted an old necktie for his own clean white one, and encased his legs in mud-spotted leggings. This done, he produced a very large and thick pocket-book, fastened by a broad elastic band, and said,

"Well, what do you think of this? Will it do for Queen's taxes, or sanitary inspection, or the gas, or the water-supply?"

"Very well indeed, I should say," I replied. "What's the case?"

"Oh, I'll tell you all about that when it's over—no time now. Oh, here you are, Kerrett. By the bye, Kerrett, I'm going out presently by the back way. Wait for about ten minutes or a quarter of an hour after I am gone, and then just go across the road and speak to that lady in black, with the veil, who is waiting in that little foot-passage opposite. Say Mr. Martin Hewitt sends his compliments, and he advises her not to wait, as he has already left his office by another door, and has been gone some little time. That's all; it would be a pity to keep the poor woman waiting all day for nothing. Now the papers. *Daily News, Standard, Telegraph, Chronicle*—yes, here it is, in the *Chronicle*."

The whole advertisement read thus:

> YOB.—H.R.
> Shop roast. You 1st. Then tonight.
> 02. 2nd top 3rd L. No. 197 red bl. straight mon.
> One at a time.

"What's this," I asked, "a cryptogram?"

"I'll see," Hewitt answered. "But I won't tell you anything about it till afterwards, so you get your lunch. Kerrett, bring the directory."

This was all I actually saw of this case myself, and I have written the rest in its proper order from Hewitt's information, as I have written some other cases entirely.[4]

To resume at the point where, for the time, I lost sight of the matter. Hewitt left by

---

[3] Sherlock Holmes prided himself on his ability to identify the typefaces and fonts used by London newspapers; Dr. Watson knew nothing of this subject. Here, Brett, identified in other Hewitt stories as a journalist, is allowed to contribute to the case.

[4] There are twenty-five Hewitt stories, and Brett, a journalist, lives with him much as Dr. Watson shared rooms with Holmes. Interestingly, this story consists in part of traditional third-person "omniscient" narration and part narration by Brett. The Holmes stories are, with only three exceptions, entirely told by Dr. Watson.

the back way and stopped an empty cab as it passed. "Abney Park Cemetery" was his direction to the driver. In little more than twenty minutes the cab was branching off down the Essex Road on its way to Stoke Newington, and in twenty minutes more Hewitt stopped it in Church Street, Stoke Newington. He walked through a street or two, and then down another, the houses of which he scanned carefully as he passed. Opposite one which stood by itself he stopped, and, making a pretense of consulting and arranging his large pocket-book, he took a good look at the house. It was rather larger, neater, and more pretentious than the others in the street, and it had a natty little coach-house just visible up the side entrance. There were red blinds hung with heavy lace in the front windows, and behind one of these blinds Hewitt was able to catch the glint of a heavy gas chandelier.

He stepped briskly up the front steps and knocked sharply at the door. "Mr. Merston?" he asked, pocket-book in hand, when a neat parlor maid opened the door.

"Yes."

"Ah!" Hewitt stepped into the hall and pulled off his hat; "it's only the meter. There's been a deal of gas running away somewhere here, and I'm just looking to see if the meters are right. Where is it?"

The girl hesitated. "I'll—I'll ask master," she said.

"Very well. I don't want to take it away, you know—only to give it a tap or two, and so on."

The girl retired to the back of the hall, and without taking her eyes off Martin Hewitt, gave his message to some invisible person in a back room, whence came a growling reply of "All right."

Hewitt followed the girl to the base-ment, apparently looking straight before him, but in reality taking in every detail of the place. The gas meter was in a very large lumber cupboard under the kitchen stairs. The girl opened the door and lit a candle. The meter stood on the floor, which was littered with hampers and boxes and odd sheets of brown paper. But a thing that at once arrested Hewitt's attention was a garment of some sort of bright blue cloth, with large brass buttons, which was lying in a tumbled heap in a corner, and appeared to be the only thing in the place that was not covered with dust. Nevertheless, Hewitt took no apparent notice of it, but stooped down and solemnly tapped the meter three times with his pencil, and listened with great gravity, placing his ear to the top. Then he shook his head and tapped again. At length he said:—

"It's a bit doubtful. I'll just get you to light the gas in the kitchen a moment. Keep your hand to the burner, and when I call out shut it off *at once;* see?"

The girl turned and entered the kitchen, and Hewitt immediately seized the blue coat—for a coat it was. It had a dull red piping in the seams, and was of the swallowtail pattern—livery coat, in fact. He held it for a moment before him, examining its pattern and color, and then rolled it up and flung it again into the corner.

"Right!" he called to the servant. "Shut off!"

The girl emerged from the kitchen as he left the cupboard.

"Well," she asked, "are you satisfied now?"

"Quite satisfied, thank you," Hewitt replied.

"Is it all right?" she continued, jerking her hand toward the cupboard.

"Well, no, it isn't; there's something

wrong there, and I'm glad I came. You can tell Mr. Merston, if you like, that I expect his gas bill will be a good deal less next quarter." And there was a suspicion of a chuckle in Hewitt's voice as he crossed the hall to leave. For a gas inspector is pleased when he finds at length what he has been searching for.

Things had fallen out better than Hewitt had dared to expect. He saw the key of the whole mystery in that blue coat; for it was the uniform coat of the hall porters at one of the banks that he had visited in the morning, though which one he could not for the moment remember. He entered the nearest post-office and dispatched a telegram to Plummer, giving certain directions and asking the inspector to meet him; then he hailed the first available cab and hurried toward the City.

At Lombard Street he alighted, and looked in at the door of each bank till he came to Buller, Clayton, Ladds & Co.'s. This was the bank he wanted. In the other banks the hall porters wore mulberry coats, brick-dust coats, brown coats, and what not, but here, behind the ladders and scaffold poles which obscured the entrance, he could see a man in a blue coat, with dull red piping and brass buttons. He sprang up the steps, pushed open the inner swing door, and finally satisfied himself by a closer view of the coat, to the wearer's astonishment. Then he regained the pavement and walked the whole length of the bank premises in front, afterwards turning up the paved passage at the side, deep in thought. The bank had no windows or doors on the side next the court, and the two adjoining houses were old and supported in place by wooden shores. Both were empty, and a great board announced that tenders would be re-ceived in a month's time for the purchase of the old materials of which they were con-structed; also that some part of the site would be let on a long building lease.

Hewitt looked up at the grimy fronts of the old buildings. The windows were crusted thick with dirt—all except the bottom window of the house nearer the bank, which was fairly clean, and seemed to have been quite lately washed. The door, too, of this house was cleaner than that of the other, though the paint was worn. Hewitt reached and fingered a hook driven into the left-hand doorpost about six feet from the ground. It was new, and not at all rusted; also a tiny splinter had been displaced when the hook was driven in, and clean wood showed at the spot.

Having observed these things, Hewitt stepped back and read at the bottom of the big board the name, "Winsor & Weekes, Surveyors and Auctioneers, Abchurch Lane." Then he stepped into Lombard Street.

Two hansoms pulled up near the post-office, and out of the first stepped Inspector Plummer and another man. This man and the two who alighted from the second hansom were unmistakably plain-clothes constables—their air, gait, and boots proclaimed it.

"What's all this?" demanded Plummer, as Hewitt approached.

"You'll soon see, I think. But, first, have you put the watch on No. 197, Hackworth Road?"

"Yes; nobody will get away from there alone."

"Very good. I am going into Abchurch Lane for a few minutes. Leave your men out here, but just go round into the court by Buller, Clayton & Ladds's, and keep your eye on the first door on the left. I think we'll find something soon. Did you get rid of Miss Shaw?"

"No, she's behind now, and Mrs. Laker's with her. They met in the Strand, and came after us in another cab. Rare fun, eh! They think we're pretty green! It's quite handy, too. So long as they keep behind me it saves all trouble of watching *them*." And Inspector Plummer chuckled and winked.

"Very good. You don't mind keeping your eye on that door, do you? I'll be back very soon," and with that Hewitt turned off into Abchurch Lane.

At Winsor & Weekes's information was not difficult to obtain. The houses were destined to come down very shortly, but a week or so ago an office and a cellar in one of them was let temporarily to a Mr. Westley. He brought no references; indeed, as he paid a fortnight's rent in advance, he was not asked for any, considering the circumstances of the case. He was opening a London branch for a large firm of cider merchants, he said, and just wanted a rough office and a cool cellar to store samples in for a few weeks till the permanent premises were ready. There was another key, and no doubt the premises might be entered if there were any special need for such a course. Martin Hewitt gave such excellent reasons that Winsor & Weekes's managing clerk immediately produced the key and accompanied Hewitt to the spot.

"I think you'd better have your men handy," Hewitt remarked to Plummer when they reached the door, and a whistle quickly brought the men over.

The key was inserted in the lock and turned, but the door would not open; the bolt was fastened at the bottom. Hewitt stooped and looked under the door.

"It's a drop bolt," he said. "Probably the man who left last let it fall loose, and then banged the door, so that it fell into its place. I must try my best with a wire or a piece of string."

A wire was brought, and with some maneuvering Hewitt contrived to pass it round the bolt, and lift it little by little, steadying it with the blade of a pocket-knife. When at length the bolt was raised out of the hole, the knife-blade was slipped under it, and the door swung open.

They entered. The door of the little office just inside stood open, but in the office there was nothing, except a board a couple of feet long in a corner. Hewitt stepped across and lifted this, turning it downward face toward Plummer. On it, in fresh white paint on a black ground, were painted the words:

BULLER, CLAYTON, LADDS & CO.,
TEMPORARY ENTRANCE.

Hewitt turned to Winsor & Weekes's clerk and asked, "The man who took this room called himself Westley, didn't he?"

"Yes."

"Youngish man, clean-shaven, and well-dressed?"

"Yes, he was."

"I fancy," Hewitt said, turning to Plummer, "*I fancy* an old friend of yours is in this—Mr. Sam Gunter."

"What, the 'Hoxton Yob'?"[5]

"I think it's possible he's been Mr. Westley for a bit, and somebody else for another bit. But let's come to the cellar."

Winsor & Weekes's clerk led the way down a steep flight of steps into a dark under-

---

[5] Eighteenth-century slang: "Boy" spelled backwards, signifying a lad who is the opposite of everything a *good* boy should be.

ground corridor, wherein they lighted their way with many successive matches. Soon the cellar corridor made a turn to the right, and as the party passed the turn, there came from the end of the passage before them a fearful yell.

"Help! Help! Open the door! I'm going mad—mad! O my God!"

And there was a sound of desperate beating from the inside of the cellar door at the extreme end. The men stopped, startled.

"Come," said Hewitt, "more matches!" and he rushed to the door. It was fastened with a bar and padlock.

"Let me out, for God's sake!" came the voice, sick and hoarse, from the inside. "Let me out!"

"All right!" Hewitt shouted. "We have come for you. Wait a moment."

The voice sank into a sort of sobbing croon, and Hewitt tried several keys from his own bunch on the padlock. None fitted. He drew from his pocket the wire he had used for the bolt of the front door, straightened it out, and made a sharp bend at the end.

"Hold a match close," he ordered shortly, and one of the men obeyed. Three or four attempts were necessary, and several different bendings of the wire were affected, but in the end Hewitt picked the lock, and flung open the door.

From within a ghastly figure fell forward among them fainting, and knocked out the matches.

"Hullo!" cried Plummer. "Hold up! Who are you?"

"Let's get him up into the open," said Hewitt. "He can't tell you who he is for a bit, but I believe he's Laker."

"Laker! What, here?"

"I think so. Steady up the steps. Don't bump him. He's pretty sore already, I expect."

Truly the man was a pitiable sight. His hair and face were caked in dust and blood, and his finger-nails were torn and bleeding. Water was sent for at once, and brandy.

"Well," said Plummer hazily, looking first at the unconscious prisoner and then at Hewitt, "but what about the swag?"

"You'll have to find that yourself," Hewitt replied. "I think my share of the case is about finished. I only act for the Guarantee Society, you know, and if Laker's proved innocent—"

"Innocent! How?"

"Well, this is what took place, as near as I can figure it. You'd better undo his collar, I think"—this to the men. "What I believe has happened is this. There has been a very clever and carefully prepared conspiracy here, and Laker has not been the criminal, but the victim."

"Been robbed himself, you mean? But how? Where?"

"Yesterday morning, before he had been to more than three banks—here, in fact."

"But then how? You're all wrong. We *know* he made the whole round, and did all the collection. And then Palmer's office, and all, and the umbrella; why—"

The man lay still unconscious. "Don't raise his head," Hewitt said. "And one of you had best fetch a doctor. He's had a terrible shock." Then turning to Plummer he went on, "As to *how* they managed the job, I'll tell you what I think. First it struck some very clever person that a deal of money might be got by robbing a walk-clerk from a bank. This clever person was one of a clever gang of thieves— perhaps the Hoxton Row gang, as I think I hinted. Now you know quite as well as I do that such a gang will spend any amount of time over a job that promises a big haul, and that for such a job they can always command the necessary capital. There are many most respectable persons living in good style in the suburbs whose chief business lies in financing such ventures, and taking the chief share of the proceeds. Well, this is their plan, carefully and intelligently carried out. They watch Laker, observe the round he takes, and his habits. They find that there is only one of the clerks with whom he does business that he is much acquainted with, and that this clerk is in a bank which is commonly second in Laker's round. The sharpest man among them—and I don't think there's a man in London could do this as well as young Sam Gunter—studies Laker's dress and habits just as an actor studies a character. They take this office and cellar, as we have seen, *because it is next door to a bank whose front entrance is being altered*— a fact which Laker must know from his daily visits. The smart man—Gunter, let us say, and I have other reasons for believing it to be he—makes up precisely like Laker, false moustache, dress, and everything, and waits here with the rest of the gang. One of the gang is dressed in a blue coat with brass buttons, like a hall-porter in Buller's bank. Do you see?"

"Yes, I think so. It's pretty clear now."

"A confederate watches at the top of the court, and the moment Laker turns in from Cornhill—having already been, mind, at the only bank where he was so well known that the disguised thief would not have passed muster—as soon as he turns in from Cornhill, I say, a signal is given, and that board"— pointing to that with the white letters—"is hung on the hook in the doorpost. The sham porter stands beside it, and as Laker approaches says, 'This way in, sir, this morning. The front way's shut for the alterations.' Laker

suspecting nothing, and supposing that the firm have made a temporary entrance through the empty house, enters. He is seized when well along the corridor, the board is taken down and the door shut. Probably he is stunned by a blow on the head—see the blood now. They take his wallet and all the cash he has already collected. Gunter takes the wallet and also the umbrella, since it has Laker's initials, and is therefore distinctive. He simply completes the walk in the character of Laker, beginning with Buller, Clayton & Ladds's just round the corner. It is nothing but routine work, which is quickly done, and nobody notices him particularly—it is the bills they examine. Meanwhile this unfortunate fellow is locked up in the cellar here, right at the end of the underground corridor, where he can never make himself heard in the street, and where next him are only the empty cellars of the deserted house next door. The thieves shut the front door and vanish. The rest is plain. Gunter, having completed the round, and bagged some £15,000 or more, spends a few pounds in a tourist ticket at Palmer's as a blind, being careful to give Laker's name. He leaves the umbrella at Charing Cross in a conspicuous place right opposite the lost property office, where it is sure to be seen, and so completes his false trail."

"Then who are the people at 197, Hackworth Road?"

"The capitalist lives there—the financier, and probably the directing spirit of the whole thing. Merston's the name he goes by there, and I've no doubt he cuts a very imposing figure in chapel every Sunday. He'll be worth picking up—this isn't the first thing he's been in, I'll warrant."

"But—but what about Laker's mother and Miss Shaw?"

"Well, what? The poor women are nearly out of their minds with terror and shame, that's all, but though they may think Laker a criminal, they'll never desert him. They've been following us about with a feeble, vague sort of hope of being able to baffle us in some way or help him if we caught him, or something, poor things. Did you ever hear of a real woman who'd desert a son or a lover merely because he was a criminal? But here's the doctor. When he's attended to him will you let your men take Laker home? I must hurry and report to the Guarantee Society, I think."

"But," said the perplexed Plummer, "where did you get your clue? You must have had a tip from some one, you know—you can't have done it by clairvoyance. What gave you the tip?"

"The *Daily Chronicle*."

"The *what*?"

"The *Daily Chronicle*. Just take a look at the 'agony column' in yesterday morning's issue, and read the message to 'Yob'—to Gunter, in fact. That's all."

By this time a cab was waiting in Lombard Street, and two of Plummer's men, under the doctor's directions, carried Laker to it. No sooner, however, were they in the court than the two watching women threw themselves hysterically upon Laker, and it was long before they could be persuaded that he was not being taken to gaol. The mother shrieked aloud, "My boy—my boy! Don't take him! Oh, don't take him! They've killed my boy! Look at his head—oh, his head!" and wrestled desperately with the men, while Hewitt attempted to soothe her, and promised to allow her to go in the cab with her son if she would only be quiet. The younger woman made no noise, but she held one of Laker's limp hands in both hers.

Hewitt and I dined together that eve-ning, and he gave me a full account of the occurrences which I have here set down. Still, when he was finished I was not able to see clearly by what process of reasoning he had arrived at the conclusions that gave him the key to the mystery, nor did I understand the "agony column" message, and I said so.

"In the beginning," Hewitt explained, "the thing that struck me as curious was the fact that Laker was said to have given his own name at Palmer's in buying his ticket. Now, the first thing the greenest and newest criminal thinks of is changing his name, so that the giving of his own name seemed unlikely to begin with. Still, he *might* have made such a mistake, as Plummer suggested when he said that criminals usually make a mistake somewhere—as they do, in fact. Still, it was the least likely mistake I could think of—especially as he actually didn't wait to be asked for his name, but blurted it out when it wasn't really wanted. And it was conjoined with another rather curious mistake, or what would have been a mistake, if the thief were Laker. Why should he conspicuously display his wallet—such a distinctive article—for the clerk to see and note? Why rather had he not got rid of it before showing himself? Suppose it should be somebody personating Laker? In any case I determined not to be prejudiced by what I had heard of Laker's betting. A man may bet without being a thief.

"But, again, supposing it *were* Laker? Might he not have given his name, and displayed his wallet, and so on, while buying a ticket for France, in order to draw pursuit after himself in that direction while he made off in another, in another name, and disguised? Each supposition was plausible. And, in either case, it might happen that whoever was laying this trail would probably lay it a little farther. Charing Cross was the next point, and there I went. I already had it from Plummer that Laker had not been recognized there. Perhaps the trail had been laid in some other manner. Something left behind with Laker's name on it, perhaps? I at once thought of the umbrella with his monogram, and, making a long shot, asked for it at the lost property office, as you know. The guess was lucky: In the umbrella, as you know, I found the scrap of paper. That, I judged, had fallen in from the hand of the man carrying the umbrella. He had torn the paper in half in order to fling it away, and one piece had fallen into the loosely flapping umbrella. It is a thing that will often happen with an omnibus ticket, as you may have noticed. Also, it was proved that the umbrella *was* unrolled when found, and rolled immediately after. So here was a piece of paper dropped by the person who had brought the umbrella to Charing Cross and left it. I got the whole advertisement, as you remember, and I studied it. 'Yob' is back-slang for 'boy,' and is often used in nicknames to denote a young smooth-faced thief. Gunter, the man I suspect, as a matter of fact, is known as the 'Hoxton Yob.' The message, then, was addressed to some one known by such a nickname. Next, 'H.R. shop roast.' Now, in thieves' slang, to 'roast' a thing or a person is to watch it or him. They call any place a shop—notably, a thieves' den. So that this meant that some resort—perhaps the 'Hoxton Row shop'—was watched. 'You 1st then tonight' would be clearer, perhaps, when the rest was understood. I thought a little over the rest, and it struck me that it must be a direction to some other house, since one was warned of as being watched. Besides, there was the number, 197, and 'red bl.,' which would be extremely likely to mean 'red blinds,'

by way of clearly distinguishing the house. And then the plan of the thing was plain. You have noticed, probably, that the map of London which accompanies the Post Office Directory is divided, for convenience of reference, into numbered squares?"

"Yes. The squares are denoted by letters along the top margin and figures down the side. So that if you consult the directory, and find a place marked as being in D-5, for instance, you find vertical divisions D, and run your finger down it till it intersects horizontal division 5, and there you are."

"Precisely. I got my Post Office Directory, and looked for 'O-2.' It was in North London, and took in parts of Abney Park Cemetery and Clissold Park; '2nd top' was the next sign. Very well, I counted the second street intersecting the top of the square—counting, in the usual way, from the left. That was Lordship Road. Then '3rd L.' From the point where Lordship Road crossed the top of the square, I ran my finger down the road till it came to '3rd L,' or, in other words, the third turning on the left—Hackworth Road. So there we were, unless my guesses were altogether wrong. 'Straight mon' probably meant 'straight moniker'—that is to say, the proper name, a thief's *real* name, in contradistinction to that he may assume. I turned over the directory till I found Hackworth Road, and found that No. 197 was inhabited by a Mr. Merston. From the whole thing I judged this. There was to have been a meeting at the 'H.R. shop,' but that was found, at the last moment, to be watched by the police for some purpose, so that another appointment was made for this house in the suburbs. 'You 1st. Then tonight'—the person addressed was to come first, and the others in the evening. They were to ask for the householder's 'straight moniker'—Mr. Merston. And they were to come one at a time.

"Now, then, what was this? What theory would fit it? Suppose this were a robbery, directed from afar by the advertiser. Suppose, on the day before the robbery, it was found that the place fixed for division of spoils were watched. Suppose that the principal thereupon advertised (as had already been agreed in case of emergency) in these terms. The principal in the actual robbery—the 'Yob' addressed—was to go first with the booty. The others were to come after, one at a time. Anyway, the thing was good enough to follow a little further, and I determined to try No. 197 Hackworth Road. I have told you what I found there, and how it opened my eyes. I went, of course, merely on chance, to see what I might chance to see. But luck favored, and I happened on that coat—brought back rolled up, on the evening after the robbery, doubtless by the thief who had used it, and flung carelessly into the handiest cupboard. *That* was this gang's mistake."

"Well, I congratulate you," I said. "I hope they'll catch the rascals."

"I rather think they will, now they know where to look. They can scarcely miss Merston, anyway. There has been very little to go upon in this case, but I stuck to the thread, however slight, and it brought me through. The rest of the case, of course, is Plummer's. It was a peculiarity of my commission that I could equally well fulfill it by catching the man with all the plunder, or by proving him innocent. Having done the latter, my work was at an end, but I left it where Plummer will be able to finish the job handsomely."

Plummer did. Sam Gunter, Merston, and one accomplice were taken—the first and last were well known to the police—and were identified by Laker. Merston, as Hewitt had suspected, had kept the lion's share for himself, so that altogether, with what was recovered from him and the other two, nearly £11,000 was saved for Messrs Liddle, Neal & Liddle. Merston, when taken, was in the act of packing up to take a holiday abroad, and there cash his notes, which were found, neatly packed in separate thousands, in his portmanteau. As Hewitt had predicted, his gas bill *was* considerably less next quarter, for less than half-way through it he began a term in gaol.

As for Laker, he was reinstated, of course, with an increase of salary by way of compensation for his broken head. He had passed a terrible twenty-six hours in the cellar, unfed and unheard. Several times he had become insensible, and again and again he had thrown himself madly against the door, shouting and tearing at it, till he fell back exhausted, with broken nails and bleeding fingers. For some hours before the arrival of his rescuers he had been sitting in a sort of stupor, from which he was suddenly aroused by the sound of voices and footsteps. He was in bed for a week, and required a rest of a month in addition before he could resume his duties. Then he was quietly lectured by Mr. Neal as to betting, and, I believe, dropped that practice in consequence. I am told that he is "at the counter" now—a considerable promotion.

M. P. Shiel

MATTHEW PHIPPS SHIEL (1865-1947) was a West Indian–born British writer who produced twenty-five novels and dozens of short stories under the name M. P. Shiel, mostly in the romantic or supernatural adventure vein. His best-remembered novel is *The Purple Cloud* (1901), a "last-man-on-Earth" tale that inspired Stephen King's *The Stand* (1978) as well as several films. The physical appearance of Shiel's detective Prince Zaleski is never described, and he only features in four stories. Chris Steinbrunner and Otto Penzler, in their essential *Encyclopedia of Mystery & Detection* (1976), call Zaleski "probably the most bizarre, erudite, and ethereal detective in literature." Shiel himself, referring to "the notorious Holmes [as] a bastard son" of Dupin, termed Zaleski "a legitimate son."

Three tales of the detective appeared in the collection titled *Prince Zaleski* in 1895. In the following story, the prince shows his power "not merely of disentangling in retrospect but of unraveling in prospect."

THE STONE OF THE
EDMUNDSBURY MONKS

M. P. SHIEL

RUSSIA," SAID PRINCE Zaleski to me one day, when I happened to be on a visit to him in his darksome sanctuary—"Russia may be regarded as land surrounded by ocean; that is to say, she is an island. In the same way, it is sheer gross irrelevancy to speak of *Britain* as an island, unless indeed the word be understood as a mere *modus loquendi*[1] arising out of a rather poor geographical pleasantry. Britain, in reality, is a small continent. Near her—a little to the south-east—is situated the large island of Europe. Thus, the enlightened French traveler passing to these shores should commune within himself: 'I now cross to the Mainland'; and retracing his steps: 'I now return to the fragment rent by wrack and earthshock from the Mother-country.' And this I say not in the way of paradox, but as the expression of a sober truth. I have in my mind merely the relative depth and extent—the *non-insularity*, in fact—of the impressions made by the several nations on the world. But this island of Europe has herself an island of her own: the name of it, Russia. She, of all lands, is the *terra incognita*, the unknown land; till quite lately she was more—she was the undiscovered, the unsuspected land. She *has* a literature, you know, and a history, and a language, and a purpose—but of all this the world has hardly so much as heard. Indeed, she, and not any Antarctic Sea whatever, is the real Ultima Thule[2] of modern times, the true Island of Mystery."

I reproduce these remarks of Zaleski here, not so much on account of the splendid tribute to my country contained in them, as because it ever seemed to me—and especially in connection with the incident I am about to recall—that in this respect at least he was a genuine son of Russia; if she is the Land, so truly was he the Man, of Mystery. I who knew him best alone knew that it was impossible to know him. He was a being little of the

[1] Way of speaking.
[2] The legendary unknown land to the far north, in the Arctic Circle.

present: with one arm he embraced the whole past; the fingers of the other heaved on the vibrant pulse of the future. He seemed to me—I say it deliberately and with fore-thought—to possess the unparalleled power not merely of disentangling in retrospect, but of unraveling in prospect, and I have known him to relate *coming* events with unimaginable minuteness of precision. He was nothing if not superlative: his diatribes, now culminating in a very *extravaganza* of hyperbole—now sailing with loose wing through the downy, witched, Dutch cloud-heaps of some quaintest tramontane[3] Nephelococcugia[4] of thought—now laying down law of the Medes[5] for the actual world of today—had oft-times the strange effect of bringing back to my mind the very singular old-epic epithet, [Greek: ænemoen]—*airy*—as applied to human thought. The mere grip of his memory was not simply extraordinary; it had in it a token, a hint, of the strange, the pythic—nay, the sibylline.[6] And as his reflecting intellect, moreover, had all the lightness of foot of a chamois kid[7], unless you could contrive to follow each dazzlingly swift successive step, by the sum of which he attained his Alp-heights, he inevitably left on you the astounding, the confounding impression of mental omnipresence.

I had brought with me a certain document, a massive book bound in iron and leather, the diary of one Sir Jocelin Saul. This I had abstracted from a gentleman of my acquaintance, the head of a firm of inquiry

agents in London, into whose hand, only the day before, it had come. A distant neighbor of Sir Jocelin, hearing by chance of his extremity, had invoked the assistance of this firm; but the aged baronet, being in a state of the utmost feebleness, terror, and indeed hysterical incoherence, had been able to utter no word in explanation of his condition or wishes, and, in silent abandonment, had merely handed the book to the agent.

A day or two after I had reached the desolate old mansion which the prince occupied, knowing that he might sometimes be induced to take an absorbing interest in questions that had proved themselves too profound, or too intricate, for ordinary solution, I asked him if he was willing to hear the details read out from the diary, and on his assenting, I proceeded to do so.

The brief narrative had reference to a very large and very valuable oval gem enclosed in the substance of a golden chalice, which chalice, in the monastery of St. Edmundsbury, had once lain centuries long within the loculus, or inmost coffin, wherein reposed the body of St. Edmund. By pressing a hidden pivot, the cup (which was composed of two equal parts, connected by minute hinges) sprang open, and in a hollow space at the bottom was disclosed the gem. Sir Jocelin Saul, I may say, was lineally connected with—though, of course, not descendant from—that same Jocelin of Brakelonda, a brother of the Edmundsbury convent, who wrote the now so celebrated *Jocelini Chronica*[8]: and the chalice

---

[3] Over the mountains.

[4] "Cloud cuckoo-land," an idealized fantasy-world.

[5] A Biblical phrase, meaning "unalterable law."

[6] That is, prophetic.

[7] A young goat.

[8] Actual record of the St. Edmunsbury monks, noted in Thomas Carlyle's *Past and Present: Chartism* (1858).

had fallen into the possession of the family, seemingly at some time prior to the suppression of the monastery about 1537. On it was inscribed in old English characters of unknown date the words:

SHULDE THIS STON STALEN BEE,
OR SHULD IT CHAUNGES DRE,
THE HOUSS OF SAWL AND HYS HED
ANOON SHAL DE.

The stone itself was an intaglio, and had engraved on its surface the figure of *a mythological animal*, together with some nearly obliterated letters, of which the only ones remaining legible were those forming the word "Has." As a sure precaution against the loss of the gem, another cup had been made and engraved in an exactly similar manner, inside of which, to complete the delusion, another stone of the same size and cut, but of comparatively valueless material, had been placed.

Sir Jocelin Saul, a man of intense nervosity, lived his life alone in a remote old manorhouse in Suffolk, his only companion being a person of Eastern origin, named Ul-Jabal. The baronet had consumed his vitality in the life-long attempt to sound the too fervid Maelstrom of Oriental research, and his mind had perhaps caught from his studies a tinge of their morbidness, their esotericism, their insanity. He had for some years past been engaged in the task of writing a stupendous work on Pre-Zoroastrian Theogonies,[9] in which, it is to be supposed, Ul-Jabal acted somewhat in the capacity of secretary. But I will give *verbatim* the extracts from his diary:

June 11.—This is my birthday. Seventy years ago exactly I slid from the belly of the great Dark into this Light and Life.

My God! My God! It is briefer than the rage of an hour, fleeter than a mid-day trance. Ul-Jabal greeted me warmly—seemed to have been looking forward to it—and pointed out that seventy is of the fateful numbers, its only factors being seven, five, and two: the last denoting the duality of Birth and Death; five, Isolation; seven, Infinity. I informed him that this was also my father's birthday; and *his* father's; and repeated the oft-told tale of how the latter, just seventy years ago today, walking at twilight by the churchyard-wall, saw the figure of *himself* sitting on a grave-stone, and died five weeks later riving with the pangs of hell. Whereat the skeptic showed his two huge rows of teeth.

What is his peculiar interest in the Edmundsbury chalice? On each successive birthday when the cup has been produced, he has asked me to show him the stone. Without any well-defined reason I have always declined, but today I yielded. He gazed long into its sky-blue depth, and then asked if I had no idea what the inscription "Has" meant. I informed him that it was one of the lost secrets of the world.

June 15.—Some new element has entered into our existence here. Something threatens me. I hear the echo of a menace against my sanity and my life. It is as if the garment which enwraps me has grown too hot, too heavy for me. A notable drowsiness has settled on my brain—a drowsiness in which thought, though slow, is a thousandfold more fiery-vivid than ever. Oh, fair goddess of Reason, desert not me, thy chosen child!

June 18.—Ul-Jabal?—that man is *the very Devil incarnate!*

June 19.—So much for my bounty, all my munificence, to this poisonous worm. I picked him up on the heights of the Mountain of Lebanon, a cultured savage

[9] Zoroaster (or Zarathustra) was an Iranian/Persian prophet, who may have lived as long ago as 6,000 B.C.E.

among cultured savages, and brought him here to be a prince of thought by my side. What though his plundered wealth—the debt I owe him—has saved me from a sort of ruin? Have not I instructed him in the sweet secret of Reason?

I lay back on my bed in the lonely morning watches, my soul heavy as with the distilled essence of opiates, and in vivid vision knew that he had entered my apartment. In the twilight gloom his glittering rows of shark's teeth seemed impacted on my eyeball—I saw *them*, and nothing else. I was not aware when he vanished from the room. But at daybreak I crawled on hands and knees to the cabinet containing the chalice. The viperous murderer! He has stolen my gem, well knowing that with it he has stolen my life. The stone is gone—gone, my precious gem. A weakness overtook me, and I lay for many dreamless hours naked on the marble floor.

Does the fool think to hide ought from my eyes? Can he imagine that I shall not recover my precious gem, my stone of Saul?

June 20.—Ah, Ul-Jabal—my brave, my noble Son of the Prophet of God! He has replaced the stone! He would not slay an aged man. The yellow ray of his eye, it is but the gleam of the great thinker, not—not—the gleam of the assassin. Again, as I lay in semi-somnolence, I saw him enter my room, this time more distinctly. He went up to the cabinet. Shaking the chalice in the dawning, some hours after he had left, I heard with delight the rattle of the stone. I might have known he would replace it; I should not have doubted his clemency to a poor man like me. But the strange being!—he has taken the *other* stone from the *other* cup—a thing of little value to any man! Is Ul-Jabal mad or I?

June 21.—Merciful Lord in Heaven! He has *not* replaced it—not *it*—but another instead of it. Today I actually

opened the chalice, and saw. He has put a stone there, the same in size, in cut, in engraving, but different in color, in quality, in value—a stone I have never seen before. How has he obtained it—whence? I must brace myself to probe, to watch; I must turn myself into an eye to search this devil's-bosom. My life, this subtle, cunning Reason of mine, hangs in the balance.

June 22.—Just now he offered me a cup of wine. I almost dashed it to the ground before him. But he looked steadfastly into my eye. I flinched: and drank—drank.

Years ago, when, as I remember, we were at Balbec, I saw him one day make an almost tasteless preparation out of pure black nicotine, which in mere wanton lust he afterwards gave to some of the dwellers by the Caspian to drink. But the fiend would surely never dream of giving to me that browse of hell—to me an aged man, and a thinker, a seer.

June 23.—The mysterious, the unfathomable Ul-Jabal! Once again, as I lay in heavy trance at midnight, has he invaded, calm and noiseless as a spirit, the sanctity of my chamber. Serene on the swaying air, which, radiant with soft beams of vermil and violet light, rocked me into variant visions of heaven, I reclined and regarded him unmoved. The man has replaced the valueless stone in the modern-made chalice, and has now stolen the false stone from the other, which *he himself* put there! In patience will I possess this my soul, and watch what shall betide. My eyes shall know no slumber!

June 24.—No more—no more shall I drink wine from the hand of Ul-Jabal. My knees totter beneath the weight of my lean body. Daggers of lambent fever race through my brain incessant. Some fibrillary twitchings at the right angle of the mouth have also arrested my attention.

June 25.—He has dared at open midday to enter my room. I watched him from an angle of the stairs pass along the corridor and open my door. But for the terrifying, death-boding thump, thump of my heart, I should have faced the traitor then, and told him that I knew all his treachery. Did I say that I had strange fibrillary twitchings at the right angle of my mouth, and a brain on fire? I have ceased to write my book—the more the pity for the world, not for me.

June 26.—Marvelous to tell, the traitor, Ul-Jabal, has now placed *another* stone in the Edmundsbury chalice—also identical in nearly every respect with the original gem. This, then, was the object of his entry into my room yesterday. So that he has first stolen the real stone and replaced it by another; then he has stolen this other and replaced it by yet another; he has beside stolen the valueless stone from the modern chalice, and then replaced it. Surely a man gone rabid, a man gone dancing, foaming, raving mad!

June 28.—I have now set myself to the task of recovering my jewel. It is here, and I shall find it. Life against life—and which is the best life, mine or this accursed Ishmaelite's?[10] If need be, I will do murder—I, with this withered hand—so that I get back the heritage which is mine.

Today, when I thought he was wandering in the park, I stole into his room, locking the door on the inside. I trembled exceedingly, knowing that his eyes are in every place. I ransacked the chamber, dived among his clothes, but found no stone. One singular thing in a drawer I saw: a long, white beard, and a wig of long and snow-white hair. As I passed out of the chamber, lo, he stood face to face with me at the door in the passage. My heart gave one bound, and then seemed wholly to cease its travail. Oh, I must be sick unto death, weaker than a bruised reed! When I woke from my swoon he was supporting me in his arms. "Now," he said, grinning down at me, "now you have at last delivered all into my hands." He left me, and I saw him go into his room and lock the door upon himself. What is it I have delivered into the madman's hands?

July 1.—Life against life—and his, the young, the stalwart, rather than mine, the mouldering, the sere. I love life. Not yet am I ready to weigh anchor, and reeve halliard,[11] and turn my prow over the watery paths of the wine-brown Deeps. Oh no. Not yet. Let *him* die. Many and many are the days in which I shall yet see the light, walk, think. I am averse to end the number of my years: there is even a feeling in me at times that this worn body shall never, never taste of death. The chalice predicts indeed that I and my house shall end when the stone is lost—a mere fiction *at first*, an idler's dream *then*, but now—now—that the prophecy has stood so long a part of the reality of things, and a fact among facts—no longer fiction, but Adamant, stern as the very word of God. Do I not feel hourly since it has gone how the surges of life ebb, ebb ever lower in my heart? Nay, nay, but there is hope. I have here beside me an Arab blade of subtle Damascene steel, insinuous[12] to pierce and to hew, with which in a street of Bethlehem I saw a Syrian's head cleft open—a gallant stroke! The edges of this I have made bright and white for a nuptial of blood.

July 2.—I spent the whole of the last night in searching every nook and crack

---

[10] Ishmael was the elder son of Abraham, and his descendants became outcasts; hence, figuratively, a despicable person.

[11] Raise a sail by tying down the halyard or rope.

[12] In a serpentine manner.

of the house, using a powerful magnifying lens. At times I thought Ul-Jabal was watching me, and would pounce out and murder me. Convulsive tremors shook my frame like earthquake. Ah me, I fear I am all too frail for this work. Yet dear is the love of life.

July 7.—The last days I have passed in carefully searching the grounds, with the lens as before. Ul-Jabal constantly found pretexts for following me, and I am confident that every step I took was known to him. No sign anywhere of the grass having been disturbed. Yet my lands are wide, and I cannot be sure. The burden of this mighty task is greater than I can bear. I am weaker than a bruised reed. Shall I not slay my enemy, and make an end?

July 8.—Ul-Jabal has been in my chamber again! I watched him through a crack in the paneling. His form was hidden by the bed, but I could see his hand reflected in the great mirror opposite the door. First, I cannot guess why, he moved to a point in front of the mirror the chair in which I sometimes sit. He then went to the box in which lie my few garments—and opened it. Ah, I have the stone—safe—safe! He fears my cunning, ancient eyes, and has hidden it in the one place where I would be least likely to seek it—*in my own trunk!* And yet I dread, most intensely I dread, to look.

July 9.—The stone, alas, is not there! At the last moment he must have changed his purpose. Could his wondrous sensitiveness of intuition have made him feel that my eyes were looking in on him?

July 10.—In the dead of night I knew that a stealthy foot had gone past my door. I rose and threw a mantle round me; I put on my head my cap of fur; I took the tempered blade in my hands; then crept out into the dark, and followed. Ul-Jabal carried a small lantern which revealed him to me. My feet were bare, but he wore felted slippers, which to

my unfailing ear were not utterly noiseless. He descended the stairs to the bottom of the house, while I crouched behind him in the deepest gloom of the corners and walls. At the bottom he walked into the pantry: there stopped, and turned the lantern full in the direction of the spot where I stood; but so agilely did I slide behind a pillar, that he could not have seen me. In the pantry he lifted the trap-door, and descended still further into the vaults beneath the house. Ah, the vaults,—the long, the tortuous, the darksome vaults,—how had I forgotten them? Still I followed, rent by seismic shocks of terror. I had not forgotten the weapon: could I creep near enough, I felt that I might plunge it into the marrow of his back. He opened the iron door of the first vault and passed in. If I could lock him in?—but he held the key. On and on he wound his way, holding the lantern near the ground, his head bent down. The thought came to me *then*, that, had I but the courage, one swift sweep, and all were over. I crept closer, closer. Suddenly he turned round, and made a quick step in my direction. I saw his eyes, the murderous grin of his jaw. I know not if he saw me—thought forsook me. The weapon fell with clatter and clangor from my grasp, and in panic fright I fled with extended arms and the headlong swiftness of a stripling, through the black labyrinths of the caverns, through the vacant corridors of the house, till I reached my chamber, the door of which I had time to fasten on myself before I dropped, gasping, panting for very life, on the floor.

July 11.—I had not the courage to see Ul-Jabal today. I have remained locked in my chamber all the time without food or water. My tongue cleaves to the roof of my mouth.

July 12.—I took heart and crept downstairs. I met him in the study. He smiled on me, and I on him, as if nothing had happened between us. Oh, our old friendship, how it has turned into bitterest hate! I had taken the false stone from the Edmundsbury chalice and put it in the pocket of my brown gown, with the bold intention of showing it to him, and asking him if he knew aught of it. But when I faced him, my courage failed again. We drank together and ate together as in the old days of love.

July 13.—I cannot think that I have not again imbibed some soporiferous drug. A great heaviness of sleep weighed on my brain till late in the day. When I woke my thoughts were in wild distraction, and a most peculiar condition of my skin held me fixed before the mirror. It is dry as parchment, and brown as the leaves of autumn.

July 14.—Ul-Jabal is gone! And I am left a lonely, a desolate old man! He said, though I swore it was false, that I had grown to mistrust him! That I was hiding something from him! That he could live with me no more! No more, he said, should I see his face! The debt I owe him he would forgive. He has taken one small parcel with him—and is gone!

July 15.—Gone! Gone! In mazeful dream I wander with uncovered head far and wide over my domain, seeking I know not what. The stone he has with him—the precious stone of Saul. I feel the life-surge ebbing, ebbing in my heart.

Here the manuscript abruptly ended.

Prince Zaleski had listened as I read aloud, lying back on his Moorish couch and breathing slowly from his lips a heavy reddish vapor, which he imbibed from a very small, carved, bismuth pipette. His face, as far as I could see in the green-grey crepuscular atmosphere of the apartment, was expressionless. But when I had finished he turned fully round on me, and said:—

"You perceive, I hope, the sinister meaning of all this?"

"*Has* it a meaning?"

Zaleski smiled.

"Can you doubt it? In the shape of a cloud, the pitch of a thrush's note, the *nuance* of a sea-shell you would find, had you only insight *enough*, inductive and deductive cunning *enough*, not only a meaning, but, I am convinced, a quite endless significance. Undoubtedly, in a human document of this kind, there is a meaning; and I may say at once that this meaning is entirely transparent to me. Pity only that you did not read the diary to me before."

"Why?"

"Because we might, between us, have prevented a crime, and saved a life. The last entry in the diary was made on the 15th of July. What day is this?"

"This is the 20th."

"Then I would wager a thousand to one that we are too late. There is still, however, the one chance left. The time is now seven o'clock: seven of the evening, I think, not of the morning; the houses of business in London are therefore closed. But why not send my man, Ham, with a letter by train to the private address of the person from whom you obtained the diary, telling him to hasten immediately to Sir Jocelin Saul, and on no consideration to leave his side for a moment? Ham would reach this person before midnight, and understanding that the matter was one of life and death, he would assuredly do your bidding."

As I was writing the note suggested by Zaleski, I turned and asked him:—

"From whom shall I say that the danger is to be expected—from the Indian?"

"From Ul-Jabal, yes; but by no means Indian—Persian."

Profoundly impressed by this knowledge of detail derived from sources which had brought me no intelligence, I handed the note to the negro, telling him how to proceed, and instructing him before starting from the station to search all the procurable papers of the last few days, and to return in case he found in any of them a notice of the death of Sir Jocelin Saul. Then I resumed my seat by the side of Zaleski.

"As I have told you," he said, "I am fully convinced that our messenger has gone on a bootless errand. I believe you will find that what has really occurred is this: either yesterday, or the day before, Sir Jocelin was found by his servant—I imagine he had a servant, though no mention is made of any—lying on the marble floor of his chamber, dead. Near him, probably by his side, will be found a gem—an oval stone, white in color—the same in fact which Ul-Jabal last placed in the Edmundsbury chalice. There will be no marks of violence—no trace of poison—the death will be found to be a perfectly natural one. Yet, in this case, a particularly wicked murder has been committed. There are, I assure you, to my positive knowledge forty-three—and in one island in the South Seas, forty-four—different methods of doing murder, any one of which would be entirely beyond the scope of the introspective agencies at the ordinary disposal of society.

"But let us bend our minds to the details of this matter. Let us ask first, *who* is this Ul-Jabal? I have said that he is a Persian, and of this there is abundant evidence in the narrative other than his mere name. Fragmentary as the document is, and not intended by the writer to afford the information, there is yet evidence of the religion of this man, of the particular sect of that religion to which he be-

longed, of his peculiar shade of color, of the object of his stay at the manor-house of Saul, of the special tribe amongst whom he formerly lived. 'What,' he asks, when his greedy eyes first light on the long-desired gem, 'what is the meaning of the inscription "Has"'—the meaning which *he* so well knew. 'One of the lost secrets of the world,' replies the baronet. But I can hardly understand a learned Orientalist speaking in that way about what appears to me a very patent circumstance: it is clear that he never earnestly applied himself to the solution of the riddle, or else—what is more likely, in spite of his rather high-flown estimate of his own 'Reason'—that his mind, and the mind of his ancestors, never was able to go farther back in time than the Edmundsbury Monks. But *they* did not make the stone, nor did they dig it from the depths of the earth in Suffolk—they got it from some one, and it is not difficult to say with certainty from whom. The stone, then, might have been engraved by that someone, or by the someone from whom *he* received it, and so on back into the dimnesses of time. And consider the character of the engraving—it consists of a mythological animal, and some words, of which the letters 'Has' only are distinguishable. But the animal, at least, is pure Persian. The Persians, you know, were not only quite worthy competitors with the Hebrews, the Egyptians, and later on the Greeks, for excellence in the glyptic art, but this fact is remarkable, that in much the same way that the figure of the *scarabaeus* on an intaglio or cameo is a pretty infallible indication of an Egyptian hand, so is that of a priest or a grotesque animal a sure indication of a Persian. We may say, then, from that evidence alone—though there is more—that this gem was certainly Persian. And having reached that point, the mystery of 'Has' vanishes: for we at once jump at the conclusion that that too is Persian. But Persian, you say, written in English characters? Yes, and it was precisely this fact that made its meaning one of what the baronet childishly calls 'the lost secrets of the world': for every successive inquirer, believing it part of an English phrase, was thus hopelessly led astray in his investigation. 'Has' is, in fact, part of the word 'Hasn-us-Sabah,' and the mere circumstance that some of it has been obliterated, while the figure of the mystic animal remains intact, shows that it was executed by one of a nation less skilled in the art of graving in precious stones than the Persians—by a rude, mediaeval Englishman, in short—the modern revival of the art owing its origin, of course, to the Medici of a later age. And of this Englishman—who either graved the stone himself, or got someone else to do it for him—do we know nothing? We know, at least, that he was certainly a fighter, probably a Norman baron, that on his arm he bore the cross of red, that he trod the sacred soil of Palestine. Perhaps, to prove this, I need hardly remind you who Hasn-us-Sabah was. It is enough if I say that he was greatly mixed up in the affairs of the Crusaders, lending his irresistible arms now to this side, now to that. He was the chief of the heterodox Mohammedan sect of the Assassins (this word, I believe, is actually derived from his name); imagined himself to be an incarnation of the Deity, and from his inaccessible rock-fortress of Alamut in the Elburz exercised a sinister influence on the intricate politics of the day. The Red Cross Knights called him Shaikh-ul-Jabal—the Old Man of the Mountains, that very nickname

connecting him infallibly with the Ul-Jabal of our own times. Now three well-known facts occur to me in connection with this stone of the House of Saul: the first, that Saladin met in battle, and defeated, *and plundered*, in a certain place, on a certain day, this Hasn-us-Sabah, or one of his successors bearing the same name; the second, that about this time there was a cordial *rapprochement* between Saladin and Richard the Lion, and between the Infidels and the Christians generally, during which a free interchange of gems, then regarded as of deep mystic importance, took place—remember 'The Talisman,' and the 'Lee Penny'[13]; the third, that soon after the fighters of Richard, and then himself, returned to England, the loculus or coffin of St. Edmund (as we are informed by the *Jocelini Chronica*) was *opened by the Abbot* at midnight, and the body of the martyr exposed. On such occasions it was customary to place gems and relics in the coffin, when it was again closed up. Now, the chalice with the stone was taken from this loculus; and is it possible not to believe that some knight, to whom it had been presented by one of Saladin's men, had in turn presented it to the monastery, first scratching uncouthly on its surface the name of Hasn to mark its semi-sacred origin, or perhaps bidding the monks to do so? But the Assassins, now called, I think, 'al Hasani' or 'Ismaili'—'that accursed *Ishmaelite*,' the baronet exclaims in one place—still live, are still a flourishing sect impelled by fervid religious fanaticisms. And where think you is their chief place of settlement? Where, but on the heights of that same 'Lebanon' on which Sir Jocelin 'picked

---

[13] The Lee Penny talisman is an amulet associated with Richard the Lion-Hearted and the subject of Sir Walter Scott's novel *The Talisman* (1825).

up' his too doubtful scribe and literary helper?

"It now becomes evident that Ul-Jabal was one of the sect of the Assassins, and that the object of his sojourn at the manor-house, of his financial help to the baronet, of his whole journey perhaps to England, was the recovery of the sacred gem which once glittered on the breast of the founder of his sect. In dread of spoiling all by over-rashness, he waits, perhaps for years, till he makes sure that the stone is the right one by seeing it with his own eyes, and learns the secret of the spring by which the chalice is opened. He then proceeds to steal it. So far all is clear enough. Now, this too is conceivable, that, intending to commit the theft, he had beforehand provided himself with another stone similar in size and shape—these being well known to him—to the other, in order to substitute it for the real stone, and so, for a time at least, escape detection. It is presumable that the chalice was not often *opened* by the baronet, and this would therefore have been a perfectly rational device on the part of Ul-Jabal. But assuming this to be his mode of thinking, how ludicrously absurd appears all the trouble he took to *engrave* the false stone in an exactly similar manner to the other. *That* could not help him in producing the deception, for that he did not contemplate the stone being *seen*, but only *heard* in the cup, is proved by the fact that he selected a stone of a different *color*. This color, as I shall afterwards show you, was that of a pale, brown-spotted stone. But we are met with something more extraordinary still when we come to the last stone, the white one—I shall prove that it was white—which Ul-Jabal placed in the cup. Is it possible that he had provided *two* substitutes, and that he had engraved these *two*, without object, in the same minutely careful manner? Your mind

refuses to conceive it; and *having* done this, declines, in addition, to believe that he had prepared even one substitute; and I am fully in accord with you in this conclusion.

"We may say then that Ul-Jabal had not *prepared* any substitute; and it may be added that it was a thing altogether beyond the limits of the probable that he could *by chance* have possessed two old gems exactly similar in every detail down to the very half-obliterated letters of the word 'Hasn-us-Sabah.' I have now shown, you perceive, that he did not make them purposely, and that he did not possess them accidentally. Nor were they the baronet's, for we have his declaration that he had never seen them before. Whence then did the Persian obtain them? That point will immediately emerge into clearness, when we have sounded his motive for replacing the one false stone by the other, and, above all, for taking away the valueless stone, and then replacing it. And in order to lead you up to the comprehension of this motive, I begin by making the bold assertion that Ul-Jabal had not in his possession the real St. Edmundsbury stone at all.

"You are surprised; for you argue that if we are to take the baronet's evidence at all, we must take it in this particular also, and he positively asserts that he saw the Persian take the stone. It is true that there are indubitable signs of insanity in the document, but it is the insanity of a diseased mind manifesting itself by fantastic exaggeration of sentiment, rather than of a mind confiding to itself its own delusions as to matters of fact. There is therefore nothing so certain as that Ul-Jabal did steal the gem; but these two things are equally evident: that by some means or other it very soon passed out of his possession, and that when it had so passed, he, for his part, believed it to be in the possession of the baronet. 'Now,' he cries in triumph, one day as he catches Sir Jocelin in his room—'*now* you have delivered all into my hands.' 'All' what, Sir Jocelin wonders. 'All,' of course, meant the stone. He believes that the baronet has done precisely what the baronet afterwards believes that *he* has done—hidden away the stone in the most secret of all places, in his own apartment, to wit. The Persian, sure now at last of victory, accordingly hastens into his chamber, and 'locks the door,' in order, by an easy search, to secure his prize. When, moreover, the baronet is examining the house at night with his lens, he believes that Ul-Jabal is spying his movements; when he extends his operations to the park, the other finds pretexts to be near him. Ul-Jabal dogs his footsteps like a shadow. But supposing he had really had the jewel, and had deposited it in a place of perfect safety—such as, with or without lenses, the extensive grounds of the manor-house would certainly have afforded—his more reasonable role would have been that of unconscious *nonchalance*, rather than of agonized interest. But, in fact, he supposed the owner of the stone to be himself seeking a secure hiding-place for it, and is resolved at all costs on knowing the secret. And again in the vaults beneath the house Sir Jocelin reports that Ul-Jabal 'holds the lantern near the ground, with his head bent down': can anything be better descriptive of the attitude of *search*? Yet each is so sure that the other possesses the gem, that neither is able to suspect that both are seekers.

"But, after all, there is far better evidence of the non-possession of the stone by the Persian than all this—and that is the murder of the baronet, for I can almost promise you that our messenger will return in a few minutes.

Now, it seems to me that Ul-Jabal was not really murderous, averse rather to murder; thus the baronet is often in his power, swoons in his arms, lies under the influence of narcotics in semi-sleep while the Persian is in his room, and yet no injury is done him. Still, when the clear necessity to murder—the clear means of gaining the stone—presents itself to Ul-Jabal, he does not hesitate a moment—indeed, he has already made elaborate preparations for that very necessity. And when was it that this necessity presented itself? It was when the baronet put the false stone in the pocket of a loose gown for the purpose of confronting the Persian with it. But what kind of pocket? I think you will agree with me, that male garments, admitting of the designation 'gown,' have usually only outer pockets—large, square pockets, simply sewed on to the outside of the robe. But a stone of that size *must* have made such a pocket bulge outwards. Ul-Jabal must have noticed it. Never before has he been perfectly sure that the baronet carried the long-desired gem about on his body; but now at last he knows beyond all doubt. To obtain it, there are several courses open to him: he may rush there and then on the weak old man and tear the stone from him; he may ply him with narcotics, and extract it from the pocket during sleep. But in these there is a small chance of failure; there is a certainty of near or ultimate detection, pursuit—and this is a land of Law, swift and fairly sure. No, the old man must die: only thus—thus surely, and thus secretly—can the outraged dignity of Hasn-us-Sabah be appeased. On the very next day he leaves the house—no more shall the mistrustful baronet, who is 'hiding something from him,' see his face. He carries with him a small parcel. Let me tell you what was in that parcel: it contained the baronet's fur cap, one of his 'brown gowns,' and a snow-white beard and wig. Of the cap we can be sure; for from the fact that, on leaving his room at midnight to follow the Persian through the *house*, he put it on his head, I gather that he wore it habitually during all his waking hours; yet after Ul-Jabal has left him he wanders *far and wide* 'with uncovered head.' Can you not picture the distracted old man seeking ever and anon with absent mind for his long-accustomed head-gear, and seeking in vain? Of the gown, too, we may be equally certain: for it was the procuring of this that led Ul-Jabal to the baronet's trunk; we now know that he did not go there to *hide* the stone, for he had it not to hide; nor to *seek* it, for he would be unable to believe the baronet childish enough to deposit it in so obvious a place. As for the wig and beard, they had been previously seen in his room. But before he leaves the house Ul-Jabal has one more work to do: once more the two eat and drink together as in 'the old days of love'; once more the baronet is drunken with a deep sleep, and when he wakes, his skin is 'brown as the leaves of autumn.' That is the evidence of which I spake in the beginning as giving us a hint of the exact shade of the Oriental's color—it was the yellowish-brown of a sered leaf. And now that the face of the baronet has been smeared with this indelible pigment, all is ready for the tragedy, and Ul-Jabal departs. He will return, but not immediately, for he will at least give the eyes of his victim time to grow accustomed to the change of color in his face; nor will he tarry long, for there is no telling whether, or whither, the stone may not disappear from that outer pocket. I therefore surmise that the tragedy took place a day or two ago. I remembered the feebleness of the old man, his highly neurotic condition; I

thought of those 'fibrillary twitchings,' indicating the onset of a well-known nervous disorder sure to end in sudden death; I recalled his belief that on account of the loss of the stone, in which he felt his life bound up, the chariot of death was urgent on his footsteps; I bore in mind his memory of his grandfather dying in agony just seventy years ago after seeing his own wraith by the churchyard-wall; I knew that such a man could not be struck by the sudden, the terrific shock of seeing *himself* sitting in the chair before the mirror (the chair, you remember, had been *placed* there by Ul-Jabal) without dropping down stone dead on the spot. I was thus able to predict the manner and place of the baronet's death—if he *be* dead. Beside him, I said, would probably be found a white stone. For Ul-Jabal, his ghastly impersonation ended, would hurry to the pocket, snatch out the stone, and finding it not the stone he sought, would in all likelihood dash it down, fly away from the corpse as if from plague, and, I hope, straightway go and—hang himself."

It was at this point that the black mask of Ham framed itself between the python-skin tapestries of the doorway. I tore from him the paper, now two days old, which he held in his hand, and under the heading, "Sudden Death of a Baronet," read a nearly exact account of the facts which Zaleski had been detailing to me.

"I can see by your face that I was not altogether at fault," he said, with one of his musical laughs; "but there still remains for us to discover whence Ul-Jabal obtained his two substitutes, his motive for exchanging one for the other, and for stealing the valueless gem; but, above all, we must find where the real stone was all the time that these two men so sedulously sought it, and where it now is. Now, let us turn our attention to this stone, and ask, first, what light does the inscription on the cup throw on its nature? The inscription assures us that if 'this stone be stolen,' or if it 'chaunges dre,' the House of Saul and its head 'anoon' (i.e. anon, at once) shall die. 'Dre,' I may remind you, is an old English word, used, I think, by Burns, identical with the Saxon '*dreogan*,' meaning to 'suffer.' So that the writer at least contemplated that the stone might 'suffer changes.' But what kind of changes—external or internal? External change—change of environment—is already provided for when he says, 'shulde this Ston stalen bee'; 'chaunges,' therefore, in *his* mind, meant internal changes. But is such a thing possible for any precious stone, and for this one in particular? As to that, we might answer when we know the name of this one. It nowhere appears in the manuscript, and yet it is immediately discoverable. For it was a 'sky-blue' stone; a sky-blue, sacred stone; a sky-blue, sacred, Persian stone. That at once gives us its name—it was a *turquoise*. But can the turquoise, to the certain knowledge of a mediaeval writer, 'chaunges dre'? Let us turn for light to old Anselm de Boot[14]: that is he in pig-skin on the shelf behind the bronze Hera."

I handed the volume to Zaleski. He pointed to a passage which read as follows:

"Assuredly the turquoise doth possess a soul more intelligent than that of man. But we cannot be wholly sure of the presence of Angels in precious stones. I do rather opine that the evil spirit doth take up his abode therein, transforming himself into an angel of light, to the end that we put our trust not in God, but in the precious stone; and thus, perhaps, doth he deceive our spirits by the turquoise: for the turquoise is of two sorts: those which keep their color, and those which lose it."*

"You thus see," resumed Zaleski, "that the turquoise was believed to have the property of changing its color—a change which was universally supposed to indicate the fading away and death of its owner. The good De Boot, alas, believed this to be a property of too many other stones beside, like the Hebrews in respect of their *urim and thummim*[15]; but in the case of the turquoise, at least, it is a well-authenticated natural phenomenon, and I have myself seen such a specimen. In some cases the change is a gradual process; in others it may occur suddenly within an hour, especially when the gem, long kept in the dark, is exposed to brilliant sunshine. I should say, however, that in this metamorphosis there is always an intermediate stage: the stone first changes from blue to a pale color spotted with brown, and, lastly, to a pure white. Thus, Ul-Jabal having stolen the stone, finds that it is of the wrong color, and soon after replaces it; he supposes that in the darkness he has selected the wrong chalice, and so takes the valueless stone from the other. This, too, he replaces,

---

* "Assurément la turquoise a une âme plus intelligente que l'âme de l'homme. Mais nous ne pouvons rien establir de certain touchant la presence des Anges dans les pierres precieuses. Mon jugement seroit plustot que le mauvais esprit, qui se transforme en Ange de lumiere se loge dans les pierres precieuses, à fin que l'on ne recoure pas à Dieu, mais que l'on repose sa creance dans la pierre precieuse; ainsi, peut-être, il deçoit nos esprits par la turquoise: car la turquoise est de deux sortes, les unes qui conservent leur couleur et les autres qui la perdent." *Anselm de Boot*, Book II.

[14] In 1609, the Dutch physician and naturalist published his influential work on mineralogy, *De Gemmis et Lapidibus*, still in use in the late 19th century.

[15] Decorative objects connected with the high priest's breastplate, used in divination.

and, infinitely puzzled, makes yet another hopeless trial of the Edmundsbury chalice, and, again baffled, again replaces it, concluding now that the baronet has suspected his designs, and substituted a false stone for the real one. But after this last replacement, the stone assumes its final hue of white, and thus the baronet is led to think that two stones have been substituted by Ul-Jabal for his own invaluable gem. All this while the gem was lying serenely in its place in the chalice. And thus it came to pass that in the Manor-house of Saul there arose a somewhat considerable Ado about Nothing."

For a moment Zaleski paused; then, turning round and laying his hand on the brown forehead of the mummy by his side, he said:—

"My friend here could tell you, and he would, a fine tale of the immensely important part which jewels in all ages have played in human history, human religions, institutions, ideas. He flourished some five centuries before the Messiah, was a Memphian priest of Amsu, and, as the hieroglyphics on his coffin assure me, a prime favorite with one Queen Amyntas. Beneath these mouldering swaddlings of the grave a great ruby still cherishes its blood-guilty secret on the forefinger of his right hand. Most curious is it to reflect how in *all* lands, and at *all* times, precious minerals have been endowed by men with mystic virtues. The Persians, for instance, believed that spinelle and the garnet were harbingers of joy. Have you read the ancient Bishop of Rennes on the subject? Really, I almost think there must be some truth in all this. The instinct of universal man is rarely far at fault. Already you have a semi-comic 'gold-cure' for alcoholism, and you have heard of the geophagism[16] of certain African tribes. What if the scientist of the future be destined to discover that the diamond, and it alone, is a specific for cholera, that powdered rubellite cures fever, and the chryso-beryl gout? It would be in exact conformity with what I have hitherto observed of a general trend towards a certain inborn perverseness and whimsicality in Nature."

Note.—As some proof of the fineness of intuition evidenced by Zaleski, as distinct from his more conspicuous powers of reasoning, I may here state that some years after the occurrence of the tragedy I have recorded above, the skeleton of a man was discovered in the vaults of the Manor-house of Saul. I have not the least doubt that it was the skeleton of Ul-Jabal. The teeth were very prominent. A rotten rope was found loosely knotted round the vertebrae of his neck.

Dick Donovan

DICK DONOVAN WAS the pseudonym of Joyce Emmerson Preston Muddock (1843-1934), an English journalist and writer, who authored more than fifty detective volumes. Many were novels, but most were collections of Donovan's supposedly autobiographical tales. The short stories regularly appeared in the *Strand Magazine* and elsewhere, the first in July 1892, contemporaneous with the Holmes tales.

The physically active Donovan was a more literate version of Nick Carter, the detective who featured in dozens of dime novels, and prefigured other "tough guys" like "Bulldog" Drummond and Mike Hammer. The following story is drawn from the 1896 collection *Riddles Read*.

THE PROBLEM OF DEAD WOOD HALL

DICK DONOVAN

MYSTERIOUS CASE IN CHESH - IRE." So ran the heading to a paragraph in all the morning papers some years ago, and prominence was given to the following particulars:

A gentleman, bearing the somewhat curious name of Tuscan Trankler, resided in a picturesque old mansion, known as Dead Wood Hall, situated in one of the most beautiful and lonely parts of Cheshire, not very far from the quaint and old-time village of Knutsford. Mr. Trankler had given a dinner-party at his house, and among the guests was a very well-known county magistrate and landowner, Mr. Manville Charnworth. It appeared that, soon after the ladies had retired from the table, Mr. Charnworth rose and went into the grounds, saying he wanted a little air. He was smoking a cigar, and in the enjoyment of perfect health. He had drunk wine, however, rather freely, as was his wont, but though on exceedingly good terms with himself and every one else, he was perfectly sober. An hour passed, but Mr. Charnworth

had not returned to the table. Though this did not arouse any alarm, as it was thought that he had probably joined the ladies, for he was what is called "a ladies' man," and preferred the company of females to that of men. A tremendous sensation, however, was caused when, a little later, it was announced that Charnworth had been found insensible, lying on his back in a shrubbery. Medical assistance was at once summoned, and when it arrived the opinion expressed was that the unfortunate gentleman had been stricken with apoplexy. For some reason or other, however, the doctors were led to modify that view, for symptoms were observed which pointed to what was thought to be a peculiar form of poisoning, although the poison could not be determined. After a time, Charnworth recovered consciousness, but was quite unable to give any information. He seemed to be dazed and confused, and was evidently suffering great pain. At last his limbs began to swell, and swelled to an enormous size; his eyes sunk, his cheeks fell in, his lips turned black, and mortification appeared in the extremities. Everything that could be done for the unfortunate man was done, but without avail. After six hours' suffering, he died in a paroxysm of raving madness, during which he had to be held down in the bed by several strong men.

The post-mortem examination, which was necessarily held, revealed the curious fact that the blood in the body had become thin and purplish, with a faint strange odor that could not be identified. All the organs were extremely congested, and the flesh presented every appearance of rapid decomposition. In fact, twelve hours after death putrefaction had taken place. The medical gentlemen who had the case in hand were greatly puzzled, and were at a loss to determine the precise cause of death. The deceased had been a very healthy man, and there was no actual organic disease of any kind. In short, everything pointed to poisoning. It was noted that on the left side of the neck was a tiny scratch, with a slightly livid appearance, such as might have been made by a small sharply pointed instrument. The viscera having been secured for purposes of analysis, the body was hurriedly, buried within thirty hours of death.

The result of the analysis was to make clear that the unfortunate gentleman had died through some very powerful and irritant poison being introduced into the blood. That it was a case of blood-poisoning there was hardly room for the shadow of a doubt, but the science of that day was quite unable to say what the poison was, or how it had got into the body. There was no reason—so far as could be ascertained—to suspect foul play, and even less reason to suspect suicide. Altogether, therefore, the case was one of profound mystery, and the coroner's jury were compelled to return an open verdict. Such were the details that were made public at the time of Mr. Charnworth's death; and from the social position of all the parties, the affair was something more than a nine days' wonder; while in Cheshire itself, it created a profound sensation. But, as no further information was forthcoming, the matter ceased to interest the outside world, and so, as far as the public were concerned, it was relegated to the limbo of forgotten things.

Two years later, Mr. Ferdinand Trankler, eldest son of Tuscan Trankler, accompanied a large party of friends for a day's shooting in Mere Forest. He was a young man, about five and twenty years of age; was in the most perfect health, and had scarcely ever had a day's illness in his life. Deservedly popular and beloved, he had a large circle of warm friends, and was about to be married to a charming young lady, a member of an old Cheshire family who were extensive landed proprietors and property owners. His prospects therefore seemed to be unclouded, and his happiness complete.

The shooting-party was divided into three sections, each agreeing to shoot over a different part of the forest, and to meet in the afternoon for refreshments at an appointed rendezvous.

Young Trankler and his companions kept pretty well together for some little time, but ultimately began to spread about a good deal. At the appointed hour the friends all met, with the exception of Trankler. He was not there. His absence did not cause any alarm, as it was thought he would soon turn up. He was known to be well acquainted with the forest, and the supposition was he had strayed further afield than the rest. By the time the repast was finished, however, he had not put in an appearance. Then, for the first time, the company began to feel some uneasiness, and vague hints that possibly an accident had happened were thrown out. Hints at last took the form of definite expressions of alarm, and search parties were at once organized to go in search of the absent young man, for only on the hypothesis of some untoward event could his prolonged absence be accounted for, inasmuch as it was not deemed in the least likely that he would show such a lack of courtesy as to go off and leave his friends without a word of explanation. For two hours the search was kept up without any result. Darkness was then closing in, and the now painfully anxious searchers began to feel that they would have to desist until daylight returned. But at last some of the more energetic and active members of the party came upon Trankler lying on his sides and nearly entirely hidden by masses of half withered bracken. He was lying near a little stream that meandered through the forest, and near a keeper's shelter that was constructed with logs and thatched with pine boughs. He was stone dead, and his appearance caused his friends to shrink back with horror, for he was not only black in the face, but his body was bloated, and his limbs seemed swollen to twice their natural size.

Among the party were two medical men, who, being hastily summoned, proceeded at once to make an examination. They expressed an opinion that the young man had been dead for some time, but they could not account for his death, as there was no wound to be observed. As a matter of fact, his gun was lying near him with both barrels loaded. Moreover, his appearance was not compatible at all with death from a gun-shot wound. How then had he died? The consternation among those who had known him can well be imagined, and with a sense of suppressed horror, it was whis-pered that the strange condition of the dead man coincided with that of Mr. Manville Charnworth, the county magistrate who had died so mysteriously two years previously.

As soon as it was possible to do so, Ferdinand Trankler's body was removed to Dead Wood Hall, and his people were stricken with profound grief when they realized that the hope and joy of their house was dead. Of course an autopsy had to be performed, owing to the ignorance of the medical men as to the cause of death. And this post-mortem examination disclosed the fact that all the extraordinary appearances which had been noticed in Mr. Charnworth's case were present in this one. There was the same purplish colored blood; the same gangrenous condition of the limbs; but as with Charnworth, so with Trankler, all the organs were healthy. There was no organic disease to account for death. As it was pretty certain, therefore, that death was not due to natural causes, a coroner's inquest was held, and while the medical evidence made it unmistakably clear that young Trankler had been cut down in the flower of his youth and while he was in radiant health by some powerful and potent means which had suddenly destroyed his life, no one had the boldness to suggest what those means were, beyond saying that blood-poisoning of a most violent character had been set up. Now, it was very obvious that blood-poisoning could not have originated without some specific cause, and the most patient investigation was directed to trying to find out the cause, while exhaustive inquiries were made, but at the end of them, the solution of the mystery was as far off as ever, for these investigations had been in the wrong channel, not one scrap of evidence was brought forward which would have justified a definite statement that this or that had been responsible for the young man's death.

It was remembered that when the post-mortem examination of Mr. Charnworth took place, a tiny bluish scratch was observed on the left side of the neck. But it was so small, and apparently so unimportant that it was not taken into consideration when attempts were made to solve the problem of "How did the man die?" When the doctors examined Mr. Trankler's body, they looked to see if there was a similar puncture or scratch, and, to their astonishment, they did find rather a curious mark on the left side of the neck, just under the ear. It was a slight abrasion of the skin, about an inch long as if he had been scratched with a pin, and this abrasion was a faint blue, approximating in color to the tattoo marks on a sailor's arm. The similarity in this scratch to that which had been observed on Mr. Charnworth's body, necessarily gave rise to a good deal of comment among the doctors, though they could not arrive at any definite conclusion respecting it. One man went so far as to express an opinion that it was due to an insect or the bite of a snake. But this theory found no supporters, for it was argued that the similar wound on Mr. Charnworth could hardly have resulted from an insect or snake bite, for he had died in his friend's garden. Besides, there was no insect or snake in England capable of killing a man as these two men had been killed. That theory, therefore, fell to the ground; and medical science as represented by the local gentlemen. had to confess itself baffled; while the coroner's jury were forced to again return an open verdict.

"There was no evidence to prove how the deceased had come by his death."

This verdict was considered highly un-satisfactory, but what other could have been returned. There was nothing to support the theory of foul play; on the other hand, no evidence was forthcoming to explain away the mystery which surrounded the deaths of Charnworth and Trankler. The two men had apparently died from precisely the same cause, and under circumstances which were as mysterious as they were startling, but what the cause was, no one seemed able to determine.

Universal sympathy was felt with the friends and relatives of young Trankler, who had perished so unaccountably while in pursuit of pleasure. Had he been taken suddenly ill at home and had died in his bed, even though the same symptoms and morbid appearances had manifested themselves, the mystery would not have been so great. But as Charnworth's end came in his host's garden after a dinner-party, so young Trankler died in a forest while he and his friends were engaged in shooting. There was certainly something truly remarkable that two men, exhibiting all the same post-mortem effects, should have died in such a way; their deaths, in point of time, being separated by a period of two years. On the face of it, it seemed impossible that it could be merely a coincidence. It will be gathered from the foregoing, that in this double tragedy were all the elements of a romance well calculated to stimulate public curiosity to the highest pitch; while the friends and relatives of the two deceased gentlemen were of opinion that the matter ought not to be allowed to drop with the return of the verdict of the coroner's jury. An investigation seemed to be urgently called for. Of course, an investigation of a kind had taken place by the local police, but something more than that was required, so thought the friends. And an application was made to me to go down to Dead Wood Hall; and bring such skill as I possessed to bear on the case, in the hope that the veil of mystery might be drawn aside, and light let in where all was then dark.

Dead Wood Hall was a curious place, with a certain gloominess of aspect which seemed to suggest that it was a fitting scene for a tragedy. It was a large, massive house, heavily timbered[1] in front in a way peculiar to many of the old Cheshire mansions. It stood in extensive grounds, and being situated on a rise commanded a very fine panoramic view which embraced the Derbyshire Hills. How it got its name of Dead Wood Hall no one seemed to know exactly. There was a tradition that it had originally been known as Dark Wood Hall; but the word "Dark" had been corrupted into "Dead." The Tranklers came into possession of the property by purchase, and the family had been the owners of it for something like thirty years.

With great circumstantiality I was told the story of the death of each man, together with the results of the post mortem examination, and the steps that had been taken by the police. On further inquiry I found that the police, in spite of the mystery surrounding the case, were firmly of opinion that the deaths of the two men were, after all, due to natural causes, and that the similarity in the appearance of the bodies after death *was* a mere coincidence. The superintendent of the county constabulary, who had had charge of the matter, waxed rather warm; for he said that all sorts of ridiculous stories had been set afloat, and absurd theories had been sug-

gested, not one of which would have done credit to the intelligence of an average school-boy.

"People lose their heads so, and make such fools of themselves in matters of this kind," he said warmly; "and of course the police are accused of being stupid, ignorant, and all the rest of it. They seem, in fact, to have a notion that we are endowed with superhuman faculties, and that nothing should baffle us. But, as a matter of fact, it is the doctors who are at fault in this instance. They are confronted with a new disease, about which they are ignorant; and, in order to conceal their want of knowledge, they at once raise the cry of 'foul play.' "

"Then you are clearly of opinion that Mr. Charnworth and Mr. Trankler died of a disease," I remarked.

"Undoubtedly I am."

"Then how do you explain the rapidity of the death in each case, and the similarity in the appearance of the dead bodies?"

"It isn't for me to explain that at all. That is doctors' work not police work. If the doctors can't explain it, how can I be expected to do so? I only know this, I've put some of my best men on to the job, and they've failed to find anything that would suggest foul play."

"And that convinces you absolutely that there has been no foul play?"

"Absolutely."

"I suppose you were personally acquainted with both gentlemen? What sort of man was Mr. Charnworth?"

"Oh, well, he was right enough, as such men go. He made a good many blunders as a

---

[1] A structure framed with exposed timbers.

[2] Magistrates, or justices of the peace, were appointed, unpaid officials who heard petty cases. There were then no qualifications for appointment, and the appointment was usually a matter of politics or went to the largest landowner.

magistrate; but all magistrates do that. You see, fellows get put on the bench who are no more fit to be magistrates than you are, sir.[2] It's a matter of influence more often as not. Mr. Charnworth was no worse and no better than a lot of others I could name."

"What opinion did you form of his private character?"

"Ah, now, there, there's another matter," answered the superintendent, in a confidential tone, and with a smile playing about his lips. "You see, Mr. Charnworth was a bachelor."

"So are thousands of other men," I answered. "But bachelorhood is not considered dishonorable in this country."

"No, perhaps not. But they say as how the reason was that Mr. Charnworth didn't get married was because he didn't care for having only one wife."

"You mean he was fond of ladies generally. A sort of general lover."

"I should think he was," said the superintendent, with a twinkle in his eye, which was meant to convey a good deal of meaning. "I've heard some queer stories about him."

"What is the nature of the stories?" I asked, thinking that I might get something to guide me.

"Oh, well, I don't attach much importance to them myself," he said, half-apologetically; "but the fact is, there was some social scandal talked about Mr. Charnworth."

"What was the nature of the scandal?"

"Mind you," urged the superintendent, evidently anxious to be freed from any responsibility for the scandal whatever it was, "I only tell you the story as I heard it. Mr. Charnworth liked his little flirtations, no doubt, as we all do; but he was a gentleman and a magistrate, and I have no right to say anything against him that I know nothing about myself."

"While a gentleman may be a magistrate, a magistrate is not always a gentleman," I remarked.

"True, true; but Mr. Charnworth was. He was a fine specimen of a gentleman, and was very liberal. He did me many kindnesses."

"Therefore, in your sight, at least, sir, he was without blemish."

"I don't go as far as that," replied the superintendent, a little warmly; "I only want to be just."

"I give you full credit for that," I answered; "but please do tell me about the scandal you spoke of. It is just possible it may afford me a clue."

"I don't think that it will. However, here is the story. A young lady lived in Knutsford by the name of Downie. She is the daughter of the late George Downie, who for many years carried on the business of a miller. Hester Downie was said to be one of the prettiest girls in Cheshire, or, at any rate, in this part of Cheshire, and rumor has it that she flirted with both Charnworth and Trankler."

"Is that all that rumor says?" I asked.

"No, there was a good deal more said. But, as I have told you, I know nothing for certain, and so must decline to commit myself to any statement for which there could be no better foundation than common gossip."

"Does Miss Downie still live in Knutsford?"

"No; she disappeared mysteriously soon after Charnworth's death."

"And you don't know where she is?"

"No; I have no idea."

As I did not see that there was much more to be gained from the superintendent I left him, and at once sought an interview with the leading medical man who had made the autopsy of the two bodies. He was a man who was somewhat puffed up with the belief in his own cleverness, but he gave me the impression that, if anything, he was a little below the average country practitioner. He hadn't a single theory to advance to account for the deaths of Charnworth and Trankler. He confessed that he was mystified; that all the appearances were entirely new to him, for neither in his reading nor his practice had he ever heard of a similar case.

"Are you disposed to think, sir, that these two men came to their end by foul play?" I asked.

"No, I am not," he answered definitely, "and I said so at the inquest. Foul play means murder, cool and deliberate; and planned and carried out with fiendish cunning. Besides, if it was murder how was the murder committed?"

"*If it was murder?*" I asked significantly. "I shall hope to answer that question later on."

"But I am convinced it wasn't murder," returned the doctor, with a self-confident air. "If a man is shot, or bludgeoned, or poisoned, there is something to go upon. I scarcely know of a poison that cannot be detected. And not a trace of poison was found in the organs of either man. Science has made tremendous strides of late years, and I doubt if she has much more to teach us in that respect.[3] Anyway, I assert without fear of contradiction that Charnworth and Trankler did not die of poison."

"What killed them, then?" I asked, bluntly and sharply.

The doctor did not like the question, and there was a roughness in his tone as he answered:—

"I'm not prepared to say. If I could have assigned a precise cause of death the coroner's verdict would have been different."

"Then you admit that the whole affair is a problem which you are incapable of solving?"

"Frankly, I do," he answered, after a pause. "There are certain peculiarities in the case that I should like to see cleared up. In fact, in the interests of my profession, I think it is most desirable that the mystery surrounding the death of the unfortunate men should be solved. And I have been trying experiments recently with a view to attaining that end, though without success."

My interview with this gentleman had not advanced matters, for it only served to show me that the doctors were quite baffled, and I confess that that did not altogether encourage me. Where they had failed, how could I hope to succeed? They had the advantage of seeing the bodies and examining them, and though they found themselves confronted with signs which were in themselves significant, they could not read them. All that I had to go upon was hearsay, and I was asked to solve a mystery which seemed unsolvable. But, as I have so often stated in the course of my chronicles, the seemingly impossible is frequently the most easy to accomplish, where a mind specially trained to deal with complex problems is brought to bear upon it.

In interviewing Mr. Tuscan Trankler, I found that he entertained a very decided opinion that there had been foul play, though he admitted that it was difficult in the extreme to suggest even a vague notion of how the deed had been accomplished. If the two

---

[3] In fact, today, with gas spectrometry, no poison is untraceable in an intact corpse. However, that was surely not the case in the Victorian age!

men had died together or within a short period of each other, the idea of murder would have seemed more logical. But two years had elapsed, and yet each man had evidently died from precisely same cause. Therefore, if it *was* murder, the same hand that had slain Mr. Charnworth slew Mr. Trankler. There was no getting away from that; and then of course arose the question of *motive*. Granted that the same hand did the deed, did the same motive prompt in each case? Another aspect of the affair that presented itself to me was that the crime, if crime it was, was not the work of any ordinary person. There was an originality of conception in it which pointed to the criminal being, in certain respects, a genius. And, moreover, the motive underlying it must have been a very powerful one; possibly, nay probably, due to a sense of some terrible wrong inflicted, and which could only be wiped out with death of the wronger. But this presupposed that each man, though unrelated, had perpetrated the same wrong. Now, it was within the grasp of intelligent reasoning that Charnworth, in his capacity of a county justice, might have given mortal offense to someone, who, cherishing the memory of it, until a mania had been set up, resolved that the magistrate should die. That theory was reasonable when taken singly, but it seemed to lose its reasonableness when connected with young Trankler, unless it was that he had been instrumental in getting somebody convicted. To determine this I made very pointed inquiries, but received the most positive assurances that never in the whole course of his life had he directly or indirectly been instrumental in prosecuting any one. Therefore, so far as he was concerned, the theory fell to the ground; and if the same person killed both men, the motive prompting in each case

was a different one, assuming that Charnworth's death resulted from revenge for a fancied wrong inflicted in the course of his administration of justice.

Although I fully recognized all the difficulties that lay in the way of a rational deduction that would square in with the theory of murder, and of murder committed by one any the same hand, I saw how necessary it was to keep in view the points I have advanced as factors in the problem that had to be worked out, and I adhered to my first impression, and felt tolerably certain that, granted the men had been murdered, they were murdered by the same hand. It may be said that this deduction required no great mental effort. I admit that that is so; but it is strange that nearly all the people in the district were opposed to the theory. Mr. Tuscan Trankler spoke very highly of Charnworth. He believed him to be an upright, conscientious man, liberal to a fault with his means, and in his position of magistrate erring on the side of mercy. In his private character he was a *bon vivant*, fond of a good dinner, good wine, and good company. He was much in request at dinner-parties and other social gatherings, for he was accounted a brilliant *raconteur*, possessed of an endless fund of racy jokes and anecdotes. I have already stated that with ladies he was an especial favorite, for he had a singularly suave, winning way, which with most women was irresistible. In age he was more than double that of young Trankler, who was only five and twenty at the time of his death, whereas Charnworth had turned sixty, though I was given to understand that he was a well-preserved, good-looking man, and apparently younger than he really was.

Coming to young Trankler, there was a consensus of opinion that he was an exemplary young man. He had been partly educated at home and partly at the Manchester Grammar School; and, though he had shown a decided talent for engineering, he had not gone in for it seriously, but had dabbled in it as an amateur, for he had ample means and good prospects, and it was his father's desire that he should lead the life of a country gentleman, devote himself to country pursuits, and to improving and keeping together the family estates. To the lady who was to have become his bride, he had been engaged but six months, and had only known her a year. His premature and mysterious death had caused intense grief in both families; and his intended wife had been so seriously affected that her friends had been compelled to take her abroad.

With these facts and particulars before me, I had to set to work and try to solve the problem which was considered unsolvable by most of the people who knew anything about it. But may I be pardoned for saying very positively that, even at this point, I did not consider it so. Its complexity could not be gainsaid; nevertheless, I felt that there were ways and means of arriving at a solution, and I set to work in my own fashion. Firstly, I started on the assumption that both men had been deliberately murdered by the same person. If that was not so, then they had died of some remarkable and unknown disease which had stricken them down under a set of conditions that were closely allied, and the coincidence in that case would be one of the most astounding the world had ever known. Now, if that was correct, a pathological conundrum was propounded which, it was for the medical world to answer, and practically I was placed out of the running, to use a sporting phrase. I found that, with few exceptions—the exceptions being Mr. Trankler and

his friends—there was an undisguised opinion that what the united local wisdom and skill had failed to accomplish, could not be accomplished by a stranger. As my experience, however, had inured me against that sort of thing, it did not affect me. Local prejudices and jealousies have always to be reckoned with, and it does not do to be thin-skinned. I worked upon my own lines, thought with my own thoughts, and, as an expert in the art of reading human nature, I reasoned from a different set of premises to that employed by the irresponsible chatterers, who cry out "Impossible," as soon as the first difficulty presents itself. Marshaling all the facts of the case so far as I had been able to gather them, I arrived at the conclusion that the problem could be solved, and, as a preliminary step to that end, I started off to London, much to the astonishment of those who had secured my services. But my reply to the many queries addressed to me was, "I hope to find the key-note to the solution in the metropolis." This reply only increased the astonishment, but later on I will explain why I took the step, which may seem to the reader rather an extraordinary one.

After an absence of five days I returned to Cheshire, and I was then in a position to say, "Unless a miracle has happened, Charnworth and Trankler were murdered beyond all doubt, and murdered by the same person in such a cunning, novel and devilish manner, that even the most astute inquirer might have been pardoned for being baffled." Of course there was a strong desire to know my reasons for the positive statement, but I felt that it was in the interests of justice itself that I should not allow them to be known at that stage of the proceedings.

The next important step was to try and find out what had become of Miss Downie, the Knutsford beauty, with whom Charnworth was said to have carried on a flirtation. Here, again, I considered secrecy of great importance.

Hester Downie was about seven and twenty years of age. She was an orphan, and was believed to have been born in Macclesfield, as her parents came from there. Her father's calling was that of a miller. He had settled in Knutsford about fifteen years previous to the period I am dealing with, and had been dead about five years. Not very much was known about the family, but it was thought there were other children living. No very kindly feeling was shown for Hester Downie, though it was only too obvious that jealousy was at the bottom of it. Half the young men, it seemed, had lost their heads about her, and all the girls in the village were consumed with envy and jealousy. It was said she was "stuck up," "above her position," "a heartless flirt," and so forth. From those competent to speak, however, she was regarded as a nice young woman, and admittedly good-looking. For years she had lived with an old aunt, who bore the reputation of being rather a sullen sort of woman, and somewhat eccentric. The girl had a little over fifty pounds a year to live upon,[4] derived from a small property left to her by her father; and she and her aunt occupied a cottage just on the outskirts of Knutsford. Hester was considered to be very exclusive, and did not associate much with the people in Knutsford. This was sufficient to account for the local bias, and as she often went away from her home for three and four weeks at a time, it was not considered extraordinary when it was known that she had left soon after Trankler's death. No-

body, however, knew where she had gone to; it is right, perhaps, that I should here state that not a soul breathed a syllable of suspicion against her, that either directly or indirectly she could be connected with the deaths of Charnworth or Trankler. The aunt, a widow by the name of Hislop, could not be described as a pleasant or genial woman, either in appearance or manner. I was anxious to ascertain for certain whether there was any truth in the rumor or not that Miss Downie had flirted with Mr. Charnworth. If it was true that she did, a clue might be afforded which would lead to the ultimate unravelling of the mystery. I had to approach Mrs. Hislop with a good deal of circumspection, for she showed an inclination to resent any inquiries being made into her family matters. She gave me the impression that she was an honest woman, and it was very apparent that she was strongly attached to her niece Hester. Trading on this fact, I managed to draw her out. I said that people in the district were beginning to say unkind things about Hester, and that it would be better for the girl's sake that there should be no mystery associated with her or her movements.

The old lady fired up at this, and declared that she didn't care a jot about what the "common people" said. Her niece was superior to all of them, and she would "have the law on any one who spoke ill of Hester."

"But there is one thing, Mrs. Hislop," I replied, "that ought to be set at rest. It is rumored—in fact, something more than rumored—that your niece and the late Mr. Charnworth were on terms of intimacy, which, to say the least, if it is true, was imprudent for a girl in her position."

---

[4] Only about £4,500 ($7,100) per year based on today's retail price index.

"Them what told you that," exclaimed the old woman, "is like the adders the woodmen get in Delamere forest: they're full of poison. Mr. Charnworth courted the girl fair and square, and led her to believe he would marry her. But, of course, he had to do the thing in secret. Some folk will talk so, and if it had been known that a gentleman like Mr. Charnworth was coming after a girl in Hester's position, all sorts of things would have been said."

"Did she believe that he was serious in his intentions toward her?"

"Of course she did."

"Why was the match broken off?"

"Because he died."

"Then do you mean to tell me seriously, Mrs. Hislop, that Mr. Charnworth, had he lived, would have married your niece?"

"Yes, I believe he would."

"Was he the only lover the girl had?"

"Oh dear no. She used to carry on with a man named Job Panton. But, though they were engaged to be married, she didn't like him much, and threw him up for Mr. Charnworth."

"Did she ever flirt with young Mr. Trankler?"

"I don't know about flirting; but he called here now and again, and made her some presents. You see, Hester is a superior sort of girl, and I don't wonder at gentlefolk liking her."

"Just so," I replied; "beauty attracts peasant and lord alike. But you will understand that it is to Hester's interest that there should be no concealment—no mystery; and I advise that she return here, for her very presence would tend to silence the tongue of scandal. By the way, where is she?"

"She's staying in Manchester with a rel-ative, a cousin of hers, named Jessie Turner."

"Is Jessie Turner a married woman?"

"Oh yes: well, that is, she has been married; but she's a widow now, and has two little children. She is very fond of Hester, who often goes to her."

Having obtained Jessie Turner's address in Manchester, I left Mrs. Hislop, feeling somehow as if I had got the key of the problem, and a day or two later I called on Mrs. Jessie Turner, who resided in a small house, situated in Tamworth Street, Hulme, Manchester.

She was a young woman, not more than thirty years of age, somewhat coarse, and vulgar-looking in appearance, and with an unpleasant, self-assertive manner. There was a great contrast between her and her cousin, Hester Downie, who was a remarkably attractive and pretty girl, with quite a classical figure, and a childish, winning way, but a painful want of education which made itself very manifest when she spoke; and a harsh, unmusical voice detracted a good deal from her winsomeness, while in everything she did, and almost everything she said, she revealed that vanity was her besetting sin.

I formed my estimate at once of this young woman indeed, of both of them. Hester seemed to me to be shallow, vain, thoughtless, giddy; and her companion, artful, cunning, and heartless.

"I want you, Miss Downie," I began, "to tell me truthfully the story of your connection, firstly, with Job Panton; secondly, with Mr. Charnworth; thirdly, with Mr. Trankler."

This request caused the girl to fall into a condition of amazement and confusion, for I had not stated what the nature of my business was, and, of course, she was unprepared for the question.

"What should I tell you my business for?" she cried snappishly, and growing very red in the face.

"You are aware," I remarked, "that both Mr. Charnworth and Mr. Trankler are dead?"

"Of course I am."

"Have you any idea how they came by their death?"

"Not the slightest."

"Will you be surprised to hear that some very hard things are being said about you?"

"About me!" she exclaimed, in amazement.

"Yes."

"Why about me?"

"Well, your disappearance from your home, for one thing."

She threw up her hands and uttered a cry of distress and horror, while sudden paleness took the place of the red flush that had dyed her cheeks. Then she burst into almost hysterical weeping, and sobbed out:

"I declare it's awful. To think that I cannot do anything or go away when I like without all the old cats in the place trying to blacken my character! It's a pity that people won't mind their own business, and not go out of the way to talk about that which doesn't concern them."

"But, you see, Miss Downie, it's the way of the world," I answered, with a desire to soothe her; "one mustn't be too thin-skinned. Human nature is essentially spiteful. However, to return to the subject, you will see, perhaps, the importance of answering my questions. The circumstances of Charnworth's and Trankler's deaths are being closely inquired into, and I am sure you wouldn't like it to be thought that you were withholding information which, in the interest of law and justice, might be valuable."

"Certainly not," she replied, suppressing a sob. "But I have nothing to tell you."

"But you knew the three men I have mentioned."

"Of course I did, but Job Panton is an ass. I never could bear him."

"He was your sweetheart, though, was he not?"

"He used to come fooling about, and declared that he couldn't live without me."

"Did you never give him encouragement?"

"I suppose every girl makes a fool of herself sometimes."

"Then you did allow him to sweetheart you?"

"If you like to call it sweethearting you can," she answered, with a toss of her pretty head. "I did walk out with him sometimes. But I didn't care much for him. You see, he wasn't my sort at all."

"In what way?"

"Well, surely I couldn't be expected to marry a gamekeeper, could I?"

"He is a gamekeeper, then?"

"Yes."

"In whose employ is he?"

"Lord Belmere's."

"Was he much disappointed when he found that you would have nothing to do with him?"

"I really don't know. I didn't trouble myself about him," she answered, with a coquettish heartlessness.

"Did you do any sweethearting with Mr. Trankler?"

"No, of course not. He used to be very civil to me, and talk to me when he met me."

"Did you ever walk out with him?"

The question brought the color back to her face, and her manner grew confused again.

"Once or twice I met him by accident, and he strolled along the road with me— that's all."

This answer was not a truthful one. Of that I was convinced by her very manner. But I did not betray my mistrust or doubts. I did not think there was any purpose to be served in so doing. So far the object of my visit was accomplished, and as Miss Downie seemed disposed to resent any further questioning, I thought it was advisable to bring the interview to a close; but before doing so, I said:—

"I have one more question to ask you, Miss Downie. Permit me to preface it, however, by saying I am afraid that, up to this point, you have failed to appreciate the situation, or grasp the seriousness of the position in which you are placed. Let me, therefore, put it before you in a somewhat more graphic way. Two men—gentlemen of good social position with whom you seem to have been well acquainted, and whose attentions you encouraged—pray do not look at me so angrily as that; I mean what I say. I repeat that you encouraged their attentions, otherwise they would not have gone after you." Here Miss Downie's nerves gave way again, and she broke into a fit of weeping, and, holding her handkerchief to her eyes, she exclaimed with almost passionate bitterness:—

"Well, whatever I did, I was egged on to do it by my cousin, Jessie Turner. She always said I was a fool not to aim at high game."

"And so you followed her promptings, and really thought that you might have made a match with Mr. Charnworth; but, he having died, you turned your thoughts to young Trankler." She did not reply, but sobbed behind her handkerchief. So I proceeded. "Now the final question I want to ask you is this:

Have you ever had anyone who has made serious love to you but Job Panton?"

"Mr. Charnworth made love to me," she sobbed out.

"He flirted with you," I suggested.

"No; he made love to me," she persisted. "He promised to marry me."

"And you believed him?"

"Of course I did."

"Did Trankler promise to marry you?"

"No."

"Then I must repeat the question, but will add Mr. Charnworth's name. Besides him and Panton, is there anyone else in existence who has courted you in the hope that you would become his wife?"

"No—no one," she mumbled in a broken voice.

As I took my departure I felt that I had gathered up a good many threads, though they wanted arranging, and, so to speak, classifying; that done, they would probably give me the clue I was seeking. One thing was clear, Miss Downie was a weak-headed, giddy, flighty girl, incapable, as it seemed to me, of seriously reflecting on anything. Her cousin was crafty and shallow, and a dangerous companion for Downie, who was sure to be influenced and led by a creature like Jessie Turner. But, let it not be inferred from these remarks that I had any suspicion that either of the two women had in any way been accessory to the crime, for crime I was convinced it was. Trankler and Charnworth had been murdered, but by whom I was not prepared to even hint at at that stage of the proceedings. The two unfortunate gentlemen had, beyond all possibility of doubt, both been attracted by the girl's exceptionally good looks, and they had amused themselves with her. This fact suggested at once the question, was Charnworth in the habit of seeing her before Trankler made her acquaintance? Now, if my theory of the crime was correct, it could be asserted with positive certainty, that Charnworth was the girl's lover before Trankler. Of course it was almost a foregone conclusion that Trankler must have been aware of her existence for a long time. The place, be it remembered, was small; she, in her way, was a sort of local celebrity, and it was hardly likely that young Trankler was ignorant of some of the village gossip in which she figured. But, assuming that he was, he was well acquainted with Charnworth, who was looked upon in the neighborhood as "a gay dog." The female conquests of such men are often matters of notoriety; though, even if that was not the case, it was likely enough that Charnworth may have discussed Miss Downie in Trankler's presence. Some men—especially those of Charnworth's characteristics—are much given to boasting of their flirtations, and Charnworth may have been rather proud of his ascendency over the simple village beauty. Of course, all this, it will be said, was mere theorizing. So it was; but it will presently be seen how it squared in with the general theory of the whole affair, which I had worked out after much pondering, and a careful weighing and nice adjustment of all the evidence, such as it was, I had been able to gather together, and the various parts which were necessary before the puzzle could be put together.

It was immaterial, however, whether Trankler did or did not know Hester Downie before or at the same time as Charnworth. A point that was not difficult to determine was this—he did not make himself conspicuous as her admirer until after his friend's death, probably not until some time afterwards. Otherwise, how came it about that the slayer of Charnworth waited two years before he took the life of young Trankler? The reader will gather from this remark how my thoughts ran at that time. Firstly, I was clearly of opinion that both men had been murdered. Secondly, the murder in each case was the outcome of jealousy. Thirdly, the murderer must, as a logical sequence, have been a rejected suitor. This would point necessarily to Job Panton as the criminal, assuming my information was right that the girl had not had any other lover. But against that theory this very strong argument could be used: By what extraordinary and secret means—means that had baffled all the science of the district—had Job Panton, who occupied the position of a gamekeeper, been able to do away with his victims, and bring about death so horrible and so sudden as to make one shudder to think of it? Herein was displayed a devilishness of cunning, and a knowledge which it was difficult to conceive that an ignorant and untravelled man was likely to be in possession of. Logic, deduction, and all the circumstances of the case were opposed to the idea of Panton being the murderer at the first blush; and yet, so far as I had gone, I had been irresistibly drawn toward the conclusion that Panton was either directly or indirectly responsible for the death of the two gentlemen. But, in order to know something more of the man whom I suspected, I disguised myself as a traveling showman on the look-out for a good pitch for my show, and I took up my quarters for a day or two at a rustic inn just on the skirts of Knutsford, and known as the Woodman. I had previously ascertained that this inn was a favorite resort of the gamekeepers for miles round about, and Job Panton was to be found there almost nightly.

In a short time I had made his acquaintance. He was a young, big-limbed, powerful man, of a pronounced rustic type. He had the face of a gipsy—swarthy and dark, with keen, small black eyes, and a mass of black curly hair, and in his ears he wore tiny, plain gold rings. Singularly enough his expression was most intelligent; but allied with—as it seemed to me—a certain suggestiveness of latent ferocity. That is to say, I imagined him liable to outbursts of temper and passion, during which he might be capable of anything. As it was, then, he seemed to me subdued, somewhat sullen, and averse to conversation. He smoked heavily, and I soon found that he guzzled beer at a terrible rate. He had received, for a man in his position, a tolerably good education. By that I mean he could write a fair hand, he read well, and had something more than a smattering of arithmetic. I was told also that he was exceedingly skilful with carpenter's tools, although he had had no training that way; he also understood something about plants, while he was considered an authority on the habit, and everything appertaining to game. The same informant thought to still further enlighten me by adding:—

"Poor Job beän't the chap he wur a year or more ago. His gal cut un, and that kind a took a hold on un. He doän't say much; but it wur a terrible blow, it wur."

"How was it his girl cut him?" I asked.

"Well, you see, maäster, it wur this way; she thought hersel' a bit too high for un. Mind you, I bään't a saying as she wur; but when a gel thinks hersel' above a chap, it's no use talking to her."

"What was the girl's name?"

"They call her Downie. Her father was a miller here in Knutsford, but his gal had too big notions of hersel'; and she chucked poor Job Panton overboard, and they do say as how she took on wi' Meäster Charnworth and also wi' Meäster Trankler. I doän't know nowt for certain myself, but there wursome rum kind o' talk going about. Leastwise, I know that Job took it badly, and he ain't been the same kind o' chap since. But there, what's the use of a breaking one's 'art about a gal? Gals is a queer lot, I tell you. My old grandfaither used to say, 'Women folk be curious folk. They be necessary evils, they be, and pleasant enough in their way, but a chap mustn't let 'em get the upper hand. They're like harses, they be, and if you want to manage 'em, you must show 'em you're their meäster.'"

The garrulous gentleman who entertained me thus with his views on women, was a tough, sinewy, weather-tanned old codger, who had lived the allotted span according to the psalmist,[5] but who seemed destined to tread the earth for a long time still; for his seventy years had neither bowed nor shrunk him. His chatter was interesting to me because it served to prove what I already suspected, which was that Job Panton had taken his jilting very seriously indeed. Job was by no means a communicative fellow. As a matter of fact, it was difficult to draw him out on any subject; and though I should have liked to have heard *his* views about Hester Downie, I did not feel warranted in tapping him straight off. I very speedily discovered, however, that his weakness was beer. His capacity for it seemed immeasurable. He soaked himself with it; but when he reached the muddled

---

[5] Psalms 90:10 records that the "days of our years [are] three-score-and-ten" (King James Version) or seventy years.

stage, there was a tendency on his part to be more loquacious, and, taking advantage at last of one of these opportunities, I asked him one night if he had travelled. The question was an exceedingly pertinent one to my theory, and I felt that to a large extent the theory I had worked out depended upon the answers he gave. He turned his beady eyes upon me, and said, with a sort of sardonic grin:—

"Yes, I've traveled a bit in my time, meäster. I've been to Manchester often, and I once tramped all the way to Edinburgh. I had to rough it, I tell thee."

"Yes, I dare say," I answered. "But what I mean is, have you ever been abroad? Have you ever been to sea?"

"No, meäster, not me."

"You've been in foreign countries?"

"No. I've never been out of this one. England was good enough for me. But I would like to go away now to Australia, or some of those places."

Why?"

"Well, meäster, I have my own reasons."

"Doubtless," I said, "and no doubt very sound reasons."

"Never thee mind whether they are, or whether they beän't," he retorted warmly. "All I've got to say is, I wouldn't care where I went to if I could only get far enough away from this place. I'm tired of it."

In the manner of giving his answer, he betrayed the latent fire which I had surmised, and showed that there was a volcanic force of passion underlying his sullen silence, for he spoke with a suppressed force which clearly indicated the intensity of his feelings, and his bright eyes grew brighter with the emotion he felt. I now ventured upon another remark. I intended it to be a test one.

"I heard one of your mates say that you had been jilted. I suppose that's why you hate the place?"

He turned upon me suddenly. His tan - ned, ruddy face took on a deeper flush of red; his upper teeth closed almost savagely on his nether lip; his chest heaved, and his great, brawny hands clenched with the working of his passion. Then, with one great bang of his ponderous fist, he struck the table until the pots and glasses on it jumped as if they were sentient and frightened; and in a voice thick with smothered passion, he growled, "Yes, damn her! She's been my ruin."

"Nonsense!" I said. "You are a young man and a young man should not talk about being ruined because a girl has jilted him."

Once more he turned that angry look upon me, and said fiercely:—

"Thou knows nowt about it, governor. Thou're a stranger to me; and I doän't allow no strangers to preach to me. So shut up! I'll have nowt more to say to thee."

There was a peremptoriness, a force of character, and a display of firmness and self-assurance in his tone and manner, which stamped him with a distinct individualism, and made it evident that in his own particular way he was distinct from the class in which his lot was cast. He, further than that, gave me the idea that he was designing and secretive; and given that he had been educated and well trained, he might have made his mark in the world. My interview with him had been in-structive, and my opinion that he might prove a very important factor in working out the problem was strengthened; but at that stage of the inquiry I would not have taken upon myself to say, with anything like definiteness, that he was directly responsible for the death of the two gentlemen, whose mysterious ending had caused such a profound sensation. But the reader of this narrative will now see for himself that of all men, so far as one could determine then, who might have been interested in the death of Mr. Charnworth and Mr. Trankler, Job Panton stood out most conspicuously. His motive for destroying them was one of the most powerful of human passions—namely, jealousy, which in his case was likely to assume a very violent form, inasmuch as there was no evenly balanced judgment, no capability of philosophical reasoning, calculated to restrain the fierce, crude passion of the determined and self-willed man.

A wounded tiger is fiercer and more dangerous than an unwounded one, and an ignorant and unreasoning man is far more likely to be led to excess by a sense of wrong, than one who is capable of reflecting and moralizing. Of course, if I had been the impossible detective of fiction, endowed with the absurd attributes of being able to tell the story of a man's life from the way the tip of his nose was formed, or the number of hairs on his head, or by the shape and size of his teeth, or by the way he held his pipe when smoking, or from the kind of liquor he consumed, or the hundred and one utterly ridiculous and burlesque signs which are so easily read by the detective prig of modern creation, I might have come to a different conclusion with reference to Job Panton. But my work had to be carried out on very different lines, and I had to be guided by certain deductive inferences, aided by an intimate knowledge of human nature, and of the laws which, more or less in every case of crime, govern the criminal.

I have already set forth my unalterable opinion that Charnworth and Trankler had been murdered; and so far as I had proceeded up to this point, I had heard and seen enough to warrant me, in my own humble judgment, in at least suspecting Job Panton of being guilty of the murder. But there was one thing that puzzled me greatly. When I first commenced my inquiries, and was made acquainted with all the extraordinary medical aspects of the case, I argued with myself that if it was murder, it was murder carried out upon very original lines. Some potent, swift and powerful poison must have been suddenly and secretly introduced into the blood of the victim. The bite of a cobra, or of the still more fearful and deadly Fer de lance of the West Indies, might have produced symptoms similar to those observed in the two men; but happily our beautiful and quiet woods and gardens of England are not infested with these deadly reptiles, and one had to search for the causes elsewhere. Now everyone knows that the notorious Lucrezia Borgia,[6] and the Marchioness of Brinvilliers,[7] made use of means for accomplishing the death of

---

[6] Lucrezia Borgia (1480-1523), a member of the infamous and powerful Italian family, is remembered as a proverbial poisoner, although there is no historical evidence that she was more than a political pawn of her father Rodrigo, married off (three times) as politically expedient.

[7] Marie-Madeleine-Marguérite d'Aubray, Marchioness de Brinvilliers (c. 1630–76), was a Frenchwoman who plotted with her lover to poison her father, her brothers, and her husband. In part, d'Aubray sought to control her family's fortunes and to end interference in her affair with J.-B. Godin de Sainte-Croix, a friend of her husband's. Sainte-Croix had his own motives, having been imprisoned at the Bastille by d'Aubray's father. After allegedly testing poisons on hospital patients, d'Aubray successfully murdered her father (in 1666) and her two brothers (in 1670), but her husband survived the attempt on his life. D'Aubray was arrested at Liège in 1676, and for her crimes was beheaded and burned. In all, the notorious murderess was reputed to have killed fifty people, and she declared under interrogation, "Half the people of quality are involved in this sort of thing, and I could ruin them if I were to talk."

those whom they were anxious to get out of the way, which were at once effective and secret. These means consisted, among others, of introducing into the blood of the intended victim some subtle poison, by the medium of a scratch or puncture. This little and fatal wound could be given by the scratch of a pin, or the sharpened stone of a ring, and in such a way that the victim would be all unconscious of it until the deadly poison so insidiously introduced began to course through his veins, and to sap the props of his life. With these facts in my mind, I asked myself if in the Dead Wood Hall tragedies some similar means had been used; and in order to have competent and authoritative opinion to guide me, I journeyed back to London to consult the eminent chemist and scientist, Professor Lucraft. This gentleman had made a lifelong study of the toxic effect of ptomaines on the human system, and of the various poisons used by savage tribes for tipping their arrows and spears. Enlightened as he was on the subject, he confessed that there were hundreds of these deadly poisons, of which the modern chemist knew absolutely nothing; but he expressed a decided opinion that there were many that would produce all the effects and symptoms observable in the cases of Charnworth and Trankler. And he particularly instanced some of the herbal extracts used by various tribes of Indians, who wander in the interior of the little known country of Ecuador, and he cited as an authority Mr. Hart Thompson, the botanist who traveled from Quito right through Ecuador to the Amazon. This gentleman reported that he found a vegetable poison in use by the natives for poisoning the tips of their arrows and spears of so deadly and virulent a nature, that a scratch even on a panther would bring about the death of the animal within an hour.

Armed with these facts, I returned to Cheshire, and continued my investigations on the assumption that some such deadly destroyer of life had been used to put Charnworth and Trankler out of the way. But necessarily I was led to question whether or not it was likely that an untravelled and ignorant man like Job Panton could have known anything about such poisons and their uses. This was a stumbling block; and while I was convinced that Panton had a strong motive for the crime, I was doubtful if he could have been in possession of the means for committing it. At last, in order to try and get evidence on this point, I resolved to search the place in which he lived. He had for a long time occupied lodgings in the house of a widow woman in Knutsford, and I subjected his rooms to a thorough and critical search, but without finding a sign of anything calculated to justify my suspicion.

I freely confess that at this stage I began to feel that the problem was a hopeless one, and that I should fail to work it out. My depression, however, did not last long. It was not my habit to acknowledge defeat so long as there were probabilities to guide me, so I began to make inquiries about Panton's relatives, and these inquiries elicited the fact that he had been in the habit of making frequent journeys to Manchester to see an uncle. I soon found that this uncle had been a sailor, and had been one of a small expedition which had traveled through Peru and Ecuador in search of gold. Now, this was a discovery indeed, and the full value of it will be understood when it is taken in connection with the information given to me by Professor Lucraft. Let us see how it works out logically.

Panton's uncle was a sailor and a traveler. He had traveled through Peru, and had been into the interior of Ecuador.

Panton was in the habit of visiting his uncle.

Could the uncle have wandered through Ecuador without hearing something of the marvelous poisons used by the natives?

Having been connected with an exploring expedition, it was reasonable to assume that he was a man of good intelligence, and of an inquiring turn of mind.

Equally probable was it that he had brought home some of the deadly poisons or poisoned implements used by the Indians. Granted that, and what more likely than that he talked of his knowledge and possessions to his nephew? The nephew, brooding on his wrongs, and seeing the means within his grasp of secretly avenging himself on those whom he counted his rivals, obtained the means from his uncle's collection of putting his rivals to death, in a way which to him would seem to be impossible to detect. I had seen enough of Panton to feel sure that he had all the intelligence and cunning necessary for planning and carrying out the deed.

A powerful link in the chain of evidence had now been forged, and I proceeded a step further. After a consultation with the chief inspector of police, who, however, by no means shared my views, I applied for a warrant for Panton's arrest, although I saw that to establish legal proof of his guilt would be extraordinarily difficult, for his uncle at that time was at sea, somewhere in the southern hemisphere. Moreover, the whole case rested upon such a hypothetical basis, that it seemed doubtful whether, even supposing a magistrate would commit, a jury would convict. But I was not daunted; and, having succeeded so far in giving a practical shape to my theory, I did not intend to draw back. So I set to work to endeavour to discover the weapon which had been used for wounding Charnworth and Trankler, so that the poison might take effect. This, of course, was the *crux* of the whole affair. The discovery of the medium by which the death-scratch was given would forge almost the last link necessary to ensure a conviction.

Now, in each case there was pretty conclusive evidence that there had been no struggle. This fact justified the belief that the victim was struck silently, and probably unknown to himself. What were the probabilities of that being the case? Assuming that Panton was guilty of the crime, how was it that he, being an inferior, was allowed to come within striking distance of his victims? The most curious thing was that both men had been scratched on the left side of the neck. Charnworth had been killed in his friend's garden on a summer night. Trankler had fallen in mid-day in the depths of a forest. There was an interval of two years between the death of the one man and the death of the other, yet each had a scratch on the left side of the neck. That could not have been a mere coincidence. It was design.

The next point for consideration was, how did Panton—always assuming that he was the criminal—get access to Mr. Trankler's grounds? Firstly, the grounds were extensive, and in connection with a plantation of young fir trees. When Charnworth was found, he was lying behind a clump of rhododendron bushes, and near where the grounds were merged into the plantation, a somewhat dilapidated oak fence separating the two. These details before us make it clear that Panton could have had no difficulty in gaining access to the plantation, and thence to the grounds. But how came it that he was there just at the time that Charnworth was strolling about? It seemed stretching a point very much to suppose that he could have been loafing about on the mere chance of seeing Charnworth. And the only hypothesis that squared in with intelligent reasoning, was that the victim had been lured into the grounds. But this necessarily presupposed a confederate. Close inquiry elicited the fact that Panton was in the habit of going to the house. He knew most of the servants, and frequently accompanied young Trankler on his shooting excursions, and periodically he spent half a day or so in the gun room at the house, in order that he might clean up all the guns, for which he was paid a small sum every month. These circumstances cleared the way of difficulties to a very considerable extent. I was unable, however, to go beyond that, for I could not ascertain the means that had been used to lure Mr. Charnworth into the garden—if he had been lured; and I felt sure that he had been. But so much had to remain for the time being a mystery.

Having obtained the warrant to arrest Panton, I proceeded to execute it. He seemed thunderstruck when told that he was arrested on a charge of having been instrumental in bringing about the death of Charnworth and Trankler. For a brief space of time he seemed to collapse, and lose his presence of mind. But suddenly, with an apparent effort, he recovered himself, and said, with a strange smile on his face:—

"You've got to prove it, and that you can never do."

His manner and this remark were hardly compatible with innocence, but I clearly recognized the difficulties of proof. From that moment the fellow assumed a self-assured air, and to those with whom he was brought in contact he would remark:

"I'm as innocent as a lamb, and them as says I done the deed have got to prove it."

In my endeavor to get further evidence to strengthen my case, I managed to obtain from Job Panton's uncle's brother, who followed the occupation of an engine-minder in a large cotton factory in Oldham, an old chest containing a quantity of lumber. The uncle, on going to sea again, had left this chest in charge of his brother. A careful examination of the contents proved that they consisted of a very miscellaneous collection of odds and ends, including two or three small, carved wooden idols from some savage country; some stone weapons, such as are used by the North American Indians; strings of cowrie shells, a pair of moccasins, feathers of various kinds; a few dried specimens of strange birds; and last, though not least, a small bamboo case containing a dozen tiny sharply pointed darts, feathered at the thick end; while in a stone box, about three inches square, was a viscid thick gummy looking substance of a very dark brown color, and giving off a sickening and most disagreeable, though faint odor. These things I at once submitted to Professor Lucraft, who expressed an opinion that the gummy substance in the stone box was a vegetable poison, used probably to poison the darts with. He lost no time in experimentalizing with this substance, as well as with the darts. With these darts he scratched guineapigs, rabbits, a dog, a cat, a hen, and a young pig, and in each case death ensued in periods of time ranging from a quarter of an hour to two hours. By means of a subcutaneous injection into a rabbit of a minute portion of the gummy substance, about the size of a pea, which had been thinned with alcohol, he produced death in exactly seven minutes. A small monkey was next procured, and slightly scratched on the neck with one of the poisoned darts. In a very short time the poor animal exhibited the most distressing symptoms, and in half an hour it was dead, and a postmortem examination revealed many of the peculiar effect which had been observed in Charnworth's and Trankler's bodies. Various other exhaustive experiments were carried out, all of which confirmed the deadly nature of these minute poison-darts, which could be puffed through a hollow tube to a great distance, and after some practice, with unerring aim. Analysis of the gummy substance in the box proved it to be a violent vegetable poison; innocuous when swallowed, but singularly active and deadly when introduced direct into the blood.

On the strength of these facts, the magistrate duly committed Job Panton to take his trial at the next assizes, on a charge of murder, although there was not a scrap of evidence forthcoming to prove that he had ever been in possession of any of the darts or the poison; and unless such evidence was forthcoming, it was felt that the case for the prosecution must break down, however clear the mere guilt of the man might seem.

In due course, Panton was put on his trial at Chester, and the principal witness against him was Hester Downie, who was subjected to a very severe cross-examination, which left not a shadow of a doubt that she and Panton had at one time been close sweethearts. But her cousin Jessie Turner proved a tempter of great subtlety. It was made clear that she poisoned the girl's mind against her humble lover. Although it could not be proved, it is highly probable that Jessie Turner was a

creature of and in the pay of Mr. Charnworth, who seemed to have been very much attracted by him. Hester's connection with Charnworth half maddened Panton, who made frantic appeals to her to be true to him, appeals to which she turned a deaf ear. That Trankler knew her in Charnworth's time was also brought out, and after Charnworth's death she smiled favorably on the young man. On the morning that Trankler's shooting-party went out to Mere Forest, Panton was one of the beaters employed by the party.

So much was proved; so much was made as clear as daylight, and it opened the way for any number of inferences. But the last and most important link was never forthcoming. Panton was defended by an able and unscrupulous counsel, who urged with tremendous force on the notice of the jury, that firstly, not one of the medical witnesses would undertake to swear that the two men had died from the effects of poison similar to that found in the old chest which had belonged to the prisoner's uncle; and secondly, there was not one scrap of evidence tending to prove that Panton had ever been in possession of poisoned darts, or had ever had access to the chest in which they were kept. These two points were also made much of by the learned judge in his summing up. He was at pains to make clear that there was a doubt involved, and that mere inference ought not to be allowed to outweigh the doubt when a human being was on trial for his life. Although circumstantially the evidence very strongly pointed to the probability of the prisoner having killed both men, nevertheless, in the absence of the strong proof which the law demanded, the way was opened for the escape of a suspected man, and it was far better to let the law be cheated of its due, than that an innocent man should suffer. At the same time, the judge went on, two gentlemen had met their deaths in a manner which had baffled medical science, and no one was forthcoming who would undertake to say that they had been killed in the manner suggested by the prosecution, and yet it had been shown that the terrible and powerful poison found in the old chest, and which there was reason to believe had been brought from some part of the little known country near the sources of the mighty Amazon, would produce all the effects which were observed in the bodies of Charnworth and Trankler. The chest, furthermore, in which the poison was discovered, was in the possession of Panton's uncle. Panton had a powerful motive in the shape of consuming jealousy for getting rid of his more favored rivals; and though he was one of the shooting-party in Mere Forest on the day that Trankler lost his life, no evidence had been produced to prove that he was on the premises of Dead Wood Hall, on the night that

Charnworth died. If, in weighing all these points of evidence, the jury were of opinion circumstantial evidence was inadequate, then it was their duty to give the prisoner—whose life was in their hands—the benefit of the doubt.

The jury retired, and were absent three long hours, and it became known that they could not agree. Ultimately, they returned into court, and pronounced a verdict of "Not guilty." In Scotland the verdict must and would have been *non-proven*.

And so Job Panton went free, but an evil odor seemed to cling about him; he was shunned by his former companions, and many a suspicious glance was directed to him, and many a bated murmur was uttered as he passed by, until in a while he went forth beyond the seas, to the far wild west, as some said, and his haunts knew him no more.

The mystery is still a mystery; but how near I came to solving the problem of Dead Wood Hall it is for the reader to judge.

George R. Sims

GEORGE ROBERT SIMS (1847-1922), English journalist, poet, and novelist, wrote much about the plight of those living in the East End of London. His obituary noted that: "He was [also] a highly successful playwright...a zealous social reformer, an expert criminologist, a connoisseur in good eating and drinking, in racing, in dogs, in boxing, and in all sorts of curious and out of the way people and things."

His important contribution to detective fiction was the creation of Dorcas Dene, a young actress who, when her husband is blinded, leaves the stage to take up detection as a profession. There are two series of tales about Dorcas, confusingly both published as *Dorcas Dene, Detective* (1897 and 1898); the following appear as succeeding chapters in the first volume.

THE HAVERSTOCK HILL MURDER
THE BEAR LAMP

GEORGE R. SIMS

THE HAVERSTOCK HILL MURDER

The blinds had been down at the house in Oak Tree Road and the house shut for nearly six weeks. I had received a note from Dorcas saying that she was engaged on a case which would take her away for some little time, and that as Paul[1] had not been very well lately she had arranged that he and her mother should accompany her. She would advise me as soon as they returned. I called once at Oak Tree Road and found it was in charge of the two servants and Toddlekins, the bulldog. The housemaid informed me that Mrs. Dene had not written, so that she did not know where she was or when she would be back, but that letters which arrived for her were forwarded by her instructions to Mr. Jackson, of Penton Street King's Cross.

Mr. Jackson, I remembered, was the ex-police-sergeant who was generally employed by Dorcas when she wanted a house watched or certain inquiries made among tradespeople. I felt that it would be unfair to go to Jackson. Had Dorcas wanted me to know where she was she would have told me in her letter.

The departure had been a hurried one. I had gone to the North in connection with a business matter of my own on a Thursday evening, leaving Dorcas at Oak Tree Road, and when I returned on Monday afternoon I found Dorcas's letter at my chambers. It was written on the Saturday, and evidently on the eve of departure.

But something that Dorcas did not tell me I learned quite accidentally from my old friend Inspector Swanage, of Scotland Yard, whom I met one cold February afternoon at Kempton Park Steeplechases.[2]

Inspector Swanage has a greater acquaint-

---

[1] Paul is the husband of Dorcas Dene, nee Lester. Dorcas is a former bit-player actress who married an artist. When he went blind, she took on a client and became a professional detective. The narrator is Saxon, a dramatist, who first met Dorcas Lester when she tried out for a part in a play of his.

[2] A popular racing venue in Sunbury-on-Thames, still in operation as Kempton Park.

ance with the fraternity known as "the boys" than any other officer. He has attended race meetings for years, and the "boys" always greet him respectfully, though they wish him further. Many a prettily-planned coup of theirs has he nipped in the bud, and many an unsuspecting greenhorn has he saved from pillage by a timely whisper that the well-dressed young gentlemen who are putting their fivers on so merrily and coming out of the enclosure with their pockets stuffed full of bank-notes are men who get their living by clever swindling, and are far more dangerous than the ordinary vulgar pickpocket.

On one occasion not many years ago I found a well-known publisher at a race meeting in earnest conversation with a beautifully-dressed, grey-haired sportsman. The publisher informed me that his new acquaintance was the owner of a horse which was certain to win the next race, and that it would start at ten to one. Only in order not to shorten the price nobody was to know the name of the horse, as the stable had three in the race. He had obligingly taken a fiver off the publisher to put on with his own money.

I told the publisher that he was the victim of a "tale-pitcher," and that he would never see his fiver again. At that moment Inspector Swanage came on the scene, and the owner of race horses disappeared as if by magic. Swanage recognized the man instantly, and having heard my publisher's story said, "If I have the man taken will you prosecute?" The publisher shook his head. He didn't want to send his authors mad with delight at the idea that somebody had eventually succeeded in getting a fiver the best of him. So Inspector Swanage strolled away. Half an hour later he came to us in the enclosure and said, "Your friend's horse doesn't run, so he's given me

that fiver back again for you." And with a broad grin he handed my friend a bank-note.

It was Inspector Swanage's skill and kindness on this occasion that made me always eager to have a chat with him when I saw him at a race meeting, for his conversation was always interesting.

The February afternoon had been a cold one, and soon after the commencement of racing there were signs of fog. Now a foggy afternoon is dear to the hearts of the "boys." It conceals their operations, and helps to cover their retreat. As the fog came up the Inspector began to look anxious, and I went up to him.

"You don't like the look of things?" I said.

"No, if this gets worse the band will begin to play—there are some very warm members of it here this afternoon. It was a day just like this last year that they held up a bookmaker going to the station, and eased him of over £500. Hullo?"

As he uttered the exclamation the Inspector pulled out his race card and seemed to be anxiously studying it.

But under his voice he said to me, "Do you see that tall man in a fur coat talking to a bookmaker? See, he's just handed him a bank-note."

"Where?—I don't see him."

"Yonder. Do you see that old gipsy-looking woman with race cards? She has just thrust her hand through the railings and offered one to the man."

"Yes, yes—I see him now."

"That's Flash George. I've missed him lately, and I heard he was broke, but he's in funds again evidently by his get-up."

"One of the boys?"

"Has been—but he's been on another lay[3] lately. He was mixed up in that big jewel case—£10,000 worth of diamonds stolen from a demi-mondaine.[4] He got rid of some of the jewels for the thieves, but we could never bring it home to him. But he was watched for a long time afterwards and his game was stopped. The last we heard of him he was hard up and borrowing from some of his pals. He's gone now. I'll just go and ask the bookie what he's betting to."

The Inspector stepped across to the bookmaker and presently returned.

"He *is* in luck again," he said. "He's put a hundred ready on the favorite for this race. By the bye, how's your friend Mrs. Dene getting on with her case?"

I confessed my ignorance as to what Dorcas was doing at the present moment—all I knew was that she was away.

"Oh, I thought you'd have known all about it," said the Inspector. "She's on the Hannaford case."

"What, the murder?"

"Yes."

"But surely that was settled by the police? The husband was arrested immediately after the inquest."

"Yes, and the case against him was very strong, but we know that Dorcas Dene has been engaged by Mr. Hannaford's family, who have made up their minds that the police, firmly believing him guilty, won't look anywhere else for the murderer—of course they are convinced of his innocence. But you must excuse me—the fog looks like thickening, and may stop racing—I must go and put my men to work."

"One moment before you go—why did you suddenly ask me how Mrs. Dene was get-

ting on? Was it anything to do with Flash George that put it in your head?"

The Inspector looked at me curiously.

"Yes," he said, "though I didn't expect you'd see the connection. It was a mere coincidence. On the night that Mrs. Hannaford was murdered Flash George, who had been lost sight of for some time by our people, was reported to have been seen by the Inspector who was going his rounds in the neighborhood. He was seen about half-past two o'clock in the morning looking rather dilapidated and seedy. When the report of the murder came in the Inspector at once remembered that he had seen Flash George in Haverstock Hill. But there was nothing in it—as the house hadn't been broken into and there was nothing stolen. You understand now why seeing Flash George carried my train of thought on to the Hannaford murder and Dorcas Dene. Good-bye."

The Inspector hurried away and a few minutes afterward the favorite came in alone for the second race on the card. The stewards immediately afterward announced that racing would be abandoned on the account of the fog increasing, and I made my way to the railway station and went home by the members' train.[5]

Directly I reached home I turned eagerly to my newspaper file and read up the Hannaford murder. I knew the leading features, but every detail of it had now a special interest to me, seeing that Dorcas Dene had taken the case up.

These were the facts as reported in the Press:

Early in the morning of January 5 a maidservant rushed out of the house, standing in its

---

[3] Among thieves, a pursuit or practice, a dodge.
[4] An adventuress, a "kept woman."
[5] Perhaps a "special" engaged by the members of Saxon's club.

own grounds on Haverstock Hill, calling "Murder!" Several people who were passing instantly came to her and inquired what was the matter, but all she could gasp was, "Fetch a policeman." When the policeman arrived he followed the terrified girl into the house and was conducted to the drawing-room, where he found a lady lying in her night-dress in the center of the room covered with blood, but still alive. He sent one of the servants for a doctor, and another to the police-station to inform the superintendent. The doctor came immediately and declared that the woman was dying. He did everything that could be done for her, and presently she partially regained consciousness. The superintendent had by this time arrived, and in the presence of the doctor asked her who had injured her.

She seemed anxious to say something, but the effort was too much for her, and presently she relapsed into unconsciousness. She died two hours later, without speaking.

The woman's injuries had been inflicted with some heavy instrument. On making a search of the room the poker was found lying between the fireplace and the body. The poker was found to have blood upon it, and some hair from the unfortunate lady's head.

The servants stated that their master and mistress, Mr. and Mrs. Hannaford, had retired to rest at their usual time, shortly before midnight. The housemaid had seen them go up together. She had been working at a dress which she wanted for next Sunday, and sat up late, using her sewing-machine in the kitchen. It was one o'clock in the morning when she passed her master and mistress's door, and she judged by what she heard that they were quarreling. Mr. Hannaford was not in the house when the murder was discovered. The house was searched thoroughly in every direction, the first idea of the police being that he had committed suicide. The telegraph was then set to work, and at ten o'clock a man answering Mr. Hannaford's description was arrested at Paddington Station, where he was taking a ticket for Uxbridge.

Taken to the police-station and informed that he would be charged with murdering his wife, he appeared to be horrified, and for some time was a prey to the most violent emotion. When he had recovered himself and was made aware of the serious position in which he stood, he volunteered a statement. He was warned, but he insisted on making it. He declared that he and his wife had quarreled violently after they had retired to rest. Their quarrel was about a purely domestic matter but he was in an irritable, nervous condition, owing to his health, and at last he had worked himself up into such a state, that he had risen, dressed himself, and gone out into the street. That would be about two in the morning. He had wandered about in a state of nervous excitement until daybreak. At seven he had gone into a coffee-house and had breakfast, and had then gone into the park and sat on a seat and fallen asleep. When he woke up it was nine o'clock. He had taken a cab to Paddington, and had intended to go to Uxbridge to see his mother, who resided there. Quarrels between himself and his wife had been frequent of late, and he was ill and wanted to get away, and he thought perhaps if he went to his mother for a day or two he might get calmer and feel better. He had been

---

[6] A member of the London Stock Exchange who deals with brokers; today, he might be called a "trader" on the floor of the Exchange.

very much worried lately over business matters. He was a stockjobber,[6] and the market in the securities in which he had been speculating was against him.

At the conclusion of the statement, which was made in a nervous, excited manner, he broke down so completely that it was deemed desirable to send for the doctor and keep him under close observation.

Police investigation of the premises failed to find any further clue. Everything pointed to the supposition that the result of the quarrel had been an attack by the husband—possibly in a sudden fit of homicidal mania—on the unfortunate woman. The police suggestion was that the lady, terrified by her husband's behavior, had risen in the night and run down the stairs to the drawing-room, and that he had followed her there, picked up the poker, and furiously attacked her. When she fell, apparently lifeless, he had run back to his bedroom, dressed himself, and made his escape quietly from the house. There was nothing missing so far as could be ascertained—nothing to suggest in any way that any third party, a burglar from outside or some person inside, had had anything to do with the matter.

The coroner's jury brought in a verdict of willful murder, and the husband was charged before a magistrate and committed for trial. But in the interval his reason gave way, and, the doctors certifying that he was undoubtedly insane, he was sent to Broadmoor.

Nobody had the slightest doubt of his guilt, and it was his mother who, broken-hearted, and absolutely refusing to believe in her son's guilt, had come to Dorcas Dene and requested her to take up the case privately and

investigate it. The poor old lady declared that she was perfectly certain that her son could not have been guilty of such a deed, but the police were satisfied, and would make no further investigation.

This I learn afterward when I went to see Inspector Swanage. All I knew when I had finished reading up the case in the newspapers was that the husband of Mrs. Hannaford was in Broadmoor, practically condemned for the murder of his wife, and that Dorcas Dene had left home to try and prove his Innocence.

The history of the Hannafords as given in the public Press was as follows:

Mrs. Hannaford was a widow when Mr. Hannaford, a man of six-and-thirty, married her. Her first husband was a Mr. Charles Drayson, a financier, who had been among the victims of the fire at the Paris Opéra Comique.[7] His wife was with him in a loge that fatal night. When the fire broke out they both tried to escape together. They became separated in the crush. She was only slightly injured, and succeeded in getting out; he was less fortunate. His gold watch, a presentation one, with an inscription, was found among a mass of charred, unrecognizable remains when the ruins were searched.

Three years after this tragedy the widow married Mr. Hannaford. The death of her first husband did not leave her well off. It was found that he was heavily in debt, and had he lived a serious charge of fraud would undoubtedly have been preferred against him. As it was, his partner, a Mr. Thomas Holmes, was arrested and sentenced to five years' penal servitude in connection with a joint fraudulent transaction.

The estate of Mr. Drayson went to sat-

[7] A terrible fire on 24 May 1887 claimed the life of eighty-four victims by asphyxiation.

isfy the creditors, but Mrs. Drayson, the widow, retained the house at Haverstock Hill, which he had purchased and settled on her, with all the furniture and contents, some years previously. She wished to continue living in the house when she married again, and Mr. Hannaford consented, and they made it their home. Hannaford himself, though not a wealthy man, was a fairly successful stock-jobber, and until the crisis, which had brought on great anxiety and helped to break down his health, had had no financial worries. But the marriage, so it was alleged, had not been a very happy one and quarrels had been frequent. Old Mrs. Hannaford was against it from the first, and to her her son always turned in his later matrimonial troubles. Now that his life had probably been spared by this mental breakdown, and he had been sent to Broadmoor, she had but one object in life—to set her son free, some day restored to reason, and with his innocence proved to the world.

It was about a fortnight after my interview with Inspector Swanage, and my study of the details of the Haverstock Hill murder, that one morning I opened a telegram and to my intense delight found that it was from Dorcas Dene. It was from London, and informed me that in the evening they would be very pleased to see me at Oak Tree Road.

In the evening I presented myself about eight o'clock. Paul was alone in the drawing-room when I entered, but his face and his voice when he greeted me showed me plainly that he had benefited greatly by the change.

"Where have you been, to look so well?" I asked. "The South of Europe, I suppose—Nice or Monte Carlo?"

"No," said Paul smiling, "we haven't been nearly so far as that. But I mustn't tell tales out of school. You must ask Dorcas."

At that moment Dorcas came in and gave me a cordial greeting.

"Well," I said, after the first conversational preliminaries, "who committed the Haverstock Hill murder?"

"Oh, so you know that I have taken that up, do you? I imagined it would get about through the Yard people. You see, Paul dear, how wise I was to give out that I had gone away."

"Give out!" I exclaimed. "*Haven't* you been away then?"

"No, Paul and mother have been staying at Hastings, and I have been down whenever I have been able to spare a day, but as a matter of fact I have been in London the greater part of the time."

"But I don't see the use of your pretending you were going away."

"I did it on purpose. I knew the fact that old Mrs. Hannaford had engaged me would get about in certain circles, and I wanted certain people to think that I had gone away to investigate some clue which I thought I had discovered. In order to baulk all possible inquirers I didn't even let the servants forward my letters. They went to Jackson, who sent them on to me."

"Then you were really investigating in London?"

"Now shall I tell you where you heard that I was on this case?"

"Yes."

"You heard it at Kempton Park Steeplechases, and your informant was Inspector Swanage."

"You have seen him and he has told you."

"No; I saw you there talking to him."

"*You*, saw me? You were at Kempton Park? I never saw you."

"Yes, you did, for I caught you looking full at me. I was trying to sell some race cards just before the second race, and was holding them between the railings of the enclosure."

"What! You were that old gypsy woman? I'm certain Swanage didn't know you."

"I didn't want him to, or anybody else."

"It was an astonishing disguise. But come, aren't you going to tell me anything about the Hannaford case? I've been reading it up, but I fail entirely to see the slightest suspicion against anyone but the husband. Everything points to his having committed the crime in a moment of madness. The fact that he has since gone completely out of his mind seems to me to show that conclusively."

"It is a good job he did go out of his mind—but for that I am afraid he would have suffered for the crime, and the poor broken-hearted old mother for whom I am working would soon have followed him to the grave."

"Then you don't share the general belief in his guilt?"

"I did at first, but I don't now."

"You have discovered the guilty party?"

"No—not yet—but I hope to."

"Tell me exactly all that has happened—there may still be a chance for your 'assistant.'"

"Yes, it is quite possible that now I may be able to avail myself of your services. You say you have studied the details of this case—let us just run through them together, and see what you think of my plan of campaign so far as it has gone. When old Mrs. Hannaford came to me, her son had already been declared insane and unable to plead, and had gone to Broadmoor. That was nearly a month after the commission of the crime, so that much valuable time had been lost. At first I declined to take the matter up—the police had so thoroughly investigated the affair. The case seemed so absolutely conclusive that I told her that it would be useless for her to incur the heavy expense of a private investigation. But she pleaded so earnestly—her faith in her son was so great—and she seemed such a sweet, dear old lady, that at last she conquered my scruples, and I consented to study the case, and see if there was the slightest alternative theory to go on. I had almost abandoned hope, for there was nothing in the published reports to encourage it, when I determined to go to the fountain-head, and see the Superintendent who had had the case in hand.

"He received me courteously, and told me everything. He was certain that the husband committed the murder. There was an entire absence of motive for anyone else in the house to have done it, and the husband's flight from the house in the middle of the night was absolutely damning. I inquired if they had found anyone who had seen the husband in the street—anyone who could fix the time at which he had left the house. He replied that no such witness had been found.

"Then I asked if the policeman on duty that night had made any report of any suspicious characters being seen about. He said 'No,' the only person he had noticed at all was a man well known to the police—a man named Flash George. I asked what time Flash George had been seen and whereabouts, and I ascertained that it was at half past two in the morning, and about a hundred yards below the scene of the crime, that when the policeman spoke to him he said he was coming from Hampstead, and was going to Covent Garden Market. He walked away in the direction of the Chalk Farm Road. I inquired what Flash George's record was, and I ascertained that he was the associate of thieves and swindlers, and he was suspected of having disposed of some jewels, the proceeds of a robbery which had made a nine days' sensation. But the police had failed to bring the charge home to him, and the jewels had never been traced. He was also a gambler, a frequenter of racecourses and certain night-clubs of evil repute, and had not been seen about for some time previous to that evening."

"And didn't the police make any further investigations in that direction?"

"No. Why should they? There was nothing missing from the house—not the slightest sign of an attempted burglary. All their efforts were directed to proving the guilt of the unfortunate woman's husband."

"And you?"

"I had a different task—mine was to prove the husband's innocence. I determined to find out something more of Flash George. I shut the house up, gave out that I had gone away, and took, among other things, to selling cards and pencils on racecourses. The day that Flash George made his reappearance on the turf after a long absence was the day that he backed the winner of the second race at Kempton Park for a hundred pounds."

"But surely that proves that if he had been connected with any crime it must have been one in which money was obtained. No one has attempted to associate the murder of Mrs. Hannaford with robbery."

"No. But one thing is certain—that on the night of the crime Flash George was in the neighborhood. Two days previously he had borrowed a few pounds of a pal because he was 'stoney broke.' When he reappears as a racing man he has on a fur coat, is evidently in first class circumstances and he bets in hundred-pound notes. He is a considerably richer man after the murder of Mrs. Hannaford than he was before and he was seen within a hundred yards of the house at half-past two o'clock on the night that the crime was committed."

"That might have been a mere accident. His sudden wealth may be the result of a lucky gamble, or a swindle of which you know nothing. I can't see that it can possibly have any bearing on the Hannaford crime, because nothing was taken from the house."

"Quite true. But here is a remarkable fact. When he went up to the betting man he went to one who was betting close to the rails. When he pulled out that hundred-pound note I was at the rails, and I pushed my cards in between and asked him to buy one. Flash George is a 'suspected character,' and quite capable on a foggy day of trying to swindle a book-maker. The book-maker took the precaution to open that note, it being for a hundred pounds, and examined it carefully. That enabled me to see the number. I had sharpened pencils to sell, and with one of them I hastily took down the number of that note—135421."

"That was clever. And you have traced it?"

"Yes."

"And has that furnished you with any clue?"

"It has placed me in possession of a most remarkable fact. The hundred-pound note which was in Flash George's possession on Kempton Park racecourse was one of a number which were paid over the counter of the Union Bank of London for a five-thousand-pound check over seven years ago. And that check was drawn by the murdered woman's husband."

"Mr. Hannaford!"

"No; her first husband—Mr. Charles Drayson."

THE BROWN BEAR LAMP

When Dorcas Dene told me that the £100 note Flash George had handed to the bookmaker at Kempton Park was one which had some years previously been paid to Mr. Charles Drayson, the first husband of the murdered woman, Mrs. Hannaford, I had to sit still and think for a moment.

It was curious certainly, but after all much more remarkable coincidences than that occur daily. I could not see what practical value there was in Dorcas's extraordinary discovery, because Mr. Charles Drayson was dead, and it was hardly likely that his wife would have kept a £100 note of his for several years. And if she had, she had not been murdered for that, because there were no signs of the house having been broken into. The more I thought the business over the more confused I became in my attempt to establish a clue from it, and so after a minute's silence I frankly confessed to Dorcas that I didn't see where her discovery led to.

"I don't say that it leads very far by itself," said Dorcas. "But you must look at *all* the circumstances. During the night of January 5 a lady is murdered in her own drawing-room. Round about the time that the attack is supposed to have been made upon her a well-known bad character is seen close to the house. That person, who just previously has been ascertained to have been so hard up that he had been borrowing of his associates, reappears on the turf a few weeks later expensively dressed and in possession of money. He bets with a £100 note, and that £100 note I have traced to the previous possession of the murdered woman's first husband, who lost his life in the Opéra Comique disaster in Paris, while on a short visit to that capital."

"Yes, it certainly is curious, but—"

"Wait a minute—I haven't finished yet. Of the bank-notes—several of them for £100—which were paid some years ago to Mr. Charles Drayson, not one had come back to the bank *before* the murder."

"Indeed!"

"Since the murder *several* of them have come in. Now, is it not a remarkable circumstance that during all those years £5,000 worth of bank-notes should have remained out!"

"It is remarkable, but after all bank-notes circulate—they may pass through hundreds of hands before returning to the bank."

"Some may, undoubtedly, but it is highly improbable that *all* would under ordinary circumstances—especially notes for £100. These are sums which are not passed from pocket to pocket. As a rule they go to the bank of one of the early receivers of them, and from that bank into the Bank of England."

"You mean that it is an extraordinary fact that for many years not one of the notes paid to Mr. Charles Drayson by the Union Bank came back to the Bank of England."

"Yes, that *is* an extraordinary fact, but there is a fact which is more extraordinary still, and that is that soon after the murder of Mrs. Hannaford that state of things ceases. It looks as though the murderer had placed the notes in circulation again."

"It does, certainly. Have you traced back any of the other notes that have come in?"

"Yes; but they have been cleverly worked. They have nearly all been circulated in the betting ring; those that have not have come in from money changers in Paris and Rotterdam. My own belief is that before long the whole of those notes will come back to the bank."

"Then, my dear Dorcas, it seems to me that your course is plain, and you ought to go to the police and get them to get the bank to circulate a list of the notes."

Dorcas shook her head. "No, thank you," she said. "I'm going to carry this case through on my own account. The police are convinced that the murderer is Mr. Hannaford, who is at present in Broadmoor, and the bank has absolutely no reason to interfere. No question has been raised of the notes having been stolen. They were paid to the man who died over seven years ago, not to the woman who was murdered last January."

"But you have traced one note to Flash George, who is a bad lot, and he was near the house on the night of the tragedy. You suspect Flash George and—"

"I do not suspect Flash George of the actual murder," she said, "and I don't see how he is to be arrested for being in possession of a bank-note which forms no part of the police case, and which he might easily say he had received in the betting ring."

"Then what *are* you going to do?"

"Follow up the clue I have. I have been shadowing Flash George all the time I have been away. I know where he lives—I know who are his companions."

"And do you think the murderer is among them?"

"No. They are all a little astonished at his sudden good fortune. I have heard them 'chip' him, as they call it, on the subject. I have carried my investigations up to a certain point and there they stop short. I am going a step further tomorrow evening, and it is in that step that I want assistance."

"And you have come to me?" I said eagerly.
"Yes."

"What do you want me to do?"

"Tomorrow morning I am going to make a thorough examination of the room in which the murder was committed. Tomorrow evening I have to meet a gentleman of whom I know nothing but his career and his name. I want you to accompany me."

"Certainly; but if I am your assistant in the evening I shall expect to be your assistant in the morning—I should very much like to see the scene of the crime."

"I have no objection. The house on Haverstock Hill is at present shut up and in charge of a caretaker, but the solicitors who are managing the late Mrs. Hannaford's estate have given me permission to go over it and examine it."

The next day at eleven o'clock I met Dorcas outside Mrs. Hannaford's house, and the caretaker, who had received his instructions, admitted us. He was the gardener, and an old servant, and had been present during the police investigation.

The bedroom in which Mr. Hannaford and his wife slept on the fatal night was on the floor above. Dorcas told me to go upstairs, shut the door, lie down on the bed, and listen. Directly a noise in the room attracted my attention, I was to jump up, open the door and call out.

I obeyed her instructions and listened intently, but lying on the bed I heard nothing for a long time. It must have been quite a quarter of an hour when suddenly I heard a sound as of a door opening with a cracking sound. I leapt up, ran to the balusters,[1] and called over, "I heard that!"

"All right, then, come down," said Dorcas, who was standing in the hall with the caretaker.

_____
[1] The railing at the side of the staircase.

She explained to me that she had been moving about the drawing-room with the man, and they had both made as much noise with their feet as they could. They had even opened and shut the drawing-room door, but nothing had attracted my attention. Then Dorcas had sent the man to open the front door. It had opened with the cracking sound that I had heard.

"Now," said Dorcas to the caretaker, "you were here when the police were coming and going—did the front door always make a sound like that?"

"Yes, madam. The door had swollen or warped, or something, and it was always difficult to open. Mrs. Hannaford spoke about it once and was going to have it eased."

"That's it, then," said Dorcas to me. "The probability is that it was the noise made by the opening of that front door which first attracted the attention of the murdered woman."

"That was Hannaford going out—if his story is correct."

"No; Hannaford went out in a rage. He would pull the door open violently, and probably bang it to. That she would understand. It was when the door *opened again* with a sharp crack that she listened, thinking it was her husband come back."

"But she was murdered in the drawing-room?"

"Yes. My theory, therefore, is that after the opening of the front door she expected her husband to come upstairs. He didn't do so, and she concluded that he had gone into one of the rooms downstairs to spend the night, and she got up and came down to find him and ask him to get over his temper and come back to bed. She went into the drawing-room to see if he was there, and was struck down from behind before she had time to utter a cry. The servants heard nothing, remember."

"They said so at the inquest—yes."

"Now come into the drawing-room. This is where the caretaker tells me the body was found—here in the center of the room—the poker with which the fatal blow had been struck was lying between the body and the fireplace. The absence of a cry and the position of the body show that when Mrs. Hannaford opened the door she *saw no one* (I am of course presuming that the murderer was *not* her husband) and she came in further. But there must have been someone in the room or she couldn't have been murdered in it."

"That is indisputable; but he might not have been in the room at the time—the person might have been hiding in the hall and followed her in."

"To suppose that we must presume that the murderer came into the room, took the poker from the fireplace, and went out again in order to come in again. That poker was secured, I am convinced, when the intruder heard footsteps coming down the stairs. He picked up the poker then and concealed himself *here.*"

"Then why, my dear Dorcas, shouldn't he have remained concealed until Mrs. Hannaford had gone out of the room again?"

"I think she was turning to go when he rushed out and struck her down. He probably thought that she had heard the noise of the door, and might go and alarm the servants."

"But just now you said she came in believing that her husband had returned and was in one of the rooms."

"The intruder could hardly be in possession of *her thoughts.*"

"In the meantime he could have got out at the front door."

"Yes; but if his object was robbery he would have to go without the plunder. He struck the woman down in order to have time to get what he wanted."

"Then you think he left her here senseless while he searched the house?"

"Nobody got anything by searching the house, ma'am," broke in the caretaker. "The police satisfied themselves that nothing had been disturbed. Every door was locked, the plate was all complete, not a bit of jewelry or anything was missing. The servants were all examined about that, and the detectives went over every room and every cupboard to prove it wasn't no burglar broke in or anything of that sort. Besides, the windows were all fastened."

"What he says is quite true," said Dorcas to me, "but something alarmed Mrs. Hannaford in the night and brought her to the drawing-room in her nightdress. If it was as I suspect, the opening of the front door, that is how the guilty person got in."

The caretaker shook his head. "It was the poor master as did it, ma'am, right enough. He was out of his mind."

Dorcas shrugged her shoulders. "If he had done it, it would have been a furious attack, there would have been oaths and cries, and the poor lady would have received a rain of blows. The medical evidence shows that death resulted from *one* heavy blow on the *back* of the skull. But let us see where the murderer could have concealed himself ready armed with the poker here in the drawing-room."

In front of the drawing-room window were heavy curtains, and I at once suggested that curtains were the usual place of concealment on the stage and might be in real life.

As soon as I had asked the question

Dorcas turned to the caretaker. "You are certain that every article of furniture is in its place exactly as it was that night?"

"Yes; the police prepared a plan of the room for the trial, and since then by the solicitors' orders we have not touched a thing."

"That settles the curtains then," continued Dorcas. "Look at the windows for yourself. In front of one, close by the curtains, is an ornamental table covered with china and glass and bric-à-brac; and in front of the other a large settee. No man could have come from behind those curtains without shifting that furniture out of his way. That would have immediately attracted Mrs. Hannaford's attention and given her time to scream and rush out of the room. No, we must find some other place for the assassin. Ah!—I wonder if—"

Dorcas's eyes were fixed on a large brown bear which stood nearly against the wall near the fireplace. The bear, a very fine, big specimen, was supported in its upright position by an ornamental iron pole, at the top of which was fixed an oil lamp covered with a yellow silk shade.

"That's a fine bear lamp," exclaimed Dorcas.

"Yes," said the caretaker, "it's been here ever since I've been in the family's service. It was bought by the poor mistress's first husband, Mr. Drayson, and he thought a lot of it. But," he added, looking at it curiously, "I always thought it stood closer to the wall than that. It used to—right against it."

"Ah," exclaimed Dorcas, "that's interesting. Pull the curtains right back and give me all the light you can."

As the man obeyed her directions she went down on her hands and knees and examined the carpet carefully.

"You are right," she said. "This has been

moved a little forward, and not so very long ago—the carpet for a square of some inches is a different color to the rest. The brown bear stands on a square mahogany stand, and the exact square now shows in the color of the carpet that has been hidden by it. Only here is a discolored portion and the bear does not now stand on it."

The evidence of the bear having been moved forward from a position it had long occupied was indisputable. Dorcas got up and went to the door of the drawing-room.

"Go and stand behind that bear," she said. "Stand as compact as you can, as though you were endeavoring to conceal yourself."

I obeyed, and Dorcas, standing in the drawing-room doorway, declared that I was completely hidden.

"Now," she said, coming to the center of the room and turning her back to me, "reach down from where you are and see if you can pick up the shovel from the fireplace without making a noise."

I reached out carefully and had the shovel in my hand without making a sound.

"I have it," I said.

"That's right. The poker would have been on the same side as the shovel, and much easier to pick up quietly. Now, while my back is turned, grasp the shovel by the handle, leap out at me, and raise the shovel as if to hit me—but don't get excited and do it, because I don't want to realize the scene *too* completely."

I obeyed. My footsteps were scarcely heard on the heavy-pile drawing-room carpet. When Dorcas turned round the shovel was above her head ready to strike.

"Thank you for letting me off," she said, with a smile. Then her face becoming serious again, she exclaimed: "The murderer of Mrs.

Hannaford concealed himself behind that brown bear lamp, and attacked her in exactly the way I have indicated. But why had he moved the bear two or three inches forward?"

"To conceal himself behind it."

"Nonsense! His concealment was a sudden act. That bear is heavy—the glass chimney of the lamp would have rattled if it had been done violently and hurriedly while Mrs. Hannaford was coming downstairs—that would have attracted her attention and she would have called out, 'Who's there?' at the doorway, and not have come in looking about for her husband."

Dorcas looked the animal over carefully, prodded it with her fingers, and then went behind it.

After a minute or two's close examination, she uttered a little cry and called me to her side.

She had found in the back of the bear a small straight slit. This was quite invisible. She had only discovered it by an accidentally violent thrust of her fingers into the animal's fur. Into this slit she thrust her hand, and the aperture yielded sufficiently for her to thrust her arm in. The interior of the bear was hollow, but Dorcas's hand as it went down struck against a wooden bottom. Then she withdrew her arm and the aperture closed up. It had evidently been specially prepared as a place of concealment, and only the most careful examination would have revealed it

"Now," exclaimed Dorcas, triumphantly, "I think we are on a straight road! This, I believe, is where those missing bank-notes lay concealed for years. They were probably placed there by Mr. Drayson with the idea that some day his frauds might be discovered or he might be made a bankrupt. This was his little nest-egg, and his death in Paris before his fraud was discovered prevented him making use of them. Mrs. Hannaford evidently knew nothing of the hidden treasure, or she would speedily have removed it. But *someone* knew, and that someone put his knowledge to practical use the night that Mrs. Hannaford was murdered. The man who got in at the front door that night, got in to relieve the bear of its valuable stuffing; he moved the bear to get at the aperture, and was behind it when Mrs. Hannaford came in. The rest is easy to understand."

"But how did he get in at the front door?"

"That's what I have to find out. I am sure now that Flash George was in it. He was seen outside, and some of the notes that were concealed in the brown bear lamp have been traced to him. Who was Flash George's accomplice we may discover tonight. I think I have an idea, and if that is correct we shall have the solution of the whole mystery before dawn tomorrow morning."

"Why do you think you will learn so much tonight?"

"Because Flash George met a man two nights ago outside the Criterion. I was selling wax matches, and followed them up, pestering them. I heard George say to his companion, whom I had never seen with him before, 'Tell him Hungerford Bridge, midnight, Wednesday. Tell him to bring the lot and I'll cash up for them!' "

"And you think the 'him'—?"

"Is the man who rifled the brown bear and killed Mrs. Hannaford."

AT ELEVEN O'CLOCK That evening I met Dorcas Dene in Villiers Street. I knew what she would be like, otherwise her disguise would have completely baffled me. She was dressed as an Italian street musician, and was with a man who looked like an Italian organ-grinder.

Dorcas took my breath away by her first words.

"Allow me to introduce you," she said, "to Mr. Thomas Holmes. This is the gentleman who was Charles Drayson's partner, and was sentenced to five years' penal servitude over the partnership frauds."

"Yes," replied the organ-grinder in excellent English. "I suppose I deserved it for being a fool, but the villain was Drayson—he had all my money, and involved me in a fraud at the finish."

"I have told Mr. Holmes the story of our discovery," said Dorcas. "I have been in communication with him ever since I discovered the notes were in circulation. He knew Drayson's affairs, and he has given me some valuable information. He is with us tonight because he knew Mr. Drayson's former associates, and he may be able to identify the man who knew the secret of the house at Haverstock Hill."

"You think that is the man Flash George is to meet?"

"I do. What else can 'Tell him to bring the lot and I'll cash up' mean but the rest of the bank-notes?"

Shortly before twelve we got on to Hungerford Bridge—the narrow footway that runs across the Thames by the side of the railway.

I was to walk ahead and keep clear of the Italians until I heard a signal.

We crossed the bridge after that once or twice, I coming from one end and the Italians from the other, and passing each other about the center.

At five minutes to midnight I saw Flash George come slowly along from the Middlesex side. The Italians were not far behind. A minute later an old man with a grey beard, and wearing an old Inverness cape, passed me, coming from the Surrey side. When he met Flash George the two stopped and leant over the parapet, apparently interested in the river. Suddenly I heard Dorcas's signal. She began to sing the Italian song, "Santa Lucia."

I had my instructions. I jostled up against the two men and begged their pardon.

Flash George turned fiercely round. At the same moment I seized the old man and shouted for help. The Italians came hastily up. Several foot passengers rushed to the scene and inquired what was the matter.

"He was going to commit suicide," I cried. "He was just going to jump into the water."

The old man was struggling in my grasp. The crowd were keeping back Flash George. They believed the old man was struggling to get free to throw himself into the water.

The Italian rushed up to me.

"Ah, poor old man!" he said. "Don't let him get away!"

He gave a violent tug to the grey beard. It came off in his hands. Then with an oath he seized the supposed would-be suicide by the throat.

"You infernal villain!" he said.

"Who is he?" asked Dorcas.

"Who is he!" exclaimed Thomas Holmes, "why, the villain who brought me to ruin—*my precious partner—Charles Drayson!*"

As the words escaped from the supposed Italian's lips, Charles Drayson gave a cry of terror, and leaping on to the parapet, plunged into the river.

Flash George turned to run, but was stopped by a policeman who had just come up.

Dorcas whispered something in the man's ear, and the officer, thrusting his hand in the rascal's pocket, drew out a bundle of bank-notes.

A few minutes later the would-be suicide was brought ashore. He was still alive, but had injured himself terribly in his fall, and was taken to the hospital.

Before he died he was induced to confess that he had taken advantage of the Paris fire to disappear. He had flung his watch down in order that it might be found as evidence of his death. He had, previously to visiting the Opéra Comique, received a letter at his hotel which told him pretty plainly the game was up, and he knew that at any moment a warrant might be issued against him. After reading his name amongst the victims, he lived as best he could abroad, but after some years, being in desperate straits, he determined to do a bold thing, return to London and endeavor to get into his house and obtain possession of the money which was lying unsuspected in the interior of the brown bear lamp. He had concealed it, well knowing that at any time the crash might come, and everything belonging to him be seized. The hiding-place he had selected was one which neither his creditors nor his relatives would suspect.

On the night he entered the house, Flash George, whose acquaintance he had made in London, kept watch for him *while he let himself in with his latch-key*, which he had carefully preserved. Mr. Hannaford's leaving the house was one of those pieces of good fortune which occasionally favor the wicked. With his dying breath Charles Drayson declared that he had no intention of killing his wife. He feared that, having heard a noise, she had come to see what it was, and might alarm the house in her terror, and as she turned to go out of the drawing-room he struck her, intending only to render her senseless until he had secured the booty.

MR. HANNAFORD, completely recovered and in his right mind, was in due time released from Broadmoor. The letter from his mother to Dorcas Dene, thanking her for clearing her son's character and proving his innocence of the terrible crime for which he had been practically condemned, brought tears to my eyes as Dorcas read it aloud to Paul and myself. It was touching and beautiful to a degree.

As she folded it up and put it away, I saw that Dorcas herself was deeply moved.

"These are the *rewards* of my profession," she said. "They compensate for everything."

Arthur Conan Doyle

ARTHUR CONAN DOYLE wrote several mysteries that do not directly involve Sherlock Holmes. The following story first appeared in the *Strand Magazine* of July 1898, five years after Holmes was presumed lost at the Reichenbach Falls; it was later included in *Round the Fire Stories* (1908). Many speculate that the "celebrated criminal investigator" mentioned in the tale was Sherlock Holmes, writing from Tibet (where he found himself in 1892); others suggest that it was secretly his brother Mycroft. Some think that Dr. Watson himself investigated the case (and its companion, "The Lost Special," which appeared in the *Strand Magazine* the following month). The mystery of the identity of the detective remains unsolved.

THE MAN WITH THE WATCHES

ARTHUR CONAN DOYLE

THERE ARE MANY who will still bear in mind the singular circumstances which, under the heading of the Rugby Mystery,[1] filled many columns of the daily Press in the spring of the year 1892. Coming as it did at a period of exceptional dullness, it attracted perhaps rather more attention than it deserved, but it offered to the public that mixture of the whimsical and the tragic which is most stimulating to the popular imagination. Interest drooped, however, when, after weeks of fruitless investigation, it was found that no final explanation of the facts was forthcoming, and the tragedy seemed from that time to the present to have finally taken its place in the dark catalogue of inexplicable and unexpiated crimes. A recent communication (the authenticity of which appears to be above question) has, however, thrown some new and clear light upon the matter. Before laying it before the public it would be as well, perhaps, that I should refresh their memories as to the singular facts upon which this commentary is founded. These facts were briefly as follows:

At five o'clock on the evening of the 18th of March in the year already mentioned a train left Euston Station for Manchester. It was a rainy, squally day, which grew wilder as it progressed, so it was by no means the weather in which anyone would travel who was not driven to do so by necessity. The train, however, is a favorite one among Manchester business men who are returning from town, for it does the journey in four hours and twenty minutes, with only three stoppages upon the way. In spite of the inclement evening it was, therefore, fairly well filled upon the occasion of which I speak. The guard of the train was a tried servant of the company—a man who had worked for twenty-two years without a blemish or complaint. His name was John Palmer.

The station clock was upon the stroke of

---

[1] A town in Warwickshire, England, celebrated for its public school that was the setting for the classic *Tom Brown's Schooldays* by Thomas Hughes (1857). The sport of Rugby-style football, now commonly known as Rugby, originated at the school.

five, and the guard was about to give the customary signal to the engine-driver when he observed two belated passengers hurrying down the platform. The one was an exceptionally tall man, dressed in a long black overcoat with astrakhan collar and cuffs. I have already said that the evening was an inclement one, and the tall traveler had the high, warm collar turned up to protect his throat against the bitter March wind. He appeared, as far as the guard could judge by so hurried an inspection, to be a man between fifty and sixty years of age, who had retained a good deal of the vigor and activity of his youth. In one hand he carried a brown leather Gladstone bag.[2] His companion was a lady, tall and erect, walking with a vigorous step which outpaced the gentleman beside her. She wore a long, fawn-colored dust-cloak, a black, close-fitting toque, and a dark veil which concealed the greater part of her face. The two might very well have passed as father and daughter. They walked swiftly down the line of carriages, glancing in at the windows, until the guard, John Palmer, overtook them.

"Now then, sir, look sharp, the train is going," said he.

"First-class," the man answered.

The guard turned the handle of the nearest door. In the carriage which he had opened, there sat a small man with a cigar in his mouth. His appearance seems to have impressed itself upon the guard's memory, for he was prepared, afterward, to describe or to identify him. He was a man of thirty-four or thirty-five years of age, dressed in some grey material, sharp-nosed, alert, with a ruddy, weather-beaten face, and a small, closely cropped, black beard. He glanced up as the door was opened. The

tall man paused with his foot upon the step.

"This is a smoking compartment. The lady dislikes smoke," said he, looking round at the guard.

"All right! Here you are, sir!" said John Palmer. He slammed the door of the smoking carriage, opened that of the next one, which was empty, and thrust the two travelers in. At the same moment he sounded his whistle and the wheels of the train began to move. The man with the cigar was at the window of his carriage, and said something to the guard as he rolled past him, but the words were lost in the bustle of the departure. Palmer stepped into the guard's van, as it came up to him, and thought no more of the incident.

Twelve minutes after its departure the train reached Willesden Junction, where it stopped for a very short interval. An examination of the tickets has made it certain that no one either joined or left it at this time, and no passenger was seen to alight upon the platform. At 5:14 the journey to Manchester was resumed, and Rugby was reached at 6:50, the express being five minutes late.

At Rugby the attention of the station officials was drawn to the fact that the door of one of the first-class carriages was open. An examination of that compartment, and of its neighbor, disclosed a remarkable state of affairs.

The smoking carriage in which the short, red-faced man with the black beard had been seen was now empty. Save for a half-smoked cigar, there was no trace whatever of its recent occupant. The door of this carriage was fastened. In the next compartment, to which attention had been originally drawn, there was no sign either of the gentleman with the

---

[2] A traveling bag or small portmanteau, opening out flat, named after W. E. Gladstone, Prime Minister of England.

astrakhan collar or of the young lady who accompanied him. All three passengers had disappeared. On the other hand, there was found upon the floor of this carriage—the one in which the tall traveler and the lady had been—a young man fashionably dressed and of elegant appearance. He lay with his knees drawn up, and his head resting against the farther door, an elbow upon either seat. A bullet had penetrated his heart and his death must have been instantaneous. No one had seen such a man enter the train, and no railway ticket was found in his pocket, neither were there any markings upon his linen, nor papers nor personal property which might help to identify him. Who he was, whence he had come, and how he had met his end were each as great a mystery as what had occurred to the three people who had started an hour and a half before from Willesden in those two compartments.

I have said that there was no personal property which might help to identify him, but it is true that there was one peculiarity about this unknown young man which was much commented upon at the time. In his pockets were found no fewer than six valuable gold watches, three in the various pockets of his waist-coat, one in his ticket-pocket, one in his breast-pocket, and one small one set in a leather strap and fastened round his left wrist. The obvious explanation that the man was a pickpocket, and that this was his plunder, was discounted by the fact that all six were of American make and of a type which is rare in England. Three of them bore the mark of the Rochester Watchmaking Company; one

was by Mason, of Elmira; one was unmarked; and the small one, which was highly jeweled and ornamented, was from Tiffany, of New York.[3] The other contents of his pocket consisted of an ivory knife with a corkscrew by Rodgers, of Sheffield; a small, circular mirror, one inch in diameter; a readmission slip to the Lyceum Theatre; a silver box full of vesta matches,[4] and a brown leather cigar-case containing two cheroots—also two pounds fourteen shillings in money. It was clear, then, that whatever motives may have led to his death, robbery was not among them. As already mentioned, there were no markings upon the man's linen, which appeared to be new, and no tailor's name upon his coat. In appearance he was young, short, smooth-cheeked, and delicately featured. One of his front teeth was conspicuously stopped with gold.

On the discovery of the tragedy an examination was instantly made of the tickets of all passengers, and the number of the passengers themselves was counted. It was found that only three tickets were unaccounted for, corresponding to the three travellers who were missing. The express was then allowed to proceed, but a new guard was sent with it, and John Palmer was detained as a witness at Rugby. The carriage which included the two compartments in question was uncoupled and side-tracked. Then, on the arrival of Inspector Vane, of Scotland Yard, and of Mr. Henderson, a detective in the service of the railway company, an exhaustive inquiry was made into all the circumstances.

That crime had been committed was

---

[3] Tiffany & Co. was founded in 1837, and by the 1860s and 1870s, "Tiffany Timers" were the preferred timepiece of numerous well-known public figures, including Vanderbilt, Morgan, Whitney, Astor, and President Ulysses S. Grant.

[4] Short matches, with shanks of thin wax tapers. In Roman mythology, Vesta was the goddess of the hearth; she was assisted by the Vestal Virgins in assuring that the sacred fire never went out.

certain. The bullet, which appeared to have come from a small pistol or revolver, had been fired from some little distance, as there was no scorching of the clothes. No weapon was found in the compartment (which finally disposed of the theory of suicide), nor was there any sign of the brown leather bag which the guard had seen in the hand of the tall gentleman. A lady's parasol was found upon the rack, but no other trace was to be seen of the travelers in either of the sections. Apart from the crime, the question of how or why three passengers (one of them a lady) could get out of the train, and one other get in during the unbroken run between Willesden and Rugby, was one which excited the utmost curiosity among the general public, and gave rise to much speculation in the London Press.

John Palmer, the guard, was able at the inquest to give some evidence which threw a little light upon the matter. There was a spot between Tring and Cheddington, according to his statement, where, on account of some repairs to the line, the train had for a few minutes slowed down to a pace not exceeding eight or ten miles an hour. At that place it might be possible for a man, or even for an exceptionally active woman, to have left the train without serious injury. It was true that a gang of platelayers[5] was there, and that they had seen nothing, but it was their custom to stand in the middle between the metals, and the open carriage door was upon the far side, so that it was conceivable that someone might have alighted unseen, as the darkness would by that time be drawing in. A steep embankment would instantly screen anyone who sprang out from the observation of the navvies.[6]

The guard also deposed that there was a good deal of movement upon the platform at Willesden Junction, and that though it was certain that no one had either joined or left the train there, it was still quite possible that some of the passengers might have changed unseen from one compartment to another. It was by no means uncommon for a gentleman to finish his cigar in a smoking carriage and then to change to a clearer atmosphere. Supposing that the man with the black beard had done so at Willesden (and the half-smoked cigar upon the floor seemed to favor the supposition), he would naturally go into the nearest section, which would bring him into the company of the two other actors in this drama. Thus the first stage of the affair might be surmised without any great breach of probability. But what the second stage had been, or how the final one had been arrived at, neither the guard nor the experienced detective officers could suggest.

A careful examination of the line between Willesden and Rugby resulted in one discovery which might or might not have a bearing upon the tragedy. Near Tring, at the very place where the train slowed down, there was found at the bottom of the embankment a small pocket Testament, very shabby and worn. It was printed by the Bible Society of London, and bore an inscription: "From John to Alice. Jan. 13th, 1856," upon the fly-leaf. Underneath was written: "James. July 4th, 1859," and beneath that again: "Edward. Nov. 1st, 1869," all the entries being in the same handwriting. This was the only clue, if it could be called a clue, which the police obtained, and the coroner's verdict of "Murder by a person or persons unknown" was the unsatisfactory ending of a singular case. Advertisement, rewards, and inquiries proved equally fruitless, and nothing could be found which was solid enough

---

[5] A workman employed to lay rails.
[6] Laborers.

to form the basis for a profitable investigation.

It would be a mistake, however, to suppose that no theories were formed to account for the facts. On the contrary, the Press, both in England and in America, teemed with suggestions and suppositions, most of which were obviously absurd. The fact that the watches were of American make, and some peculiarities in connection with the gold stopping of his front tooth, appeared to indicate that the deceased was a citizen of the United States, though his linen, clothes and boots were undoubtedly of British manufacture. It was surmised, by some, that he was concealed under the seat, and that, being discovered, he was for some reason, possibly because he had overheard their guilty secrets, put to death by his fellow-passengers. When coupled with generalities as to the ferocity and cunning of anarchical and other secret societies, this theory sounded as plausible as any.

The fact that he should be without a ticket would be consistent with the idea of concealment, and it was well known that women played a prominent part in the Nihilistic propaganda.[7] On the other hand, it was clear, from the guard's statement, that the man must have been hidden there *before* the others arrived, and how unlikely the coincidence that conspirators should stray exactly into the very compartment in which a spy was

already concealed! Besides, this explanation ignored the man in the smoking carriage, and gave no reason at all for his simultaneous disappearance. The police had little difficulty in showing that such a theory would not cover the facts, but they were unprepared in the absence of evidence to advance any alternative explanation.

There was a letter in the *Daily Gazette*,[8] over the signature of a well-known criminal investigator,[9] which gave rise to considerable discussion at the time. He had formed a hypothesis which had at least ingenuity to recommend it, and I cannot do better than append it in his own words.

"Whatever may be the truth," said he, "it must depend upon some bizarre and rare combination of events, so we need have no hesitation in postulating such events in our explanation. In the absence of data we must abandon the analytic or scientific method of investigation, and must approach it in the synthetic fashion. In a word, instead of taking known events and deducing from them what has occurred, we must build up a fanciful explanation if it will only be consistent with known events. We can then test this explanation by any fresh facts which may arise. If they all fit into their places, the probability is that we are upon the right track, and with each fresh fact this probability increases in a geo-

---

[7] Nihilists were dedicated to the rejection of aestheticism and the destruction of the existing social order; they loathed ignorance and trusted only in the pursuit of scientific knowledge. Admission to a train without a ticket would, by the uneducated, be seen as a typical nihilistic act, a rejection of authority. The convergence of nihilist approval of scientific knowledge and an increased consciousness of women's education and rights led to many women, especially in Russia, seeking a scientific education. Russian women were among the first to receive doctorates in medicine, chemistry, mathematics, zoology, and related sciences. Of course, women who rejected prevailing social values, such as the "New Women" and the Suffragettes, would be tarred as "nihilists" in the press.

[8] A fictitious newspaper.

[9] The question of the identity of the "well-known criminal investigator" has long been debated by students of Sherlock Holmes and Doyle. Many assert that the letters were written by Holmes himself; others have suggested that Dr. Watson filled in for Holmes, while still others suggest Holmes's brother Mycroft. Some have even daringly suggested that Arthur Conan Doyle himself wrote the letters!

metrical progression until the evidence becomes final and convincing.

"Now, there is one most remarkable and suggestive fact which has not met with the attention which it deserves. There is a local train running through Harrow and King's Langley, which is timed in such a way that the express must have overtaken it at or about the period when it eased down its speed to eight miles an hour on account of the repairs of the line. The two trains would at that time be traveling in the same direction at a similar rate of speed and upon parallel lines. It is within every one's experience how, under such circumstances, the occupant of each carriage can see very plainly the passengers in the other carriages opposite to him. The lamps of the express had been lit at Willesden, so that each compartment was brightly illuminated, and most visible to an observer from outside.

"Now, the sequence of events as I reconstruct them would be after this fashion. This young man with the abnormal number of watches was alone in the carriage of the slow train. His ticket, with his papers and gloves and other things, was, we will suppose, on the seat beside him. He was probably an American, and also probably a man of weak intellect. The excessive wearing of jewelry is an early symptom in some forms of mania.[10]

"As he sat watching the carriages of the express which were (on account of the state of the line) going at the same pace as himself, he suddenly saw some people in it whom he knew. We will suppose for the sake of our theory that these people were a woman whom he loved and a man whom he hated—and who in return hated him. The young man was excitable and impulsive. He opened the door of his carriage, stepped from the footboard of the local train to the footboard of the express, opened the other door, and made his way into the presence of these two people. The feat (on the supposition that the trains were going at the same pace) is by no means so perilous as it might appear.

"Having now got our young man, without his ticket, into the carriage in which the elder man and the young woman are traveling, it is not difficult to imagine that a violent scene ensued. It is possible that the pair were also Americans, which is the more probable as the man carried a weapon—an unusual thing in England. If our supposition of incipient mania is correct, the young man is likely to have assaulted the other. As the upshot of the quarrel the elder man shot the intruder, and then made his escape from the carriage, taking the young lady with him. We will suppose that all this happened very rapidly, and that the train was still going at so slow a pace that it was not difficult for them to leave it. A woman might leave a train going at eight miles an hour. As a matter of fact, we know that this woman *did* do so.

"And now we have to fit in the man in the smoking carriage. Presuming that we have, up to this point, reconstructed the tragedy correctly, we shall find nothing in this other man to cause us to reconsider our conclusions. According to my theory, this man saw the young fellow cross from one train to the other, saw him open the door, heard the pistol-shot, saw the two fugitives spring out on to the line, realized that murder had been done, and sprang out himself in pursuit. Why he has never been heard of since—whether he met his own death

[10] Modern psychologists associate excessive jewelry with the manic phase of bipolar disorder (a condition with which at least one scholar diagnoses Sherlock Holmes). Another interpretation is that the "mania" referred to here is transvestism; numerous points in the tale support this thesis.

in the pursuit, or whether, as is more likely, he was made to realize that it was not a case for his interference—is a detail which we have at present no means of explaining. I acknowledge that there are some difficulties in the way. At first sight, it might seem improbable that at such a moment a murderer would burden himself in his flight with a brown leather bag. My answer is that he was well aware that if the bag were found his identity would be established. It was absolutely necessary for him to take it with him. My theory stands or falls upon one point, and I call upon the railway company to make strict inquiry as to whether a ticket was found unclaimed in the local train through Harrow and King's Langley upon the 18th of March. If such a ticket were found my case is proved. If not, my theory may still be the correct one, for it is conceivable either that he traveled without a ticket or that his ticket was lost."

To this elaborate and plausible hypothesis the answer of the police and of the company was, first, that no such ticket was found; secondly, that the slow train would never run parallel to the express; and, thirdly, that the local train had been stationary in King's Langley Station when the express, going at fifty miles an hour, had flashed past it. So perished the only satisfying explanation, and five years have elapsed without supplying a new one. Now, at last, there comes a statement which covers all the facts, and which must be regarded as authentic. It took the shape of a letter dated from New York, and addressed to the same criminal investigator whose theory I have quoted. It is given here in extenso, with

the exception of the two opening paragraphs, which are personal in their nature:

"You'll excuse me if I'm not very free with names. There's less reason now than there was five years ago when mother was still living. But for all that, I had rather cover up our tracks all I can. But I owe you an explanation, for if your idea of it was wrong, it was a mighty ingenious one all the same. I'll have to go back a little so as you may understand all about it.

"My people came from Bucks, England, and emigrated to the States in the early fifties. They settled in Rochester, in the State of New York, where my father ran a large dry goods store. There were only two sons: myself, James, and my brother, Edward. I was ten years older than my brother, and after my father died I sort of took the place of a father to him, as an elder brother would. He was a bright, spirited boy, and just one of the most beautiful creatures that ever lived. But there was always a soft spot in him, and it was like mold in cheese, for it spread and spread, and nothing that you could do would stop it. Mother saw it just as clearly as I did, but she went on spoiling him all the same, for he had such a way with him that you could refuse him nothing. I did all I could to hold him in, and he hated me for my pains.

"At last he fairly got his head, and nothing that we could do would stop him. He got off into New York, and went rapidly from bad to worse. At first he was only fast, and then he was criminal; and then, at the end of a year or two, he was one of the most notorious young crooks in the city. He had formed a friendship with Sparrow MacCoy, who was at

[11] Bunco, originally a card game, became a gambling pastime in the 19th century, and eventually referred to all kinds of swindles. A "bunco-steerer" was a confidence man who inveigled intended victims into the confidence game at hand.

[12] A "green-goodsman" was a slang reference to a forger who passes bad currency, "greenbacks."

the head of his profession as a bunco-steerer,[11] green goodsman[12] and general rascal. They took to card-sharping, and frequented some of the best hotels in New York. My brother was an excellent actor (he might have made an honest name for himself if he had chosen), and he would take the parts of a young Englishman of title, of a simple lad from the West, or of a college undergraduate, whichever suited Sparrow MacCoy's purpose. And then one day he dressed himself as a girl, and he carried it off so well, and made himself such a valuable decoy, that it was their favorite game afterward. They had made it right with Tammany[13] and with the police, so it seemed as if nothing could ever stop them, for those were in the days before the Lexow Commission,[14] and if you only had a pull, you could do pretty nearly everything you wanted.

"And nothing would have stopped them if they had only stuck to cards and New York, but they must needs come up Rochester way, and forge a name upon a check. It was my brother that did it, though everyone knew that it was under the influence of Sparrow Mac-Coy. I bought up that check, and a pretty sum it cost me. Then I went to my brother, laid it before him on the table, and swore to him that I would prosecute if he did not clear out of the country. At first he simply laughed. I could not prosecute, he said, without breaking our mother's heart, and he knew that I would not do that. I made him understand, however, that our mother's heart was being broken in any case, and that I had set firm on the point that

I would rather see him in Rochester gaol than in a New York hotel. So at last he gave in, and he made me a solemn promise that he would see Sparrow MacCoy no more, that he would go to Europe, and that he would turn his hand to any honest trade that I helped him to get. I took him down right away to an old family friend, Joe Willson, who is an exporter of American watches and clocks, and I got him to give Edward an agency in London, with a small salary and a fifteen percent commission on all business. His manner and appearance were so good that he won the old man over at once, and within a week he was sent off to London with a case full of samples.

"It seemed to me that this business of the check had really given my brother a fright, and that there was some chance of his settling down into an honest line of life. My mother had spoken with him, and what she said had touched him, for she had always been the best of mothers to him and he had been the great sorrow of her life. But I knew that this man Sparrow MacCoy had a great influence over Edward and my chance of keeping the lad straight lay in breaking the connection between them. I had a friend in the New York detective force, and through him I kept a watch upon MacCoy. When, within a fortnight of my brother's sailing, I heard that MacCoy had taken a berth in the *Etruria*, I was as certain as if he had told me that he was going over to England for the purpose of coaxing Edward back again into the ways that he had left. In an instant I had resolved to go

---

[13] Tammany Hall was the Democratic Party political machine that played a major role in controlling New York City politics from the 1790s to the 1960s. It was associated in mid-19th century with "Boss" Tweed and other corrupt politicians, although in 1901, the Tammany forces were unable to prevent the election of a reformer to the position of mayor.

[14] The Lexow Commission on Criminal and Political Corruption (1894-1895), chaired by State Senator Clarence Lexow, investigated New York City police and government and disclosed massive institutionalized and routinized payoffs of politicians and police officials.

also, and to pit my influence against Mac-Coy's. I knew it was a losing fight, but I thought, and my mother thought, that it was my duty. We passed the last night together in prayer for my success, and she gave me her own Testament that my father had given her on the day of their marriage in the Old Country, so that I might always wear it next my heart.

"I was a fellow-traveler, on the steamship, with Sparrow MacCoy, and at least I had the satisfaction of spoiling his little game for the voyage. The very first night I went into the smoking-room, and found him at the head of a card-table, with a half a dozen young fellows who were carrying their full purses and their empty skulls over to Europe. He was settling down for his harvest, and a rich one it would have been. But I soon changed all that.

" 'Gentlemen,' said I, 'are you aware whom you are playing with?'

" 'What's that to you? You mind your own business!' said he, with an oath.

" 'Who is it, anyway?' asked one of the dudes.

" 'He's Sparrow MacCoy, the most notorious card-sharper in the States.'

"Up he jumped with a bottle in his hand, but he remembered that he was under the flag of the effete Old Country, where law and order run, and Tammany has no pull. Gaol and the gallows wait for violence and murder, and there's no slipping out by the back door on board an ocean liner.

" 'Prove your words, you—!' said he.

" 'I will!' said I. 'If you will turn up your right shirt-sleeve to the shoulder, I will either prove my words or I will eat them.'

"He turned white and said not a word. You see, I knew something of his ways, and I was aware of that part of the mechanism which he and all such sharpers use consists of an elastic down the arm with a clip just above the wrist. It is by means of this clip that they withdraw from their hands the cards which they do not want, while they substitute other cards from another hiding place. I reckoned on it being there, and it was.[15] He cursed me, slunk out of the saloon, and was hardly seen again during the voyage. For once, at any rate, I got level with Mister Sparrow MacCoy.

"But he soon had his revenge upon me, for when it came to influencing my brother he outweighed me every time. Edward had kept himself straight in London for the first few weeks, and had done some business with his American watches, until this villain came across his path once more. I did my best, but the best was little enough. The next thing I heard there had been a scandal at one of the Northumberland Avenue hotels: a traveler had been fleeced of a large sum by two confederate card-sharpers, and the matter was in the hands of Scotland Yard. The first I learned of it was in the evening paper, and I was at once certain that my brother and MacCoy were back at their old games. I hurried at once to Edward's lodgings. They told me that he and a tall gentleman (whom I recognized as MacCoy) had gone off together, and that he had left the lodgings and taken his things with him. The landlady had heard them give several directions to the cabman, ending with Euston Station, and she had accidentally overheard the tall gentleman saying some-

---

[15] The mechanism in question is known as a holdout device and came in many varieties in the nineteenth century. This particular version seems to be the type known as a "bean shooter"; the clip (known as a "thief") could be attached to a card, the card allowed to travel up a sleeve. All were designed to allow the cheating gambler to remove and "hold out" an extra card, to be added to a hand (usually a poker hand) when needed.

thing about Manchester. She believed that that was their destination.

"A glance at the time-table showed me that the most likely train was at five, though there was another at 4:35 which they might have caught. I had only time to get the later one, but found no sign of them either at the depot or in the train. They must have gone on by the earlier one, so I determined to follow them to Manchester and search for them in the hotels there. One last appeal to my brother by all that he owed to my mother might even now be the salvation of him. My nerves were overstrung, and I lit a cigar to steady them. At that moment, just as the train was moving off, the door of my compartment was flung open, and there were MacCoy and my brother on the platform.

"They were both disguised, and with good reason, for they knew that the London police were after them. MacCoy had a great astrakhan collar drawn up, so that only his eyes and nose were showing. My brother was dressed like a woman, with a black veil half down his face, but of course it did not deceive me for an instant, nor would it have done so even if I had not known that he had often used such a dress before. I started up, and as I did so MacCoy recognized me. He said something, the conductor slammed the door, and they were shown into the next compartment. I tried to stop the train so as to follow them, but the wheels were already moving, and it was too late.

"When we stopped at Willesden, I instantly changed my carriage. It appears that I was not seen to do so, which is not surprising, as the station was crowded with people. Mac-Coy, of course, was expecting me, and he had spent the time between Euston and Willesden in saying all he could to harden my brother's heart and set him against me. That is what I fancy, for I had never found him so

impossible to soften or to move. I tried this way and I tried that; I pictured his future in an English gaol; I described the sorrow of his mother when I came back with the news; I said everything to touch his heart, but all to no purpose. He sat there with a fixed sneer upon his handsome face, while every now and then Sparrow MacCoy would throw in a taunt at me, or some word of encouragement to hold my brother to his resolutions.

" 'Why don't you run a Sunday-school?' he would say to me, and then, in the same breath: 'He thinks you have no will of your own. He thinks you are just the baby brother and that he can lead you where he likes. He's only just finding out that you are a man as well as he.'

"It was those words of his which set me talking bitterly. We had left Willesden, you understand, for all this took some time. My temper got the better of me, and for the first time in my life I let my brother see the rough side of me. Perhaps it would have been better had I done so earlier and more often.

" 'A man!' said I. 'Well, I'm glad to have your friend's assurance of it, for no one would suspect it to see you like a boarding-school missy. I don't suppose in all this country there is a more contemptible-looking creature than you are as you sit there with that Dolly pinafore[16] upon you.' He colored up at that, for he was a vain man, and he winced from ridicule.

" 'It's only a dust-cloak,' said he, and he slipped it off. 'One has to throw the coppers off one's scent, and I had no other way to do it.' He took his toque off with the veil attached, and he put both it and the cloak into his brown bag. 'Anyway, I don't need to wear it until the conductor comes round,' said he.

" 'Nor then, either,' said I, and taking the

16 A girl's dress.

bag I slung it with all my force out of the window. 'Now,' said I, 'you'll never make a Mary Jane[17] of yourself while I can help it. If nothing but that disguise stands between you and a gaol, then to gaol you shall go.'

"That was the way to manage him. I felt my advantage at once. His supple nature was one which yielded to roughness far more readily than to entreaty. He flushed with shame, and his eyes filled with tears. But MacCoy saw my advantage also, and was determined that I should not pursue it.

" 'He's my pard, and you shall not bully him,' he cried.

" 'He's my brother, and you shall not ruin him,' said I. 'I believe a spell of prison is the very best way of keeping you apart, and you shall have it, or it will be no fault of mine.'

" 'Oh, you would squeal, would you?' he cried, and in an instant he whipped out his revolver. I sprang for his hand, but saw that I was too late, and jumped aside. At the same instant he fired, and the bullet which would have struck me passed through the heart of my unfortunate brother.

"He dropped without a groan upon the floor of the compartment, and MacCoy and I, equally horrified, knelt at each side of him, trying to bring back some signs of life. MacCoy still held the loaded revolver in his hand, but his anger against me and my resentment toward him had both for the moment been swallowed up in this sudden tragedy. It was he who first realized the situation. The train was for some reason going very slowly at the moment, and he saw his opportunity for escape. In an instant he had the door open, but I was as quick as he, and jumping upon him the two of us fell off the footboard and rolled in each other's arms down a steep embankment. At the bottom I struck my head against a stone, and I remembered nothing more. When I came to myself I was lying among some low bushes, not far from the railroad track, and somebody was bathing my head with a wet handkerchief. It was Sparrow MacCoy.

" 'I guess I couldn't leave you,' said he. 'I didn't want to have the blood of two of you on my hands in one day. You loved your brother, I've no doubt; but you didn't love him a cent more than I loved him, though you'll say that I took a queer way to show it. Anyhow, it seems a mighty empty world now that he is gone, and I don't care a continental whether you give me over to the hangman or not.'

"He had turned his ankle in the fall, and there we sat, he with his useless foot, and I with my throbbing head, and we talked and talked until gradually my bitterness began to soften and to turn into something like sympathy. What was the use of revenging his death upon a man who was as much stricken by that death as I was? And then, as my wits gradually returned, I began to realize also that I could do nothing against MacCoy which would not recoil upon my mother and myself. How could we convict him without a full account of my brother's career being made public—the very thing which of all others we wished to avoid? It was really as much our interest as his to cover the matter up, and from being an avenger of crime I found myself changed to a conspirator against Justice. The place in which we found ourselves was one of those pheasant preserves which are so common in the Old Country, and as we groped

---

[17] "Mary Jane" was a common name applied to household servants, and *Mary Jane's Memoirs* (1887) was a popular "yellow back" novel by George R. Sims purporting to be the memoirs of a housemaid.

our way through it I found myself consulting the slayer of my brother as to how far it would be possible to hush it up.

"I soon realized from what he said that unless there were some papers of which we knew nothing in my brother's pockets, there was really no possible means by which the police could identify him or learn how he had got there. His ticket was in MacCoy's pocket, and so was the ticket for some baggage which they had left at the depot. Like most Americans, he had found it cheaper and easier to buy an outfit in London than to bring one from New York, so that all his linen and clothes were new and unmarked. The bag, containing the dust-cloak, which I had thrown out of the window, may have fallen among some bramble patch where it is still concealed, or may have been carried off by some tramp, or may have come into the possession of the police, who kept the incident to themselves. Anyhow, I have seen nothing about it in the London papers. As to the watches, they were a selection from those which had been entrusted to him for business purposes. It may have been for the same business purposes that he was taking them to Manchester, but—well, it's too late to enter into that.

"I don't blame the police for being at fault. I don't see how it could have been otherwise. There was just one little clue that they might have followed up, but it was a small one. I mean that small, circular mirror which was found in my brother's pocket. It isn't a very common thing for a young man to carry about with him, is it? But a gambler might have told you what such a mirror may mean to a card-sharper. If you sit back a little from the table, and lay the mirror, face up-wards, upon your lap, you can see, as you deal, every card that you give to your adversary.[18] It is not hard to say whether you see a man or raise him when you know his cards as well as your own. It was as much a part of a sharper's outfit as the elastic clip upon Sparrow Mac-Coy's arm. Taking that, in connection with the recent frauds at the hotels, the police might have got hold of one end of the string.

"I don't think there is much more for me to explain. We got to a village called Amer-sham that night in the character of two gentlemen upon a walking tour, and afterward we made our way quietly to London, whence MacCoy went on to Cairo and I returned to New York. My mother died six months afterward, and I am glad to say that to the day of her death she never knew what happened. She was always under the delusion that Edward was earning an honest living in London, and I never had the heart to tell her the truth. He never wrote; but, then, he never did write at any time, so that made no difference. His name was the last upon her lips.

"There's just one other thing that I have to ask you, sir, and I should take it as a kind return for all this explanation, if you could do it for me. You remember that Testament that was picked up. I always carried it in my inside pocket, and it must have come out in my fall. I value it very highly, for it was the family book with my birth and my brother's marked by my father in the beginning of it. I wish you would apply at the proper place and have it sent to me. It can be of no possible value to anyone else. If you address it to X, Bassano's Library, Broadway, New York, it is sure to come to hand."

---

[18] The mirror was a common card-sharper's tool in the nineteenth century and was known variously as a "shiner," a "glim," a "reflector," a "light," or a "flick."

Rodriguez Ottolengui

RODRIGUEZ OTTOLENGUI (1861-1937) was an American writer of Sephardic descent; he was also a pioneer of American dentistry. He was the editor of *Items of Interest: A Monthly Magazine of Dental Art, Science, and Literature* for thirty-five years. Ottolengui wrote four novels and several short stories, but his fiction remained largely unappreciated. His collection *Final Proof* (1898) merited the attention of Ellery Queen in his *Queen's Quorum*. It was the third outing for his two rival criminologists—the professional Mr. Barnes and the amateur Robert Leroy Mitchel; the pair had previously appeared in *An Artist in Crime* (1892) and *The Crime of a Century* (1896).

The following story was included in the 1898 collection, having first appeared in February 1895 in *The Idler* magazine, which rarely published detective stories. Along with "The Azteck Opal," which appeared in the April 1895 issue of *The Idler*, this remains the duo's most popular adventure.

THE MONTEZUMA EMERALD

RODRIGUEZ OTTOLENGUI

IS THE INSPECTOR in?"

Mr. Barnes immediately recognized the voice, and turned to greet the speaker. The man was Mr. Leroy Mitchel's English valet. Contrary to all precedent and tradition, he did not speak in cockney dialect, not even stumbling over the proper distribution of the letter "h" throughout his vocabulary. That he was English, however, was apparent to the ear, because of a certain rather attractive accent, peculiar to his native island, and to the eye because of a deferential politeness of manner, too seldom observed in American servants. He also always called Mr. Barnes "Inspector," oblivious of the fact that he was not a member of the regular police, and mindful only of the English application of the word to detectives.

"Step right in, Williams," said Mr. Barnes. "What is the trouble?"

"I don't rightly know, Inspector," said Williams. "Won't you let me speak to you alone? It's about the master."

"Certainly. Come into my private room." He led the way and Williams followed, re-maining standing, although Mr. Barnes waved his hand toward a chair as he seated himself in his usual place at his desk. "Now then," continued the detective, "what's wrong? Nothing serious I hope?"

"I hope not, sir, indeed. But the master's disappeared."

"Disappeared, has he." Mr. Barnes smiled slightly. "Now Williams, what do you mean by that? You did not see him vanish, eh?"

"No, sir, of course not. If you'll excuse my presumption, Inspector, I don't think this is a joke, sir, and you're laughing."

"All right, Williams," answered Mr. Barnes, assuming a more serious tone. "I will give your tale my sober consideration. Proceed."

"Well, I hardly know where to begin, Inspector. But I'll just give you the facts, with-out any unnecessary opinions of my own."

Williams rather prided himself upon his ability to tell what he called "a straight story." He placed his hat on a chair, and, standing behind it, with one foot resting on a rung, checked off the points of his narrative, as he made them, by tapping the palm of one hand with the index finger of the other.

"To begin then," said he. "Mrs. Mitchel and Miss Rose sailed for England, Wednesday morning of last week. That same night, quite unexpected, the master says to me, says he, 'Williams, I think you have a young woman you're sweet on down at Newport?' 'Well, sir,' says I, 'I do know a person as answers that description,' though I must say to you, Inspector, that how he ever came to know it beats me. But that's aside, and digression is not my habit. 'Well, Williams,' the master went on, 'I shan't need you for the rest of this week, and if you'd like to take a trip to the seashore, I shan't mind standing the expense, and letting you go.' Of course, I thanked him very much, and I went, promising to be back on Monday morning as directed. And I kept my word, Inspector; though it was a hard wrench to leave the young person last Sunday in time to catch the boat; the moon being bright and everything most propitious for a stroll, it being her Sunday off, and all that. But, as I said, I kept my word, and was up to the house Monday morning only a little after seven, the boat having got in at six. I was a little surprised to find that the master was not at home, but then it struck me as how he must have gone out of town over Sunday, and I looked for him to be in for dinner. But he did not come to dinner, nor at all that night. Still, I did not worry about it. It was the master's privilege to stay away as long as he liked. Only I could not help thinking I might just as well have had that stroll in the moonlight, Sunday night. But when all Tuesday and Tuesday night went by, and no word from the master, I must confess that I got uneasy; and now here's Wednesday noon, and no news; so I just took the liberty to come down and ask your

opinion in the matter, seeing as how you are a particular friend of the family, and an Inspector to boot."

"Really, Williams," said Mr. Barnes, "all I see in your story is that Mr. Mitchel, contemplating a little trip off somewhere with friends, let you go away. He expected to be back by Monday, but, enjoying himself, has remained longer."

"I hope that's all, sir, and I've tried to think so. But this morning I made a few investigations of my own, and I'm bound to say what I found don't fit that theory."

"Ah, you have some more facts. What are they?"

"One of them is this cablegram that I found only this morning under a book on the table in the library." He handed a blue paper to Mr. Barnes, who took it and read the following, on a cable blank:

"Emerald. Danger. Await letter."

For the first time during the interview Mr. Barnes's face assumed a really serious expression. He studied the dispatch silently for a full minute, and then, without raising his eyes, said:—

"What else?"

"Well, Inspector, I don't know that this has anything to do with the affair, but the master had a curious sort of jacket, made of steel links, so tight and so closely put together, that I've often wondered what it was for. Once I made so bold as to ask him, and he said, said he, 'Williams, if I had an enemy, it would be a good idea to wear that, because it would stop a bullet or a knife.' Then he laughed, and went on: 'Of course, I shan't need it for myself. I bought it when I was abroad once, merely as a curiosity.' Now, Inspector, that jacket's disappeared also."

"Are you quite sure?"

"I've looked from dining-room to garret for it. The master's derringer is missing, too. It's a mighty small affair. Could be held in the hand without being noticed, but it carries a nasty-looking ball."

"Very well, Williams, there may be something in your story. I'll look into the matter at once. Meanwhile, go home, and stay there so that I may find you if I want you."

"Yes, sir; I thank you for taking it up. It takes a load off my mind to know you're in charge, Inspector. If there's harm come to the master, I'm sure you'll track the party down. Good morning, sir."

"Good morning, Williams."

After the departure of Williams, the detective sat still for several minutes, lost in thought. He was weighing two ideas. He seemed still to hear the words which Mr. Mitchel had uttered after his success in unraveling the mystery of Mr. Goldie's lost identity. "Next time I will assign myself the chief role," or words to that effect, Mr. Mitchel had said. Was this disappearance a new riddle for Mr. Barnes to solve? If so, of course he would undertake it, as a sort of challenge which his professional pride could not reject. On the other hand, the cable dispatch and the missing coat of mail might portend ominously. The detective felt that Mr. Mitchel was somewhat in the position of the fabled boy who cried "Wolf!" so often that, when at last the wolf really appeared, no assistance was sent to him. Only Mr. Barnes decided that he must chase the "wolf," whether it be real or imaginary. He wished, though, that he knew which.

Ten minutes later he decided upon a course of action, and proceeded to a telegraph office, where he found that, as he had supposed, the dispatch had come from the Paris firm of jewelers from which Mr. Mitchel had frequently bought gems. He sent a lengthy message to them, asking for an immediate reply.

While waiting for the answer, the detective was not inactive. He went direct to Mr. Mitchel's house, and once more questioned the valet, from whom he obtained an accurate description of the clothes which his master must have worn, only one suit being absent. This fact alone, seemed significantly against the theory of a visit to friends out of town. Next, Mr. Barnes interviewed the neighbors, none of whom remembered to have seen Mr. Mitchel during the week. At the sixth house below, however, he learned something definite. Here he found Mr. Mordaunt, a personal acquaintance, and member of one of Mr. Mitchel's clubs. This gentleman stated that he had dined at the club with Mr. Mitchel on the previous Thursday, and had accompanied him home, in the neighborhood of eleven o'clock, parting with him at the door of his own residence. Since then he had neither seen nor heard from him. This proved that Mr. Mitchel was at home one day after Williams went to Newport.

Leaving the house, Mr. Barnes called at the nearest telegraph office and asked whether a messenger summons had reached them during the week, from Mr. Mitchel's house. The record slips showed that the last call had been received at 12.30 A.M., on Friday. A cab had been demanded, and was sent, reaching the house at one o'clock. At the stables, Mr. Barnes questioned the cab-driver, and learned that Mr. Mitchel had alighted at Madison Square.

"But he got right into another cab," added the driver. "It was just a chance I seen him, 'cause he made as if he was goin' into the Fifth Avenoo; but luck was agin' him, for I'd scarcely gone two blocks back, when I had to get down to fix my harness, and while I was doin' that, who should I see but my fare go by in another cab."

"You did not happen to know the driver of that vehicle?" suggested Mr. Barnes.

"That's just what I did happen to know. He's always by the Square, along the curb by the Park. His name's Jerry. You'll find him easy enough, and he'll tell you where he took that fly bird."

Mr. Barnes went down town again, and did find Jerry, who remembered driving a man at the stated time, as far as the Imperial Hotel; but beyond that the detective learned nothing, for at the hotel no one knew Mr. Mitchel, and none recollected his arrival early Friday morning.

From the fact that Mr. Mitchel had changed cabs, and doubled on his track, Mr. Barnes concluded that he was after all merely hiding away for the pleasure of baffling him, and he felt much relieved to divest the case of its alarming aspect. However, he was not long permitted to hold this opinion. At the telegraph office he found a cable dispatch awaiting him, which read as follows:

> Montezuma Emerald forwarded Mitchel tenth. Previous owner murdered London eleventh. Mexican suspected. Warned Mitchel.

This assuredly looked very serious. Casting aside all thought of a practical joke, Mr. Barnes now threw himself heart and soul into the task of finding Mitchel, dead or alive. From the telegraph office he hastened to the Custom-House, where he learned that an emerald, the invoiced value of which was no less than twenty thousand dollars, had been delivered to Mr. Mitchel in person, upon payment of the custom duties, at noon of the previous Thursday. Mr. Barnes, with this know -

ledge, thought he knew why Mr. Mitchel had been careful to have a friend accompany him to his home on that night. But why had he gone out again? Perhaps he felt safer at a hotel than at home, and, having reached the Imperial, taking two cabs to mystify the villain who might be tracking him, he might have registered under an alias. What a fool he had been not to examine the registry, as he could certainly recognize Mr. Mitchel's handwriting, though the name signed would of course be a false one.

Back, therefore, he hastened to the Imperial, where, however, his search for familiar chirography[1] was fruitless. Then an idea occurred to him. Mr. Mitchel was so shrewd that it would not be unlikely that, meditating a disappearance to baffle the men on his track, he had registered at the hotel several days prior to his permanently stopping there. Turning the page over, Mr. Barnes still failed to find what he sought, but a curious name caught his eye.

"Miguel Palma—City of Mexico."

Could this be the London murderer? Was this the suspected Mexican? If so, here was a bold and therefore dangerous criminal who openly put up at one of the most prominent hostelries. Mr. Barnes was turning this over in his mind, when a diminutive newsboy rushed into the corridor, shouting:

"Extra *Sun*! Extra *Sun*! All about the horrible murder. Extra!"

Mr. Barnes purchased a paper and was stupefied at the headlines:

ROBERT LEROY MITCHEL DROWNED!
His Body Found Floating in the East River.
A DAGGER IN HIS BACK.
Indicates Murder.

[1] Penmanship.

Mr. Barnes rushed out of the hotel, and, quickly finding a cab, instructed the man to drive rapidly to the Morgue. On the way, he read the details of the crime as recounted in the newspaper. From this he gathered that the body had been discovered early in the morning by two boatmen, who towed it to shore and handed it over to the police. An examination at the Morgue had established the identity by letters found on the corpse and the initials marked on the clothing. Mr. Barnes was sad at heart, and inwardly fretted because his friend had not asked his aid when in danger.

Jumping from the cab almost before it had fully stopped in front of the Morgue, he stumbled and nearly fell over a decrepit-looking beggar, upon whose breast was a printed card soliciting alms for the blind. Mr. Barnes dropped a coin, a silver quarter, into his outstretched palm, and hurried into the building. As he did so he was jostled by a tall man who was coming out, and who seemed to have lost his temper, as he muttered an imprecation under his breath in Spanish. As the detective's keen ear noted the foreign tongue an idea occurred to him which made him turn and follow the stranger. When he reached the street again he received a double surprise. The stranger had already signaled the cab which Mr. Barnes had just left, and was entering it, so that he had only a moment in which to observe him. Then the door was slammed, and the driver whipped up his horses and drove rapidly away. At the same moment the blind beggar jumped up, and ran in the direction taken by the cab. Mr. Barnes watched them till both cab and beggar disappeared around the next corner, and then he went into the building again, deeply thinking over the episode.

He found the Morgue-keeper, and was taken to the corpse. He recognized the clothing at once, both from the description given by Williams, and because he now remembered to have seen Mr. Mitchel so dressed. It was evident that the body had been in the water for several days, and the marks of violence plainly pointed to murder. Still sticking in the back was a curious dagger of foreign make, the handle projecting between the shoulders. The blow must have been a powerful stroke, for the blade was so tightly wedged in the bones of the spine that it resisted ordinary efforts to withdraw it. Moreover, the condition of the head showed that a crime had been committed, for the skull and face had been beaten into a pulpy mass with some heavy instrument. Mr. Barnes turned away from the sickening sight to examine the letters found upon the corpse. One of these bore the Paris postmark, and he was allowed to read it. It was from the jewelers, and was the letter alluded to in the warning cable. Its contents were:

"DEAR SIR:—
"As we have previously advised you the Montezuma Emerald was shipped to you on the tenth instant. On the following day the man from whom we had bought it was found dead in Dover Street, London, killed by a dagger-thrust between the shoulders. The meager accounts telegraphed to the papers here, state that there is no clue to the assassin. We were struck by the name, and remembered that the deceased had urged us to buy the emerald, because, as he declared, he feared that a man had followed him from Mexico, intending to murder him to get possession of it. Within an hour of reading the newspaper story, a gentlemanly looking man, giving the name of Miguel Palma, entered our store, and asked if we had purchased the Montezuma

Emerald. We replied negatively, and he smiled and left. We notified the police, but they have not yet been able to find this man. We deemed it our duty to warn you, and did so by cable."

The signature was that of the firm from which Mr. Barnes had received the cable in the morning. The plot seemed plain enough now. After the fruitless murder of the man in London, the Mexican had traced the emerald to Mr. Mitchel, and had followed it across the water. Had he succeeded in obtaining it? Among the things found on the corpse was an empty jewel-case, bearing the name of the Paris firm. It seemed from this that the gem had been stolen. But, if so, this man, Miguel Palma, must be made to explain his knowledge of the affair.

Once more visiting the Imperial, Mr. Barnes made inquiry, and was told that Mr. Palma had left the hotel on the night of the previous Thursday, which was just a few hours before Mr. Mitchel had undoubtedly reached there alive. Could it be that the man at the Morgue had been he? If so, why was he visiting that place to view the body of his victim? This was a problem over which Mr. Barnes puzzled, as he was driven up to the residence of Mr. Mitchel. Here he found Williams, and imparted to that faithful servant the news of his master's death, and then inquired for the address of the family abroad, that he might notify them by cable, before they could read the bald statement in a newspaper.

"As they only sailed a week ago today," said Williams, "they're hardly more than due in London. I'll go up to the master's desk and get the address of his London bankers."

As Williams turned to leave the room, he started back amazed at the sound of a bell.

"That's the master's bell, Inspector! Someone is in his room! Come with me!"

The two men bounded upstairs, two steps at a time, and Williams threw open the door of Mr. Mitchel's boudoir, and then fell back against Mr. Barnes, crying:

"The master himself!"

Mr. Barnes looked over the man's shoulder, and could scarcely believe his eyes when he observed Mr. Mitchel, alive and well, brushing his hair before a mirror.

"I've rung for you twice, Williams," said Mr. Mitchel, and then, seeing Mr. Barnes, he added, "Ah, Mr. Barnes. You are very welcome. Come in. Why, what is the matter, man? You are as white as though you had seen a ghost."

"Thank God, you are safe!" fervently ejaculated the detective, going forward and grasping Mr. Mitchel's hand. "Here, read this, and you will understand. " He drew out the afternoon paper and handed it to him.

"Oh, that," said Mr. Mitchel, carelessly. "I've read that. Merely a sensational lie, worked off upon a guileless public. Not a word of truth in it, I assure you."

"Of course not, since you are alive; but there is a mystery about this which is yet to be explained."

"What! A mystery, and the great Mr. Barnes has not solved it? I am surprised. I am, indeed. But then, you know, I told you after Goldie made a fizzle of our little joke that if I should choose to play the principal part you would not catch me. You see I have beaten you this time. Confess. You thought that was my corpse which you gazed upon at the Morgue?"

"Well," said Mr. Barnes, reluctantly, "the identification certainly seemed complete, in spite of the condition of the face, which made recognition impossible."

"Yes; I flatter myself the whole affair was artistic."

"Do you mean that this whole thing is nothing but a joke? That you went so far as to invent cables and letters from Paris just for the trifling amusement of making a fool of me?"

Mr. Barnes was evidently slightly angry, and Mr. Mitchel, noting this fact, hastened to mollify him.

"No, no; it is not quite so bad as that," he said. "I must tell you the whole story, for there is yet important work to do, and you must help me. No, Williams, you need not go out. Your anxiety over my absence entitles you to a knowledge of the truth. A short time ago I heard that a very rare gem was in the market, no less a stone than the original emerald which Cortez stole from the crown of Montezuma. The emerald was offered in Paris, and I was notified at once by the dealer, and authorized the purchase by cable. A few days later I received a dispatch warning me that there was danger. I understood at once, for similar danger had lurked about other large stones which are now in my collection. The warning meant that I should not attempt to get the emerald from the Custom-House until further advices reached me, which would indicate the exact nature of the danger. Later, I received the letter which was found on the body now at the Morgue, and which I suppose you have read?"

Mr. Barnes nodded assent.

"I readily located the man Palma at the Imperial, and from his openly using his name I knew that I had a dangerous adversary. Criminals who disdain aliases have brains, and use them. I kept away from the Custom-House until I had satisfied myself that I was being dogged by a veritable cutthroat, who, of course, was the tool hired by Palma to rob, perhaps to kill me. Thus acquainted with my adversaries, I was ready for the enterprise."

"Why did you not solicit my assistance?" asked Mr. Barnes.

"Partly because I wanted all the glory, and partly because I saw a chance to make you admit that I am still the champion detective-baffler. I sent my wife and daughter to Europe that I might have time for my scheme. On the day after their departure I boldly went to the Custom-House and obtained the emerald. Of course I was dogged by the hireling, but I had arranged a plan which gave him no advantage over me. I had constructed a pair of goggles which looked like simple smoked glasses, but in one of these I had a little mirror so arranged that I could easily watch the man behind me, should he approach too near. However, I was sure that he would not attack me in a crowded thoroughfare, and I kept in crowds until time for dinner, when, by appointment, I met my neighbor Mordaunt, and remained in his company until I reached my own doorway late at night. Here he left me, and I stood on the stoop until he disappeared into his own house. Then I turned, and apparently had much trouble to place my latch-key in the lock. This offered the assassin the chance he had hoped for, and, gliding stealthily forward, he made a vicious stab at me. But, in the first place, I had put on a chain-armor vest, and, in the second, expecting the attack to occur just as it did, I turned swiftly and with one blow with a club I knocked the weapon from the fellow's hand, and with another I struck him over the head so that he fell senseless at my feet."

"Bravo!" cried Mr. Barnes. "You have a cool nerve."

"I don't know. I think I was very much excited at the crucial moment, but with my chain armor, a stout loaded club in one hand and a derringer in the other, I never was in any real danger. I took the man down to the wine-cellar and locked him in one of the vaults. Then I called a cab, and went down to the Imperial, in search of Palma; but I was too late. He had vanished."

"So I discovered," interjected Mr. Barnes.

"I could get nothing out of the fellow in the cellar. Either he cannot or he will not speak English. So I have merely kept him a prisoner, visiting him at midnight only, to avoid Williams, and giving him rations for another day. Meanwhile, I disguised myself and looked for Palma. I could not find him. I had another card, however, and the time came at last to play it. I deduced from Palma's leaving the hotel on the very day when I took the emerald from the Custom-House, that it was prearranged that his hireling should stick to me until he obtained the gem, and then meet him at some rendezvous, previously appointed. Hearing nothing during the past few days, he has perhaps thought that I had left the city, and that his man was still upon my track. Meanwhile I was perfecting my grand *coup*. With the aid of a physician, who is a confidential friend, I obtained a corpse from one of the hospitals, a man about my size, whose face we battered beyond description. We dressed him in my clothing, and fixed the dagger which I had taken from my would-be assassin so tightly in the backbone that it would not drop out. Then one night we took our dummy to the river and securely anchored it in the water. Last night I simply cut it loose and let it drift down the river."

"You knew of course that it would be taken to the Morgue," said Mr. Barnes.

"Precisely. Then I dressed myself as a blind beggar, posted myself in front of the Morgue, and waited."

"You were the beggar?" ejaculated the detective.

"Yes. I have your quarter, and shall prize it as a souvenir. Indeed, I made nearly four dollars during the day. Begging seems to be lucrative. After the newspapers got on the street with the account of my death, I looked for developments. Palma came in due time, and went in. I presume that he saw the dagger, which was placed there for his special benefit, as well as the empty jewel-case, and at once concluded that his man had stolen the gem and meant to keep it for himself. Under these circumstances he would naturally be angry, and therefore less cautious and more easily shadowed. Before he came out, you turned up and stupidly brought a cab, which allowed my man to get a start of me. However, I am a good runner, and as he only rode as far as Third Avenue, and then took the elevated railroad, I easily followed him to his lair. Now I will explain to you what I wish you to do, if I may count on you?"

"Assuredly."

"You must go into the street, and when I release the man in the cellar, you must track him. I will go to the other place, and we will see what happens when the men meet. We will both be there to see the fun."

An hour later, Mr. Barnes was skillfully dogging a sneaking Mexican, who walked rapidly through one of the lowest streets on the East Side, until finally he dodged into a blind alley, and before the detective could make sure which of the many doors had allowed him ingress he had disappeared. A moment later a low whistle attracted his attention, and across in a doorway he saw a figure which beckoned to him. He went over and found Mr. Mitchel.

"Palma is here. I have seen him. You see I was right. This is the place of appointment, and the cutthroat has come here straight. Hush! What was that?"

There was a shriek, followed by another, and then silence.

"Let us go up," said Mr. Barnes. "Do you know which door?"

"Yes; follow me."

Mr. Mitchel started across, but, just as they reached the door, footsteps were heard rapidly descending the stairs. Both men stood aside and waited. A minute later a cloaked figure bounded out, only to be gripped instantly by those in hiding. It was Palma, and he fought like a demon, but the long, powerful arms of Mr. Barnes encircled him, and, with a hug that would have made a bear envious, the scoundrel was soon subdued. Mr. Barnes then manacled him, while Mr. Mitchel ascended the stairs to see about the other man. He lay sprawling on the floor, face downward, stabbed in the heart.

George Griffith

GEORGE CHETWYND GRIFFITH-JONES (1857-1906) was best known for his science-fiction novels and tales of exploring the world (he traveled around the world in sixty-five days, then a record). Overshadowed by H. G. Wells and Arthur Conan Doyle, he still achieved great popularity, and his work formed the template for much later "steampunk" writing, combining Victorian sensibilities and futuristic technology.

Griffith also wrote a series of stories for *Pearson's Magazine* known as "I.D.B." ("illicit diamond buyers"), later collected as *Knave of Diamonds: Being Tales of Mine and Veld* (1899). These focused on investigations in the rough-and-tumble world of the South African diamond mines and often featured a Gentile investigator and Jewish criminals.

FIVE HUNDRED CARATS

GEORGE GRIFFITH

IT WAS SEVERAL months after the brilliant if somewhat mysterious recovery of the £15,000 parcel from the notorious but now vanished Seth Salter that I had the pleasure, and I think I may fairly add the privilege, of making the acquaintance of Inspector Lipinzki.

I can say without hesitation that in the course of wanderings which have led me over considerable portion of the lands and seas of the world I have never met a more interesting man than he was. I say "was," poor fellow, for he is now no longer anything but a memory of bitterness to the I.D.B.—but that is a yarn with another twist.

There is no need of further explanation of the all too brief intimacy which followed our introduction, than the statement of the fact that the greatest South African detective of his day was after all a man as well as a detective, and hence not only justifiably proud of the many brilliant achievements which illustrated his career, but also by no means loath that some day the story of them should,

with all due and proper precautions and reservations, be told to a wider and possibly less prejudiced audience than the motley and migratory population of the Camp as it was in his day.

I had not been five minutes in the cozy, tastily-furnished sanctum of his low, broad-roofed bungalow in New De Beers Road before I saw it was a museum as well as a study. Specimens of all sorts of queer apparatus employed by the I.D.B.'s for smuggling diamonds were scattered over the tables and mantelpiece.

There were massive, handsomely-carved briar and meerschaum pipes which seemed to hold wonderfully little tobacco for their size; rough sticks of firewood ingeniously hollowed out, which must have been worth a good round sum in their time; hollow handles of traveling trunks; ladies' boot heels of the fashion affected on a memorable occasion by Mrs. Michael Mosenstein; and novels, hymn-books, church-services, and bibles, with cavities cut out of the center of their leaves which had once held thousands of pounds' worth of illicit stones on their unsuspected passage through the book-post.

But none of these interested, or, indeed, puzzled me so much as did a couple of curiously-assorted articles which lay under a little glass case on a wall bracket. One was an ordinary piece of heavy lead tubing, about three inches long and an inch in diameter, sealed by fusing at both ends, and having a little brass tap fused into one end. The other was a small ragged piece of dirty red sheet-India rubber, very thin—in fact almost transparent—and, roughly speaking, four or five inches square.

I was looking at these things, wondering what on earth could be the connection between them, and what manner of strange story might be connected with them, when the Inspector came in.

"Good-evening. Glad to see you!" he said, in his quiet and almost gentle voice, and without a trace of foreign accent, as we shook hands. "Well, what do you think of my museum? I daresay you've guessed already that if some of these things could speak they could keep your readers entertained for some little time, eh?"

"Well, there is no reason why their owner shouldn't speak for them," I said, making the obvious reply, "provided always, of course, that it wouldn't be giving away too many secrets of state."

"My dear sir," he said, with a smile which curled up the ends of his little, black, carefully-trimmed moustache ever so slightly, "I should not have made you the promise I did at the club the other night if I had not been prepared to rely absolutely on your discretion—and my own. Now, there's whisky-and-soda or brandy; which would you prefer? You smoke, of course, and I think you'll find these

pretty good, and that chair I can recommend. I have unraveled many a knotty problem in it, I can tell you.

"And now," he went on when we were at last comfortably settled, "may I ask which of my relics has most aroused your professional curiosity?"

It was already on the tip of my tongue to ask for the story of the gas-pipe and piece of India-rubber, but the Inspector forestalled me by saying:

"But perhaps that is hardly a fair question, as they will all probably seem pretty strange to you. Now, for instance, I saw you looking at two of my curios when I came in. You would hardly expect them to be associated, and very intimately too, with about the most daring and skillfully planned diamond robbery that ever took place on the Fields, or off them, for the matter of that, would you?"

"Hardly," I said. "And yet I think I have learned enough of the devious ways of the I.D.B. to be prepared for a perfectly logical explanation of the fact."

"As logical as I think I may fairly say romantic," replied the Inspector as he set his glass down. "In one sense it was the most ticklish problem that I've ever had to tackle. Of course you've heard some version or other of the disappearance of the Great De Beers' Diamond?"

"I should rather think I had!" I said, with a decided thrill of pleasurable anticipation, for I felt sure that now, if ever, I was going to get to the bottom of the great mystery. "Everybody in Camp seems to have a different version of it, and, of course, everyone seems to think that if he had only had the management of the case the mystery would have been solved long ago."

"It is invariably the case," said the

Inspector, with another of his quiet, pleasant smiles, "that everyone can do work better than those whose reputation depends upon the doing of it. We are not altogether fools at the Department, and yet I have to confess that I myself was in ignorance as to just how that diamond disappeared, or where it got to, until twelve hours ago.

"Now, I am going to tell you the facts exactly as they are, but under the condition that you will alter all the names except, if you choose, my own, and that you will not publish the story for at least twelve months to come. There are personal and private reasons for this which you will probably understand without my stating them. Of course it will, in time, leak out into the papers, although there has been, and will be, no prosecution; but anything in the newspapers will of necessity be garbled and incorrect, and—well, I may as well confess that I am sufficiently vain to wish that my share in the transaction shall not be left altogether to the tender mercies of the imaginative penny-a-liner."[1]

I acknowledged the compliment with a bow as graceful as the easiness of the Inspector's chair would allow me to make, but I said nothing, as I wanted to get to the story.

"I had better begin at the beginning," the Inspector went on, as he meditatively snipped the end of a fresh cigar. "As I suppose you already know, the largest and most valuable diamond ever found on these fields was a really magnificent stone, a perfect octahedron, pure white, without a flaw, and weighing close on 500 carats. There's a photograph of it there on the mantelpiece. I've got another one by me; I'll give it you before you leave Kimberley.

"Well, this stone was found about six months ago in one of the drives on the 800-foot level of the Kimberley Mine. It was taken by the overseer straight to the De Beers' office and placed on the Secretary's desk—you know where he sits, on the right hand side as you go into the Board Room through the green baize doors. There were several of the Directors present at the time, and, as you may imagine, they were pretty well pleased at the find, for the stone, without any exaggeration, was worth a prince's ransom.

"Of course, I needn't tell you that the value per carat of a diamond which is perfect and of a good color increases in a sort of geometrical progression with the size. I dare say that stone was worth anywhere between one and two millions, according to the depth of the purchaser's purse. It was worthy to adorn the proudest crown in the world instead of—but there, you'll think me a very poor storyteller if I anticipate.

"Well, the diamond, after being duly admired, was taken upstairs to the Diamond Room by the Secretary himself, accompanied by two of the Directors. Of course, you have been through the new offices of De Beers, but still, perhaps I had better just run over the ground, as the locality is rather important.

"You know that when you get upstairs and turn to the right on the landing from the top of the staircase there is a door with a little grille in it. You knock, a trap-door is raised, and, if you are recognized and your business warrants it, you are admitted. Then you go along a little passage out of which a room opens on the left, and in front of you is another door leading into the Diamond Rooms themselves.

---

[1] A hack writer or journalist, paid at this rate. However, by 1871, an Australian newspaper declared that the expression was obsolete—no newspaper paid so little.

"You know, too, that in the main room fronting Stockdale Street and Jones Street the diamond tables run round the two sides under the windows, and are railed off from the rest of the room by a single light wooden rail. There is a table in the middle of the room, and on your right hand as you go in there is a big safe standing against the wall. You will remember, too, that in the corner exactly facing the door stands the glass case containing the diamond scales. I want you particularly to recall the fact that these scales stand diagonally across the corner by the window. The secondary room, as you know, opens out on to the left, but that is not of much consequence."

I signified my remembrance of these details and the Inspector went on.

"The diamond was first put in the scale and weighed in the presence of the Secretary and the two Directors by one of the higher officials, a licensed diamond broker and a most trusted employee of De Beers, whom you may call Phillip Marsden when you come to write the story. The weight, as I told you, in round figures was 500 carats. The stone was then photographed, partly for purposes of identification and partly as a reminder of the biggest stone ever found in Kimberley in its rough state.

"The gem was then handed over to Mr. Marsden's care pending the departure of the Diamond Post to Vryburg on the following Monday—this was a Tuesday. The Secretary saw it locked up in the big safe by Mr. Marsden, who, as usual, was accompanied by another official, a younger man than himself, whom you can call Henry Lomas, a connection of his, and also one of the most trusted members of the staff.

"Every day, and sometimes two or three times a day, either the Secretary or one or other of the Directors came up and had a look at the big stone, either for their own satisfaction or to show it to some of their more intimate friends. I ought, perhaps, to have told you before that the whole Diamond Room staff were practically sworn to secrecy on the subject, because, as you will readily understand, it was not considered desirable for such an exceedingly valuable find to be made public property in a place like this. When Saturday came it was decided not to send it down to Cape Town, for some reasons connected with the state of the market. When the safe was opened on Monday morning the stone was gone.

"I needn't attempt to describe the absolute panic which followed. It had been seen two or three times in the safe on the Saturday, and the Secretary himself was positive that it was there at closing time, because he saw it just as the safe was being locked for the night. In fact, he actually saw it put in, for it had been taken out to show to a friend of his a few minutes before.

"The safe had not been tampered with, nor could it have been unlocked, because when it is closed for the night it cannot be opened again unless either the Secretary or the Managing Director is present, as they have each a master-key without which the key used during the day is of no use.

"Of course I was sent for immediately, and I admit that I was fairly staggered. If the Secretary had not been so positive that the stone was locked up when he saw the safe closed on the Saturday I should have worked upon the theory—the only possible one, as it seemed—that the stone had been abstracted from the safe during the day, concealed in the room, and somehow or other smuggled out, although even that would have been almost impossible in consequence of the strictness of the searching system and the almost certain discovery which must have followed an attempt to get it out of the town.

"Both the rooms were searched in every nook and cranny. The whole staff, naturally feeling that everyone of them must be suspected, immediately volunteered to submit to any process of search that I might think satisfactory, and I can assure you the search was a very thorough one.

"Nothing was found, and when we had done there wasn't a scintilla of evidence to warrant us in suspecting anybody. It is true that the diamond was last actually seen by the Secretary in charge of Mr. Marsden and Mr. Lomas. Mr. Marsden opened the safe, Mr. Lomas put the tray containing the big stone and several other fine ones into its usual compartment, and the safe door was locked. Therefore that fact went for nothing.

"You know, I suppose, that one of the Diamond Room staff always remains all night in the room; there is at least one night-watchman on every landing; and the frontages are patrolled all night by armed men of the special police. Lomas was on duty on the Saturday night. He was searched as usual when he came off duty on Sunday morning. Nothing was found, and I recognized that it was absolutely impossible that he could have brought the diamond out of the room or passed it to any confederate in the street without being discovered. Therefore, though at first sight suspicion might have pointed to him as being the one who was apparently last in the room with the diamond, there was absolutely no reason to connect that fact with its disappearance."

"I must say that that is a great deal plainer and more matter-of-fact than any of the other stories that I have heard of the mysterious disappearance," I said, as the Inspector paused to re-fill his glass and ask me to do likewise.

"Yes," he said drily, "the truth *is* more commonplace up to a certain point than the sort of stories that a stranger will find floating about Kimberley, but still I daresay you have found in your own profession that it sometimes has a way of—to put it in sporting language—giving Fiction a seven-pound[2] and beating it in a canter."

"For my own part," I answered with an affirmative nod, "my money would go on Fact every time. Therefore it would go on now if I were betting. At any rate, I may say that none of the fiction that I have so far heard has offered even a reasonable explanation of the disappearance of that diamond, given the conditions which you have just stated, as far as I can see, I admit that I couldn't give the remotest guess at the solution of the mystery."

"That's exactly what I said to myself after I had been worrying day and night for more than a week over it," said the Inspector. "And then," he went on, suddenly getting up from his seat and beginning to walk up and down the room with quick, irregular strides, "all of a sudden in the middle of a very much smaller puzzle, just one of the common I.D.B. cases we have almost every week, the whole of the work that I was engaged upon vanished from my mind, leaving it for the moment a perfect blank. Then, like a lightning flash out of a black cloud, there came a momentary ray of light which showed me the clue to the mystery. That was the idea. These," he said,

---

[2] In horse-racing, a handicap (weight penalty) given to a horse to equalize the field's chances of winning.

stopping in front of the mantelpiece and putting his finger on the glass case which covered the two relics that had started the story, "these were the materialization of it."

"And yet, my dear Inspector," I ventured to interrupt, "you will perhaps pardon me for saying that your ray of light leaves me just as much in the dark as ever."

"But your darkness shall be made day all in good course," he said with a smile. I could see that he had an eye for dramatic effect, and so I thought it was better to let him tell the story uninterrupted and in his own way, so I simply assured him of my ever-increasing interest and waited for him to go on. He took a couple of turns up and down the room in silence, as though he were considering in what form he should spring the solution of the mystery upon me, then he stopped and said abruptly:

"I didn't tell you that the next morning— that is to say, Sunday—Mr. Marsden went out on horseback, shooting in the veld up towards that range of hills which lies over yonder to the north-westward between here and Barkly West. I can see by your face that you are already asking yourself what that has got to do with spiriting a million or so's worth of crystallized carbon out of the safe at De Beers'. Well, a little patience, and you shall see.

"Early that same Sunday morning, I was walking down Stockdale Street, in front of the De Beers' offices, smoking a cigar, and, of course, worrying my brains about the diamond. I took a long draw at my weed, and quite involuntarily put my head back and blew it up into the air-there, just like that— and the cloud drifted diagonally across the street dead in the direction of the hills on which Mr. Philip Marsden would just then be hunting buck. At the same instant the revela-tion which had scattered *my* thoughts about the other little case that I mentioned just now came back to me. I saw, with my mind's eye, of course—well, now, what do you think I saw?"

"If it wouldn't spoil an incomparable detective," I said, somewhat irrelevantly, "I should say that you would make an excellent storyteller. Never mind what I think. I'm in the plastic condition just now. I am receiving impressions, not making them. Now, what did you see?"

"I saw the Great De Beers' Diamond— say from ten to fifteen hundred thousand pounds' worth of concentrated capital—floating from the upper storey of the De Beers' Consolidated Mines, rising over the house-tops, and drifting down the wind to Mr. Philip Marsden's hunting-ground."

To say that I stared in the silence of blank amazement at the Inspector, who made this astounding assertion with a dramatic gesture and inflection which naturally cannot be reproduced in print, would be to utter the merest commonplace. He seemed to take my stare for one of incredulity rather than wonder, for he said almost sharply:

"Ah, I see you are beginning to think that I am talking fiction now; but never mind, we will see about that later on. You have followed me, I have no doubt, closely enough to understand that, having exhausted all the resources of my experience and such native wit as the Fates have given me, and having made the most minute analysis of the circumstances of the case, I had come to the fixed conclusion that the great diamond had not been carried out of the room on the person of a human being, nor had it been dropped or thrown from the windows to the street—yet it was equally undeniable that it had got out of the safe and out of the room."

"And therefore it flew out, I suppose!" I could not help interrupting, nor, I am afraid, could I quite avoid a suggestion of incredulity in my tone.

"Yes, my dear sir!" replied the Inspector, with an emphasis which he increased by slapping the four fingers of his right hand on the palm of his left. "Yes, it flew out. It flew some seventeen or eighteen miles before it returned to the earth in which it was born, if we may accept the theory of the terrestrial origin of diamonds. So far, as the event proved, I was absolutely correct, wild and all as you may naturally think my hypothesis to have been.

"But," he continued, stopping in his walk and making an eloquent gesture of apology, "being only human, I almost instantly deviated from truth into error. In fact, I freely confess to you that there and then I made what I consider to be the greatest and most fatal mistake of my career.

"Absolutely certain as I was that the diamond had been conveyed through the air to the Barkly Hills, and that Mr. Philip Marsden's shooting expedition had been undertaken with the object of recovering it, I had all the approaches to the town watched till he came back. He came in by the Old Transvall Road about an hour after dark. I had him arrested, took him into the house of one of my men who happened to live out that way, searched him, as I might say, from the roots of his hair to the soles of his feet, and found—nothing.

"Of course he was indignant, and of course I looked a very considerable fool. In fact, nothing would pacify him but that I should meet him the next morning in the Board Room at De Beers', and, in the presence of the Secretary and at least three directors, apologize to him for my unfounded

suspicions and the outrage that they had led me to make upon him. I was, of course, as you might say, between the devil and the deep sea. I had to do it, and I did it; but my convictions and my suspicions remained exactly what they were before.

"Then there began a very strange, and, although you may think the term curious, a very pathetic, waiting game between us. He knew that in spite of his temporary victory I had really solved the mystery and was on the right track. I knew that the great diamond was out yonder somewhere among the hills or on the veld, and I knew, too, that he was only waiting for my vigilance to relax to go out and get it.

"Day after day, week after week, and month after month the game went on in silence. We met almost every day. His credit had been completely restored at De Beers'. Lomas, his connection and, as I firmly believed, his confederate, had been, through his influence, sent on a mission to England, and when he went I confess to you that I thought the game was up—that Marsden had somehow managed to recover the diamond, and that Lomas had taken it beyond our reach.

"Still I watched and waited, and as time went on I saw that my fears were groundless and that the gem was still on the veld or in the hills. He kept up bravely for weeks, but at last the strain began to tell upon him. Picture to yourself the pitiable position of a man of good family in the Old Country, of expensive tastes and very considerable ambition, living here in Kimberley on a salary of some £12 a week, worth about £5 in England, and knowing that within a few miles of him, in a spot that he alone knew of, there lay a concrete fortune of say, fifteen hundred thousand pounds, which was his for the picking up if he only dared to go and take it, and yet he dared not do so.

"Yes, it is a pitiless trade this of ours, and professional thief-catchers can't afford to have much to do with mercy, and yet I tell you that as I watched that man day after day, with the fever growing hotter in his blood and the unbearable anxiety tearing ever harder and harder at his nerves, I pitied him—yes, I pitied him so much that I even found myself growing impatient for the end to come. Fancy that, a detective, a thief-catcher getting impatient to see his victim out of his misery!

"Well, I had to wait six months—that is to say, I had to wait until five o'clock this morning—for the end. Soon after four one of my men came and knocked me up; he brought a note into my bed-room and I read it in bed. It was from Philip Marsden asking me to go and see him at once and alone. I went, as you may be sure, with as little delay as possible. I found him in his sitting-room. The lights were burning. He was fully dressed, and had evidently been up all night.

"Even I, who have seen the despair that comes of crime in most of its worst forms, was shocked at the look of him. Still he greeted me politely and with perfect composure. He affected not to see the hand that I held out to him, but asked me quite kindly to sit down and have a chat with him. I sat down, and when I looked up I saw him standing in front of me, covering me with a brace of revolvers. My life, of course, was absolutely at his mercy, and whatever I might have thought of myself or the situation, there was obviously nothing to do but to sit still and wait for developments.

"He began very quietly to tell me why he had sent for me. He said: 'I wanted to see you, Mr. Lipinzki, to clear up this matter about the big diamond. I have seen for a long time—in fact from that Sunday night—that you had worked out a pretty correct notion as to the way that diamond vanished. You are quite right; it did fly across the veld to the Barkly Hills. I am a bit of a chemist you know, and when I had once made up my mind to steal it—for there is no use in mincing words now—I saw that it would be perfectly absurd to attempt to smuggle such a stone out by any of the ordinary methods.

" 'I daresay you wonder what these revolvers are for. They are to keep you there in that chair till I've done, for one thing. If you attempt to get out of it or utter a sound I shall shoot you. If you hear me out you will not be injured, so you may as well sit still and keep your ears open.

" 'To have any chance of success I must have had a confederate, and I made young Lomas one. If you look on that little table beside your chair you will see a bit of closed lead piping with a tap in it and a piece of thin sheet India-rubber. That is the remains of the apparatus that I used. I make them a present to you; you may like to add them to your collection.

" 'Lomas, when he went on duty that Saturday night, took the bit of tube charged with compressed hydrogen and an empty child's toy balloon with him. You will remember that that night was very dark, and that the wind had been blowing very steadily all day toward the Barkly Hills. Well, when everything was quiet he filled the balloon with gas, tied the diamond—'

" 'But how did he get the diamond out of the safe? The Secretary saw it locked up that evening!' I exclaimed, my curiosity getting the better of my prudence.

" 'It was not locked up in the safe at all

that night,' he answered, smiling with a sort of ghastly satisfaction. 'Lomas and I, as you know, took the tray of diamonds to the safe, and, as far as the Secretary could see, put them in, but as he put the tray into its compartment he palmed the big diamond as I had taught him to do in a good many lessons before. At the moment that I shut the safe and locked it, the diamond was in his pocket.

" 'The Secretary and his friends left the room, Lomas and I went back to the tables, and I told him to clean the scales as I wanted to test them. While he was doing so he slipped the diamond behind the box, and there it lay between the box and the corner of the wall until it was wanted.

" 'We all left the room as usual, and, as you know, we were searched. When Lomas went on night-duty there was the diamond ready for its balloon voyage. He filled the balloon just so that it lifted the diamond and no more. The lead pipe he just put where the diamond had been—the only place you never looked in. When the row was over on the Monday I locked it up in the safe. We were all searched that day; the next I brought it away and now you may have it.

" 'Two of the windows were open on account of the heat. He watched his opportunity, and committed it to the air about two hours before dawn. You know what a sudden fall there is in the temperature here just before daybreak. I calculated upon that to contract the volume of the gas sufficiently to destroy the balance and bring the balloon to the ground, and I knew that, if Lomas had obeyed my instructions, it would fall either on the veld or on this side of the hills.

" 'The balloon was a bright red, and, to make a long story short, I started out before daybreak that morning, as you know, to look for buck. When I got outside the camp I took compass bearings and rode straight down the wind toward the hills. By good luck or good calculation, or both, I must have followed the course of the balloon almost exactly, for in three hours after I left the camp I saw the little red speck ahead of me up among the stones on the hillside.

" 'I dodged about for a bit as though I were really after buck, in case anybody was watching me. I worked round to the red spot, put my foot on the balloon, and burst it. I folded the India-rubber up, as I didn't like to leave it there, and put it in my pocket-book. You remember that when you searched me you didn't open my pocketbook, as, of course, it was perfectly flat, and the diamond couldn't possibly have been in it. That's how you missed your clue, though I don't suppose it would have been much use to you as you'd already guessed it. However, there it is at your service now.'

" 'And the diamond?'

"As I said these three words his whole manner suddenly changed. So far he had spoken quietly and deliberately, and without even a trace of anger in his voice, but now his white, sunken cheeks suddenly flushed a bright fever red and his eyes literally blazed at me. His voice sank to a low, hissing tone that was really horrible to hear.

" 'The diamond!' he said. 'Yes, curse it, and curse you, Mr. Inspector Lipinzki—for it and you have been a curse to me! Day and night I have seen the spot where I buried it, and day and night you have kept your nets spread about my feet so that I could not move a step to go and take it. I can bear the suspense no longer. Between you—you and that infernal stone—you have wrecked my health and driven me mad. If I had all the wealth of

De Beers' now it wouldn't be any use to me, and tonight a new fear came to me—that if this goes on much longer I shall go mad, really mad, and in my delirium rob myself of my revenge on you by letting out where I hid it.

" 'Now listen. Lomas has gone. He is beyond your reach. He has changed his name—his very identity. I have sent him by different posts, and to different name and addresses, two letters. One is a plan and the other is a key to it. With those two pieces of paper he can find the diamond. Without them you can hunt for a century and never go near it.

" 'And now that you know that—that your incomparable stone, which should have been mine, is out yonder somewhere where you can never find it, you and the De Beers' people will be able to guess at the tortures of Tantalus that you have made me endure. That is all you have got by your smartness. That is my legacy to you—curse you! If I had my way I would send you all out there to hunt for it without food or drink till you died of hunger and thirst of body, as you have made me die a living death of hunger and thirst of mind.'

"As he said this, he covered me with one revolver, and put the muzzle of the other into his mouth. With an ungovernable impulse, I sprang to my feet. He pulled both triggers at once. One bullet passed between my arm and my body, ripping a piece out of my coat sleeve; the other—well, I can spare you the details. He dropped dead instantly."

"And the diamond?" I said.

"The reward is £20,000, and it is at your service," replied the Inspector, in his suavest manner, "provided that you can find the stone—or Mr. Lomas and his plans."

Clifford Ashdown

CLIFFORED ASHDOWN as the pseudonym of R. Austin Freeman (see below) and John James Pitcairn (1860-1936). The latter, a prison doctor, was never acknowledged by Freeman as his collaborator, but Freeman's wife revealed this in 1946. Pitcairn also collaborated with Freeman on *The Queen's Treasure*, a novel not published until 1986, and a series of medical mysteries which ran in *Cassell's Magazine* in 1904 and 1905, collected as *From a Surgeon's Diary* in 1975.

The following story, about detective-rogue Romney Pringle, appeared in *Cassell's Magazine* in June 1902 and was collected in the *Adventures of Romney Pringle* (1902). A second series of stories, *The Further Adventures of Romney Pringle*, ran in *Cassell's* in 1903 but did not appear in book form until 1970.

THE ASSYRIAN REJUVENATOR

CLIFFORD ASHDOWN

As six o'clock struck, the procession of the un-dined began to stream beneath the electric arcade which graces the entrance to Cristiani's. The doors swung unceasingly; the mirrors no longer reflected a mere squadron of tables and erect serviettes;[1] a hum of conversation now mingled with the clatter of knives and the popping of corks; and the brisk scurry of waiters' slippers replaced the stillness of the afternoon.

Although the restaurant had been crowded some time before he arrived, Mr. Romney Pringle had secured his favorite seat opposite the feminine print after Gainsborough, and in the intervals of feeding listened to a selection from Mascagni through a convenient electrophone,[2] price sixpence in the slot. It was a warm night for the time of year, a muggy spell having succeeded a week of biting north-east wind, and as the evening wore on the atmosphere grew somewhat oppressive, more particularly to those who had dined well. Its effects were not very visible on Pringle, whose complexion (a small port-wine mark on his right cheek its only blemish) was of that fairness which imparts to its fortunate possessor the air of youth until long past forty; especially in a man who shaves clean, and habitually goes to bed before two in the morning.

As the smoke from Pringle's havana wreathed upward to an extractor, his eye fell, not for the first time, upon a diner at the next table. He was elderly, probably on the wrong side of sixty, but with his erect figure might easily have claimed a few years' grace, while the retired soldier spoke in his scrupulous neatness, and in the trim of a carefully tended moustache. He had finished his dinner some little time, but remained seated, studying a letter with an intentness more due to its subject than to its length, which Pringle could see was

[1] Napkins (here, folded).
[2] A device patented in 1897, an early form of coin-operated "jukebox" that played music through a telephone headset

by no means excessive. At last, with a gesture almost equally compounded of weariness and disgust, he rose and was helped into his overcoat by a waiter, who held the door for him in the obsequious manner of his kind.

The languid attention which Pringle at first bestowed on his neighbor had by this time given place to a deeper interest, and as the swing-doors closed behind the old gentleman, he scarcely repressed a start, when he saw lying beneath the vacant table the identical letter which had received such careful study. His first impulse was to run after the old gentleman and restore the paper, but by this time he had disappeared, and the waiter being also invisible, Pringle sat down and read:

> The Assyrian Rejuvenator Co.,
> 82, Barbican, E.C. April 5th
> Dear Sir—
> We regret to hear of the failure of the "Rejuvenator" in your hands. This is possibly due to your not having followed the directions for its use sufficiently closely, but I must point out that we do not guarantee its infallible success. As it is an expensive preparation, we do not admit the justice of your contention that our charges are exorbitant. In any case we cannot entertain your request to return the whole or any part of the fees. Should you act upon your threat to take proceedings for the recovery of the same, we must hold your good self responsible for any publicity which may follow your trial of the preparation.
> > Yours faithfully,
> > Henry Jacobs,
> > Secretary.
> > Lieut.-Col. Sandstream,
> > 272, Piccadilly, W.

To Pringle this businesslike communication hardly seemed to deserve so much consideration as Colonel Sandstream had given it, but having read and pondered it over afresh, he walked back to his chambers in Furnival's Inn.

He lived at No. 33, on the left as you enter from Holborn, and anyone who, scaling the stone stairs, reached the second floor, might observe on the entrance to the front set of chambers the legend:

Mr. Romney Pringle,
Literary Agent.

According to high authority, the reason of being of the literary agent is to act as a buffer between the ravening publisher and his prey. But although a very fine oak bureau with capacious pigeon-holes stood conspicuously in Pringle's sitting-room, it was tenanted by no rolls of MS, or type-written sheets. Indeed, little or no business appeared to be transacted in the chambers. The buffer[3] was at present idle, if it could be said to have ever worked! It was "resting," to use the theatrical expression.[4]

Mr. Pringle was an early riser, and as nine o'clock chimed the next morning from the brass lantern-clock which ticked sedately on a mantel unencumbered by the usual litter of a bachelor's quarters, he had already spent some time in consideration of last night's incident, and a further study of the letter had only served thoroughly to arouse his curiosity, and decided him to investigate the affair of the mysterious "Rejuvenator." Unlocking a cupboard in the bottom of the bureau, he disclosed a regiment of bottles and jars. Sprin-

---

[3] Pringle, that is, the "literary agent."

[4] In the anonymously written book of social journalism titled *Victorian London* (1889), the author recounts, "acknowledged burlesque performers take to the music-hall as a stop-gap whilst they are what is technically called 'resting'—in other words, out of work."

kling a few drops from one on to a hare's-foot, he succeeded, with a little friction, in entirely removing the port-wine mark from his cheek. Then from another vial he saturated a sponge and rubbed it into his eyebrows, which turned in the process from their original yellow to a jetty black. From a box of several, he selected a waxed moustache (that most facile article of disguise), and having attached it with a few drops of spirit-gum, covered his scalp with a black wig, which, as is commonly the case, remained an aggressive fraud in spite of the most assiduous adjustment. Satisfied with the completeness of his disguise, he sallied out in search of the offices of the "Assyrian Rejuvenator," affecting a military bearing which his slim but tall and straight-backed figure readily enabled him to assume.

"My name is Parkins—Major Parkins," said Pringle, as he opened the door of a mean-looking room on the second floor of No. 82, Barbican. He addressed an oleaginous-looking[5] gentleman, whose curly locks and beard suggested the winged bulls of Nineveh, and who appeared to be the sole representative of the concern. The latter bowed politely, and handed him a chair.

"I have been asked," Pringle continued, "by a friend who saw your advertisement to call upon you for some further information."

Now the subject of rejuvenation being a delicate one, especially where ladies are concerned, the business of the company was mainly transacted through the post. So seldom, indeed, did a client desire a personal interview, that the Assyrian-looking gentleman jumped to the conclusion that his visitor was interested in quite another matter.

"Ah yes! You refer to 'Pelosia'," he said briskly. "Allow me to read you an extract from the prospectus."

And before Pringle could reply he proceeded to read from a small leaflet with unctuous elocution:

Pelosia. The sovereign remedy of Mud has long been used with the greatest success in the celebrated baths of Schwalbach and Franzensbad.[6] The proprietors of Pelosia having noted the beneficial effect which many of the lower animals derive from the consumption of earth with their food, have been led to investigate the internal uses of mud. The success which has crowned the treatment of some of the longest-standing cases of dyspepsia (the disease so characteristic of this neurotic age), has induced them to admit the world at large to its benefits. To thoroughly safeguard the public, the proprietors have secured the sole right to the alluvial deposits of a stream remote from human habitation, and consequently above any suspicion of contamination. Careful analysis has shown that the deposit in this particular locality, consisting of finely divided mineral particles, practically free from organic admixture, is calculated to give the most gratifying results. The proprietors are prepared to quote special terms for public institutions.

"Many thanks," said Pringle, as the other momentarily paused for breath; "but I think you are under a slight misapprehension. I called on you with reference to the 'Assyrian Rejuvenator.' Have I mistaken the offices?"

"Pray excuse my absurd mistake! I am secretary of the 'Assyrian Rejuvenator Company,' who are also the proprietors of 'Pelosia'." And in evident concern he regarded Pringle fixedly.

---

[5] Greasy-looking.

[6] Both were famous spas of the day, the former in Germany, the latter in Bohemia (now the Czech Republic).

It was not the first time he had known a diffident person to assume an interest in the senility of an absent friend, and he mentally decided that Pringle's waxed moustache, its blue-blackness speaking loudly of hair-dye, together with the unmistakable wig, were evidence of the decrepitude for which his new customer presumably sought the Company's assistance.

"Ours, my dear sir," he resumed, leaning back in his chair, and placing the tips of his fingers in apposition—"Ours is a world-renowned specific for removing the ravages which time effects in the human frame.[7] It is a secret which has been handed down for many generations in the family of the original proprietor. Its success is frequently remarkable, and its absolute failure is impossible. It is not a drug, it is not a cosmetic, yet it contains the properties of both. It is agreeable and soothing to use, and being best administered during the hours of sleep does not interfere with the ordinary avocations of every-day life. The price is so moderate—ten and sixpence, including the Government stamp[8]—that it could only prove remunerative with an enormous sale. If you—ah, on behalf of your friend!—would care to purchase a bottle, I shall be most happy to explain its operation."

Mr. Pringle laid a half sovereign and a sixpence on the table, and the secretary, diving into a large packing-case which stood on one side, extracted a parcel. This contained a cardboard box adorned with a representation of Blake's preposterous illustration to "The Grave," in which a centenarian on crutches is hobbling into a species of banker's strong-room with a rocky top, whereon is seated a youth clothed in nothing, and with an ecstatic expression.

"This," said Mr. Jacobs impressively, "is the entire apparatus!" And he opened the box, displaying a moderate-sized vial and a spirit-lamp with a little tin dish attached. "On retiring to rest, a teaspoonful of the contents of the bottle is poured into the receptacle above the lamp, which is then lighted, and the preparation being vaporized is inhaled by the patient. It is best to concentrate the thoughts on some object of beauty while the delicious aroma sooths the patient to sleep."

"But how does it act?" inquired the Major a trifle impatiently.

"In this way," replied the imperturbable secretary. "Remember that the appearance of age is largely due to wrinkles; that is to say, to the skin losing its *elasticity* and fullness—so true is it that beauty is only skin-deep." Here he laughed gaily. "The joints grow stiff from loss of their natural tone, the figure stoops, and the vital organs decline their functions from the same cause. In a word, old age is due

---

[7] Drugs that allegedly produced "rejuvenation" first became popular in the late nineteenth century and were marketed through the 1920s. French physiologist Charles Edouard Brown-Séquard (1817-1894), already recognized for having discovered the importance of the spinal cord, announced in June 1889—to much sensation in the Paris and London journals—that he had injected himself with the testicular secretions of guinea pigs and dogs and felt "rejuvenated" as a result. Among other findings, he reported that he was now able to engage in sexual relations with his new, younger wife, whereas previously he had found his capabilities limited. Brown-Séquard did not, however, end up prolonging his lifespan in any meaningful way. Later, experiments were conducted with transplanted monkey glands as well as extracts, all to no avail. However, the failures of science did little to slow the successes of commerce.

[8] A stamp duty (tax) imposed on patent medicines.

to a loss of elasticity, and that is the very property which the 'Rejuvenator' imparts to the system, if inhaled for a few hours daily."

Mr. Pringle diplomatically succeeded in maintaining his gravity while the merits of the "Rejuvenator" were expounded, and it was not until he had bidden Mr. Jacobs a courteous farewell, and was safely outside the office, that he allowed the fastening of his moustache to be disturbed by an expansive grin.

About nine o'clock the same evening the housekeeper of the Barbican offices was returning from market, her thoughts centered on the savory piece of fried fish she was carrying home for supper.

"Mrs. Smith?" said a man's voice behind her, as she produced her latch-key.

"My name's 'Odges," she replied unguardedly, dropping the key in her agitation.

"You're the housekeeper, aren't you?" said the stranger, picking up the key and handing it to her politely.

"Lor', sir! You did give me a turn," she faltered.

"Very sorry, I'm sure. I only want to know where I can find Mr. Jacobs, of the Assyrian Rejuvenator Company."

"Well, sir, he told me I wasn't to give his address to anyone. Not that I know it either, sir, for I always send the letters to Mr. Weeks."

"I'll see you're not found fault with. I know he won't mind your telling me." A sovereign clinked against the latch-key in her palm.

For a second she hesitated, then her eye caught the glint of the gold, and she fell.

"All I know, sir, is that when Mr. Jacobs is away I send the letters—and a rare lot there are—to Mr. Newton Weeks, at the Northumberland Avenue Hotel."

"Is he one of the firm?"

"I don't know, sir, but there's no one comes here but Mr. Jacobs."

"Thank you very much, and good night," said the stranger; and he strode down Barbican, leaving Mrs. Hodges staring at the coin in her hand as if doubting whether, like fairy gold, it might not disappear even as she gazed.

The next day Mr. Jacobs received a letter at his hotel:

April 7th
Sir—
My friend Col. Sandstream informs me he has communicated with the police, and has sworn an information against you in respect of the moneys you have obtained from him, as he alleges, by false pretenses. Although I am convinced that his statements are true, a fact which I can more readily grasp after my interview with you today, I give you this warning in order that you may make your escape before it is too late. Do not misunderstand my motives; I have not the slightest desire to save you from the punishment you so richly deserve. I am simply anxious to rescue my old friend from the ridiculous position he will occupy before the world should he prosecute you.
　　　Your obedient servant,
　　　Joseph Parkins, Major.
　　　Newton Weeks, Esq.,
　　　Northumberland Avenue Hotel.

Mr. Jacobs read this declaration of war with very mixed feelings.

So his visitor of yesterday was the friend of Colonel Sandstream! Obviously come to get up evidence against him. Knowing old dog, that Sandstream! But then how had they run him to earth? That looked as if the police had got their fingers in the pie. Mrs. Hodges was discreet. She would never have given the address to any but the police. It was annoying, though, after all his precautions; seemed as if the game was really up at last. Well, it was bound to come some day, and he had been in tighter places before. He could hardly complain; the "Rejuvenator" had been going very well lately. But suppose the whole thing was a plant—a dodge to intimidate him?

He read the letter through again. The writer had been careful to omit his address, but it seemed plausible enough on the face of it. Anyhow, whatever the major's real motive might be, he couldn't afford to neglect the warning, and the one clear thing was that London was an unhealthy place for him just at present. He would pack up, so as to be ready for all emergencies, and drive round to Barbican and reconnoiter. Then, if things looked fishy, he could go to Cannon Street and catch the 11:05 Continental.[9] He'd show them that Harry Jacobs wasn't the man to be bluffed out of his claim!

Mr. Jacobs stopped his cab some doors from the "Rejuvenator" office, and was in the act of alighting when he paused, spellbound at the apparition of Pringle. The latter was loitering outside No. 82, and as the cab drew up he ostentatiously consulted a large pocket-book, and glanced several times from its pages to the countenance of his victim as if comparing a description. Attired in a long overcoat, a bowler hat, and wearing thick boots of a constabulary pattern to the nervous imagination of Mr. Jacobs, he afforded startling evidence of the police interest in the establishment; and this idea was confirmed when Pringle, as if satisfied with his scrutiny, drew a paper from the pocket-book and made a movement in his direction. Without waiting

for further developments, Mr. Jacobs retreated into the cab and hoarsely whispered through the trap-door, "Cannon Street as hard as you can go!"

The cabman wrenched the horse's head round. He had been an interested spectator of the scene, and sympathized with the evident desire of his fare to escape what appeared to be the long arm of the law. At this moment a "crawling" hansom came up, and was promptly hailed by Pringle.

"Follow that cab and don't lose it on any account!" he cried, as he stood on the step and pointed vigorously after the receding hansom.

While Mr. Jacobs careered down Barbican, his cabman looked back in time to observe this expressive pantomime, and with the instinct of a true sportsman lashed the unfortunate brute into a hand-gallop. But the observant eye of a policeman checked this moderate exhibition of speed just as they were rounding the sharp corner into Aldersgate Street, and had not a lumbering railway van intervened Pringle would have caught him up and brought the farce to an awkward finish. But the van saved the situation. The moment's respite was all that the chase needed, and in response to the promises of largesse, frantically roared by Mr. Jacobs through the trap-door, he was soon bounding and bumping over the wood pavement with Pringle well in the rear.

Then ensued a mad stampede down Aldersgate Street.

In and out, between the crowded files of vans and buses, the two cabs wound a zig-zag course; the horses slipping and skating over the greasy surface, or plowing up the mud as

---

[9] Prior to its destruction in World War II, the Cannon Street Station was a grand train shed stretching over the Thames, with high brick walls, lofty towers, and a magnificent hotel. It provided service to the City of London and, prior to 1914, served as the principal terminus for Continental boat express trains.

their bits skidded them within inches of a collision. In vain did policemen roar to them to stop—the order fell on heedless ears. In vain did officious boys wave intimidating arms, or make futile grabs at the harness of the apparent runaways. Did a cart dart unexpectedly from out a side street, the inevitable disaster failed to come off. Did an obstacle loom dead ahead of them, it melted into thin air as they approached. Triumphantly they piloted the narrowest of straits, and dashed unscathed into St. Martin's-le-Grand.

There was a block in Newgate Street, and the cross traffic was stopped. Mr. Jacobs' hansom nipped through a temporary gap, grazing the pole of an omnibus, and being lustily anathematized in the process. But Pringle's cabman, attempting to follow, was imperiously waved back by a policeman.

"No go, I'm afraid, sir!" was the man's comment, as they crossed into St. Paul's Churchyard after a three minutes' wait. "I can't see him nowhere."

"Never mind," said Pringle cheerfully. "Go to Charing Cross telegraph office."

There he sent the following message:

"To Mrs. Hodges, 82, Barbican. Called away to country. Mr. Weeks will take charge of office—Jacobs."

About two the same afternoon, Pringle, wearing the wig and moustache of Major Parkins, rang the housekeeper's bell at 82.

"I'm Mr. Weeks," he stated, as Mrs. Hodges emerged from the bowels of the earth. "Mr. Jacobs has had to leave town, and has asked me to take charge of the office."

"Oh yes, sir! I've had a telegram from Mr. Jacobs to say so. You know the way up, I suppose."

"I think so. But Mr. Jacobs forgot to send me the office key."

"I'd better lend you mine, then, sir, till you can hear from Mr. Jacobs." She fumbled in her voluminous pocket. "I hope nothing's the matter with him?"

"Oh dear no! He found he needed a short holiday, that's all," Pringle reassured her, and taking the key from the confiding woman he climbed to the second floor.

Sitting down at the secretarial desk, he sent a quick glance round the office. A poor creature, that Jacobs, he reflected, for all his rascality, or he wouldn't have been scared so easily. And he drew a piece of wax from his pocket and took a careful impression of the key.

He had not been in possession of the "Rejuvenator" offices for very long before he discovered that Mr. Jacobs' desire to break out in a fresh place had proved abortive. It will be remembered that on the occasion of his interview with that gentleman, Mr. Jacobs assumed that Pringle's visit had reference to "Pelosia," whose virtues he extolled in a leaflet composed in his own very pronounced style. A large package in the office Pringle found to contain many thousands of these effusions, which had apparently been laid aside for some considerable time. From the absence in the daily correspondence of any inquiries thereafter, it was clear that the public had failed to realize the advantages of the internal administration of mud, so that Mr. Jacobs had been forced to stick to the swindle that was already in existence. After all, the latter was a paying concern—eminently so! Besides, the patent-medicine trade is rather overdone.

The price of the "Assyrian Rejuvenator" was such as to render the early cashing of remittances an easy matter. Ten-and-sixpence being a sum for which the average banker demurs to honor a cheque, the payments were usually made in postal orders;[10] and Pringle acquired a larger faith in Carlyle's opinion of the majority of his fellow-creatures[11] as he cashed the previous day's takings at the General Post Office on his way up to Barbican each morning. The business was indeed a flourishing one, and his satisfaction was only alloyed by the probability of some legal interference, at the instance of Colonel Sandstream, with the further operations of the Company. But for the present Fortune smiled, and Pringle continued energetically to dispatch parcels of the "Rejuvenator" in response to the daily shower of postal orders. In this indeed he had little trouble, for he had found many gross of parcels duly packed and ready for posting.

One day while engaged in the process, which had grown quite a mechanical one by that time, he listened absently to a slow but determined step which ascended the stairs and paused on the landing outside. Above, on the third floor, was an importer of cigars made in Germany, and the visitor evidently delayed the further climb until he had regained his wind. Presently, after a preliminary pant or two, he got under weigh again, but proceeded only as far as the "Rejuvenator" door, to which he gave a peremptory thump, and, opening it, walked in without further ceremony.

There was no need for him to announce himself. Pringle recognized him at first glance, although he had never seen him since the eventful evening at Cristiani's restaurant.

"I'm Colonel Sandstream!" he growled, looking round him savagely.

"Delighted to see you, sir," said Pringle with assurance. "Pray be seated," he added politely.

"Who am I speaking to?"

"My name is Newton Weeks. I am—"

"I don't want to see *you!*" interrupted the Colonel testily. "I want to see the secretary of this concern. I've no time to waste either."

"I regret to say that Mr. Jacobs—"

"Ah, yes! That's the name. Where is he?" again interrupted the old gentleman.

"Mr. Jacobs is at present out of town."

"Well, I'm not going to run after him. When will he be here again?"

"It is quite impossible for me to tell. But I was just now going to say that as the managing director of the company I am also acting as secretary during Mr. Jacobs' absence."

"What do you say your name is?" demanded the other, still ignoring the chair which Pringle had offered him.

"Newton Weeks."

"Newton Weeks," repeated the Colonel, making a note of the name on the back of an envelope.

"Managing director," added Pringle suavely.

"Well, Mr. Weeks, if you represent the *company*—" this with a contemptuous glance from the middle of the room at his surroundings—"I've called with reference to a letter you've had the impertinence to send me."

"What was the date of it?" inquired Pringle innocently.

"I don't remember!" snapped the Colonel.

"May I ask what was the subject of the correspondence?"

"Why, this confounded 'Rejuvenator' of yours, of course!"

---

[10] Postal orders of the era did not designate a payee, so that anyone could cash them at the Post Office.

[11] Thomas Carlyle, the master of the epigram, expressed so many opinions about humanity that it is not possible to pick out which opinion Pringle had in mind.

"You see we have a very large amount of correspondence concerning the 'Rejuvenator,' and I'm afraid unless you have the letter with you—"

"I've lost it or mislaid it somewhere."

"That is unfortunate! Unless you can remember the contents I fear it will be quite impossible for *me* to do so."

"I remember them well enough! I'm not likely to forget them in a hurry. I asked you to return me the money your 'Rejuvenator,' as you call it, has cost me, because it's been quite useless, and in your reply you not only refused absolutely, but hinted that I dare not prosecute you."

As Pringle made no reply, he continued more savagely: "Would you like to hear my candid opinion of you?"

"We are always pleased to hear the opinion of our clients."

Pringle's calmness only appeared to exasperate the Colonel the more.

"Well, sir, you shall have it. I consider that letter the most impudent attempt at blackmail that I have ever heard of!" He ground out the words from between his clenched teeth in a voice of concentrated passion.

"Blackmail!" echoed Pringle, allowing an expression of horror to occupy his countenance.

"Yes, sir! Blackmail!" asseverated the Colonel, nodding his head vigorously.

"Of course," said Pringle, with a deprecating gesture, "I am aware that some correspondence has passed between us, but I cannot attempt to remember every word of it. At the same time, although you are pleased to put such an unfortunate construction upon it, I am sure there is some misunderstanding in the matter. I must positively decline to admit that there has been any attempt on the part of the company of such a nature as you allege."

"Oh! So you don't admit it, don't you? Perhaps you won't admit taking pounds and pounds of my money for your absurd concoction, which hasn't done me the least little bit of good in the world—nor ever will! And perhaps you won't admit refusing to return me my money? Eh? Perhaps you won't admit daring me to take proceedings because it would show up what an ass I've been! Don't talk to me, sir! Haugh!"

"I'm really very sorry that this unpleasantness has arisen," began Pringle, "but—"

"Pleasant or unpleasant, sir, I'm going to stop your little game! I mislaid your letter or I'd have called upon you before this. As you're the managing director I'm better pleased to see you than your precious secretary. Anyhow, I've come to tell you that you're a set of swindlers! Of swindlers, sir!"

"I can make every allowance for your feelings," said Pringle, drawing himself up with an air of pained dignity, "but I regret to see a holder of His Majesty's commission so deficient in self-control."

"Like your impertinence, sir!" vociferated the veteran. "I'll let the money go, and I'll prosecute the pair of you, no matter what it costs me! Yes, you, and your rascally secretary too! I'll go and swear an information against you this very day!" He bounced out of the room, and explosively snorted downstairs.

Pringle followed in the rear, and reached the outer door in time to hear him exclaim, "Mansion House Police Court," to the driver of a motor-cab, in which he appropriately clanked and rumbled out of sight.

Returning upstairs, Pringle busied himself in making a bonfire of the last few days' correspondence. Then, collecting the last batch of postal orders, he proceeded to cash them at the General Post Office, and walked back to

Furnival's Inn. After all, the farce couldn't have lasted much longer.

Arrived at Furnival's Inn, Pringle rapidly divested himself of the wig and moustache, and, assuming his official port-wine mark, became once more the unemployed literary agent.

It was now half-past one, and, after lunching lightly at a near restaurant, he lighted a cigar and strolled leisurely eastward.

By the time he reached Barbican three o'clock was reverberating from St Paul's. He entered the private bar of a tavern nearly opposite, and sat down by a window which commanded a view of No. 82.

As time passed and the quarters continued to strike in rapid succession, Pringle felt constrained to order further refreshment; and he was lighting a third cigar before his patience was rewarded. Happening to glance up at the second floor window, he caught a glimpse of a strange man engaged in taking a momentary survey of the street below.

The march of events had been rapid. He had evidently resigned the secretaryship not a moment too soon!

Not long after the strange face had disappeared from the window, a four-wheeled cab stopped outside the tavern, and an individual wearing a pair of large blue spectacles, and carrying a Gladstone bag, got out and carefully scrutinized the offices of the "Rejuvenator." Mr. Jacobs, for it was he, did not intend to be caught napping this time.

At length, being satisfied with the normal appearance of the premises, he crossed the road, and to Pringle's intense amusement, disappeared into the house opposite. The spectator had not long to wait for the next act of the drama.

About ten minutes after Mr. Jacobs' disappearance, the man who had looked out of the window emerged from the house and beckoned to the waiting cab. As it drew up at the door, a second individual came down the steps, fast-holding Mr. Jacobs by the arm. The latter, in very crestfallen guise, re-entered the vehicle, being closely followed by his captor; and the first man having taken his seat with them, the party adjourned to a destination as to which Pringle had no difficulty in hazarding a guess. Satisfying the barmaid, he sallied into the street. The "Rejuvenator" offices seemed once more to be deserted, and the postman entered in the course of his afternoon round. Pringle walked a few yards up the street and then, crossing as the postman re-appeared, turned back and entered the house boldly. Softly mounting the stairs, he knocked at the door. There was no response. He knocked again more loudly, and finally turned the handle. As he expected, it was locked securely, and, satisfied that the coast was clear, he inserted his own replica of the key and entered. The books tumbled on the floor in confused heaps, the wide-open and empty drawers, and the overturned packing-cases, showed how thoroughly the place had been ransacked in the search for compromising evidence. But Pringle took no further interest in these things. The letter-box was the sole object of his attention. He tore open the batch of newly-delivered letters, and crammed the postal orders into his pockets; then, secreting the correspondence behind a rifled packing-case, he silently locked the door.

As he strolled down the street, on a last visit to the General Post Office, the two detectives passed him on their way back in quest of the "Managing Director."

Baroness Orczy

BARONESS EMMA MAGDOLNA Rozália Mária Jozefa Borbála "Emmuska" Orczy de Orczi (1864-1947) was a Hungarian-born English novelist, dramatist, and painter. She is best remembered for creating the Scarlet Pimpernel, about whom she wrote four novels, a play, and numerous short stories. However, she also created a number of memorable detectives: Lady Molly Robertson-Kirk of Scotland Yard, who heads the "Female Department" (her cases are collected in *Lady Molly of Scotland Yard,* 1910); Monsieur Fernand, a Napoleonic-era secret agent (*The Man in Grey,* 1918); and Patrick Mulligan, a shady attorney (*Skin o' My Tooth,* 1928).

Her greatest detective was the Old Man in the Corner, probably the first of the "armchair" detectives. He sits in a chair in a London tea shop, unraveling knots and intricate cases brought to him by Polly Burton, a young reporter. Twelve of the several dozen stories of the detective were made into short films in 1924. The following tale first appeared in *The Royal Magazine* for July 1901 and was later collected in *The Old Man in the Corner* (1909).

THE MYSTERIOUS DEATH ON
THE UNDERGROUND RAILWAY

BARONESS ORCZY

It was all very well for Mr. Richard Frobisher (of the *London Mail*) to cut up rough about it. Polly did not altogether blame him.

She liked him all the better for that frank outburst of manlike ill-temper which, after all said and done, was only a very flattering form of masculine jealousy.

Moreover, Polly distinctly felt guilty about the whole thing. She had promised to meet Dickie—that is Mr. Richard Frobisher—at two o'clock sharp outside the Palace Theatre, because she wanted to go to a Maud Allan[1] matinee, and because he naturally wished to go with her.

But at two o'clock sharp she was still in Norfolk Street, Strand, inside an A.B.C. shop,[2] sipping cold coffee opposite a grotesque old man who was fiddling with a bit of string.

How could she be expected to remember Maud Allan or the Palace Theatre, or Dickie himself for a matter of that? The man in the corner had begun to talk of that mysterious death on the underground railway, and Polly had lost count of time, of place, and circumstance.

She had gone to lunch quite early, for she was looking forward to the matinee at the Palace.

The old scarecrow was sitting in his accustomed place when she came into the A.B.C. shop, but he had made no remark all the time that the young girl was munching her scone and butter. She was just busy thinking how rude he was not even to have said "Good morning," when an abrupt remark from him caused her to look up.

"Will you be good enough," he said suddenly, "to give me a description of the man who sat next to you just now, while you were having your cup of coffee and scone."

Involuntarily Polly turned her head toward the distant door, through which a man

---

[1] American actor-dancer (1873-1956). She appeared in only one film, in 1915.
[2] The Aerated Bread Company was the proprietor of a large chain of tea shops in England.

in a light overcoat was even now quickly passing. That man had certainly sat at the next table to hers, when she first sat down to her coffee and scone: he had finished his luncheon—whatever it was—moments ago, had paid at the desk and gone out. The incident did not appear to Polly as being of the slightest consequence.

Therefore she did not reply to the rude old man, but shrugged her shoulders, and called to the waitress to bring her bill.

"Do you know if he was tall or short, dark or fair?" continued the man in the corner, seemingly not the least disconcerted by the young girl's indifference. "Can you tell me at all what he was like?"

"Of course I can," rejoined Polly impatiently, "but I don't see that my description of one of the customers of an A.B.C. shop can have the slightest importance."

He was silent for a minute, while his nervous fingers fumbled about in his capacious pockets in search of the inevitable piece of string. When he had found this necessary "adjunct to thought," he viewed the young girl again through his half-closed lids, and added maliciously:

"But supposing it were of paramount importance that you should give an accurate description of a man who sat next to you for half an hour today, how would you proceed?"

"I should say that he was of medium height—"

"Five foot eight, nine, or ten?" he interrupted quietly.

"How can one tell to an inch or two?" rejoined Polly crossly. "He was between colors."

"What's that?" he inquired blandly.

"Neither fair nor dark—his nose—"

"Well, what was his nose like? Will you sketch it?"

"I am not an artist. His nose was fairly straight—his eyes—"

"Were neither dark nor light—his hair had the same striking peculiarity—he was neither short nor tall—his nose was neither aquiline nor snub—" he recapitulated sarcastically.

"No," she retorted; "he was just ordinary looking."

"Would you know him again—say tomorrow, and among a number of other men who were 'neither tall nor short, dark nor fair, aquiline nor snub-nosed,' etc.?"

"I don't know—I might—he was certainly not striking enough to be specially remembered."

"Exactly," he said, while he leant forward excitedly, for all the world like a Jack-in-the-box let loose. "Precisely; and you are a journalist—call yourself one, at least—and it should be part of your business to notice and describe people. I don't mean only the wonderful personage with the clear Saxon features, the fine blue eyes, the noble brow and classic face, but the ordinary person—the person who represents ninety out of every hundred of his own kind—the average Englishman, say, of the middle classes, who is neither very tall nor very short, who wears a moustache which is neither fair nor dark, but which masks his mouth, and a top hat which hides the shape of his head and brow, a man, in fact, who dresses like hundreds of his fellow-creatures, moves like them, speaks like them, has no peculiarity.

"Try to describe him, to recognize him, say a week hence, among his other eighty-nine doubles; worse still, to swear his life away, if he happened to be implicated in some crime, wherein your recognition of him would place the halter round his neck.

"Try that, I say, and having utterly failed you will more readily understand how one of the greatest scoundrels unhung is still at large, and why the mystery on the Underground Railway was never cleared up.

"I think it was the only time in my life that I was seriously tempted to give the police the benefit of my own views upon the matter. You see, though I admire the brute for his cleverness, I did not see that his being unpunished could possibly benefit any one.

"In these days of tubes and motor traction of all kinds, the old-fashioned 'best, cheapest, and quickest route to City and West End' is often deserted, and the good old Metropolitan Railway carriages cannot at any time be said to be overcrowded. Anyway, when that particular train steamed into Aldgate at about 4:00 p.m. on March 18th last, the first-class carriages were all but empty.

"The guard marched up and down the platform looking into all the carriages to see if anyone had left a halfpenny evening paper behind for him, and opening the door of one of the first-class compartments, he noticed a lady sitting in the further corner, with her head turned away toward the window, evidently oblivious of the fact that on this line Aldgate is the terminal station.

"'Where are you for, lady?' he said.

"The lady did not move, and the guard stepped into the carriage, thinking that perhaps the lady was asleep. He touched her arm lightly and looked into her face. In his own poetic language, he was 'struck all of a 'eap.' In the glassy eyes, the ashen color of the cheeks, the rigidity of the head, there was the unmistakable look of death.

"Hastily the guard, having carefully locked the carriage door, summoned a couple of porters, and sent one of them off to the police-station, and the other in search of the station-master.

"Fortunately at this time of day the up platform is not very crowded, all the traffic tending westward in the afternoon. It was only when an inspector and two police constables, accompanied by a detective in plain clothes and a medical officer, appeared upon the scene, and stood round a first-class railway compartment, that a few idlers realized that something unusual had occurred, and crowded round, eager and curious.

"Thus it was that the later editions of the evening papers, under the sensational heading, 'Mysterious Suicide on the Underground Railway,' had already an account of the extraordinary event. The medical officer had very soon come to the decision that the guard had not been mistaken, and that life was indeed extinct.

"The lady was young, and must have been very pretty before the look of fright and horror had so terribly distorted her features. She was very elegantly dressed, and the more frivolous papers were able to give their feminine readers a detailed account of the unfortunate woman's gown, her shoes, hat, and gloves.

"It appears that one of the latter, the one on the right hand, was partly off, leaving the thumb and wrist bare. That hand held a small satchel, which the police opened, with a view to the possible identification of the deceased, but which was found to contain only a little loose silver, some smelling-salts, and a small empty bottle, which was handed over to the medical officer for purposes of analysis.

"It was the presence of that small bottle which had caused the report to circulate freely that the mysterious case on the Underground Railway was one of suicide. Certain it was that neither about the lady's person, nor in the appearance of the railway carriage, was there the slightest sign of struggle or even of resistance. Only the look in the poor woman's eyes spoke of sudden terror, of the rapid vision of an unexpected and violent death, which probably only lasted an infinitesimal fraction of a second, but which had left its indelible mark upon the face, otherwise so placid and so still.

"The body of the deceased was conveyed to the mortuary. So far, of course, not a soul had been able to identify her, or to throw the slightest light upon the mystery which hung around her death.

"Against that, quite a crowd of idlers—genuinely interested or not—obtained admission to view the body, on the pretext of having lost or mislaid a relative or a friend. At about 8:30 p.m. a young man, very well dressed, drove up to the station in a hansom, and sent in his card to the superintendent. It was Mr. Hazeldene, shipping agent, of 11, Crown Lane, E.C., and No. 19, Addison Row, Kensington.

"The young man looked in a pitiable state of mental distress; his hand clutched nervously a copy of the St. James's Gazette, which contained the fatal news. He said very little to the superintendent except that a person who was very dear to him had not returned home that evening.

"He had not felt really anxious until half an hour ago, when suddenly he thought of looking at his paper. The description of the deceased lady, though vague, had terribly alarmed him. He had jumped into a hansom, and now begged permission to view the body, in order that his worst fears might be allayed.

"You know what followed, of course," continued the man in the corner, "the grief of the young man was truly pitiable. In the woman lying there in a public mortuary before him, Mr. Hazeldene had recognized his wife.

"I am waxing melodramatic," said the man in the corner, who looked up at Polly with a mild and gentle smile, while his nervous fingers vainly endeavored to add another knot on the scrappy bit of string with which he was continually playing, "and I fear that the whole story savors of the penny novelette, but you must admit, and no doubt you remember, that it was an intensely pathetic and truly dramatic moment.

"The unfortunate young husband of the deceased lady was not much worried with questions that night. As a matter of fact, he was not in a fit condition to make any coherent statement. It was at the coroner's inquest on the following day that certain facts came to light, which for the time being seemed to clear up the mystery surrounding Mrs. Hazeldene's death, only to plunge that same mystery, later on, into denser gloom than before.

"The first witness at the inquest was, of course, Mr. Hazeldene himself. I think every one's sympathy went out to the young man as he stood before the coroner and tried to throw what light he could upon the mystery. He was well dressed, as he had been the day before, but he looked terribly ill and worried, and no doubt the fact that he had not shaved gave his face a careworn and neglected air.

"It appears that he and the deceased had been married some six years or so, and that they had always been happy in their married life. They had no children. Mrs. Hazeldene seemed to enjoy the best of health till lately, when she had had a slight attack of influenza, in which Dr. Arthur Jones had attended her. The doctor was present at this moment, and would no doubt explain to the coroner and the jury whether he thought that Mrs. Hazeldene had the slightest tendency to heart disease, which might have had a sudden and fatal ending.

"The coroner was, of course, very considerate to the bereaved husband. He tried by circumlocution to get at the point he wanted, namely, Mrs. Hazeldene's mental condition lately. Mr. Hazeldene seemed loath to talk about this. No doubt he had been warned as to the existence of the small bottle found in his wife's satchel.

" 'It certainly did seem to me at times,' he at last reluctantly admitted, 'that my wife did not seem quite herself. She used to be very gay and bright, and lately I often saw her in the evening sitting, as if brooding over some matters, which evidently she did not care to communicate to me.'

"Still the coroner insisted, and suggested the small bottle.

" 'I know, I know,' replied the young man, with a short, heavy sigh. 'You mean—the question of suicide—I cannot understand it at all—it seems so sudden and so terrible— she certainly had seemed listless and troubled lately—but only at times—and yesterday morning, when I went to business, she appeared quite herself again, and I suggested that we should go to the opera in the evening. She was delighted, I know, and told me she would do some shopping, and pay a few calls in the afternoon.'

" 'Do you know at all where she intended to go when she got into the Underground Railway?'

" 'Well, not with certainty. You see, she may have meant to get out at Baker Street, and go down to Bond Street to do her shopping. Then, again, she sometimes goes to a shop in St. Paul's Churchyard, in which case she would take a ticket to Aldersgate Street; but I cannot say.'

" 'Now, Mr. Hazeldene,' said the coroner at last very kindly, 'will you try to tell me if there was anything in Mrs. Hazeldene's life which you know of, and which might in some measure explain the cause of the distressed state of mind, which you yourself had noticed? Did there exist any financial difficulty which might have preyed upon Mrs. Hazeldene's mind; was there any friend—to whose intercourse with Mrs. Hazeldene—you—er—at any time took exception? In fact,' added the coroner, as if thankful that he had got over an unpleasant moment, 'can you give me the slightest indication which would tend to confirm the suspicion that the unfortunate lady, in a moment of mental anxiety or derangement, may have wished to take her own life?'

"There was silence in the court for a few moments. Mr. Hazeldene seemed to every one there present to be laboring under some terrible moral doubt. He looked very pale and wretched, and twice attempted to speak before he at last said in scarcely audible tones:

" 'No; there were no financial difficulties of any sort. My wife had an independent fortune of her own—she had no extravagant tastes—'

" 'Nor any friend you at any time objected to?' insisted the coroner.

" 'Nor any friend, I—at any time objected to,' stammered the unfortunate young man, evidently speaking with an effort.

"I was present at the inquest," resumed the man in the corner, after he had drunk a glass of milk and ordered another, "and I can assure you that the most obtuse person there plainly realized that Mr. Hazeldene was telling a lie. It was pretty plain to the meanest intelligence that the unfortunate lady had not fallen into a state of morbid dejection for nothing, and that perhaps there existed a third person who could throw more light on her strange and sudden death than the unhappy, bereaved young widower.

"That the death was more mysterious even than it had at first appeared became very soon apparent. You read the case at the time, no doubt, and must remember the excitement in the public mind caused by the evidence of the two doctors. Dr. Arthur Jones, the lady's usual medical man, who had attended her in a last very slight illness, and who had seen her in a professional capacity fairly recently, declared most emphatically that Mrs. Hazeldene suffered from no organic complaint which could possibly have been the cause of sudden death. Moreover, he had assisted Mr. Andrew Thornton, the district medical officer, in making a postmortem examination, and together they had come to the conclusion that death was due to the action of prussic acid, which had caused instantaneous failure of the heart, but how the drug had been administered neither he nor his colleague were at present able to state.

" 'Do I understand, then, Dr. Jones, that the deceased died, poisoned with prussic acid?'

" 'Such is my opinion,' replied the doctor.

" 'Did the bottle found in her satchel contain prussic acid?'

" 'It had contained some at one time, certainly.'

" 'In your opinion, then, the lady caused her own death by taking a dose of that drug?'

"'Pardon me, I never suggested such a thing; the lady died poisoned by the drug, but how the drug was administered we cannot say. By injection of some sort, certainly. The drug certainly was not swallowed; there was not a vestige of it in the stomach.'

" 'Yes,' added the doctor in reply to another question from the coroner, 'death had probably followed the injection in this case almost immediately; say within a couple of minutes, or perhaps three. It was quite possible that the body would not have more than one quick and sudden convulsion, perhaps not that; death in such cases is absolutely sudden and crushing.'

"I don't think that at the time any one in the room realized how important the doctor's statement was, a statement which, by the way, was confirmed in all its details by the district medical officer, who had conducted the postmortem. Mrs. Hazeldene had died suddenly from an injection of prussic acid, administered no one knew how or when. She had been traveling in a first-class railway carriage in a busy time of the day. That young and elegant woman must have had singular nerve and coolness to go through the process of a self-inflicted injection of a deadly poison in the presence of perhaps two or three other persons.

"Mind you, when I say that no one there realized the importance of the doctor's statement at that moment, I am wrong; there were three persons, who fully understood at once the gravity of the situation, and the astounding development which the case was beginning to assume.

"Of course, I should have put myself out of the question," added the weird old man, with that inimitable self-conceit peculiar to himself. "I guessed then and there in a moment where the police were going wrong, and where they would go on going wrong until the mysterious death on the Underground Railway had sunk into oblivion, together with the other cases which they mismanage from time to time.

"I said there were three persons who understood the gravity of the two doctors' statements—the other two were, firstly, the detective who had originally examined the railway carriage, a young man of energy and plenty of misguided intelligence, the other was Mr. Hazeldene.

"At this point the interesting element of the whole story was first introduced into the proceedings, and this was done through the humble channel of Emma Funnel, Mrs. Hazeldene's maid, who, as far as was known then, was the last person who had seen the unfortunate lady alive and had spoken to her.

" 'Mrs. Hazeldene lunched at home,' explained Emma, who was shy, and spoke almost in a whisper; 'she seemed well and cheerful. She went out at about half-past three, and told me she was going to Spence's, in St. Paul's Churchyard, to try on her new tailor-made gown. Mrs. Hazeldene had meant to go there in the morning, but was prevented as Mr. Errington called.'

" 'Mr. Errington?' asked the coroner casually. 'Who is Mr. Errington?'

"But this Emma found difficult to explain. Mr. Errington was—Mr. Errington, that's all.

" 'Mr. Errington was a friend of the family. He lived in a flat in the Albert Mansions. He very often came to Addison Row, and generally stayed late.'

"Pressed still further with questions, Emma at last stated that latterly Mrs. Hazeldene had been to the theatre several times with Mr. Errington, and that on those nights the master looked very gloomy, and was very cross.

"Recalled, the young widower was strangely reticent. He gave forth his answers very grudgingly, and the coroner was evidently absolutely satisfied with himself at the marvelous way in which, after a quarter of an hour of firm yet very kind questionings, he had elicited from the witness what information he wanted.

"Mr. Errington was a friend of his wife. He was a gentleman of means, and seemed to have a great deal of time at his command. He himself did not particularly care about Mr. Errington, but he certainly had never made any observations to his wife on the subject.

" 'But who is Mr. Errington?' repeated the coroner once more. 'What does he do? What is his business or profession?'

" 'He has no business or profession.'

" 'What is his occupation, then?'

" 'He has no special occupation. He has ample private means. But he has a great and very absorbing hobby.'

" 'What is that?'

" 'He spends all his time in chemical experiments, and is, I believe, as an amateur, a very distinguished toxicologist.' "

"Did you ever see Mr. Errington, the gentleman so closely connected with the mysterious death on the Underground Railway?" asked the man in the corner as he placed one or two of his little snap-shot photos before Miss Polly Burton. "There he is, to the very life. Fairly good-looking, a pleasant face enough, but ordinary, absolutely ordinary.

"It was this absence of any peculiarity which very nearly, but not quite, placed the halter round Mr. Errington's neck.

"But I am going too fast, and you will lose the thread.

"The public, of course, never heard how it actually came about that Mr. Errington, the wealthy bachelor of Albert Mansions, of the Grosvenor, and other young dandies' clubs, one fine day found himself before the magistrates at Bow Street, charged with being concerned in the death of Mary Beatrice Hazeldene, late of No. 19, Addison Row.

"I can assure you both press and public were literally flabbergasted. You see, Mr. Errington was a well-known and very popular member of a certain smart section of London society. He was a constant visitor at the opera, the racecourse, the Park, and the Carlton, he had a great many friends, and there was consequently quite a large attendance at the police court that morning.

"What had transpired was this:

"After the very scrappy bits of evidence which came to light at the inquest, two gentlemen bethought themselves that perhaps they had some duty to perform toward the State and the public generally. Accordingly they had come forward, offering to throw what light they could upon the mysterious affair on the Underground Railway.

"The police naturally felt that their information, such as it was, came rather late in the day, but as it proved of paramount importance, and the two gentlemen, moreover, were of undoubtedly good position in the world, they were thankful for what they could get, and acted accordingly; they accordingly brought Mr. Errington up before the magistrate on a charge of murder.

"The accused looked pale and worried when I first caught sight of him in the court that day, which was not to be wondered at, considering the terrible position in which he found himself.

"He had been arrested at Marseilles, where he was preparing to start for Colombo.

"I don't think he realized how terrible his position really was until later in the proceedings, when all the evidence relating to the arrest had been heard, and Emma Funnel had repeated her statement as to Mr. Errington's call at 19, Addison Row, in the morning, and Mrs. Hazeldene starting off for St. Paul's Churchyard at 3.30 in the afternoon.

"Mr. Hazeldene had nothing to add to the statements he had made at the coroner's inquest. He had last seen his wife alive on the morning of the fatal day. She had seemed very well and cheerful.

"I think every one present understood that he was trying to say as little as possible that could in any way couple his deceased wife's name with that of the accused.

"And yet, from the servant's evidence, it undoubtedly leaked out that Mrs. Hazeldene, who was young, pretty, and evidently fond of admiration, had once or twice annoyed her husband by her somewhat open, yet perfectly innocent, flirtation with Mr. Errington.

"I think every one was most agreeably impressed by the widower's moderate and dignified attitude. You will see his photo there, among this bundle. That is just how he appeared in court. In deep black, of course, but without any sign of ostentation in his mourning. He had allowed his beard to grow lately, and wore it closely cut in a point.

"After his evidence, the sensation of the day occurred. A tall, dark-haired man, with the word 'City' written metaphorically all over him, had kissed the book, and was waiting to tell the truth, and nothing but the truth.

"He gave his name as Andrew Campbell, head of the firm of Campbell & Co., brokers, of Throgmorton Street.

"In the afternoon of March 18th Mr. Campbell, traveling on the Underground Railway, had noticed a very pretty woman in the same carriage as himself. She had asked him if she was in the right train for Aldersgate. Mr. Campbell replied in the affirmative, and then buried himself in the Stock Exchange quotations of his evening paper.

"At Gower Street, a gentleman in a tweed suit and bowler hat got into the carriage, and took a seat opposite the lady.

"She seemed very much astonished at seeing him, but Mr. Andrew Campbell did not recollect the exact words she said.

"The two talked to one another a good deal, and certainly the lady appeared animated and cheerful. Witness took no notice of them; he was very much engrossed in some calculations, and finally got out at Farringdon Street. He noticed that the man in the tweed suit also got out close behind him, having shaken hands with the lady, and said in a pleasant way: 'Au revoir! Don't be late tonight.' Mr. Campbell did not hear the lady's reply, and soon lost sight of the man in the crowd.

"Every one was on tenter-hooks,[3] and eagerly waiting for the palpitating moment when witness would describe and identify the man who last had seen and spoken to the unfortunate woman, within five minutes probably of her strange and unaccountable death.

"Personally I knew what was coming before the Scotch stockbroker spoke.

"I could have jotted down the graphic and lifelike description he would give of a probable murderer. It would have fitted equally well the man who sat and had luncheon at this table just now; it would certainly have described five out of every ten young Englishmen you know.

"The individual was of medium height, he wore a moustache which was not very fair nor yet very dark, his hair was between colors.

He wore a bowler hat, and a tweed suit—and—and—that was all—Mr. Campbell might perhaps know him again, but then again, he might not—he was not paying much attention—the gentleman was sitting on the same side of the carriage as himself—and he had his hat on all the time. He himself was busy with his newspaper—yes—he might know him again—but he really could not say.

"Mr. Andrew Campbell's evidence was not worth very much, you will say. No, it was not in itself, and would not have justified any arrest were it not for the additional statements made by Mr. James Verner, manager of Messrs. Rodney & Co., color printers.

"Mr. Verner is a personal friend of Mr. Andrew Campbell, and it appears that at Farringdon Street, where he was waiting for his train, he saw Mr. Campbell get out of a first-class railway carriage. Mr. Verner spoke to him for a second, and then, just as the train was moving off, he stepped into the same compartment which had just been vacated by the stockbroker and the man in the tweed suit. He vaguely recollects a lady sitting in the opposite corner to his own, with her face turned away from him, apparently asleep, but he paid no special attention to her. He was like nearly all business men when they are traveling—engrossed in his paper. Presently a special quotation interested him; he wished to make a note of it, took out a pencil from his waistcoat pocket, and seeing a clean piece of paste-board on the floor, he picked it up, and scribbled on it the memorandum, which he wished to keep. He then slipped the card into his pocket-book.

" 'It was only two or three days later,' added Mr. Verner in the midst of breathless

---

3 Literally, hooks used to stretch a cloth on a drying frame; figuratively, in a state of tension.

silence, 'that I had occasion to refer to these same notes again.

" 'In the meanwhile the papers had been full of the mysterious death on the Underground Railway, and the names of those connected with it were pretty familiar to me. It was, therefore, with much astonishment that on looking at the paste-board which I had casually picked up in the railway carriage I saw the name on it, "Frank Errington." '

"There was no doubt that the sensation in court was almost unprecedented. Never since the days of the Fenchurch Street mystery, and the trial of Smethurst, had I seen so much excitement. Mind you, I was not excited—I knew by now every detail of that crime as if I had committed it myself. In fact, I could not have done it better, although I have been a student of crime for many years now. Many people there—his friends, mostly—believed that Errington was doomed. I think he thought so, too, for I could see that his face was terribly white, and he now and then passed his tongue over his lips, as if they were parched.

"You see he was in the awful dilemma—a perfectly natural one, by the way—of being absolutely incapable of proving an alibi. The crime—if crime there was—had been committed three weeks ago. A man about town like Mr. Frank Errington might remember that he spent certain hours of a special afternoon at his club, or in the Park, but it is very doubtful in nine cases out of ten if he can find a friend who could positively swear as to having seen him there. No! No! Mr. Errington was in a tight corner, and he knew it. You see, there were—besides the evidence—two or three circumstances which did not improve matters for him. His hobby in the direction of toxicology, to begin with. The police had found in his room every description of poisonous substances, including prussic acid.

"Then, again, that journey to Marseilles, the start for Colombo, was, though perfectly innocent, a very unfortunate one. Mr. Errington had gone on an aimless voyage, but the public thought that he had fled, terrified at his own crime. Sir Arthur Inglewood, however, here again displayed his marvelous skill on behalf of his client by the masterly way in which he literally turned all the witnesses for the Crown inside out.

"Having first got Mr. Andrew Campbell to state positively that in the accused he certainly did *not* recognize the man in the tweed suit, the eminent lawyer, after twenty minutes' cross-examination, had so completely upset the stockbroker's equanimity that it is very likely he would not have recognized his own office-boy.

"But through all his flurry and all his annoyance Mr. Andrew Campbell remained very sure of one thing; namely, that the lady was alive and cheerful, and talking pleasantly with the man in the tweed suit up to the moment when the latter, having shaken hands with her, left her with a pleasant 'Au revoir! Don't be late tonight.' He had heard neither scream nor struggle, and in his opinion, if the individual in the tweed suit had administered a dose of poison to his companion, it must have been with her own knowledge and free will; and the lady in the train most emphatically neither looked nor spoke like a woman prepared for a sudden and violent death.

"Mr. James Verner, against that, swore equally positively that he had stood in full view of the carriage door from the moment that Mr. Campbell got out until he himself stepped into the compartment, that there was no one else in that carriage between Farringdon Street and Aldgate, and that the lady, to the best of his belief, had made no movement during the whole of that journey.

"No; Frank Errington was *not* committed for trial on the capital charge," said the man in the corner with one of his sardonic smiles, "thanks to the cleverness of Sir Arthur Inglewood, his lawyer. He absolutely denied his identity with the man in the tweed suit, and swore he had not seen Mrs. Hazeldene since eleven o'clock in the morning of that fatal day. There was no *proof* that he had; moreover, according to Mr. Campbell's opinion, the man in the tweed suit was in all probability not the murderer. Common sense would not admit that a woman could have a deadly poison injected into her without her knowledge, while chatting pleasantly to her murderer.

"Mr. Errington lives abroad now. He is about to marry. I don't think any of his real friends for a moment believed that he committed the dastardly crime. The police think they know better. They do know this much, that it could not have been a case of suicide, that if the man who undoubtedly traveled with Mrs. Hazeldene on that fatal afternoon had no crime upon his conscience he would long ago have come forward and thrown what light he could upon the mystery.

"As to who that man was, the police in their blindness have not the faintest doubt. Under the unshakable belief that Errington is guilty they have spent the last few months in unceasing labor to try and find further and stronger proofs of his guilt. But they won't find them, because there are none. There are no positive proofs against the actual murderer, for he was one of those clever blackguards who think of everything, foresee every even-

tuality, who know human nature well, and can foretell exactly what evidence will be brought against them, and act accordingly.

"This blackguard from the first kept the figure, the personality, of Frank Errington before his mind. Frank Errington was the dust which the scoundrel threw metaphorically in the eyes of the police, and you must admit that he succeeded in blinding them—to the extent even of making them entirely forget the one simple little sentence, overheard by Mr. Andrew Campbell, and which was, of course, the clue to the whole thing—the only slip the cunning rogue made—'Au revoir! Don't be late tonight.' Mrs. Hazeldene was going that night to the opera with her husband—

"You are astonished?" he added with a shrug of the shoulders, "you do not see the tragedy yet, as I have seen it before me all along. The frivolous young wife, the flirtation with the friend?—all a blind, all pretence. I took the trouble which the police should have taken immediately, of finding out something about the finances of the Hazeldene *ménage*. Money is in nine cases out of ten the keynote to a crime.

"I found that the will of Mary Beatrice Hazeldene had been proved by the husband, her sole executor, the estate being sworn at £15,000. I found out, moreover, that Mr. Edward Sholto Hazeldene was a poor shipper's clerk when he married the daughter of a wealthy builder in Kensington—and then I made note of the fact that the disconsolate widower had allowed his beard to grow since the death of his wife.

"There's no doubt that he was a clever rogue," added the strange creature, leaning excitedly over the table, and peering into Polly's face. "Do you know how that deadly poison was injected into the poor woman's system? By the simplest of all means, one known to every scoundrel in Southern Europe. A ring—yes! A ring, which has a tiny hollow needle capable of holding a sufficient quantity of prussic acid to have killed two persons instead of one. The man in the tweed suit shook hands with his fair companion— probably she hardly felt the prick, not sufficiently in any case to make her utter a scream. And, mind you, the scoundrel had every facility, through his friendship with Mr. Errington, of procuring what poison he required, not to mention his friend's visiting card. We cannot gauge how many months ago he began to try and copy Frank Errington in his style of dress, the cut of his moustache, his general appearance, making the change probably so gradual, that no one in his own *entourage* would notice it. He selected for his model a man his own height and build, with the same colored hair."

"But there was the terrible risk of being identified by his fellow-traveler in the Underground," suggested Polly.

"Yes, there certainly was that risk; he chose to take it, and he was wise. He reckoned that several days would in any case elapse before that person, who, by the way, was a business man absorbed in his newspaper, would actually see him again. The great secret of successful crime is to study human nature," added the man in the corner, as he began looking for his hat and coat. "Edward Hazeldene knew it well."

"But the ring?"

"He may have bought that when he was on his honeymoon," he suggested with a grim chuckle; "the tragedy was not planned in a week, it may have taken years to mature. But you will own that there goes a frightful scoundrel unhung. I have left you his photograph as he was a year ago, and as he is now. You will see he has shaved his beard again, but also his moustache. I fancy he is a friend now of Mr. Andrew Campbell."

He left Miss Polly Burton wondering, not knowing what to believe.

And that is why she missed her appointment with Mr. Richard Frobisher (of the *London Mail*) to go and see Maud Allan dance at the Palace Theatre that afternoon.

❦

B. Fletcher Robinson

BERTRAM FLETCHER ROBINSON (1870-1937) was a sportsman, journalist, and writer probably best remembered for his friendship with Arthur Conan Doyle and his role in the creation of *The Hound of the Baskervilles* (1902). His principal contribution to mystery fiction was a little-known book called *The Chronicles of Addington Peace* (1905), noted by Ellery Queen in his *Queen's Quorum*, and featuring a Sherlock Holmes–type detective, whose adventures are chronicled by a Watson-like companion. The following story, echoing elements of *The Hound*, appeared in *Ladies' Home Journal* in 1904 and shows the little, rotund Scotland Yard detective at his best.

THE TERROR IN THE SNOW

B. FLETCHER ROBINSON

HENDRY, MY SERVANT, saw to it that I should not forget Inspector Addington Peace. Shortly after the adventure which I have already narrated, I left London for a round of country visits. And if a paragraph concerning that eminent detective chanced to appear in a newspaper, the substance of it was brought to me with my shaving-water in the morning.

"I see as 'e 'as bin up to 'is games again, sir," was Hendry's usual overture. "My word, but 'e's a sly one, by all accounts," was the customary conclusion.

I believe that Hendry often gained considerable notoriety in the servants' hall by a boasted friendship with Peace. To this I attribute the fact of his being consulted by Mr. Heavitree's butler on the occasion of the burglary that took place while I was staying at Crandon. Hendry's ludicrous fiasco, which resulted in a law-suit for false imprisonment, need not be narrated here, though it was considered a remarkably good joke against me at the time.

Toward the end of December, I returned to London for a few days, and on the third night after my arrival I decided to visit the inspector. Hendry had discovered that he was a bachelor, and lived in two little rooms on the third floor. The floors that separated us were let out as offices, so that Peace at the top and I at the bottom had the old house to ourselves after seven o'clock.

The little man was at home, and seemed pleased to see me. With his sparrow-like agility he hopped about, producing glasses and a bottle of whisky. Finally, with our pipes in full blast, we sat facing each other across the fire, and soon dropped into a conversation which to me, at least, was of unusual interest. A very curious knowledge of London and its peoples had Inspector Addington Peace.

An hour quickly slipped by, and when I rose to go I asked him if he would dine with me on my return from Cloudsham in Norfolk, where I was spending Christmas. He would be pleased, he told me; and then, as he stooped to light a spill in the coals:—

"You stay with the Baron Steen, I suppose?" he asked.

"Yes."

"And why?"

"Why?" I echoed in some surprise.

"You have relatives or other friends?"

"My nearest relative is a sour old uncle in Bradford, who calls me hard names for using the gifts Providence gave me instead of adding up figures in office. As for friends— well, I am a fairly rich man, Inspector, and, as such, have many friends. What is there against the Baron Steen?"

"Oh, nothing," he said, puffing at his pipe, so that he spoke as from a cloud, mistily.

"I know that he has played a bold game on the Stock Exchange," I continued, "and there may be a few outwitted financiers growling at his heels. But it would be hard to find a more thoughtful host. Yes, I am going to Cloudsham tomorrow."

We shook hands warmly on parting, and as I descended the stairs he leaned over the rail, smiling down upon me.

"Remember your dinner engagement," I called up to him. "I shall see you after the New Year."

"Yes, if not before," he said; and I seemed to catch the faint echo of a laugh as I turned the corner.

It was on the afternoon of December 24th that I stepped from the train at the little station of Cloudsham. Fresh snow had fallen, and the wind came bitterly over the frozen levels of the fen country.[1] A distant clock was striking four as the carriage passed into the crested entrance-gates and tugged up a slope of park land dotted with ragged oaks and storm-bowed spinnies,[2] which showed as black stains upon its snow-clad undulations. At the summit the road bent sharply, and I saw below me the old manor of Cloudsham, beyond which a somber plain, losing itself in the evening mists that swathed the horizon— stretched the restless waters of the North Sea.

The house lay in a broad depression, in shape as the hollow of a hand, on the seaward side, where the line of cliff bit into it like the grip teeth. The grey front looked up, across a slope of grass land, to a semicircle of forest that swept away in dark shadings of fir and oak. From the long oblong of the main buildings were thrust back two wings, flanked on the nearer side by a chapel.

From the back of the house to the edge of the sea cliffs, a distance of some quarter of a mile, ran an irregular avenue of firs with clipped yew walks and laurel-edged flower gardens on either hand.

A dozen men sweeping the paths and a telegraph boy on a pony mounting the hill toward me showed as black pygmies against the drifts of snow.

My bachelor host was absent when I was ushered into the great central hall where the house-party were met together for their tea. I am by nature shy of strangers, taken in large doses, and it was with relief that I recognized Jack Talman, the grizzled cynic of an Academician,[3] sitting in a corner seat well out of reach of draughts and female conversation.

"Hello, Phillips," he welcomed me. "And what financial gale brings you here?"

"What do you mean?"

---

[1] A marshy region. "The Fens" is an area in the east of England, and Cloudsham may be presumed to be located there in light of the North Sea vista described following.

[2] Small woods or copses.

[3] A member of the Royal Academy of Arts.

"Don't put on frills with me. I've come to paint old Steen's picture, if he will give me the fifteen hundred that I'm asking for it. Lord Tommy Retford yonder is here to unload some of his old furniture—you know Tommy's rooms in Piccadilly, don't you? Furnished by a dealer in Bond Street, and twenty-five per cent. commission to Tommy on everything he can sell out of them. That's Mrs. Talbot Slingsly talking to him. Pretty woman, got into trouble in New York, was cut by all America, and captured Slingsly and London Society at one blow. Scandal never does cross the Atlantic somehow—all the dirty linen gets washed in the herring-pond. That's old Lord Blane by the fire; very respectable, and lends money on the sly. 'Private gentleman will make advances on note of hand'—you know. Fine woman Mrs. Billy Blades—that's she on the sofa. She's been making desperate love to Steen, but no go. The gay old dog's too clever for her. That long chap's her husband. Watch him prowling round, looking to see if he can pouch a silver ashtray or something, I expect. By Jove, Phillips, but it's as good as a play, ain't it?"

"And this is London Society?" I exclaimed.

"No," he cackled, shaking with vast amusement. "No, man; no. It's the Smart Set, that advertised, criticized, glorious, needy brigade of rogues and vagabonds—the Smart Set. Bless 'em all, say I; they're the best of company, but it's as well to lock up your valuables before you become too intimate with them."

I finished off my tea while old Talman sucked at his cigarette in great entertainment.

"You'd like to see the house," he commenced again, "Come along, I'll show you round—I want a walk before dinner."

It was a most interesting ramble. We passed from room to room admiring the carved oak, the splendid pictures, the Sheraton furniture,[4] the cabinets of old china, the armor, and the tapestry. For the manor was filled with the heirlooms of the de Launes, from whom the Baron Steen rented it. And though the present peer, a broken-down old drunkard, was living in a little villa at Eastbourne on eight hundred pounds a year,[5] the family had been a great and glorious one, finding mention on many a page in English history.

At the end of the great dining-room, set in the black-oak wainscot[6] above the fire, was the portrait of a boy. It was a Reynolds,[7] and a worthy effort of that master hand. The lad could have been no more than fifteen years of age, but in his eyes was that grave, distracted expression that usually comes with the painful wisdom of later years. In more closely examining the picture, I noticed that a large portion of it at the bottom right-hand corner had been repaired or painted out. I called Talman's attention to this misfortune, asking if he knew the cause.

"They painted out the wolf," he said, "and with good enough reason, too."

"A wolf?" I said.

"If old de Laune were to hear me gossiping about it he'd kick me out of the place—he would, by Jove! But with Steen in possession it's safe enough. Mind you, though, you mustn't mention it to the ladies—on your word now."

---

[4] Furniture designed by renowned furniture-maker Thomas Sheraton (1751-1806).
[5] Over $100,000 per year, based on the current retail price index.
[6] Wooden paneling.
[7] Sir Joshua Reynolds (1723-1792), the most influential portrait painter of his day.

"Yes, yes," I said eagerly; "go on."

"Such things frighten the women," he explained. "Well, it was in this way. Phillip, and he was the sixth earl, was our ambassador at St. Petersburg somewhere about the year 1790. Once when he was out hunting he shot an old she-wolf that was peering from the mouth of a cave, and inside they found a thriving family of four cubs. One of them was white, an albino, I suspect. He saved it from the dogs and took it home. When he came back to Cloudsham the next year, he brought it along with his wife and his boy—an only son. They say it was a great pet at first, but it grew sulky with age, and finally was kept chained in the stables.

"One Christmas Eve, just as dusk was closing in, de Laune was trotting down the drive—he had been hunting at a distant meeting—when he heard a fearful screaming from the lower gardens toward the cliff. He put spurs to his horse, and in two minutes was galloping through the shadows of the fir avenue toward the sea. All of a sudden his horse pulled up dead, threw him, and bolted. When he got to his feet—he wasn't hurt, luckily—what did he see but the body of his son, lying with his throat torn out, and the white wolf standing over him, the broken chain dangling at its neck.

"They say he was a giant, this Philip de Laune, and of a very wild and passionate temper. Anyway, he went straight for the beast, and, though he was dreadfully mauled, he killed it—Heaven knows how—with his bare hands. That's why the present branch of the family came by the place. Pretty gruesome, isn't it?"

"A strange story," I told him; "but why must it be kept a secret from the ladies?"

"Because the beast walks, man. There's not a laborer in Norfolk who would go into the lower gardens on any night of the year, much less on Christmas Eve."

"My good Talman, do you mean to say you believe this?"

"I don't know—but I wouldn't go into the lower gardens tonight, if I could walk round. Think of it, Phillips, the white shape with the bloody jaws lurking in the shadows! Ugh—let's go and get a cocktail before—"

"I beg your pardon, sir, but the Baron is looking for you."

He was a tall, hatchet-faced fellow, with that mixture of respect and dignity that marks the well-trained British manservant. Upon the soft pile of the rugs we had not heard his footsteps.

"He asked me to find you, sir," he continued, addressing himself to me with a slight bow. "He is waiting in his room."

As he preceded us thither, Talman whispered that Henderson—meaning thereby our conductor—was Steen's valet, and a very clever follow by all accounts.

The Baron, fat, high-colored, and hearty, welcomed me with an open sincerity of pleasure well calculated to place a guest at his ease. A remarkable old boy was the Baron Steen. He always seemed to carry with him a jovial atmosphere of his own, in which those to whom he spoke were lost and blinded out of their better judgment. He was kind enough to pay me some compliments upon my watercolor work. Whatever else can be brought against him, no one can deny that he was a sound judge of art.

The dinner passed pleasantly enough that night, with free and witty conversation. Our bachelor host was in his most humorous mood, keeping those about him in shouts of laughter. Facing him, at the extremity of the table, was his secretary, a thin, melancholy youth of about four-and-twenty. My fair neighbor told me that Terry, as he was named, had been intended for the Church, but that his father, having ruined himself on the Stock Exchange, had persuaded the Baron to give him work. He was devoted to his patron, which, she smiled, was not surprising, seeing that he must be well on his way to rebuilding the fortune his father had lost.

I am not an ardent gambler, and when I do play I admit a preference for games in which brains are of some account. The roulette-table soon bored me, and after I had seen the last of a few pounds, I contented myself by watching the changing fortunes of the rest of the party. Just before eleven the Baron, who had parted with considerable sums of money in perfect good humor, excused himself, and before the rest had settled down to the table again I slipped away to my bedroom, where a selection of novels and a favorite pipe offered more congenial attractions.

The room was of considerable size and majestically furnished. It was on the first floor at the extremity of the right-hand wing, and looked out over the gardens on the cliff. A branch road from the main drive ran beneath the windows to an entrance at the back of the house.

They had steam heat on the upper floors, and the high temperature of my room had drawn stale and heavy odors from the tapestry on the walls and the ancient hangings that fringed the huge four-post bedstead. It was the atmosphere of an old clothes shop on a July day. I pulled back the curtains, opened the window and thrust out my head for a mouthful of fresh air.

It was a quiet, moonless night, lit by the stars that blinked in their thousand constella- tions. Though the snow lay deep, the air struck mildly. Indeed, if it were freezing, it could not have been by more than two degrees. Upon the edge of the distant cliffs robes of confus- ing mist curled in veils as thin as moonlight; but in the foreground the yew walks and aisles of ancient laurel showed clearly upon the white carpet. About the central avenue of firs which carved the gardens into two the dark- ness lay in impenetrable pools of shadow. As I waited, the silence was startled by a bell. It rang the four quarters in a tinkling measure, followed by eleven musical strokes. I know that the sound must come from the little church that lay to my right; but, though I leant from my window, the angle of the wing in which I was hid the building from me.

I feel that the story which I have now to tell may well turn me into an object for ridicule. I can only describe that which I saw; as for the conclusions at which I arrived there are many more practical people in the world than myself who would have judged no dif- ferently. At best it was a ghastly business.

I HAD RETURNED to the dressing-table and was changing my dress-coat for a comfortable smoking-jacket when I heard it—a faint and distant cry, yet a cry which was crowded with such terror that I clung to a chair with my white face and goggling eyes staring back at me from the mirror on the table. Again it sounded, and again; then silence fell like the shutter of a camera. I rushed to the window, peering out into the night.

The great gardens lay sleeping in the dusky shadows. There was nothing to be heard; nothing moved save the curling wreaths of mist that came creeping up over the cliffs like the ghosts of drowned sailormen from their burial sands below. Could it have been some trick of the imagination? Could it—and the suggestion which I despised thrust itself upon me—could it bear reference to that grim tragedy that had been played in the old fir avenue so many years ago?

And then I first saw the *thing* that came toward me.

It was moving up a narrow path, hedged with yew, that led from the gardens and passed to the right of the wing in which I stood. The yew had been clipped into walls some five feet high, but the eastern gales had beaten out gaps and ragged indentations in the lines of greenery, so that in my sideways view of it the path itself was here and there exposed. It was through one of these breaches in the walls that I noticed a sign of movement. I waited straining my eyes. Yes, there it showed again, a something, moving swiftly toward the house with a clumsy rolling stride.

It was never nearer to me than fifty yards, and the stars gave a shifty light. Yet it left me with an impression that it was about four feet in height and of a dull white color. I remember that its body contrasted plainly with the dark hedges, but melted into uncertainty against a patch of snow. Once it stopped and half raised itself on its hind legs as if listening. Then again it tumbled forward in its shambling, ungainly fashion—now hidden by the yew wall, now thrust into momentary sight by a ragged gap until it disappeared around the angle of the house. Doubtless it would turn to the left, round the old chapel, across the snow-bound park, and so to the woods—where a wolf should be!

I was still staring from the window in the blank fear of the unknown, when I heard the swift tap of feet upon the road beneath me. Around the corner of the wing came a man, running with a patter of little strides, while a dozen yards behind him were a pair of less active followers. What they wanted I did not consider; for at that moment the sight of my own kind was joy enough for me. The electric lamps in the room behind me threw a broad golden patch upon the snow, and as the leader reached it he stopped, glancing up at where I stood. The light struck him fairly in the face. It was Addington Peace!

"Did you hear that cry?" he panted; and then, with a sudden nod of recognition: "I see who it is, Mr. Phillips—well, and did you hear it?"

"It came from over there—in the fir avenue," said I, pointing with a trembling finger. "I don't understand it, Inspector; I don't indeed. There was something that came up that yew walk behind you about a minute afterward. I should have thought it would have passed you."

"No, I saw nothing. What was it like?"

"A sort of a dog," I stammered; for under his steady eye I had not nerve enough to tell him of my private imaginings.

"A dog—that's curious. Are all the rest of you in bed?"

"No; they're gambling!"

"Very good. I see there is a door at the back there. Will you come down and let me in, after I've had I look round the gardens?"

"Certainly."

"If you meet any of your friends, you need not mention that I have arrived. Do you understand?"

I nodded, and he hopped away across the lawn with his two companions at his heels.

I slipped on an overcoat and made my way quietly down the stairs. From the roulette-room, as I passed it, came the chink of money and the murmur of merry voices. They would not disturb us, that was certain. I reached the garden doors in the center of the main build-ing, turned the key, and walked out into the gloom of a great square porch.

As I have said, the temperature was scarcely below freezing-point, and if I shiv-ered in my fur-lined overcoat it was more from excitement than any great chill in the air. For a good twenty minutes I waited listening and peering into the night. It was not a pleas-ant time, for my nerves were jangled, and I searched the shadows with timorous eyes, half fearing, half expecting, Heaven knows what hideous apparition. It was with a start which set my heart thumping that I saw Peace turn the corner of the right-hand wing and come trotting down the drive toward me. There was something in his aspect that told a story of calamity.

"What is it?" I asked him, as he panted up.

"I want you—come along," he whis-pered, and started back by the way he had come.

We passed round the right-hand wing, under my bedroom window, and stopped where the yew walk ended. To right and left of the entrance two stone fauns leered upon us under the starlight.

"This thing you call a dog—could you see it as far as this?"

"No; the angle of the wing prevented me."

"YOU SAW IT pass in this direction. Are you certain it did not go back the way it came?"

"Yes. I am quite certain."

"Then it must either have turned up the road, in which case I should have met it; or down the road, where you would have seen it as it passed under your windows: or else have run straight on. If we take these facts as proved, it must have run straight on."

"That is so."

We had our backs to the laughing fauns. Before us lay a broad triangle of even snow, with the chapel and wing of the house for its sides, and for its base the carriage-drive on which we stood. There was no shrub or tree in any part of it that might conceal a fugitive. Close to the wall of the house ran a path end-ing in a small side door. The chapel, which was joined to the mansion, had no entrance on the garden side.

"'If it entered this triangle and disap-peared—for I am certain it was not here when I ran by—we may conclude that it found its way into the house. It had no other method of escape. Kindly stay here, Mr. Phillips. This snow is fortunate, but I wish the sweepers had not been so conscientious about their work on the paths."

He drew a little electric lantern from his coat, touched the spring, and with an eye of light moving before him, turned into the path under the wall. He walked slowly, bending double as he swept the brilliant circle now on the exposed ground, now on the snow ridges to right and left. The sills of the ground-floor window were carefully examined and when he reached the door he searched the single step before it with minute attention. A curious spectacle he made; this little atom of a man, as he peeped and peered his way like some slow-hunting beast on a cold scent.

It was not until he left the path for the snow-covered grass-plot that I saw him give any sign of success. He dropped on his knees with a little chirrup of satisfaction like the note of a bird. Then he rose again, shaking his head and staring up at the windows above him in a cautious, suspicious manner. Finally he came slowly back to me, with his head on one side, staring at the ground before him.

"You thought it was a dog?" he asked. "Why a dog?"

"It looked to me like a big dog—or a wolf." I told him boldly.

"Whether it be beast or man, or both. I believe the thing that killed him is in the house now."

I jumped back, staring at him with a sudden exclamation.

"Who has been killed?" I stammered out.

"Baron Steen. We found him on the cliffs yonder. He was badly cut about."

"It's impossible, Inspector," I cried. "He left the roulette-table not a quarter of an hour before you came."

"Ah—he was a cool hand, Mr. Phillips. It was like him to put off bolting till the last minute. The warrant against him for company frauds is in my pocket now. But some one gave the game away to him, for his yacht is lying off the beach there, with a boat from her waiting at the foot of the cliff. But we've no time to lose—come along."

Before the big garden porch the inspector's two companions were waiting. He drew them aside for a minute's whispered conversation before they separated, and disappeared into the night. What had they done with the body? I had not the courage to inquire.

We entered the house, moving very softly. In the hall Peace took me by the arm.

"You're a bit shaken, Mr. Phillips, and I'm not surprised. But I want your assistance badly. Can you pull yourself together and help me to see this through?"

"I'll do what I can."

"Take me up to your room, then."

We were in luck, for we tip-toed up the great stairs and down the long passages without meeting a guest or servant. Once in my room, the inspector walked across and pushed the electric bell. Three, four minutes went by before the summons was answered, and then it was by a flushed and disordered footman who bounced into the room and halted, staring open-mouthed from me to my companion.

"Sorry to disturb your dance," said Peace, beaming upon him.

"Beg pardon, sir, but you startled me— yes, we was 'aving a little dance in the servants' 'all; but it's of no consequence, sir."

"A slippery floor, eh, with so much French chalk on it?"

The young man glanced at the powder on his shoes and grinned.

"So you are all dancing in the servants' hall, are you?"

"I believe so, sir, barring Edward, who is waiting on the party, and Mr. Henderson."

"And where is Mr. Henderson?"

"He is the baron's man, sir. I should not presume to inquire where he was. Beg pardon, sir, but are you staying here tonight?"

"This is a friend of mine," I interposed. "He will stay the night; but you need not trouble about that now."

"A smart fellow like you can keep his mouth shut," continued the inspector, sweetly. "You wouldn't go shouting all over the house if you were let into a secret—now, would you?"

"Oh no, sir; on my word I wouldn't."

And so Peace told him of the projected arrest, of the murder, and of his own identity. The color faded from the young man's cheeks, but he stood stiff and silent, never taking his eyes from the little detective's face.

"And what can I do, sir?" he asked, when the tale was over. "He was a good master to us, sir; whatever there was against him, he was good to us. You can trust me to help catch the scoundrel who killed him if I can."

"I see this room is warmed by steam heat. Is that the case with all the bedrooms and passages?"

"Yes, sir. The only open fires are in the reception-rooms. When the baron made the alterations last year, they left the grates for the sake of appearance; but they are never lighted, save on the ground-floor."

"And in what reception-rooms are there fires at the present moment?"

"The dining-room fire has died out by now," said the young man, ticking off the numbers on his fingers. "But there is one in the big hall, one in the library where the party is playing, one in the little drawing-room, and one in the baron's room."

"And the kitchen?"

"Of course, sir, one in the kitchen and one in the servants' hall."

"That is all. Are you certain?"

"Quite certain, sir."

"Good; and now for the bath-rooms."

"The bath-rooms, sir?"

"Exactly."

"There are two bath-rooms in each wing; some of the gentlemen have tubs in their own rooms besides."

"Now, I think we know where we are," said the inspector, briskly. "No chance of the roulette party breaking up, is there?"

"Oh no, sir; not for another two hours, at least."

"I want you to return, Mr. Phillips, and try your luck at the tables for a spell," he said, with a quick glance at me. "It is now eleven thirty; be back in this room at twelve fifteen. I am going to take a walk around the house with our young friend here in the meanwhile. The baron had a secretary, I believe?"

"Yes, a man called Terry."

"Bring him up with you when you come.

I shall want a talk with him. Is all quite plain?"

"Yes," I told him; and so we parted.

When I stepped into the roulette-room I stood for a moment blinking at the players like a yokel at a pantomime. The scene was to me something unreal, a clever piece of stage effect, with its flushed and covetous faces, its frocks and its diamonds, its piles of sparkling gold, and the cry of the banker as he twirled the wheel. How could they be doing this with that bloodstained patch on the cliff edge, with that unknown horror slinking through the snow—how could they be doing this if they were not acting a part! An odd figure I must have looked, if there had been anyone to notice me. But they were too eager in the game to hear the opening of the door, or to see who went and came. I walked over to the fireplace, lit a cigarette, and watched them, my nerves growing steadier in the merry chatter of tongues. They were all there, the men and women of that careless house-party, all there—save one who lay silent wherever they had laid him.

Half an hour had slipped by, until, at last, with an effort, I walked to the table and threw down two sovereigns on the red.

It won, and I laughed at the melancholy omen; not, perhaps, without an odd note in my voice, for the man over whose shoulder I leaned to gather my winnings glanced up with a startled expression. It was young Terry, the secretary; the very person I wanted to see.

"Anything the matter, Mr. Phillips?" he asked. "You're not looking very well."

"Don't worry about me," I told him. "But I want a word with you in private."

"Certainly—just one moment."

He had been winning heavily, and it took him some time to crowd the banknotes into his pockets. A sovereign slipped from his fingers and rolled under the table as he rose; but he paid no attention to it.

"I have something to tell you. Can you come up to my room?" I asked him.

He hesitated, looking regretfully at the table, where Fortune had been so kind to him.

"It happens to be rather important," I said.

He followed me without another word. I did not attempt to explain until we had passed up the stairs and through the corridors to my room. He seated himself on the great bed with a shiver of cold, drawing the heavy curtains about his shoulders. And there I told him the story from the beginning to the end, hiding nothing, not even my belief in the supernatural nature of the thing which I had seen.

He never moved, but his face grew so pale and drawn that toward the end it seemed as if it were a powdered mask that stared at me from the shadows of the curtains.

"My God," he cried, and fell back upon the bed in a passion of hysterical tears.

I tried to help him, but he thrust me fiercely away, so I thought it best to let him get over it himself. He was still lying on the thick quilt, sobbing and shivering, when the door opened and Peace stepped into the room. I explained the situation in a hurried whisper; but when I turned again Terry had got to his feet and was watching us, clinging to the bed-post.

"THIS IS INSPECTOR Addington Peace," I told him. "Perhaps you can give him some information?"

"Not tonight," he cried, "don't ask me tonight, gentlemen. You cannot tell what this means to me; tomorrow, perhaps—"

He dropped down upon the bed, cover-ing his face with his hands. He seemed a help-less sort of creature, and my heart went out to him in his calamity.

"A night's rest is what you want," I said, patting him on the shoulder. "Come, let me give you an arm."

He took it at once, with a grateful glance, and I led him down the corridor, with Peace in sympathetic attendance. Fortunately, his room was in the same wing, so we had not far to go. When we reached it, he thanked us for our care of him. And so we left him, returning to my bedroom in silence, for indeed, the scene had been a painful one.

"Peace," I said, when the door had closed behind us, "what was the thing I saw in the yew walk?"

He had seated himself in an easy-chair, and was polishing the bowl of a well-stained meerschaum pipe, with a silk pocket-hand-kerchief.

"I think you already have an explana-tion," he answered cheerfully.

"If it amuses you to sneer at my super-stition—"

"You refer to the legend of the de Laune's. I have heard the story before, Mr. Phillips; nor am I surprised that you believed it to be the ghost wolf."

"I did—but now I want you to disprove it."

"On the contrary, all my evidence sup-ports your theory."

I stared at him, with a creeping horror in my blood. I was beginning to be afraid—seri-ously afraid. Peace leaned back in his chair, with his eyes, vacant in expression, fixed on the wall. He seemed rather to be arguing with himself than addressing a listener.

"Baron Steen," he said, "met with his death on an open path between a shallow duck-pond and a little pavilion. He had fought hard for life, had rolled and struggled with his enemy. There were four or five punctured wounds in his throat and neck, from which he had bled profusely. And now for the thing that killed him—whatever it was. It could not have fled down the cliff path, for the boat's crew waiting below had heard the screams, and had come running up by that way. They were with him when we arrived, and assured me they had seen nothing. It could not have turned to the right or left, for, though the paths had been swept clean—doubtless by the baron's orders, for he would not desire his way of escape to be easily traced—the snow on either side lay in unbroken levels. It could only have retired by the yew avenue, and it did not break through the hedge. That, again, the snow proved clearly. So, we may take it, that whatever the thing may have been which you saw—it killed Baron Steen; further, it escaped into the house—this, you will remember, we decided in the garden. Let us imagine it was a man—that you were deceived by the uncertain light. His clothes must of necessity have been drenched in blood. He could not have struggled so fiercely with his victim and escaped those fatal signs. Yet, he cannot have burned his clothes, for the fires are downstairs where people were passing. Nor can he have washed them, for neither the bathrooms nor the bedroom basins have been recently used. I have spent some time in searching boxes and wardrobes with no result. Stranger still, as far as my limited information goes, everyone in the house can prove an *alibi*—save two."

"And who are they?" I asked eagerly.

"Mr. Henderson, the baron's valet—and yourself."

"Inspector Peace—" I began angrily.

"Tut, tut, my dear Mr. Phillips. I was merely stating the facts. Mr. Henderson's case, however, presents an interesting feature, for he has run away."

"Run away," I said. "Then that settles it."

"Not altogether, I'm afraid. I think it is more a matter of theft than murder with Mr. Henderson."

I stared at him in silence as he sat there, with his little hands clasped upon his lap, a picture of irritating composure.

"Peace," I said, struggling to control my voice. "What are you hiding from me? It is something inhuman, unnatural that has done this dreadful thing."

The little detective stretched himself, yawned, and then rose to his feet.

"I have no opinion except that I think you had better get to bed. Don't lock your door, for I may find time for an hour's sleep on your sofa before morning."

THE NEWS WAS OUT after breakfast—the news that led to mild hysterics and scurrying lady's-maids to the packing of boxes, and the chastened sorrow of those gentlemen who owed the baron money. Through all the turmoil of the morning moved the little detective, the most sympathetic of men. It was he who apologized so humbly for the locked doors of the bath-rooms; he who superintended the lighting of fires, and the making of the beds, and the packing of trunks for the station so closely that the housemaids were convinced that he entertained a secret passion for each one of them; it was he who announced Henderson's robbery of the gold plate, following it by information as to the culprit's arrest. The establishment had by this time become convinced that Henderson was the murderer, and breathed relief at the news.

They had brought the body of Baron Steen to the house early in the morning—it had been laid in the garden pavilion on its first discovery.

With death in so strange a form present among us, I was disgusted by the noise and bustle, the gossip and chatter among the guests of the dead man. I wandered off in search of the one person who had seemed sincerely affected by the news, the young secretary, Maurice Terry. He was nowhere to be found. A servant of whom I inquired told me that the secretary had kept to his bed, being greatly unnerved by the tragedy, and I strolled up the stairs on an errand of consolation. The door was locked, and there came no answer to my continued tapping.

"Terry," I called through the keyhole. "It is I, Phillips; won't you let me in?"

"I have a key that will fit, if you will kindly stand aside," suggested a modest voice.

I rose from my knees to find the inspector at my elbow.

"It would be a gross intrusion," I told him. "If he wishes to be alone with his sorrow, we have no right to disturb him."

"He is seriously ill."

"How did you discover that?"

"By borrowing a gardener's ladder and looking through his window. He is unconscious, or was ten minutes ago."

A skillful twist or two with a bit of wire and the key was pushed from the lock. The duplicate opened the door. Peace walked into the room, and I followed at his heels.

On his bed, fully dressed, lay poor Terry, with a face paler than his pillows. His breath came and went in short, painful gasps. One hand strayed continuously about his throat, groping and plucking at his collar with feverish unrest. It was a very painful spectacle.

"I will send for a doctor at once," I whispered, stepping to the bell. But Peace held up a warning hand.

"Come here," he said, "I have something to show you."

With movements as tender as a woman's he unfastened the man's collar and slipped out the stud. Then he paused. The eyes that watched me had turned cold and hard.

"If it is as I suspect, you may be called as a witness. Do you object?"

"Yes; but I shall not leave you on that account?"

"Very well," he said, as he opened the shirt and the vest beneath it.

Smeared and patched in dark etching upon the white shin was a broad stain of blood, of dried and clotted blood, the life's blood of a man.

"He is wounded. Peace," I cried. "Poor fellow, he must have nearly bled to death."

"Do not alarm yourself," said the inspector, drily. "It is the blood of Baron Steen."

A WEEK HAD GONE by, and I was sitting alone in my Keble Street rooms, when Peace walked in, with a heavy traveling-coat over his arm.

"Thank Heaven, you have come at last," I cried. "How is Maurice Terry?"

"Dead—poor fellow," he said, with an honest sorrow in his voice. "Yet, after all, Mr. Phillips, it was the best that could have happened to him."

"And his story—the causes—the method?" I demanded.

"It has taken some hard work, but the bits of the puzzle are fitted together at last. You wish to hear it, I suppose?"

"According to your promise," I reminded him.

"It is a case of unusual interest," he said.

"Though it bears a certain similarity to the Gottstein trial at Kiel in '89."[8]

He paused to light his big pipe, and then sat back in his chair, with his eyes fixed in abstract contemplation.

"I was convinced that the murderer was in the house; and that he had entered by the side door, toward which you had seen him pass. When studying the spot I made a discovery of some importance. Steen had left by the same exit. Also he had reason to fear some person in that wing, for he had turned from the path and made a circuit over the grass. I had already noted his broad-toed boots when examining his body and the footprints in the snow were unmistakable. Who was his enemy in that wing? It was a problem to be solved.

"I discovered no stained clothing, and no signs of its cleansing or destruction. From what information I could gather, all the house party had been in the roulette-room save you yourself; and all the servants had been at the dance save Henderson and a man waiting on the guests. But in the course of my search the footman who accompanied me discovered that a quantity of gold plate was missing. It was reasonable to imagine that Henderson was the thief. Probably the confidential valet had learned of the Baron's projected flight and of the warrant for his arrest. It was a moment for judicious robbery, the traces of which would be covered by the confusion of the news. But was Henderson also a murderer? I did not think so. The death of his master was the one thing which would wreck his scheme. In the early morning I interviewed the fanner on whose cart he had driven into Norbridge. He told me that, acting on orders he had received from Henderson, he met that person at the corner of the stables at eleven o'clock precisely—five minutes before the murder occurred. That finally eliminated the valet from the list.

"On my return from the farm I examined the gardens again with great minuteness. At the corner of the little pavilion, about fifteen feet from where the body had lain, there was a patch of bloody snow. This puzzled me a good deal until the solution offered itself that the murderer had tried to wash his hands in the snow, the water of the pond being frozen hard. Yet his clothing would also bear the stain. What had he worn that showed so white to you in the starlight? Could it have been that he wore no clothes at all?

"A naked man! The suggestion was full of possibilities.

"It was fortunate that I had brought assistants to help me in Steen's capture. Their presence gave me a wider scope, for they were both good men. I left them to search the pavilion and laurels for the clothing, which the murderer might have concealed when he realized how fatal was its evidence. As I walked back to the house I began to understand the situation more clearly. The main drive, curving down the slope of the park, was in view of a tall man coming up by the yew walk. The murderer might have noticed our approach. What more natural than that he should have bent double as he ran, thus obtaining the cover of the left-hand hedge, which was not more than four to five feet high? Did not this answer to your description of the thing you had seen? It would have been cold work for him. I made a note to be on the look-out for chills.

"For a couple of hours I devoted myself

---

[8] Peace is a "walking calendar of crime," as Sherlock Holmes is described in *A Study in Scarlet* (1887).

to speeding those guests who caught the eleven-thirty train. I do not think a trunk left for the station of which I have not a complete inventory. Indeed, the baron's creditors have to thank me for the return of several trifles of value, which were included, accidentally, no doubt, in the ladies' dressing-bags.

"After the carriages had started I went in search of Terry, and discovered that he had not left his room. Equally to the point, his windows looked down upon the spot where the baron made his *detour* over the grass while escaping. I became interested in this young man. The score was creeping up against him. A ladder from an obliging gardener allowed me to observe him from the window. A visit to the housekeeper gave me a duplicate key to his door. What happened in the room you know, Mr. Phillips."

"But, the motive—why did he kill his patron?" I asked him eagerly.

"I doubt if we shall ever learn the truth on that point," he said. "As far as I can make out, Steen was directly responsible for the ruin and disgrace of Terry's father. Probably the son did not fully realize this when the baron, with a pity most unusual in the man, gave him the secretaryship. But of all participation in the flight he was certainly innocent, for he was in bed at the time."

"In bed!" I cried.

"Don't interrupt, if you please. What happened I take to be as follows:—Terry was in bed when the old man tried to creep past his window. Somehow he heard him, and, looking out, understood what was up. Perhaps that rascal Henderson had told him the truth

about his father; perhaps Steen had promised him compensation—he had a mother and sister dependent on him—which promise the financier meant to avoid, along with many more serious obligations, by running away. At any rate, passion, revenge, the sense of injustice—call it what you like—took hold of the lad. He caught up the first handy weapon; it chanced to be a dagger paper-knife—dangerous things, I hate them—and rushed down a back staircase and through the side door in pursuit of his enemy.

"When that had happened, which happened, the fear that comes to all amateurs in crime took him by the throat. He wiped his hands in the snow; he tore off his sleeping suit—that is how I know he had been in bed—and thrust it, with its terrible evidences of murder, into the thatch of the little pavilion. We found it there a day later. Then he started back to the house as naked as a baby.

"He saw us running down the hill, and made for the side door, bending double behind the hedge. Who were we? Had we noticed him? Believe me, Mr. Phillips, whether he had held the murder righteous or no, it was only the rope he saw dangling before him. Might not the alarm be given at any moment? He dared not wash himself, and the stains had dried upon him, He hurried on his clothes, shivering in the chill that had struck home, and so to the safest place he could find—the roulette-table."

"It is well that he died," I said simply.

"It saved the law some trouble," remarked the inspector, with a grim little nod at the wall.

Arnold Bennett

ENOCH ARNOLD BENNETT (1867-1931) was an English novelist, playwright, and journalist, whose novels and plays generally reflected middle-class life in north Staffordshire, where he lived. However, his excellent detective fiction includes *The Loot of Cities* (1905), six stories about Cecil Thorold, a rogue-detective millionaire "in search of joy" and not above blackmail and theft to corral his criminals. The following story first appeared in the *Windsor Magazine* for August 1905.

A BRACELET IN BRUGES

ARNOLD BENNETT

I.

The bracelet had fallen into the canal. And the fact that the canal was the most picturesque canal in the old Flemish city of Bruges,[1] and that the ripples caused by the splash of the bracelet had disturbed reflections of wondrous belfries, towers, steeples, and other unique examples of Gothic architecture, did nothing whatever to assuage the sudden agony of that disappearance. For the bracelet had been given to Kitty Sartorius by her grateful and lordly manager, Lionel Belmont (U.S.A.), upon the completion of the unexampled run of *The Delmonico Doll* at the Regency Theatre, London. And its diamonds were worth five hundred pounds,[2] to say nothing of the gold.

The beautiful Kitty, and her friend Eve Fincastle the journalist, having exhausted Ostend,[3] had duly arrived at Bruges in the course of their holiday tour. The question of Kitty's jewelry had arisen at the start. Kitty had insisted that she must travel with all her jewels, according to the custom of theatrical stars of great magnitude. Eve had equally insisted that Kitty must travel without jewels, and had exhorted her to remember the days of her simplicity. They compromised. Kitty was allowed to bring the bracelet, but nothing else save the usual half-dozen rings. The ravishing creature could not have persuaded herself to leave the bracelet behind, because it was so recent a gift and still new and strange and heavenly to her. But, since prudence forbade even Kitty to let the trifle lie about in hotel bedrooms, she was obliged always to wear it. And she had been wearing it this bright afternoon in early October when the girls, during a stroll, had met one

---

[1] Bruges is the capital of West Flanders, in the Flemish Region (the northern part) of Belgium. In the latter part of the ninteenth century, it was an important tourist destination for English and French travelers.

[2] Using the increase in the retail price index since 1905, these diamonds would sell for almost £40,000 today.

[3] A popular sea side resort in Belgium.

of their new friends, Madame Lawrence, on the world-famous Quai du Rosaire,[4] just at the back of the Hotel de Ville and the Halles.

Madame Lawrence resided permanently in Bruges. She was between twenty-five and forty-five, dark, with the air of continually subduing a natural instinct to dash, and well dressed in black. Equally interested in the peerage and in the poor, she had made the acquaintance of Eve and Kitty at the Hotel de la Grande Place, where she called from time to time to induce English travellers to buy genuine Bruges lace wrought under her own supervision by her own paupers. She was Belgian by birth, and when complimented on her fluent and correct English, she gave all the praise to her deceased husband, an English barrister. She had settled in Bruges like many people settle there, because Bruges is inexpensive, picturesque, and inordinately respectable; besides an English church and chaplain, it has two cathedrals and an episcopal palace with a real bishop in it.

"What an exquisite bracelet! May I look at it?"

It was these simple but ecstatic words, spoken with Madame Lawrence's charming foreign accent, which had begun the tragedy. The three women had stopped to admire the always admirable view from the little quay, and they were leaning over the rails when Kitty unclasped the bracelet for the inspection of the widow. The next instant there was a *plop*, an affrighted exclamation from Madame Lawrence in her native tongue, and the bracelet was engulfed before the very eyes of all three.

The three looked at each other, nonplussed. Then they looked around, but not a single person was in sight. Then, for some reason which doubtless psychology can explain, they stared hard at the water, though the water there was just as black and foul as it is everywhere else in the canal system of Bruges.

"Surely you've not dropped it!" Eve Fincastle exclaimed in a voice of horror. Yet she knew positively that Madame Lawrence had.

The delinquent took a handkerchief from her muff and sobbed into it. And between her sobs she murmured: "We must inform the police."

"Yes, of course," said Kitty, with the lightness of one to whom a five-hundred-pound bracelet is a bagatelle. "They'll fish it up in no time."

"Well," Eve decided, "you go to the police at once, Kitty; and Madame Lawrence will go with you, because she speaks French; and I'll stay here to mark the exact spot."

The other two started, but Madame Lawrence, after a few steps, put her hand to her side. "I can't," she sighed, pale. "I am too upset. I cannot walk. You go with Miss Sartorius," she said to Eve, "and I will stay." And she leaned heavily against the railings.

Eve and Kitty ran off, just as if it were an affair of seconds, and the bracelet had to be saved from drowning. But they had scarcely turned the corner, thirty yards away, when they reappeared in company with a high official of police, whom, by the most lucky chance in the world, they had encountered in the covered passage leading to the Place du Bourg. This official, instantly enslaved by Kitty's beauty, proved to be the very mirror of politeness and optimism. He took their names and addresses, and a full description of the bracelet, and informed them that at that place the canal was nine feet deep. He said that the bracelet should

---

[4] A beautiful canal in Bruges, the inspiration for Bruges's reputation as "the Venice of the north."

undoubtedly be recovered on the morrow, but that, as dusk was imminent, it would be futile to commence angling that night. In the meantime, the loss should be kept secret; and to make all sure, a succession of gendarmes should guard the spot during the night.

Kitty grew radiant and rewarded the gallant officer with smiles; Eve was satisfied; and the face of Madame Lawrence wore a less mournful hue.

"And now," said Kitty to Madame, when everything had been arranged, and the first of the gendarmes was duly installed at the exact spot against the railings, "you must come and take tea with us in our winter-garden; and be gay! Smile: I insist. And I insist that you don't worry."

Madame Lawrence tried feebly to smile.

"You are very good-natured," she stammered.

Which was decidedly true.

II.

THE WINTER-GARDEN of the Hotel de la Grande Place, referred to in all the hotel's advertisements, was merely the inner court of the hotel roofed in by glass at the height of the first storey. Cane flourished there, in the shape of lounge-chairs, but no other plant. One of the lounge-chairs was occupied when, just as the carillon in the belfry at the other end of the Place began to play Gounod's "Nazareth," indicating the hour of five o'clock, the three ladies entered the winter-garden. Apparently the toilettes of two of them had been adjusted and embellished as for a somewhat ceremonious occasion.

"Lo!" cried Kitty Sartorius, when she perceived the occupant of the chair, "the millionaire! Mr. Thorold, how charming of

you to reappear like this! I invite you to tea."

Cecil Thorold rose with appropriate eagerness.

"Delighted!" he said, smiling, and then explained that he had arrived from Ostend about two hours before and had taken rooms in the hotel.

"You knew we were staying here?" Eve asked as he shook hands with her.

"No," he replied; "but I am very glad to find you again."

"Are you?" She spoke languidly, but her color heightened and those eyes of hers sparkled.

"Madame Lawrence," Kitty chirruped, "let me present Mr. Cecil Thorold. He is appallingly rich, but we mustn't let that frighten us."

From a mouth less adorable than the mouth of Miss Sartorius such an introduction might have been judged lacking in the elements of good form, but for more than two years now Kitty had known that whatever she did or said was perfectly correct because she did or said it. The new acquaintances laughed amiably and a certain intimacy was at once established.

"Shall I order tea, dear?" Eve suggested.

"No, dear," said Kitty quietly. "We will wait for the Count."

"The Count?" demanded Cecil Thorold.

"The Comte d'Avrec," Kitty explained. "He is staying here."

"A French nobleman, doubtless?"

"Yes," said Kitty; and she added, "you will like him. He is an archeologist, and a musician—oh, and lots of things!"

"If I am one minute late, I entreat pardon," said a fine tenor voice at the door.

It was the Count. After he had been introduced to Madame Lawrence, and Cecil

Thorold had been introduced to him, tea was served. Now, the Comte d'Avrec was everything that a French count ought to be. As dark as Cecil Thorold, and even handsomer, he was a little older and a little taller than the millionaire, and a short, pointed, black beard, exquisitely trimmed, gave him an appearance of staid reliability which Cecil lacked. His bow was a vertebrate poem, his smile a consolation for all misfortunes, and he managed his hat, stick, gloves, and cup with the dazzling assurance of a conjurer. To observe him at afternoon tea was to be convinced that he had been specially created to shine gloriously in drawing-rooms, winter-gardens, and *tables d'hôte*. He was one of those men who always do the right thing at the right moment, who are capable of speaking an indefinite number of languages with absolute purity of accent (he spoke English much better than Madame Lawrence), and who can and do discourse with *verve* and accuracy on all sciences, arts, sport, and regions. In short, he was a phoenix[5] of a count; and this was certainly the opinion of Miss Kitty Sartorius and of Miss Eve Fincastle, both of whom reckoned that what they did not know about men might be ignored. Kitty and the Count, it soon became evident, were mutually attracted; their souls were approaching each other with a velocity which increased inversely as the square of the lessening distance between them.[6] And Eve was watching this approximation with undisguised interest and relish.

Nothing of the least importance occurred, save the Count's marvelous exhibition of how to behave at afternoon tea, until the refection[7] was nearly over; and then, during a brief pause in the talk, Cecil, who was sitting to the left of Madame Lawrence, looked sharply around at the right shoulder of his tweed coat; he repeated the gesture a second and yet a third time.

"What is the matter with the man?" asked Eve Fincastle. Both she and Kitty were extremely bright, animated, and even excited.

"Nothing. I thought I saw something on my shoulder, that's all," said Cecil. "Ah! It's only a bit of thread." And he picked off the thread with his left hand and held it before Madame Lawrence. "See! It's a piece of thin black silk, knotted. At first I took it for an insect—you know how queer things look out of the corner of your eye. Pardon!" He had dropped the fragment on to Madame Lawrence's black silk dress. "Now it's lost."

"If you will excuse me, kind friends," said Madame Lawrence, "I will go." She spoke hurriedly and as though in mental distress.

"Poor thing!" Kitty Sartorius exclaimed when the widow had gone. "She's still dreadfully upset"; and Kitty and Eve proceeded jointly to relate the story of the diamond bracelet, upon which hitherto they had kept silence (though with difficulty), out of regard for Madame Lawrence's feelings.

Cecil made almost no comment.

The Count, with the sympathetic excitability of his race, walked up and down the winter-garden, asseverating earnestly that such clumsiness amounted to a crime; then he grew calm and confessed that he shared the optimism of the police as to the recovery of the bracelet; lastly he complimented Kitty on her equable demeanor under this affliction.

---

[5] In this context, meaning a paragon, someone of the highest quality.

[6] Bennett makes a joke of the physical formula, in which distance equals acceleration multiplied by time squared over two ($D = a \ t^2/2$).

[7] A refreshment with food and drink.

"Do you know, Count," said Cecil Thorold, later, after they had all four ascended to the drawing-room overlooking the Grande Place, "I was quite surprised when I saw at tea that you had to be introduced to Madame Lawrence."

"Why so, my dear Mr. Thorold?" the Count inquired suavely.

"I thought I had seen you together in Ostend a few days ago."

The Count shook his wonderful head.

"Perhaps you have a brother—?" Cecil paused.

"No," said the Count. "But it is a favorite theory of mine that everyone has his double somewhere in the world."[8] Previously the Count had been discussing Planchette[9]—he was a great authority on the supernatural, the subconscious, and the subliminal. He now deviated gracefully to the discussion of the theory of doubles.

"I suppose you aren't going out for a walk, dear, before dinner?" said Eve to Kitty.

"No, dear," said Kitty positively.

"I think I shall," said Eve.

And her glance at Cecil Thorold intimated in the plainest possible manner that she wished not only to have a companion for her stroll, but to leave Kitty and the Count in dual solitude.

"I shouldn't, if I were you, Miss Fincastle," Cecil remarked with calm and studied blindness. "It's risky here in the evenings—with these canals exhaling miasma and mosquitoes and bracelets and all sorts of things."

"I will take the risk, thank you," said Eve in an icy tone, and she haughtily departed; she would not cower before Cecil's millions. As for Cecil, he joined in the discussion of the theory of doubles.

III.

ON THE NEXT afternoon but one, policemen were still fishing, without success, for the bracelet, and raising from the ancient duct long-buried odors which threatened to destroy the inhabitants of the quay. (When Kitty Sartorius had hinted that perhaps the authorities might see their way to drawing off the water from the canal, the authorities had intimated that the death-rate of Bruges was already as high as convenient.) Nevertheless, though nothing had happened, the situation had somehow developed, and in such a manner that the bracelet itself was in danger of being partially forgotten; and of all places in Bruges, the situation had developed on the top of the renowned Belfry which dominates the Grande Place in particular and the city in general.

The summit of the Belfry is three hundred and fifty feet high, and it is reached by four hundred and two winding stone steps, each a separate menace to life and limb. Eve Fincastle had climbed those steps alone, perhaps in quest of the view at the top, perhaps in quest of spiritual calm. She had not been leaning over the parapet more than a minute before Cecil Thorold had appeared, his fieldglasses slung over his shoulder. They had begun to talk a little, but nervously and only in snatches. The wind blew free up there among the forty-eight bells, but the social atmosphere was oppressive.

---

[8] A popular theory. See, e.g., Edgar Allan Poe's story "William Wilson," in which the protagonist's doppelgänger acts as his conscience.

[9] The "little plank" used with a Ouija board to receive spiritual messages. The device was very popular (see, e.g., *Planchette; or the Despair of Science*, by Epes Sargent [Boston, Roberts Brothers, 1869]).

"The Count is a most charming man," Eve was saying, as if in defense of the Count.

"He is," said Cecil; "I agree with you."

"Oh, no, you don't, Mr. Thorold! Oh, no, you don't!"

Then there was a pause, and the twain looked down upon Bruges, with its venerable streets, its grass-grown squares, its waterways, and its innumerable monuments, spread out maplike beneath them in the mellow October sunshine. Citizens passed along the thoroughfare in the semblance of tiny dwarfs.

"If you didn't hate him," said Eve, "you wouldn't behave as you do."

"How do I behave, then?"

Eve schooled her voice to an imitation of jocularity—

"All Tuesday evening, and all day yesterday, you couldn't leave them alone. You know you couldn't."

Five minutes later the conversation had shifted.

"You actually saw the bracelet fall into the canal?" said Cecil.

"I actually saw the bracelet fall into the canal. And no one could have got it out while Kitty and I were away, because we weren't away half a minute."

But they could not dismiss the subject of the Count, and presently he was again the topic.

"Naturally it would be a good match for the Count—for *any* man," said Eve: "but then it would also be a good match for Kitty. Of course, he is not so rich as some people, but he is rich."

Cecil examined the horizon with his glasses, and then the streets near the Grande Place.

"Rich, is he? I'm glad of it. By the by, he's gone to Ghent[10] for the day, hasn't he?"

"Yes. He went by the 9:27, and returns by the 4:38."

Another pause.

"Well," said Cecil at length, handing the glasses to Eve Fincastle, "kindly glance down there. Follow the line of the Rue St. Nicolas. You see the cream-colored house with the enclosed courtyard? Now, do you see two figures standing together near a door—a man and a woman, the woman on the steps? Who are they?"

"I can't see very well," said Eve.

"Oh, yes, my dear lady, you can," said Cecil. "These glasses are the very best. Try again."

"They look like the Comte d'Avrec and Madame Lawrence," Eve murmured.

"But the Count is on his way from Ghent! I see the steam of the 4:38 over there. The curious thing is that the Count entered the house of Madame Lawrence, to whom he was introduced for the first time the day before yesterday, at ten o'clock this morning. Yes. It would be a very good match for the Count. When one comes to think of it, it usually is that sort of man that contrives to marry a brilliant and successful actress. There! He's just leaving, isn't he? Now let us descend and listen to the recital of his day's doings in Ghent—shall we?"

"You mean to insinuate," Eve burst out in sudden wrath, "that the Count is an—an *adventurer*, and that Madame Lawrence—Oh! Mr. Thorold!" She laughed condescendingly. "This jealousy is too absurd. Do you suppose I haven't noticed how impressed you were with Kitty at the Devonshire Mansion that night, and again at Ostend, and again here? You're simply carried away by jeal-

---

[10] The capital city of East Flanders, a mere twenty-four miles from Bruges.

ousy; and you think because you are a million-aire you must have all you want. I haven't the slightest doubt that the Count—"

"Anyhow," said Cecil, "let us go down and hear about Ghent."

His eyes made a number of remarks (indulgent, angry, amused, protective, admiring, perspicacious, puzzled) too subtle for the medium of words.

They groped their way down to earth in silence, and it was in silence they crossed the Grande Place. The Count was seated on the *terrasse* in front of the hotel, with a liqueur glass before him, and he was making graceful and expressive signs to Kitty Sartorius, who leaned her marvelous beauty out of a first-storey[11] window. He greeted Cecil Thorold and Eve with an equal grace.

"And how is Ghent?" Cecil inquired.

"Did you go to Ghent, after all, Count?" Eve put in. The Comte d'Avrec looked from one to another, and then, instead of replying, he sipped at his glass. "No," he said, "I didn't go. The rather curious fact is that I happened to meet Madame Lawrence, who offered to show me her collection of lace. I have been an amateur of lace for some years, and really Madame Lawrence's collection is amazing. You have seen it? No? You should do so. I'm afraid I have spent most of the day there."

When the Count had gone to join Kitty in the drawing· room, Eve Fincastle looked victoriously at Cecil, as if to demand of him: "Will you apologize?"

"My dear journalist," Cecil remarked simply, "you gave the show away."

THAT EVENING THE continued obstinacy of the bracelet, which still refused to be caught,

[11] The second floor by American reckoning.

began at last to disturb the birdlike mind of Kitty Sartorius. Moreover, the secret was out, and the whole town of Bruges was discussing the episode and the chances of success.

"Let us consult Planchette," said the Count. The proposal was received with enthusiasm by Kitty. Eve had disappeared.

Planchette was produced; and when asked if the bracelet would be recovered, it wrote, under the hands of Kitty and the Count, a trembling "Yes." When asked: "By whom?" it wrote a word which faintly resembled "Avrec."

The Count stated that he should personally commence dragging operations at sunrise.

"You will see," he said, "I shall succeed."

"Let me try this toy, may I?" Cecil asked blandly, and upon Kitty agreeing, he addressed Planchette in a clear voice: "Now, Planchette, who will restore the bracelet to its owner?"

And Planchette wrote "Thorold," but in characters as firm and regular as those of a copy-book.

"Mr. Thorold is laughing at us," observed the Count, imperturbably bland.

"How horrid you are, Mr. Thorold!" Kitty exclaimed.

IV.

OF THE FOUR persons more or less interested in the affair, three were secretly active that night, in and out of the hotel. Only Kitty Sartorius, chief mourner for the bracelet, slept placidly in her bed. It was toward three o'clock in the morning that a sort of preliminary crisis was reached.

From the multiplicity of doors which ventilate its rooms, one would imagine that the average foreign hotel must have been designed immediately after its architect had been to see a Palais Royal farce,[12] in which every room opens into every other room in every act. The Hotel de la Grande Place was not peculiar in this respect; it abounded in doors. All the chambers on the second storey, over the public rooms, fronting the Place, communicated one with the next, but naturally most of the communicating doors were locked. Cecil Thorold and the Comte d'Avrec had each a bedroom and a sitting-room on that floor. The Count's sitting-room adjoined Cecil's; and the door between was locked, and the key in the possession of the landlord.

Nevertheless, at three a.m. this particular door opened noiselessly from Cecil's side, and Cecil entered the domain of the Count. The moon shone, and Cecil could plainly see not only the silhouette of the Belfry across the Place, but also the principal objects within the room. He noticed the table in the middle, the large easy-chair turned toward the hearth, the old-fashioned sofa; but not a single article did he perceive which might have been the personal property of the Count. He cautiously passed across the room through the moonlight to the floor of the Count's bedroom, which apparently, to his immense surprise, was not only shut, but locked, and the key in the lock on the sitting-room side. Silently unlocking it, he entered the bedroom and disappeared....

In less than five minutes he crept back into the Count's sitting-room, closed the door and locked it.

"Odd!" he murmured reflectively; but he seemed quite happy.

There was a sudden movement in the region of the hearth, and a form rose from the armchair. Cecil rushed to the switch and turned on the electric light. Eve Fincastle stood before him. They faced each other.

"What are you doing here at this time, Miss Fincastle?" he asked sternly. "You can talk freely; the Count will not waken."

"I may ask you the same question," Eve replied with cold bitterness.

"Excuse me. You may not. You are a woman. This is the Count's room—"

"You are in error," she interrupted him. "It is not the Count's room. It is mine. Last night I told the Count I had some important writing to do, and I asked him as a favor to relinquish this room to me for twenty-four hours. He very kindly consented. He removed his belongings, handed me the key of that door, and the transfer was made in the hotel books. And now," she added, "may I inquire, Mr. Thorold, what you are doing in my room?"

"I–I thought it was the Count's," Cecil faltered, decidedly at a loss for a moment. "In offering my humblest apologies, permit me to say that I admire you, Miss Fincastle."

"I wish I could return the compliment," Eve exclaimed, and she repeated with almost plaintive sincerity: "I do wish I could."

Cecil raised his arms and let them fall to his side.

"You meant to catch me," he said. "You suspected something, then? The 'important writing' was an invention." And he added, with a faint smile: "You really ought not to have fallen asleep. Suppose I had not wakened you?"

"Please don't laugh, Mr. Thorold. Yes, I did suspect. There was something in the demeanor of your servant Lecky that gave me the idea.... I did mean to catch you. Why you, a millionaire, should be a burglar, I cannot understand. I never understood that incident

---

[12] The 750-seat Théâtre du Palais-Royal was and is a popular venue in Paris for comedies.

at the Devonshire Mansion; it was beyond me. I am by no means sure that you didn't have a great deal to do with the Rainshore affair at Ostend.[13] But that you should have stooped to slander is the worst. I confess you are a mystery. I confess that I can make no guess at the nature of your present scheme. And what I shall do, now that I have caught you, I don't know. I can't decide; I must think. If, however, anything is missing tomorrow morning, I shall be bound in any case to denounce you. You grasp that?"

"I grasp it perfectly, my dear journalist," Cecil replied. "And something will not improbably be missing. But take the advice of a burglar and a mystery, and go to bed, it is half past three."

And Eve went. And Cecil bowed her out and then retired to his own rooms. And the Count's apartment was left to the moonlight.

V.

"PLANCHETTE IS A very safe prophet," said Cecil to Kitty Sartorius the next morning, "provided it has firm guidance."

They were at breakfast.

"What do you mean?"

"I mean that Planchette prophesied last night that I should restore to you your bracelet. I do."

He took the lovely gewgaw from his pocket and handed it to Kitty.

"Ho-ow did you find it, you dear thing?" Kitty stammered, trembling under the shock of joy.

"I fished it up out—out of the mire by a contrivance of my own."

"But when?"

"Oh! Very early. At three o'clock a.m. You see, I was determined to be first."

"In the dark, then?"

"I had a light. Don't you think I'm rather clever?"

Kitty's scene of ecstatic gratitude does not come into the story. Suffice it to say that not until the moment of its restoration did she realize how precious the bracelet was to her.

It was ten o'clock before Eve descended. She had breakfasted in her room, and Kitty had already exhibited to her the prodigal bracelet.

"I particularly want you to go up the Belfry with me, Miss Fincastle," Cecil greeted her; and his tone was so serious and so urgent that she consented. They left Kitty playing waltzes on the piano in the drawing-room.

"And now, O man of mystery?" Eve questioned, when they had toiled to the summit, and saw the city and its dwarfs beneath them.

"We are in no danger of being disturbed here," Cecil began; "but I will make my explanation—the explanation which I certainly owe you—as brief as possible. Your Comte d'Avrec is an adventurer (please don't be angry), and your Madame Lawrence is an adventuress. I knew that I had seen them together. They work in concert, and for the most part make a living on the gaming-tables of Europe. Madame Lawrence was expelled from Monte Carlo last year for being too intimate with a croupier. You may be aware that at a roulette-table one can do a great deal with the aid of the croupier. Madame Lawrence appropriated the bracelet 'on her own,' as it were. The Count (he may be a real Count, for anything I know) heard first of that enterprise from the lips of Miss Sartorius. He was annoyed, angry—because he was really a little in

---

[13] These references are to earlier stories in Bennett's *The Loot of Cities*.

love with your friend, and he saw golden prospects. It is just this fact—the Count's genuine passion for Miss Sartorius—that renders the case psychologically interesting. To proceed, Madame Lawrence became jealous. The Count spent six hours yesterday in trying to get the bracelet from her, and failed. He tried again last night, and succeeded, but not too easily, for he did not re-enter the hotel till after one o'clock. At first I thought he had succeeded in the daytime, and I had arranged accordingly, for I did not see why he should have the honor and glory of restoring the bracelet to its owner. Lecky and I fixed up a sleeping-draught for him. The minor details were simple. When you caught me this morning, the bracelet was in my pocket, and in its stead I had left a brief note for the perusal of the Count, which has had the singular effect of inducing him to decamp: probably he has not gone alone. But isn't it amusing that, since you so elaborately took his sitting-room, he will be convinced that you are a party to his undoing—you, his staunchest defender?"

Eve's face gradually broke into an embarrassed smile.

"You haven't explained," she said, "how Madame Lawrence got the bracelet."

"Come over here," Cecil answered. "Take these glasses and look down at the Quai du Rosaire. You see everything plainly?" Eve could, in fact, see on the quay the little mounds of mud which had been extracted from the canal in the quest of the bracelet. Cecil continued: "On my arrival in Bruges on Monday, I had a fancy to climb the Belfry at once. I witnessed the whole scene between you and Miss Sartorius and Madame Law-

rence, through my glasses. Immediately your backs were turned, Madame Lawrence, her hands behind her, and her back against the railing, began to make a sort of rapid, drawing-up motion with her forearms. Then I saw a momentary glitter…. Considerably mystified, I visited the spot after you had left it, chatted with the gendarme on duty and got round him, and then it dawned on me that a robbery had been planned, prepared, and executed with extraordinary originality and ingenuity. A long, thin thread of black silk must have been ready tied to the railing, with perhaps a hook at the other end. As soon as Madame Lawrence held the bracelet, she attached the hook to it and dropped it. The silk, especially as it was the last thing in the world you would look for, would be as good as invisible. When you went for the police, Madame retrieved the bracelet, hid it in her muff, and broke off the silk. Only, in her haste, she left a bit of silk tied to the railing. That fragment I carried to the hotel. All along she must have been a little uneasy about me…. And that's all. Except that I wonder you thought I was jealous of the Count's attentions to your friend." He gazed at her admiringly.

"I'm glad you are not a thief, Mr. Thorold," said Eve.

"Well," Cecil smiled, "as for that, I left him a couple of louis[14] for fares, and I shall pay his hotel bill."

"Why?"

"There were notes for nearly ten thousand francs with the bracelet. Ill-gotten gains, I am sure. A trifle, but the only reward I shall have for my trouble. I shall put them to good use." He laughed, serenely gay.

---

[14] French coins.

Robert Barr

ROBERT BARR (1849-1912) is one of the forgotten literary greats of the late nineteenth century. A Scottish short story writer and novelist, in 1892 he moved to London and, together with Jerome K. Jerome, founded *The Idler*, one of the most popular and amusing magazines of the day. As its editor, Barr became friends with everyone who was anyone in the literary world, including Arthur Conan Doyle, Rudyard Kipling, Bram Stoker, Bret Harte, and Stephen Crane. He wrote one of the first series of parodies of Sherlock Holmes, the wonderful "Detective Stories Gone Wrong: The Adventures of Sherlaw Kombs" (by "Luke Sharp"), which appeared in the May 1892 issue of *The Idler* (later included in the incredibly rare collection *The Face and the Mask* [1894]); he also parodied Holmes in his *Jenny Baxter, Journalist* (1899).

In mystery-fan circles, Barr is probably best remembered for his tales of the French detective Eugéne Valmont. The former chief investigator of the French government, Valmont was a significant influence on Agatha Christie's Poirot. The following story first appeared in the *Saturday Evening Post* of May 13, 1905; it was collected later in *The Triumphs of Eugéne Valmont* (1906).

THE ABSENT-MINDED COTERIE

ROBERT BARR

The question of lighting is an important one in a room such as mine, and electricity offers a good deal of scope to the ingenious.[1] Of this fact I have taken full advantage. I can manipulate the lighting of my room so that any particular spot is bathed in brilliancy, while the rest of the space remains in comparative gloom, and I arranged the lamps so that the full force of their rays impinged against the door that Wednesday evening, while I sat on one side of the table in semidarkness and Hale sat on the other, with a light beating down on him from above which gave him the odd, sculptured look of a living statue of Justice, stern and triumphant. Anyone entering the room would first be dazzled by the light, and next would see the gigantic form of Hale in the full uniform of his order.

When Angus Macpherson was shown into this room, he was quite visibly taken aback, and paused abruptly on the threshold, his gaze riveted on the huge policeman. I think his first purpose was to turn and run, but the door closed behind him, and he doubtless heard, as we all did, the sound of the bolt being thrust in its place, thus locking him in.

"I—I beg your pardon," he stammered, "I expected to meet Mr. Webster."

As he said this, I pressed the button under my table, and was instantly enshrouded with light. A sickly smile overspread the countenance of Macpherson as he caught sight of me, and he made a very creditable attempt to carry off the situation with nonchalance.

"Oh, there you are, Mr. Webster; I did not notice you at first."

It was a tense moment. I spoke slowly and impressively.

"Sir, perhaps you are not unacquainted with the name of Eugene Valmont."

---

[1] Incandescent lighting was first sold commercially around 1880, and by 1905, when this story was published, electricity was widely available throughout London from a multiplicity of private, quasi-private, and municipal power stations.

He replied brazenly:—

"I am sorry to say, sir, I never heard of the gentleman before."

At this came a most inopportune "Haw-haw" from that blockhead Spenser Hale, completely spoiling the dramatic situation I had elaborated with such thought and care. It is little wonder the English possess no drama, for they show scant appreciation of the sensational moments in life; they are not quickly alive to the lights and shadows of events.

"Haw-haw," brayed Spenser Hale, and at once reduced the emotional atmosphere to a fog of commonplace. However, what is a man to do? He must handle the tools with which it pleases Providence to provide him. I ignored Hale's untimely laughter.

"Sit down, sir," I said to Macpherson, and he obeyed.

"You have called on Lord Semptam this week," I continued sternly.

"Yes, sir."

"And collected a pound from him?"

"Yes, sir."

"In October, 1893, you sold Lord Semptam a carved antique table for fifty pounds?"

"Quite right, sir."

"When you were here last week you gave me Ralph Summertrees as the name of a gentleman living in Park Lane. You knew at the time that this man was your employer?"

Macpherson was now looking fixedly at me, and on this occasion made no reply. I went on calmly:

"You also knew that Summertrees, of Park Lane, was identical with Simpson, of Tottenham Court Road?"

"Well, sir," said Macpherson, "I don't exactly see what you're driving at, but it's quite usual for a man to carry on a business under an assumed name. There is nothing illegal about that."

"We will come to the illegality in a moment, Mr. Macpherson. You and Rogers and Tyrrel and three others are confederates of this man Simpson."

"We are in his employ; yes, sir, but no more confederates than clerks usually are."

"I think, Mr. Macpherson, I have said enough to show you that the game is what you call up. You are now in the presence of Mr. Spenser Hale, from Scotland Yard, who is waiting to hear your confession."

Here the stupid Hale broke in with his:

"And remember, sir, that anything you say will be—"

"Excuse me, Mr. Hale," I interrupted hastily, "I shall turn over the case to you in a very few moments, but I ask you to remember our compact, and to leave it for the present entirely in my hands. Now, Mr. Macpherson, I want your confession, and I want it at once."

"Confession? Confederates?" protested Macpherson, with admirably simulated surprise. "I must say you use extraordinary terms, Mr.—Mr.— What did you say the name was?"

"Haw-haw," roared Hale. "His name is Monsieur Valmont."

"I implore you, Mr. Hale, to leave this man to me for a very few moments. Now, Macpherson, what have you to say in your defense?"

"Where nothing criminal has been alleged, Monsieur Valmont, I see no necessity for defense. If you wish me to admit that somehow you have acquired a number of details regarding our business, I am perfectly willing to do so, and to subscribe to their accuracy. If you will be good enough to let me know of what you complain, I shall endeavor to make the point clear to you, if I can. There has evidently been some misapprehension, but for the life of me, without further explanation, I am as much in a fog as I was on my way coming here, for it is getting a little thick outside."

Macpherson certainly was conducting himself with great discretion, and presented, quite unconsciously, a much more diplomatic figure than my friend Spenser Hale, sitting stiffly opposite me. His tone was one of mild expostulation, mitigated by the intimation that all misunderstanding speedily would be cleared away. To outward view he offered a perfect picture of innocence, neither protesting too much nor too little. I had, however, another surprise in store for him, a trump card, as it were, and I played it down on the table.

"There!" I cried with vim, "have you ever seen that sheet before?"

He glanced at it without offering to take it in his hand.

"Oh, yes," he said, "that has been abstracted from our file. It is what I call my visiting list."

"Come, come, sir," I cried sternly, "you refuse to confess, but I warn you we know all about it. You never heard of Dr. Willoughby, I suppose?"

"Yes, he is the author of the silly pamphlet on Christian Science."[2]

"You are in the right, Mr. Macpherson; on Christian Science and Absent-Mindedness."

"Possibly. I haven't read it for a long while."

"Have you ever met this learned doctor, Mr. Macpherson?"

"Oh, yes. Dr. Willoughby is the pen name of Mr. Summertrees. He believes in Christian Science and that sort of thing, and writes about it."

"Ah, really. We are getting your confession bit by bit, Mr. Macpherson. I think it would be better to be quite frank with us."

"I was just going to make the same suggestion to you, Monsieur Valmont. If you will tell me in a few words exactly what is your charge against either Mr. Summertrees or myself, I will know then what to say."

"We charge you, sir, with obtaining money under false pretenses, which is a crime that has landed more than one distinguished financier in prison."

Spenser Hale shook his fat forefinger at me, and said:

"Tut, tut, Valmont; we mustn't threaten, we mustn't threaten, you know"; but I went on without heeding him.

"Take, for instance, Lord Semptam. You sold him a table for fifty pounds, on the installment plan. He was to pay a pound a week, and in less than a year the debt was liquidated. But he is an absent-minded man, as all your clients are. That is why you came to me. I had answered the bogus Willoughby's advertisement. And so you kept on collecting and collecting for something more than three years. Now do you understand the charge?"

Mr. Macpherson's head, during this accusation, was held slightly inclined to one side. At first his face was clouded by the most clever imitation of anxious concentration of mind I had ever seen, and this was gradually cleared away by the dawn of awakening

---

[2] The system of thought founded by Mary Baker Eddy in 1866 based on her reading of the Christian Bible. Her book *Science & Health With a Key to the Scriptures* (1875) is the principal text of the First Church of Christ, Scientist (along with the Bible) and emphasizes the teachings of Jesus as a means of healing.

perception. When I had finished, an ingratiating smile hovered about his lips.

"Really, you know," he said, "that is rather a capital scheme. The absent-minded league, as one might call them. Most ingenious. Summertrees, if he had any sense of humor, which he hasn't, would be rather taken by the idea that his innocent fad for Christian Science had led him to be suspected of obtaining money under false pretenses. But, really, there are no pretensions about the matter at all. As I understand it, I simply call and receive the money through the forgetfulness of the persons on my list, but where I think you would have both Summertrees and myself, if there was anything in your audacious theory, would be an indictment for conspiracy. Still, I quite see how the mistake arises. You have jumped to the conclusion that we sold nothing to Lord Semptam except that carved table three years ago. I have pleasure in pointing out to you that his lordship is a frequent customer of ours, and has had many things from us at one time or another. Sometimes he is in our debt; sometimes we are in his. We keep a sort of running contract with him by which he pays us a pound a week. He and several other customers deal on the same plan, and in return, for an income that we can count upon, they get the first offer of anything in which they are supposed to be interested. As I have told you, we call these sheets in the office our visiting lists, but to make the visiting lists complete you need what we term our encyclopedia. We call it that because it is in so many volumes; a volume for each year, running back I don't know how long. You will notice little figures here from time to time above the amount stated on this visiting list. These figures refer to the page of the encyclopedia for the current year, and on that page is noted the new sale and the amount of it, as it might be set down, say, in a ledger."

"That is a very entertaining explanation, Mr. Macpherson. I suppose this encyclopedia, as you call it, is in the shop at Tottenham Court Road?"

"Oh, no, sir. Each volume of the encyclopedia is self-locking. These books contain the real secret of our business, and they are kept in the safe at Mr. Summertrees's house in Park Lane. Take Lord Semptam's account, for instance. You will find in faint figures under a certain date, 102. If you turn to page 102 of the encyclopedia for that year, you will then see a list of what Lord Semptam has bought, and the prices he was charged for them. It is really a very simple matter. If you will allow me to use your telephone for a moment, I will ask Mr. Summertrees, who has not yet begun dinner, to bring with him here the volume for 1893, and within a quarter of an hour you will be perfectly satisfied that everything is quite legitimate."

I confess that the young man's naturalness and confidence staggered me, the more so as I saw by the sarcastic smile on Hale's lips that he did not believe a single word spoken. A portable telephone stood on the table, and as Macpherson finished his explanation, he reached over and drew it toward him. Then Spenser Hale interfered.

"Excuse *me*," he said, "I'll do the telephoning. What is the call number of Mr. Summertrees?"

"One forty Hyde Park."

Hale at once called up Central, and presently was answered from Park Lane. We heard him say:

"Is this the residence of Mr. Summertrees? Oh, is that you, Podgers? Is Mr. Summertrees in? Very well. This is Hale. I am in Valmont's flat—Imperial Flats—you know. Yes, where you went with me the other day. Very well, go to Mr. Summertrees, and say to him that Mr. Macpherson wants the encyclopedia for 1893. Do you get that? Yes, encyclopedia. Oh, don't understand what it is. Mr. Macpherson. No, don't mention my name at all. Just say Mr. Macpherson wants the encyclopedia for the year 1893, and that you are to bring it. Yes, you may tell him that Mr. Macpherson is at Imperial Flats, but don't mention my name at all. Exactly. As soon as he gives you the book, get into a cab, and come here as quickly as possible with it. If Summertrees doesn't want to let the book go, then tell him to come with you. If he won't do that, place him under arrest, and bring both him and the book here. All right. Be as quick as you can; we're waiting."

Macpherson made no protest against Hale's use of the telephone; he merely sat back in his chair with a resigned expression on his face which, if painted on canvas, might have been entitled, "The Falsely Accused." When Hale rang off, Macpherson said:

"Of course you know your own business best, but if your man arrests Summertrees, he will make you the laughingstock of London. There is such a thing as unjustifiable arrest, as well as getting money under false pretenses, and Mr. Summertrees is not the man to forgive an insult. And then, if you will allow me to say so, the more I think over your absent-minded theory, the more absolutely grotesque it seems, and if the case ever gets into the newspapers, I am sure, Mr. Hale, you'll experience an uncomfortable half hour with your chiefs at Scotland Yard."

"I'll take the risk of that, thank you," said Hale stubbornly.

"Am I to consider myself under arrest?" inquired the young man.

"No, sir."

"Then, if you will pardon me, I shall withdraw. Mr. Summertrees will show you everything you wish to see in his books, and can explain his business much more capably than I, because he knows more about it; therefore, gentlemen, I bid you good night."

"No you don't. Not just yet awhile," exclaimed Hale, rising to his feet simultaneously with the young man.

"Then I *am* under arrest," protested Macpherson.

"You're not going to leave this room until Podgers brings that book."

"Oh, very well," and he sat down again.

And now, as talking is dry work, I set out something to drink, a box of cigars, and a box of cigarettes. Hale mixed his favorite brew, but Macpherson, shunning the wine of his country, contented himself with a glass of plain mineral water, and lit a cigarette. Then he awoke my high regard by saying pleasantly, as if nothing had happened:

"While we are waiting, Monsieur Valmont, may I remind you that you owe me five shillings?"

I laughed, took the coin from my pocket, and paid him, whereupon he thanked me.

"Are you connected with Scotland Yard, Monsieur Valmont?" asked Macpherson, with the air of a man trying to make conversation to bridge over a tedious interval; but before I could reply Hale blurted out:

"Not likely!"

"You have no official standing as a detective, then, Monsieur Valmont?"

"None whatever," I replied quickly, thus getting in my oar ahead of Hale.

"That is a loss to our country," pursued

this admirable young man, with evident sincerity.

I began to see I could make a good deal of so clever a fellow if he came under my tuition.

"The blunders of our police," he went on, "are something deplorable. If they would but take lessons in strategy, say, from France, their unpleasant duties would be so much more acceptably performed, with much less discomfort to their victims."

"France," snorted Hale in derision, "why, they call a man guilty there until he's proven innocent."

"Yes, Mr. Hale, and the same seems to be the case in Imperial Flats. You have quite made up your mind that Mr. Summertrees is guilty, and will not be content until he proves his innocence. I venture to predict that you will hear from him before long in a manner that may astonish you."

Hale grunted and looked at his watch. The minutes passed very slowly as we sat there smoking and at last even I began to get uneasy. Macpherson, seeing our anxiety, said that when he came in the fog was almost as thick as it had been the week before, and that there might be some difficulty in getting a cab. Just as he was speaking the door was unlocked from the outside, and Podgers entered, bearing a thick volume in his hand. This he gave to his superior, who turned over its pages in amazement, and then looked at the back, crying:

" 'Encyclopedia of Sport, 1893'! What sort of a joke is this, Mr. Macpherson?"

There was a pained look on Mr. Macpherson's face as he reached forward and took the book. He said with a sigh:

"If you had allowed me to telephone, Mr. Hale, I should have made it perfectly plain to

Summertrees what was wanted. I might have known this mistake was liable to occur. There is an increasing demand for out-of-date books of sport, and no doubt Mr. Summertrees thought this was what I meant. There is nothing for it but to send your man back to Park Lane and tell Mr. Summertrees that what we want is the locked volume of accounts for 1893, which we call the encyclopedia. Allow me to write an order that will bring it. Oh, I'll show you what I have written before your man takes it," he said, as Hale stood ready to look over his shoulder.

On my note paper he dashed off a request such as he had outlined, and handed it to Hale, who read it and gave it to Podgers.

"Take that to Summertrees, and get back as quickly as possible. Have you a cab at the door?"

"Yes, sir."

"Is it foggy outside?"

"Not so much, sir, as it was an hour ago. No difficulty about the traffic now, sir."

"Very well, get back as soon as you can."

Podgers saluted, and left with the book under his arm. Again the door was locked, and again we sat smoking in silence until the stillness was broken by the tinkle of the telephone. Hale put the receiver to his ear.

"Yes, this is the Imperial Flats. Yes. Valmont. Oh, yes; Macpherson is here. What? Out of what? Can't hear you. Out of print. What, the encyclopedia's out of print? Who is that speaking? Dr. Willoughby; thanks."

Macpherson rose as if he would go to the telephone, but instead (and he acted so quietly that I did not notice what he was doing until the thing was done) he picked up the sheet which he called his visiting list, and walking quite without haste, held it in the glowing coals of the fireplace until it disappeared in a flash of flame up the chimney. I sprang to my feet indignant, but too late to make even a motion toward saving the sheet. Macpherson regarded us both with that self-depreciatory smile which had several times lighted up his face.

"How dared you burn that sheet?" I demanded.

"Because, Monsieur Valmont, it did not belong to you; because you do not belong to Scotland Yard; because you stole it; because you had no right to it; and because you have no official standing in this country. If it had been in Mr. Hale's possession I should not have dared, as you put it, to destroy the sheet, but as this sheet was abstracted from my master's premises by you, an entirely unauthorized person, whom he would have been justified in shooting dead if he had found you housebreaking, and you had resisted him on his discovery, I took the liberty of destroying the document. I have always held that these sheets should not have been kept, for, as has been the case, if they fell under the scrutiny of so intelligent a person as Eugéne Valmont, improper inferences might have been drawn. Mr. Summertrees, however, persisted in keeping them, but made this concession, that if I ever telegraphed him or telephoned him the word 'Encyclopedia,' he would at once burn these records, and he, on his part, was to telegraph or telephone to me 'The encyclopedia is out of print,' whereupon I would know that he had succeeded.

"Now, gentlemen, open this door, which will save me the trouble of forcing it. Either put me formally under arrest, or cease to restrict my liberty. I am very much obliged to Mr. Hale for telephoning, and I have made no protest to so gallant a host as Monsieur Valmont is, because of the locked door. However, the farce is now terminated. The proceedings I have sat through were entirely illegal, and if you will pardon me, Mr. Hale, they have been a little too French to go down here in old England, or to make a report in the newspapers that would be quite satisfactory to your chiefs. I demand either my formal arrest or the unlocking of that door."

In silence I pressed a button, and my man threw open the door. Macpherson walked to the threshold, paused, and looked back at Spenser Hale, who sat there silent as a sphinx.

"Good evening, Mr. Hale."

There being no reply, he turned to me with the same ingratiating smile:

"Good evening, Monsieur Eugéne Valmont," he said. "I shall give myself the pleasure of calling next Wednesday at six for my five shillings."

Jacques Futrelle

JACQUES FUTRELLE (1875-1912), American journalist and writer who died heroically on the *Titanic*, is best remembered as the creator of the Thinking Machine, Professor Augustus S. F. X. Van Dusen. The Professor solves cases brought to him by a reporter, Hutchinson Hatch. Van Dusen is dwarfish in appearance, with a huge head, and claims to solve problems by applied logic. He regards crime-solving as a minor annoyance, being more importantly engaged in various scientific endeavors. Although the Professor appeared in several dozen stories, the following is the most popular, widely anthologized. It first appeared in the *Boston American* newspaper from October 30 to November 5, 1905; it was later collected in *The Thinking Machine* (1907).

THE PROBLEM OF CELL 13

JACQUES FUTRELLE

I.

PRACTICALLY ALL THOSE letters remaining in the alphabet after Augustus S. F. X. Van Dusen was named were afterward acquired by that gentleman in the course of a brilliant scientific career, and, being honorably acquired, were tacked on to the other end. His name, therefore, taken with all that belonged to it, was a wonderfully imposing structure. He was a Ph.D., an LL.D., an F.R.S.,[1] an M.D., and an M.D.S.[2] He was also some other things—just what he himself couldn't say—through recognition of his ability by various foreign educational and scientific institutions.

In appearance he was no less striking than in nomenclature. He was slender with the droop of the student in his thin shoulders and the pallor of a close, sedentary life on his clean-shaven face. His eyes wore a perpetual, forbidding squint—the squint of a man who studies little things—and when they could be seen at all through his thick spectacles, were mere slits of watery blue. But above his eyes was his most striking feature. This was a tall, broad brow, almost abnormal in height and width, crowned by a heavy shock of bushy, yellow hair. All these things conspired to give him a peculiar, almost grotesque, personality.

Professor Van Dusen was remotely German. For generations his ancestors had been noted in the sciences; he was the logical result, the master mind. First and above all he was a logician. At least thirty-five years of the half-century or so of his existence had been devoted exclusively to proving that two and two always equal four, except in unusual cases, where they equal three or five, as the case may be. He stood broadly on the general proposition that all things that start must go somewhere, and was able to bring the concentrated

---

[1] Fellow of the Royal Society (the premier scientific body of England, of which Isaac Newton had been a prominent member).
[2] Master of Dental Surgery.

mental force of his forefathers to bear on a given problem. Incidentally it may be remarked that Professor Van Dusen wore a No. 8 hat.[3]

The world at large had heard vaguely of Professor Van Dusen as the Thinking Machine. It was a newspaper catch-phrase applied to him at the time of a remarkable exhibition at chess; he had demonstrated then that a stranger to the game might, by the force of inevitable logic, defeat a champion who had devoted a lifetime to its study. The Thinking Machine! Perhaps that more nearly described him than all his honorary initials, for he spent week after week, month after month, in the seclusion of his small laboratory from which had gone forth thoughts that staggered scientific associates and deeply stirred the world at large.

It was only occasionally that The Thinking Machine had visitors, and these were usually men who, themselves high in the sciences, dropped in to argue a point and perhaps convince themselves. Two of these men, Dr. Charles Ransome and Alfred Fielding, called one evening to discuss some theory which is not of consequence here.

"Such a thing is impossible," declared Dr. Ransome emphatically, in the course of the conversation.

"Nothing is impossible," declared The Thinking Machine with equal emphasis. He always spoke petulantly. "The mind is master of all things. When science fully recognizes that fact a great advance will have been made."

"How about the airship?" asked Dr. Ransome.[4]

"That's not impossible at all," asserted The Thinking Machine. "It will be invented some time. I'd do it myself, but I'm busy."

Dr. Ransome laughed tolerantly.

"I've heard you say such things before," he said. "But they mean nothing. Mind may be master of matter, but it hasn't yet found a way to apply itself. There are some things that can't be *thought* out of existence, or rather which would not yield to any amount of thinking."

"What, for instance?" demanded The Thinking Machine.

Dr. Ransome was thoughtful for a moment as he smoked.

"Well, say prison walls," he replied. "No man can *think* himself out of a cell. If he could, there would be no prisoners."

"A man can so apply his brain and ingenuity that he can leave a cell, which is the same thing," snapped The Thinking Machine.

Dr. Ransome was slightly amused.

"Let's suppose a case," he said, after a moment. "Take a cell where prisoners under sentence of death are confined—men who are desperate and, maddened by fear, would take any chance to escape—suppose you were locked in such a cell. Could you escape?"

"Certainly," declared The Thinking Machine.

"Of course," said Mr. Fielding, who entered the conversation for the first time, "you might wreck the cell with an explosive—but inside, a prisoner, you couldn't have that."

"There would be nothing of that kind," said The Thinking Machine. "You might treat me precisely as you treated prisoners under

---

[3] This would translate to an extra-extra-large hat. Big head = big brain = super-intelligence was a popular view in the late nineteenth century.

[4] While the Wright brothers' first flight had occurred two years earlier than the date this story first appeared, commercial (indeed, passenger) airships were still in the future.

sentence of death, and I would leave the cell."

"Not unless you entered it with tools prepared to get out," said Dr. Ransome.

The Thinking Machine was visibly annoyed and his blue eyes snapped.

"Lock me in any cell in any prison anywhere at any time, wearing only what is necessary, and I'll escape in a week," he declared, sharply.

Dr. Ransome sat up straight in the chair, interested. Mr. Fielding lighted a new cigar.

"You mean you could actually *think* yourself out?" asked Dr. Ransome.

"I would get out," was the response.

"Are you serious?"

"Certainly I am serious."

Dr. Ransome and Mr. Fielding were silent for a long time.

"Would you be willing to try it?" asked Mr. Fielding, finally.

"Certainly," said Professor Van Dusen, and there was a trace of irony in his voice. "I have done more asinine things than that to convince other men of less important truths."

The tone was offensive and there was an undercurrent strongly resembling anger on both sides. Of course it was an absurd thing, but Professor Van Dusen reiterated his willingness to undertake the escape and it was decided upon.

"To begin now," added Dr. Ransome.

"I'd prefer that it begin tomorrow," said The Thinking Machine, "because—"

"No, now," said Mr. Fielding, flatly. "You are arrested, figuratively, of course, without any warning locked in a cell with no chance to communicate with friends, and left there with identically the same care and attention that would be given to a man under sentence of death. Are you willing?"

"All right, now, then," said the Thinking Machine, and he arose.

"Say, the death-cell in Chisholm Prison."

"The death-cell in Chisholm Prison."

"And what will you wear?"

"As little as possible," said The Thinking Machine. "Shoes, stockings, trousers and a shirt."

"You will permit yourself to be searched, of course?"

"I am to be treated precisely as all prisoners are treated," said The Thinking Machine. "No more attention and no less."

There were some preliminaries to be arranged in the matter of obtaining permission for the test, but all three were influential men and everything was done satisfactorily by telephone, albeit the prison commissioners, to whom the experiment was explained on purely scientific grounds, were sadly bewildered. Professor Van Dusen would be the most distinguished prisoner they had ever entertained.

When The Thinking Machine had donned those things which he was to wear during his incarceration he called the little old woman who was his housekeeper, cook and maid servant all in one.

"Martha," he said, "it is now twenty-seven minutes past nine o'clock. I am going away. One week from tonight, at half-past nine, these gentlemen and one, possibly two, others will take supper with me here. Remember Dr. Ransome is very fond of artichokes."

The three men were driven to Chisholm Prison, where the Warden was awaiting them, having been informed of the matter by telephone. He understood merely that the eminent Professor Van Dusen was to be his prisoner, if he could keep him, for one week; that he had committed no crime, but that he was to be treated as all other prisoners were treated.

"Search him," instructed Dr. Ransome.

The Thinking Machine was searched. Nothing was found on him; the pockets of the trousers were empty; the white, stiff-bosomed shirt had no pocket. The shoes and stockings were removed, examined, then replaced. As he watched all these preliminaries—the rigid search and noted the pitiful, childlike physical weakness of the man, the colorless face, and the thin, white hands—Dr. Ransome almost regretted his part in the affair.

"Are you sure you want to do this?" he asked.

"Would you be convinced if I did not?" inquired The Thinking Machine in turn.

"No."

"All right. I'll do it."

What sympathy Dr. Ransome had was dissipated by the tone. It nettled him, and he resolved to see the experiment to the end; it would be a stinging reproof to egotism.

"It will be impossible for him to communicate with anyone outside?" he asked.

"Absolutely impossible," replied the warden. "He will not be permitted writing materials of any sort."

"And your jailers, would they deliver a message from him?"

"Not one word, directly or indirectly," said the warden. "You may rest assured of that. They will report anything he might say or turn over to me anything he might give them."

"That seems entirely satisfactory," said Mr. Fielding, who was frankly interested in the problem.

"Of course, in the event he fails," said Dr. Ransome, "and asks for his liberty, you understand you are to set him free?"

"I understand," replied the warden.

The Thinking Machine stood listening, but had nothing to say until this was all ended, then:—

"I should like to make three small requests. You may grant them or not, as you wish."

"No special favors, now," warned Mr. Fielding.

"I am asking none," was the stiff response. "I would like to have some tooth powder—buy it yourself to see that it is tooth powder—and I should like to have one five-dollar and two ten-dollar bills."

Dr. Ransome, Mr. Fielding and the warden exchanged astonished glances. They were not surprised at the request for tooth powder, but were at the request for money.

"Is there any man with whom our friend would come in contact that he could bribe with twenty-five dollars?" asked Dr. Ransome of the warden.

"Not for twenty-five hundred dollars," was the positive reply.

"Well, let him have them," said Mr. Fielding. "I think they are harmless enough."

"And what is the third request?" asked Dr. Ransome.

"I should like to have my shoes polished."

Again the astonished glances were exchanged. This last request was the height of absurdity, so they agreed to it. These things all being attended to, The Thinking Machine was led back into the prison from which he had undertaken to escape.

"Here is Cell 13," said the warden, stopping three doors down the steel corridor. "This is where we keep condemned murderers. No one can leave it without my permission; and no one in it can communicate with the outside. I'll stake my reputation on that. It's only three doors back of my office and I can readily hear any unusual noise."

"Will this cell do, gentlemen?" asked The Thinking Machine. There was a touch of irony in his voice.

"Admirably," was the reply.

The heavy steel door was thrown open, there was a great scurrying and scampering of tiny feet, and The Thinking Machine passed into the gloom of the cell. Then the door was closed and double locked by the warden.

"What is that noise in there?" asked Dr. Ransome, through the bars.

"Rats—dozens of them," replied The Thinking Machine, tersely.

The three men, with final good-nights, were turning away when The Thinking Machine called:

"What time is it exactly, warden?"

"Eleven seventeen," replied the warden.

"Thanks. I will join you gentlemen in your office at half-past eight o'clock one week from tonight," said The Thinking Machine.

"And if you do not?"

"There is no 'if' about it."

II.

CHISHOLM PRISON WAS a great, spreading structure of granite, four stories in all, which stood in the center of acres of open space. It was surrounded by a wall of solid masonry eighteen feet high, and so smoothly finished inside and out as to offer no foothold to a climber, no matter how expert. Atop of this fence, as a further precaution, was a five-foot fence of steel rods, each terminating in a keen point. This fence in itself marked an absolute deadline between freedom and imprisonment, for, even if a man escaped from his cell, it would seem impossible for him to pass the wall.

The yard, which on all sides of the prison building was twenty-five feet wide, that being the distance from the building to the wall, was by day an exercise ground for those prisoners to whom was granted the boon of occasional semi-liberty. But that was not for those in Cell 13. At all times of the day there were armed guards in the yard, four of them, one patrolling each side of the prison building.

By night the yard was almost as brilliantly lighted as by day. On each of the four sides was a great arc light which rose above the prison wall and gave to the guards a clear sight. The lights, too, brightly illuminated the spiked top of the wall. The wires which fed the arc lights ran up the side of the prison building on insulators and from the top story led out to the poles supporting the arc lights.

All these things were seen and comprehended by The Thinking Machine, who was only enabled to see out his closely barred cell window by standing on his bed. This was on the morning following his incarceration. He gathered, too, that the river lay over there beyond the wall somewhere, because he heard faintly the pulsation of a motor boat and high up in the air saw a river bird. From that same direction came the shouts of boys at play and the occasional crack of a batted ball. He knew then that between the prison wall and the river was an open space, a playground.

Chisholm Prison was regarded as absolutely safe. No man had ever escaped from it. The Thinking Machine, from his perch on the bed, seeing what he saw, could readily understand why. The walls of the cell, though built he judged twenty years before, were perfectly solid, and the window bars of new iron had not a shadow of rust on them. The window itself, even with the bars out, would be a difficult mode of egress because it was small.

Yet, seeing these things, The Thinking Machine was not discouraged. Instead, he thoughtfully squinted at the great arc light—there was bright sunlight now—and traced with his eyes the wire which led from it to the building. That electric wire, he reasoned, must come down the side of the building not a great distance from his cell. That might be worth knowing.

Cell 13 was on the same floor with the offices of the prison—that is, not in the basement, nor yet upstairs. There were only four steps up to the office floor, therefore the level of the floor must be only three or four feet above the ground. He couldn't see the ground directly beneath his window, but he could see it further out toward the wall. It would be an easy drop from the window. Well and good.

Then The Thinking Machine fell to remembering how he had come to the cell. First, there was the outside guard's booth, a part of the wall. There were two heavily barred gates there, both of steel. At this gate was one man always on guard. He admitted persons to the prison after much clanking of keys and locks, and let them out when ordered to do so. The warden's office was in the prison building, and in order to reach that official from the prison yard one had to pass a gate of solid steel with only a peep-hole in it. Then coming from that inner office to Cell 13, where he was now, one must pass a heavy wooden door and two steel doors into the corridors of the prison; and always there was the double-locked door of Cell 13 to reckon with.

There were then, The Thinking Machine recalled, seven doors to be overcome before one could pass from Cell 13 into the outer world, a free man. But against this was the fact that he was rarely interrupted. A jailer appeared at his cell door at six in the morning with a breakfast of prison fare; he would come again at noon, and again at six in the afternoon. At nine o'clock at night would come the inspection tour. That would be all.

"It's admirably arranged, this prison system," was the mental tribute paid by The Thinking Machine. "I'll have to study it a little when I get out. I had no idea there was such great care exercised in the prisons."

There was nothing, positively nothing, in his cell, except his iron bed, so firmly put together that no man could tear it to pieces save with sledges or a file. He had neither of these. There was not even a chair, or a small table, or a bit of tin or crockery. Nothing! The jailer stood by when he ate, then took away the wooden spoon and bowl which he had used.

One by one these things sank into the brain of The Thinking Machine. When the last possibility had been considered he began an examination of his cell. From the roof, down the walls on all sides, he examined the stones and the cement between them. He stamped over the floor carefully time after time, but it was cement, perfectly solid. After the examination he sat on the edge of the iron bed and was lost in thought for a long time. For Professor Augustus S. F. X. Van Dusen, The Thinking Machine, had something to think about.

He was disturbed by a rat, which ran across his foot, then scampered away into a dark corner of the cell, frightened at its own daring. After awhile The Thinking Machine, squinting steadily into the darkness of the corner where the rat had gone, was able to make out in the gloom many little beady eyes staring at him. He counted six pair, and there were perhaps others; he didn't see very well.

Then The Thinking Machine, from his seat on the bed, noticed for the first time the bottom of his cell door. There was an opening there of two inches between the steel bar and the floor. Still looking steadily at this opening, The Thinking Machine backed suddenly into the corner where he had seen the beady eyes. There was a great scampering of tiny feet, several squeaks of frightened rodents, and then silence.

None of the rats had gone out the door, yet there were none in the cell. Therefore there must be another way out of the cell, however small. The Thinking Machine, on hands and knees, started a search for this spot, feeling in the darkness with his long, slender fingers.

At last his search was rewarded. He came upon a small opening in the floor, level with the cement. It was perfectly round and somewhat larger than a silver dollar. This was the way the rats had gone. He put his fingers deep into the opening; it seemed to be a disused drainage pipe and was dry and dusty.

Having satisfied himself on this point, he sat on the bed again for an hour, then made another inspection of his surroundings through the small cell window. One of the outside guards stood directly opposite, beside the wall, and happened to be looking at the window of Cell 13 when the head of The Thinking Machine appeared. But the scientist didn't notice the guard.

Noon came and the jailer appeared with the prison dinner of repulsively plain food. At home The Thinking Machine merely ate to live; here he took what was offered without comment. Occasionally he spoke to the jailer who stood outside the door watching him.

"Any improvements made here in the last few years?" he asked.

"Nothing particularly," replied the jailer. "New wall was built four years ago."

"Anything done to the prison proper?"

"Painted the woodwork outside, and I believe about seven years ago a new system of plumbing was put in."

"Ah!" said the prisoner. "How far is the river over there?"

"About three hundred feet. The boys have a baseball ground between the wall and the river."

The Thinking Machine had nothing further to say just then, but when the jailer was ready to go he asked for some water.

"I get very thirsty here," he explained. "Would it be possible for you to leave a little water in a bowl for me?"

"I'll ask the warden," replied the jailer, and he went away. Half an hour later he returned with water in a small earthen bowl.

"The warden says you may keep this bowl," he informed the prisoner. "But you must show it to me when I ask for it. If it is broken, it will be the last."

"Thank you," said The Thinking Machine. "I shan't break it."

The jailer went on about his duties. For just the fraction of a second it seemed that The Thinking Machine wanted to ask a question, but he didn't.

Two hours later this same jailer, in passing the door of Cell No. 13, heard a noise inside and stopped. The Thinking Machine was down on his hands and knees in a corner of the cell, and from that same corner came several frightened squeaks. The jailer looked on interestedly.

"Ah, I've got you," he heard the prisoner say.

"Got what?" he asked, sharply.

"One of these rats," was the reply. "See?" And between the scientist's long fingers the jailer saw a small gray rat struggling. The prisoner brought it over to the light and looked at it closely. "It's a water rat," he said.

"Ain't you got anything better to do than to catch rats?" asked the jailer.

"It's disgraceful that they should be here at all," was the irritated reply. "Take this one away and kill it. There are dozens more where it came from."

The jailer took the wriggling, squirmy rodent and flung it down on the floor violently. It gave one squeak and lay still. Later he reported the incident to the warden, who only smiled.

Still later that afternoon the outside armed guard on Cell 13 side of the prison looked up again at the window and saw the prisoner looking out. He saw a hand raised to the barred window and then something white fluttered to the ground, directly under the window of Cell 13. It was a little roll of linen, evidently of white shirting material, and tied around it was a five-dollar bill. The guard looked up at the window again, but the face had disappeared.

With a grim smile he took the little linen roll and the five-dollar bill to the warden's office. There together they deciphered something which was written on it with a queer sort of ink, frequently blurred. On the outside was this:

"Finder of this please deliver to Dr. Charles Ransome."

"Ah," said the warden, with a chuckle. "Plan of escape number one has gone wrong." Then, as an afterthought: "But why did he address it to Dr. Ransome?"

"And where did he get the pen and ink to write with?" asked the guard.

The warden looked at the guard and the guard looked at the warden. There was no apparent solution of that mystery. The warden studied the writing carefully, then shook his head.

"Well, let's see what he was going to say to Dr. Ransome," he said at length, still puzzled, and he unrolled the inner piece of linen.

"Well, if that—what—what do you think of that?" he asked, dazed.

The guard took the bit of linen and read this:

"Epa cseot d'net niiy awe htto n'si sih. T."

III.

THE WARDEN SPENT an hour wondering what sort of a cipher it was, and half an hour wondering why his prisoner should attempt to communicate with Dr. Ransome, who was the cause of him being there. After this the warden devoted some thought to the question of where the prisoner got writing materials, and what sort of writing materials he had. With the idea of illuminating this point, he examined the linen again. It was a torn part of a white shirt and had ragged edges.

Now it was possible to account for the linen, but what the prisoner had used to write with was another matter. The warden knew it would have been impossible for him to have either pen or pencil, and, besides, neither pen nor pencil had been used in this writing. What, then? The warden decided to personally investigate. The Thinking Machine was his prisoner; he had orders to hold his prisoners; if this one sought to escape by sending cipher messages to persons outside, he would stop it, as he would have stopped it in the case of any other prisoner.

The warden went back to Cell 13 and

found The Thinking Machine on his hands and knees on the floor, engaged in nothing more alarming than catching rats. The prisoner heard the warden's step and turned to him quickly.

"It's disgraceful," he snapped, "these rats. There are scores of them."

"Other men have been able to stand them," said the warden. "Here is another shirt for you—let me have the one you have on."

"Why?" demanded The Thinking Machine, quickly. His tone was hardly natural, his manner suggested actual perturbation.

"You have attempted to communicate with Dr. Ransome," said the warden severely. "As my prisoner, it is my duty to put a stop to it."

The Thinking Machine was silent for a moment.

"All right," he said, finally. "Do your duty."

The warden smiled grimly. The prisoner arose from the floor and removed the white shirt, putting on instead a striped convict shirt the warden had brought. The warden took the white shirt eagerly, and then there compared the pieces of linen on which was written the cipher with certain torn places in the shirt. The Thinking Machine looked on curiously.

"The guard brought you those, then?" he asked.

"He certainly did," replied the warden triumphantly. "And that ends your first attempt to escape."

The Thinking Machine watched the warden as he, by comparison, established to his own satisfaction that only two pieces of linen had been torn from the white shirt.

"What did you write this with?" demanded the warden.

"I should think it a part of your duty to find out," said The Thinking Machine, irritably.

The warden started to say some harsh things, then restrained himself and made a minute search of the cell and of the prisoner instead. He found absolutely nothing; not even a match or toothpick which might have been used for a pen. The same mystery surrounded the fluid with which the cipher had been written. Although the warden left Cell 13 visibly annoyed, he took the torn shirt in triumph.

"Well, writing notes on a shirt won't get him out, that's certain," he told himself with some complacency. He put the linen scraps into his desk to await developments. "If that man escapes from that cell I'll—hang it—I'll resign."

On the third day of his incarceration The Thinking Machine openly attempted to bribe his way out. The jailer had brought his dinner and was leaning against the barred door, waiting, when The Thinking Machine began the conversation.

"The drainage pipes of the prison lead to the river, don't they?" he asked.

"Yes," said the jailer.

"I suppose they are very small?"

"Too small to crawl through, if that's what you're thinking about," was the grinning response.

There was silence until The Thinking Machine finished his meal. Then:

"You know I'm not a criminal, don't you?"

"Yes."

"And that I've a perfect right to be freed if I demand it?"

"Yes."

"Well, I came here believing that I could make my escape," said the prisoner, and his squint eyes studied the face of the jailer.

"Would you consider a financial reward for aiding me to escape?"

The jailer, who happened to be an honest man, looked at the slender, weak figure of the prisoner, at the large head with its mass of yellow hair, and was almost sorry.

"I guess prisons like these were not built for the likes of you to get out of," he said, at last.

"But would you consider a proposition to help me get out?" the prisoner insisted, almost beseechingly.

"No," said the jailer, shortly.

"Five hundred dollars," urged The Thinking Machine. "I am not a criminal."

"No," said the jailer.

"A thousand?"

"No," again said the jailer, and he started away hurriedly to escape further temptation. Then he turned back. "If you should give me ten thousand dollars I couldn't get you out. You'd have to pass through seven doors, and I only have the keys to two."

Then he told the warden all about it.

"Plan number two fails," said the warden, smiling grimly. "First a cipher, then bribery."

When the jailer was on his way to Cell 13 at six o'clock, again bearing food to The Thinking Machine, he paused, startled by the unmistakable scrape, scrape of steel against steel. It stopped at the sound of his steps, then craftily the jailer, who was beyond the prisoner's range of vision, resumed his tramping, the sound being apparently that of a man going away from Cell 13. As a matter of fact he was in the same spot.

After a moment there came again the steady scrape, scrape, and the jailer crept cautiously on tiptoes to the door and peered between the bars. The Thinking Machine was standing on the iron bed working at the bars of the little window. He was using a file, judging from the backward and forward swing of his arms.

Cautiously the jailer crept back to the office, summoned the warden in person, and they returned to Cell 13 on tiptoes. The steady scrape was still audible. The warden listened to satisfy himself and then suddenly appeared at the door.

"Well?" he demanded, and there was a smile on his face.

The Thinking Machine glanced back from his perch on the bed and leaped suddenly to the floor, making frantic efforts to hide something. The warden went in, with hand extended.

"Give it up," he said.

"No," said the prisoner, sharply.

"Come, give it up," urged the warden. "I don't want to have to search you again."

"No," repeated the prisoner.

"What was it, a file?" asked the warden.

The Thinking Machine was silent and stood squinting at the warden with something very nearly approaching disappointment on his face—nearly, but not quite. The warden was almost sympathetic.

"Plan number three fails, eh?" he asked, good-naturedly. "Too bad, isn't it?"

The prisoner didn't say.

"Search him," instructed the warden.

The jailer searched the prisoner carefully. At last, artfully concealed in the waist band of the trousers, he found a piece of steel about two inches long, with one side curved like a half moon.

"Ah," said the warden, as he received it from the jailer. "From your shoe heel," and he smiled pleasantly.

The jailer continued his search and on

the other side of the trousers waist band found another piece of steel identical with the first. The edges showed where they had been worn against the bars of the window.

"You couldn't saw a way through those bars with these," said the warden.

"I could have," said The Thinking Machine firmly.

"In six months, perhaps," said the warden, good-naturedly.

The warden shook his head slowly as he gazed into the slightly flushed face of his prisoner.

"Ready to give it up?" he asked.

"I haven't started yet," was the prompt reply.

Then came another exhaustive search of the cell. Carefully the two men went over it, finally turning out the bed and searching that. Nothing. The warden in person climbed upon the bed and examined the bars of the window where the prisoner had been sawing. When he looked he was amused.

"Just made it a little bright by hard rubbing," he said to the prisoner, who stood looking on with a somewhat crestfallen air. The warden grasped the iron bars in his strong hands and tried to shake them. They were immovable, set firmly in the solid granite. He examined each in turn and found them all satisfactory. Finally he climbed down from the bed.

"Give it up, professor," he advised.

The Thinking Machine shook his head and the warden and jailer passed on again. As they disappeared down the corridor The Thinking Machine sat on the edge of the bed with his head in his hands.

"He's crazy to try to get out of that cell," commented the jailer.

"Of course he can't get out," said the warden. "But he's clever. I would like to know what he wrote that cipher with."

It was four o'clock next morning when an awful, heart-racking shriek of terror resounded through the great prison. It came from a cell somewhere about the center, and its tone told a tale of horror, agony, terrible fear. The warden heard and with three of his men rushed into the long corridor leading to Cell 13.

IV.

As they ran there came again that awful cry. It died away in a sort of wail. The white faces of prisoners appeared at cell doors upstairs and down, staring out wonderingly, frightened.

"It's that fool in Cell 13," grumbled the warden.

He stopped and stared in as one of the jailers flashed a lantern. "That fool in Cell 13" lay comfortably on his cot, flat on his back with his mouth open, snoring. Even as they looked there came again the piercing cry, from somewhere above. The warden's face blanched a little as he started up the stairs. There on the top floor he found a man in Cell 43, directly above Cell 13, but two floors higher, cowering in a corner of his cell.

"What's the matter?" demanded the warden.

"Thank God you've come," exclaimed the prisoner, and he cast himself against the bars of his cell.

"What is it?" demanded the warden again.

He threw open the door and went in. The prisoner dropped on his knees and clasped the warden about the body. His face was white with terror, his eyes were widely distended, and he was shuddering. His hands, icy cold, clutched at the warden's.

"Take me out of this cell, please take me out," he pleaded.

"What's the matter with you, anyhow?" insisted the warden, impatiently.

"I heard something—something," said the prisoner, and his eyes roved nervously around the cell.

"What did you hear?"

"I—I can't tell you," stammered the prisoner. Then, in a sudden burst of terror: "Take me out of this cell—put me anywhere—but take me out of here."

The warden and the three jailers exchanged glances.

"Who is this fellow? What's he accused of?" asked the warden.

"Joseph Ballard," said one of the jailers. "He's accused of throwing acid in a woman's face. She died from it."

"But they can't prove it," gasped the prisoner. "They can't prove it. Please put me in some other cell."

He was still clinging to the warden, and that official threw his arms off roughly. Then for a time he stood looking at the cowering wretch, who seemed possessed of all the wild, unreasoning terror of a child.

"Look here, Ballard," said the warden, finally, "if you heard anything, I want to know what it was. Now tell me."

"I can't, I can't," was the reply. He was sobbing.

"Where did it come from?"

"I don't know. Everywhere—nowhere. I just heard it."

"What was it—a voice?"

"Please don't make me answer," pleaded the prisoner.

"You must answer," said the warden, sharply.

"It was a voice—but—but it wasn't human," was the sobbing reply.

"Voice, but not human?" repeated the warden, puzzled.

"It sounded muffled and—and far away—and ghostly," explained the man.

"Did it come from inside or outside the prison?"

"It didn't seem to come from anywhere—it was just here, here, everywhere. I heard it. I heard it."

For an hour the warden tried to get the story, but Ballard had become suddenly obstinate and would say nothing—only pleaded to be placed in another cell, or to have one of the jailers remain near him until daylight. These requests were gruffly refused.

"And see here," said the warden, in conclusion, "if there's any more of this screaming, I'll put you in the padded cell."

Then the warden went his way, a sadly puzzled man. Ballard sat at his cell door until daylight, his face, drawn and white with terror, pressed against the bars, and looked out into the prison with wide, staring eyes.

That day, the fourth since the incarceration of The Thinking Machine, was enlivened considerably by the volunteer prisoner, who spent most of his time at the little window of his cell. He began proceedings by throwing another piece of linen down to the guard, who picked it up dutifully and took it to the warden. On it was written:

"Only three days more."

The warden was in no way surprised at what he read; he understood that The Thinking Machine meant only three days more of his imprisonment, and he regarded the note as a boast. But how was the thing written? Where had The Thinking Machine found this new piece of linen? Where? How? He carefully examined the linen. It was white, of fine texture, shirting material. He took the shirt which he had taken and carefully fitted the two original pieces of the linen to the torn places. This third piece was entirely superfluous; it didn't fit anywhere, and yet it was unmistakably the same goods.

"And where—where does he get anything to write with?" demanded the warden of the world at large.

Still later on the fourth day The Thinking Machine, through the window of his cell, spoke to the armed guard outside.

"What day of the month is it?" he asked.

"The fifteenth," was the answer.

The Thinking Machine made a mental astronomical calculation and satisfied himself that the moon would not rise until after nine o'clock that night. Then he asked another question: "Who attends to those arc lights?"

"Man from the company."

"You have no electricians in the building?"

"No."

"I should think you could save money if you had your own man."

"None of my business," replied the guard.

The guard noticed The Thinking Machine at the cell window frequently during that day, but always the face seemed listless and there was a certain wistfulness in the squint eyes behind the glasses. After a while he accepted the presence of the leonine head as a matter of course. He had seen other prisoners do the same thing; it was the longing for the outside world.

That afternoon, just before the day guard was relieved, the head appeared at the window again, and The Thinking Machine's hand held something out between the bars. It fluttered to the ground and the guard picked it up. It was a five-dollar bill.

"That's for you," called the prisoner.

As usual, the guard took it to the warden. That gentleman looked at it suspiciously; he looked at everything that came from Cell 13 with suspicion.

"He said it was for me," explained the guard.

"It's a sort of a tip, I suppose," said the warden. "I see no particular reason why you shouldn't accept—"

Suddenly he stopped. He had remembered that The Thinking Machine had gone into Cell 13 with one five-dollar bill and two ten-dollar bills; twenty-five dollars in all. Now a five-dollar bill had been tied around the first pieces of linen that came from the cell. The warden still had it, and to convince himself he took it out and looked at it. It was five dollars; yet here was another five dollars, and The Thinking Machine had only had ten-dollar bills.

"Perhaps somebody changed one of the bills for him," he thought at last, with a sigh of relief.

But then and there he made up his mind. He would search Cell 13 as a cell was never before searched in this world. When a man could write at will, and change money, and do other wholly inexplicable things, there was something radically wrong with his prison. He planned to enter the cell at night—three o'clock would be an excellent time. The Thinking Machine must do all the weird things he did sometime. Night seemed the most reasonable.

Thus it happened that the warden stealthily descended upon Cell 13 that night at three-o'clock. He paused at the door and listened. There was no sound save the steady, regular breathing of the prisoner. The keys unfastened the double locks with scarcely a clank, and the warden entered, locking the door behind him. Suddenly he flashed his dark-lantern[5] in the face of the recumbent figure.

If the warden had planned to startle The Thinking Machine he was mistaken, for that individual merely opened his eyes quietly, reached for his glasses and inquired, in a most matter-of-fact tone:

"Who is it?"

It would be useless to describe the search that the warden made. It was minute. Not one inch of the cell or the bed was overlooked. He found the round hole in the floor, and with a flash of inspiration thrust his thick fingers into it. After a moment of fumbling there he drew up something and looked at it in the light of his lantern.

"Ugh!" he exclaimed.

The thing he had taken out was a rat—a dead rat. His inspiration fled as a mist before the sun. But he continued the search. The Thinking Machine, without a word, arose and kicked the rat out of the cell into the corridor.

The warden climbed on the bed and tried the steel bars in the tiny window. They were perfectly rigid; every bar of the door was the same.

Then the warden searched the prisoner's clothing, beginning at the shoes. Nothing hidden in them! Then the trousers waist band. Still nothing! Then the pockets of the trousers. From one side he drew out some paper money and examined it.

"Five one-dollar bills," he gasped.

"That's right," said the prisoner.

"But the—you had two tens and a five—what the—how do you do it?"

"That's my business," said the Thinking Machine.

"Did any of my men change this money for you—on your word of honor?"

The Thinking Machine paused just a fraction of a second.

"No," he said.

"Well, do you make it?" asked the warden. He was prepared to believe anything.

"That's my business," again said the prisoner.

The warden glared at the eminent scientist fiercely. He felt—he *knew*—that this man was making a fool of him, yet he didn't know how. If he were a real prisoner he would get the truth—but, then, perhaps, those inexplicable things which had happened would not have been brought before him so sharply. Neither of the men spoke for a long time, then suddenly the warden turned fiercely and left the cell, slamming the door behind him. He didn't dare to speak, then.

He glanced at the clock. It was ten minutes to four. He had hardly settled himself in bed when again came that heart-breaking shriek through the prison. With a few muttered words, which, while not elegant, were highly expressive, he relighted his lantern and rushed through the prison again to the cell on the upper floor.

Again Ballard was crushing himself against the steel door, shrieking, shrieking at the top of his voice. He stopped only when the warden flashed his lamp in the cell.

"Take me out, take me out," he screamed. "I did it, I did it, I killed her. Take it away."

"Take what away?" asked the warden.

---

[5] A Victorian "flashlight"—a lantern that could be darkened by sliding a shutter over the lamp.

"I threw the acid in her face—I did it—I confess. Take me out of here."

Ballard's condition was pitiable; it was only an act of mercy to let him out into the corridor. There he crouched in a corner, like an animal at bay, and clasped his hands to his ears. It took half an hour to calm him sufficiently for him to speak. Then he told incoherently what had happened. On the night before at four o'clock he had heard a voice—a sepulchral voice, muffled and wailing in tone.

"What did it say?" asked the warden, curiously.

"Acid—acid—acid!" gasped the prisoner. "It accused me. Acid! I threw the acid, and the woman died. Oh!" It was a long, shuddering wail of terror.

"Acid?" echoed the warden, puzzled. The case was beyond him.

"Acid. That's all I heard—that one word, repeated several times. There were other things, too, but I didn't hear them."

"That was last night, eh?" asked the warden. "What happened tonight—what frightened you just now?"

"It was the same thing," gasped the prisoner. "Acid—acid—acid!" He covered his face with his hands and sat shivering. "It was acid I used on her, but I didn't mean to kill her. I just heard the words. It was something accusing me—accusing me." He mumbled, and was silent.

"Did you hear anything else?"

"Yes—but I couldn't understand—only a little bit—just a word or two."

"Well, what was it?"

"I heard 'acid' three times, then I heard a long, moaning sound, then—then—I heard 'No. 8 hat.' I heard that twice."

"No. 8 hat," repeated the warden. "What the devil—No. 8 hat? Accusing voices of con-

science have never talked about No. 8 hats, so far as I ever heard. "

"He's insane," said one of the jailers, with an air of finality.

"I believe you," said the warden. "He must be. He probably heard something and got frightened. He's trembling now. No. 8 hat! What the—"

V.

WHEN THE FIFTH day of The Thinking Machine's imprisonment rolled around the warden was wearing a hunted look. He was anxious for the end of the thing. He could not help but feel that his distinguished prisoner had been amusing himself. And if this were so, The Thinking Machine had lost none of his sense of humor. For on this fifth day he flung down another linen note to the outside guard, bearing the words: "Only two days more." Also he flung down half a dollar.

Now the warden knew—he knew—that the man in Cell 13 didn't have any half dollars—he couldn't have any half dollars, no more than he could have pen and ink and linen, and yet he did have them. It was a condition, not a theory; that is one reason why the warden was wearing a hunted look.

That ghastly, uncanny thing, too, about "Acid" and "No. 8 hat" clung to him tenaciously. They didn't mean anything, of course, merely the ravings of an insane murderer who had been driven by fear to confess his crime, still there were so many things that "didn't mean anything" happening in the prison now since The Thinking Machine was there.

On the sixth day the warden received a postal stating that Dr. Ransome and Mr. Fielding would be at Chisholm Prison on the following evening, Thursday, and in the event

Professor Van Dusen had not yet escaped—and they presumed he had not because they had not heard from him—they would meet him there.

"In the event he had not yet escaped!" The warden smiled grimly. Escaped!

The Thinking Machine enlivened this day for the warden with three notes. They were on the usual linen and bore generally on the appointment at half-past eight o'clock Thursday night, which appointment the scientist had made at the time of his imprisonment.

On the afternoon of the seventh day the warden passed Cell 13 and glanced in. The Thinking Machine was lying on the iron bed, apparently sleeping lightly. The cell appeared precisely as it always did to a casual glance. The warden would swear that no man was going to leave it between that hour—it was then four o'clock—and half-past eight o'clock that evening.

On his way back past the cell the warden heard the steady breathing again, and coming close to the door looked in. He wouldn't have done so if The Thinking Machine had been looking, but now—well, it was different.

A ray of light came through the high window and fell on the face of the sleeping man. It occurred to the warden for the first time that his prisoner appeared haggard and weary. Just then The Thinking Machine stirred slightly and the warden hurried on up the corridor guiltily. That evening after six o'clock he saw the jailer.

"Everything all right in Cell 13?" he asked.

"Yes, sir," replied the jailer. "He didn't eat much, though."

It was with a feeling of having done his duty that the warden received Dr. Ransome and Mr. Fielding shortly after seven o'clock.

He intended to show them the linen notes and lay before them the full story of his woes, which was a long one. But before this came to pass, the guard from the river side of the prison yard entered the office.

"The arc light in my side of the yard won't light," he informed the warden.

"Confound it, that man's a hoodoo," thundered the official. "Everything has happened since he's been here."

The guard went back to his post in the darkness, and the warden 'phoned to the electric light company.

"This is Chisholm Prison," he said through the 'phone. "Send three or four men down here quick, to fix an arc light."

The reply was evidently satisfactory, for the warden hung up the receiver and passed out into the yard. While Dr. Ransome and Mr. Fielding sat waiting the guard at the outer gate came in with a special delivery letter. Dr. Ransome happened to notice the address, and, when the guard went out, looked at the letter more closely.

"By George!" he exclaimed.

"What is it?" asked Mr. Fielding.

Silently the doctor offered the letter. Mr. Fielding examined it closely.

"Coincidence," he said. "It must be."

It was nearly eight o'clock when the warden returned to his office. The electricians had arrived in a wagon, and were now at work. The warden pressed the buzz-button communicating with the man at the outer gate in the wall.

"How many electricians came in?" he asked, over the short 'phone. "Four? Three workmen in jumpers and overalls and the manager? Frock coat and silk hat? All right. Be certain that only four go out. That's all."

He turned to Dr. Ransome and Mr.

Fielding. "We have to be careful here—particularly," and there was broad sarcasm in his tone, "since we have scientists locked up."

The warden picked up the special delivery letter carelessly, and then began to open it.

"When I read this I want to tell you gentlemen something about how—Great Caesar!" he ended, suddenly, as he glanced at the letter. He sat with mouth open, motionless, from astonishment.

"What is it?" asked Mr. Fielding.

"A special delivery from Cell 13," gasped the warden. "An invitation to supper."

"What?" and the two others arose, unanimously.

The warden sat dazed, staring at the letter for a moment, then called sharply to a guard outside in the corridor.

"Run down to Cell 13 and see if that man's in there."

The guard went as directed, while Dr. Ransome and Mr. Fielding examined the letter.

"It's Van Dusen's handwriting; there's no question of that," said Dr. Ransome. "I've seen too much of it."

Just then the buzz on the telephone from the outer gate sounded, and the warden, in a semi-trance, picked up the receiver.

"Hello! Two reporters, eh? Let 'em come in." He turned suddenly to the doctor and Mr. Fielding. "Why, the man *can't* be out. He must be in his cell."

Just at that moment the guard returned.

"He's still in his cell, sir," he reported. "I saw him. He's lying down."

"There, I told you so," said the warden, and he breathed freely again. "But how did he mail that letter?"

There was a rap on the steel door which led from the jail yard into the warden's office.

"It's the reporters," said the warden. "Let them in," he instructed the guard; then to the two other gentlemen: "Don't say anything about this before them, because I'd never hear the last of it."

The door opened, and the two men from the front gate entered.

"Good-evening, gentlemen," said one. That was Hutchinson Hatch; the warden knew him well.

"Well?" demanded the other, irritably. "I'm here."

That was The Thinking Machine.

He squinted belligerently at the warden, who sat with mouth agape. For the moment that official had nothing to say. Dr. Ransome and Mr. Fielding were amazed, but they didn't know what the warden knew. They were only amazed; he was paralyzed. Hutchinson Hatch, the reporter, took in the scene with greedy eyes.

"How—how—how did you do it?" gasped the warden, finally.

"Come back to the cell," said The Thinking Machine, in the irritated voice which his scientific associates knew so well.

The warden, still in a condition bordering on trance, led the way.

"Flash your light in there," directed The Thinking Machine.

The warden did so. There was nothing unusual in the appearance of the cell, and there—there on the bed lay the figure of The Thinking Machine. Certainly! There was the yellow hair! Again the warden looked at the man beside him and wondered at the strangeness of his own dreams.

With trembling hands he unlocked the cell door and The Thinking Machine passed inside.

"See here," he said.

He kicked at the steel bars in the bottom of the cell door and three of them were pushed out of place. A fourth broke off and rolled away in the corridor.

"And here, too," directed the erstwhile prisoner as he stood on the bed to reach the small window. He swept his hand across the opening and every bar came out.

"What's this in the bed?" demanded the warden, who was slowly recovering.

"A wig," was the reply. "Turn down the cover."

The warden did so. Beneath it lay a large coil of strong rope, thirty feet or more, a dagger, three files, ten feet of electric wire, a thin, powerful pair of steel pliers, a small tack hammer with its handle, and—and a Derringer pistol.

"'How did you do it?" demanded the warden.

"You gentlemen have an engagement to supper with me at half past nine o'clock," said The Thinking Machine. "Come on, or we shall be late."

"But how did you do it?" insisted the warden.

"Don't ever think you can hold any man who can use his brain," said The Thinking Machine. "Come on; we shall be late."

VI.

IT WAS AN impatient supper party in the rooms of Professor Van Dusen and a somewhat silent one. The guests were Dr. Ransome, Albert Fielding, the warden, and Hutchinson Hatch, reporter. The meal was served to the minute, in accordance with Professor Van Dusen's instructions of one week before; Dr. Ransome found the artichokes delicious. At last the supper was finished and The Thinking Machine turned full on Dr. Ransome and squinted at him fiercely.

"Do you believe it now?" he demanded.

"I do," replied Dr. Ransome.

"Do you admit that it was a fair test?"

"I do."

With the others, particularly the warden, he was waiting anxiously for the explanation.

"Suppose you tell us how—" began Mr. Fielding.

"Yes, tell us how," said the warden.

The Thinking Machine readjusted his glasses, took a couple of preparatory squints at his audience, and began the story. He told it from the beginning logically; and no man ever talked to more interested listeners.

"My agreement was," he began, "to go into a cell, carrying nothing except what was necessary to wear, and to leave that cell within a week. I had never seen Chisholm Prison. When I went into the cell I asked for tooth powder, two ten and one five-dollar bills, and also to have my shoes blacked. Even if these requests had been refused it would not have mattered seriously. But you agreed to them.

"I knew there would be nothing in the cell which you thought I might use to advantage. So when the warden locked the door on me I was apparently helpless, unless I could turn three seemingly innocent things to use. They were things which would have been permitted any prisoner under sentence of death, were they not, warden?"

"Tooth powder and polished shoes, yes, but not money," replied the warden.

"Anything is dangerous in the hands of a man who knows how to use it," went on The Thinking Machine. "I did nothing that first night but sleep and chase rats." He glared at the warden. "When the matter was broached

I knew I could do nothing that night, so suggested next day. You gentlemen thought I wanted time to arrange an escape with outside assistance, but this was not true. I knew I could communicate with whom I pleased, when I pleased."

The warden stared at him a moment, then went on smoking solemnly.

"I was aroused next morning at six o'clock by the jailer with my breakfast," continued the scientist. "He told me dinner was at twelve and supper at six. Between these times, I gathered, I would be pretty much to myself. So immediately after breakfast I examined my outside surroundings from my cell window. One look told me it would be useless to try to scale the wall, even should I decide to leave my cell by the window, for my purpose was to leave not only the cell, but the prison. Of course, I could have gone over the wall, but it would have taken me longer to lay my plans that way. Therefore, for the moment, I dismissed all idea of that.

"From this first observation I knew the river was on that side of the prison, and that there was also a playground there. Subsequently these surmises were verified by a keeper. I knew then one important thing—that anyone might approach the prison wall from that side if necessary without attracting any particular attention. That was well to remember. I remembered it.

"But the outside thing which most attracted my attention was the feed wire to the arc light which ran within a few feet—probably three or four—of my cell window. I knew that would be valuable in the event I found it necessary to cut off that arc light."

"Oh, you shut it off tonight, then?" asked the warden.

"Having learned all I could from that window," resumed The Thinking Machine, without heeding the interruption, "I considered the idea of escaping through the prison proper. I recalled just how I had come into the cell, which I knew would be the only way. Seven doors lay between me and the outside. So, also for the time being I gave up the idea of escaping that way. And I couldn't go through the solid granite walls of the cell."

The Thinking Machine paused for a moment and Dr. Ransome lighted a new cigar. For several minutes there was silence, then the scientific jail-breaker went on:

"While I was thinking about these things a rat ran across my foot. It suggested a new line of thought. There were at least half a dozen rats in the cell—I could see their beady eyes. Yet I had noticed none come under the cell door. I frightened them purposely and watched the cell door to see if they went out that way. They did not, but they were gone. Obviously they went another way. Another way meant another opening.

"I searched for this opening and found it. It was an old drain pipe, long unused and partly choked with dirt and dust. But this was the way the rats had come. They came from somewhere. Where? Drain pipes usually lead outside prison grounds. This one probably led to the river, or near it. The rats must therefore come from that direction. If they came a part of the way, I reasoned that they came all the way, because it was extremely unlikely that a solid iron or lead pipe would have any hole in it except at the exit.

"When the jailer came with my luncheon he told me two important things, although he didn't know it. One was that a new system of plumbing had been put in the prison seven years before; another that the river was only three hundred feet away. Then I knew positively that the pipe was a part of an old system; I knew, too, that it slanted generally toward the river. But did the pipe end in the water or on land?

"This was the next question to be decided. I decided it by catching several of the rats in the cell. My jailer was surprised to see me engaged in this work. I examined at least a dozen of them. They were perfectly dry; they had come through the pipe, and, most important of all, they were *not house rats, but field rats.* The other end of the pipe was on land, then, outside the prison walls. So far, so good.

"Then, I knew that if I worked freely from this point I must attract the warden's attention in another direction. You see, by telling the warden that I had come there to escape you made the test more severe, because I had to trick him by false scents."

The warden looked up with a sad expression in his eyes.

"The first thing was to make him think I was trying to communicate with you, Dr. Ransome. So I wrote a note on a piece of linen I tore from my shirt, addressed it to Dr. Ransome, tied a five-dollar bill around it and threw it out of the window. I knew the guard would take it to the warden, but I rather hoped the warden would send it as addressed. Have you that first linen note, warden?"

The warden produced the cipher.

"What the deuce does it mean, anyhow?" he asked.

"Read it backward, beginning with the 'T' signature and disregard the division into words," instructed The Thinking Machine.

The warden did so.

"T-h-i-s, this," he spelled, studied it a moment, then read it off, grinning:

"This is not the way I intend to escape."

"Well, now what do you think o' that?" he demanded, still grinning.

"I knew that would attract your attention, just as it did," said The Thinking Machine, "and if you really found out what it was, it would be a sort of gentle rebuke."

"What did you write it with?" asked Dr. Ransome, after he had examined the linen and passed it to Mr. Fielding.

"This," said the erstwhile prisoner, and he extended his foot. On it was the shoe he had worn in prison, though the polish was gone—scraped off clean. "The shoe blacking, moistened with water, was my ink; the metal tip of the shoe lace made a fairly good pen."

The warden looked up and suddenly burst into a laugh, half of relief, half of amusement.

"You're a wonder," he said, admiringly. "Go on."

"That precipitated a search of my cell by the warden, as I had intended," continued The Thinking Machine. "I was anxious to get the warden into the habit of searching my cell, so that finally, constantly finding nothing, he would get disgusted and quit. This at last happened, practically."

The warden blushed.

"He then took my white shirt away and gave me a prison shirt. He was satisfied that those two pieces of the shirt were all that was missing. But while he was searching my cell I had another piece of that same shirt, about nine inches square, rolled into a small ball in my mouth."

"Nine inches off that shirt?" demanded the warden. "Where did it come from?"

"The bosoms of all stiff white shirts are of triple thickness," was the explanation. "I tore out the inside thickness, leaving the bosom only two thicknesses. I knew you wouldn't see it. So much for that."

There was a little pause, and the warden looked from one to another of the men with a sheepish grin.

"Having disposed of the warden for the time being by giving him something else to think about, I took my first serious step toward freedom," said Professor Van Dusen. "I knew, within reason, that the pipe led somewhere to the playground outside; I knew a great many boys played there; I knew that rats came into my cell from out there. Could I communicate with some one outside with these things at hand?

"First was necessary, I saw, a long and fairly reliable thread, so—but here," he pulled up his trousers legs and showed that the tops of both stockings, of fine, strong lisle, were gone. "I unraveled those—after I got them started it wasn't difficult—and I had easily a quarter of a mile of thread that I could depend on.

"Then on half of my remaining linen I wrote, laboriously enough I assure you, a letter explaining my situation to this gentleman here," and he indicated Hutchinson Hatch. "I knew he would assist me for the value of the newspaper story. I tied firmly to this linen letter a ten-dollar bill—there is no surer way of attracting the eye of anyone—and wrote on the linen: 'Finder of this deliver to Hutchinson Hatch, *Daily American*, who will give another ten dollars for the information.'

"The next thing was to get this note outside on that playground where a boy might find it. There were two ways, but I chose the best. I took one of the rats—I became adept in catching them—tied the linen and money firmly to one leg, fastened my lisle thread to another, and turned him loose in the drain pipe. I reasoned that the natural fright of the rodent would make him run until he was outside the pipe and then out on earth he would probably stop to gnaw off the linen and money.

"From the moment the rat disappeared into that dusty pipe I became anxious. I was taking so many chances. The rat might gnaw the string, of which I held one end; other rats might gnaw it; the rat might run out of the pipe and leave the linen and money where they would never be found; a thousand other things might have happened. So began some nervous hours, but the fact that the rat ran on until only a few feet of the string remained in my cell made me think he was outside the pipe. I had carefully instructed Mr. Hatch what to do in case the note reached him. The question was: Would it reach him?

"This done, I could only wait and make other plans in case this one failed. I openly attempted to bribe my jailer, and learned from him that he held the keys to only two of seven doors between me and freedom. Then I did something else to make the warden nervous. I took the steel supports out of the heels of my shoes and made a pretense of sawing the bars of my cell window. The warden raised a pretty row about that. He developed, too, the habit of shaking the bars of my cell window to see if they were solid. They were—then."

Again the warden grinned. He had ceased being astonished.

"With this one plan I had done all I could and could only wait to see what happened," the scientist went on. "I couldn't know whether my note had been delivered or even found, or whether the rat had gnawed it up. And I didn't dare to draw back through the pipe that one slender thread which connected me with the outside.

"When I went to bed that night I didn't sleep, for fear there would come the slight signal twitch at the thread which was to tell me that Mr. Hatch had received the note. At half-past three o'clock, I judge, I felt this twitch, and no prisoner actually under sentence of death ever welcomed a thing more heartily."

The Thinking Machine stopped and turned to the reporter.

"You'd better explain just what you did," he said.

"The linen note was brought to me by a small boy who had been playing baseball," said Mr. Hatch. "I immediately saw a big story in it, so I gave the boy another ten dollars, and got several spools of silk, some twine, and a roll of light, pliable wire. The professor's note suggested that I have the finder of the note show me just where it was picked up, and told me to make my search from there, beginning at two o'clock in the morning. If I found the other end of the thread I was to twitch it gently three times, then a fourth.

"I began the search with a small bulb electric light. It was an hour and twenty minutes before I found the end of the drain pipe, half hidden in weeds. The pipe was very large there, say twelve inches across. Then I found the end of the lisle thread, twitched it as directed and immediately I got an answering twitch.

"Then I fastened the silk to this and Professor Van Dusen began to pull it into his cell. I nearly had heart disease for fear the string would break. To the end of the silk I fastened the twine, and when that had been pulled in, I tied on the wire. Then that was drawn into the pipe and we had a substantial line, which rats couldn't gnaw, from the mouth of the drain into the cell."

The Thinking Machine raised his hand and Hatch stopped.

"All this was done in absolute silence," said the scientist. "But when the wire reached my hand I could have shouted. Then we tried another experiment, which Mr. Hatch was prepared for. I tested the pipe as a speaking tube. Neither of us could hear very clearly, but I dared not speak loud for fear of attracting attention in the prison. At last I made him understand what I wanted immediately. He seemed to have great difficulty in understanding when I asked for nitric acid, and I repeated the word 'acid' several times.

"Then I heard a shriek from a cell above me. I knew instantly that some one had overheard, and when I heard you coming, Mr. Warden, I feigned sleep. If you had entered my cell at that moment that whole plan of escape would have ended there. But you passed on. That was the nearest I ever came to being caught.

"Having established this improvised trolley it is easy to see how I got things in the cell and made them disappear at will. I merely dropped them back into the pipe. You, Mr. Warden, could not have reached the connecting wire with your fingers; they are too large. My fingers, you see, are longer and more slender. In addition I guarded the top of that pipe with a rat—you remember how."

"I remember," said the warden, with a grimace.

"I thought that if any one were tempted to investigate that hole the rat would dampen his ardor. Mr. Hatch could not send me anything useful through the pipe until next night, although he did send me change for ten dollars as a test, so I proceeded with other parts of my plan. Then I evolved the method of escape, which I finally employed.

"In order to carry this out successfully it was necessary for the guard in the yard to get accustomed to seeing me at the cell window. I arranged this by dropping linen notes to him, boastful in tone, to make the warden believe, if possible, one of his assistants was communicating with the outside for me. I would stand at my window for hours gazing out, so the guard could see, and occasionally I spoke to him. In that way I learned that the prison had no electricians of its own, but was dependent upon the lighting company if anything should go wrong.

"That cleared the way to freedom perfectly. Early in the evening of the last day of my imprisonment, when it was dark, I planned to cut the feed wire which was only a few feet from my window, reaching it with an acid-tipped wire I had. That would make that side of the prison perfectly dark while the electricians were searching for the break. That would also bring Mr. Hatch into the prison yard.

"There was only one more thing to do before I actually began the work of setting myself free. This was to arrange final details with Mr. Hatch through our speaking tube. I did this within half an hour after the warden left my cell on the fourth night of my imprisonment. Mr. Hatch again had serious difficulty in understanding me, and I repeated the word 'acid' to him several times, and later the words: 'Number eight hat'—that's my size—and these were the things which made a prisoner upstairs confess to murder, so one of the jailers told me next day. This prisoner heard our voices, confused of course, through the pipe, which also went to his cell. The cell directly over me was not occupied, hence no one else heard.

"Of course the actual work of cutting the steel bars out of the window and door was comparatively easy with nitric acid, which I got through the pipe in thin bottles, but it took time. Hour after hour on the fifth and sixth and seventh days the guard below was looking at me as I worked on the bars of the window with the acid on a piece of wire. I used the tooth powder to prevent the acid spreading. I looked away abstractedly as I worked and each minute the acid cut deeper into the metal. I noticed that the jailers always tried the door by shaking the upper part, never the lower bars, therefore I cut the lower bars, leaving them hanging in place by thin strips of metal. But that was a bit of daredeviltry. I could not have gone that way so easily."

The Thinking Machine sat silent for several minutes.

"I think that makes everything clear," he went on. "Whatever points I have not explained were merely to confuse the warden and jailers. These things in my bed I brought in to please Mr. Hatch, who wanted to improve the story. Of course, the wig was necessary in my plan. The special delivery letter I wrote and directed in my cell with Mr. Hatch's fountain pen, then sent it out to him and he mailed it. That's all, I think."

"But your actually leaving the prison grounds and then coming in through the outer gate to my office?" asked the warden.

"Perfectly simple," said the scientist. "I cut the electric light wire with acid, as I said, when the current was off. Therefore when the current was turned on, the arc light didn't light. I knew it would take some time to find out what was the matter and make repairs. When the guard went to report to you the yard was dark, I crept out the window—it was a tight fit, too—replaced the bars by standing on a narrow ledge and remained in a shadow until the force of electricians arrived. Mr. Hatch was one of them.

"When I saw him I spoke and he handed me a cap, a jumper and overalls, which I put on within ten feet of you, Mr. Warden, while you were in the yard. Later Mr. Hatch called me, presumably as a workman, and together we went out the gate to get something out of the wagon. The gate guard let us pass out readily as two workmen who had just passed in. We changed our clothing and reappeared, asking to see you. We saw you. That's all."

There was silence for several minutes. Dr. Ransome was first to speak.

"Wonderful!" he exclaimed. "Perfectly amazing."

"How did Mr. Hatch happen to come with the electricians?" asked Mr. Fielding.

"His father is manager of the company," replied The Thinking Machine.

"But what if there had been no Mr. Hatch outside to help?"

"Every prisoner has one friend outside who would help him escape if he could."

"Suppose—just suppose—there had been no old plumbing system there?" asked the warden, curiously.

"There were two other ways out," said The Thinking Machine, enigmatically.

Ten minutes later the telephone bell rang. It was a request for the warden.

"Light all right, eh?" the warden asked, through the 'phone. "Good. Wire cut beside Cell 13? Yes, I know. One electrician too many? What's that? Two came out?"

The warden turned to the others with a puzzled expression.

"He only let in four electricians, he has let out two and says there are three left."

"I was the odd one," said The Thinking Machine.

"Oh," said the warden. "I see." Then through the 'phone: "Let the fifth man go. He's all right."

R. Austin Freeman

RICHARD AUSTIN FREEMAN (1862-1943) was a physician and mystery writer. Like Conan Doyle, Freeman tried at first to establish a medical practice but his health caused him to give it up, and he turned to writing. Freeman is credited with inventing, in *The Singing Bone* (1912), the "inverted" mystery story, in which the criminal is known and the suspense arises out of the means by which the criminal is caught. Made famous on television by the Columbo mysteries by William Link and Richard Levinson, the form was developed extensively by Freeman's contemporary Marie Belloc Lowndes, in *The Chink in the Armour* (1912) and later by Anthony Berkeley, writing as Francis Iles in a series of novels, beginning with *Malice Aforethought* (1931).

Freeman's great invention, the premier scientific detective Dr. John Thorndyke, appeared in dozens of stories and novels, the first being *The Red Thumb Mark* (1907). He was always accompanied by his "inevitable green case" (his research kit) and frequently aided by his laboratory assistant and butler Nathaniel Polton; his stories are chronicled by Christopher Jervis, who, like Dr. Watson, usually sees but does not observe. The following tale is an early one (the last of the Thorndyke mysteries appeared in 1942); it first appeared in *Pearson's Magazine* (March, 1909) and was collected in *John Thorndyke's Cases* (1909).

THE MANDARIN'S PEARL

R. AUSTIN FREEMAN

Mr. Brodribb stretched out his toes on the curb[1] before the blazing fire with the air of a man who is by no means insensible to physical comfort.

"You are really an extraordinarily polite fellow, Thorndyke," said he.

He was an elderly man, rosy-gilled, portly, and convivial, to whom a mass of bushy, white hair, an expansive double chin, and a certain prim sumptuousness of dress imparted an air of old-world distinction. Indeed, as he dipped an amethystine[2] nose into his wine-glass, and gazed thoughtfully at the glowing end of his cigar, he looked the very type of the well-to-do lawyer of an older generation.

"You are really an extraordinarily polite fellow, Thorndyke," said Mr. Brodribb.

"I know," replied Thorndyke. "But why this reference to an admitted fact?"

"The truth has just dawned on me," said the solicitor. "Here am I, dropping in on you, uninvited and unannounced, sitting in your own armchair before your fire, smoking your cigars, drinking your Burgundy—and deuced good Burgundy, too, let me add—and you have not dropped a single hint of curiosity as to what has brought me here."

"I take the gifts of the gods, you see, and ask no questions," said Thorndyke.

"Devilish handsome of you, Thorndyke—unsociable beggar like you, too," rejoined Mr. Brodribb, a fan of wrinkles spreading out genially from the corners of his eyes; "but the fact is I have come, in a sense, on business—always glad of a pretext to look you up, as you know—but I want to take your opinion on a rather queer case. It is about young Calverley. You remember Horace Calverley? Well, this is his son. Horace and I were schoolmates, you know, and after his death the boy, Fred, hung on to me rather. We're near neighbors down at Weybridge, and very good friends. I like Fred. He's a good fellow, though cranky, like all his people."

[1] The metal border around the firebox of a fireplace.
[2] Purple.

"What has happened to Fred Calverley?" Thorndyke asked, as the solicitor paused.

"Why, the fact is," said Mr. Brodribb, "just lately he seems to be going a bit queer—not mad, mind you—at least, I think not—but undoubtedly queer. Now, there is a good deal of property, and a good many highly interested relatives, and, as a natural consequence, there is some talk of getting him certified. They're afraid he may do something involving the estate or develop homicidal tendencies, and they talk of possible suicide—you remember his father's death—but I say that's all bunkum. The fellow is just a bit cranky, and nothing more."

"What are his symptoms?" asked Thorndyke.

"Oh, he thinks he is being followed about and watched, and he has delusions; sees himself in the glass with the wrong face, and that sort of thing, you know."

"You are not highly circumstantial," Thorndyke remarked.

Mr. Brodribb looked at me with a genial smile.

"What a glutton for facts this fellow is, Jervis. But you're right, Thorndyke; I'm vague. However, Fred will be here presently. We travel down together, and I took the liberty of asking him to call for me. We'll get him to tell you about his delusions, if you don't mind. He's not shy about them. And meanwhile I'll give you a few preliminary facts. The trouble began about a year ago. He was in a railway accident, and that knocked him all to pieces. Then he went for a voyage to recruit,[3] and the ship broke her propeller-shaft in a storm and became helpless. That didn't improve the state

of his nerves. Then he went down the Mediterranean, and after a month or two, back he came, no better than when he started. But here he is, I expect."

He went over to the door and admitted a tall, frail young man whom Thorndyke welcomed with quiet geniality, and settled in a chair by the fire. I looked curiously at our visitor. He was a typical neurotic—slender, fragile, eager. Wide-open blue eyes with broad pupils, in which I could plainly see the characteristic "hippus"[4]—that incessant change of size that marks the unstable nervous equilibrium—parted lips, and wandering taper fingers, were as the stigmata of his disorder. He was of the stuff out of which prophets and devotees, martyrs, reformers, and third-rate poets are made.

"I have been telling Dr. Thorndyke about these nervous troubles of yours," said Mr. Brodribb presently. "I hope you don't mind. He is an old friend, you know, and he is very much interested."

"It is very good of him," said Calverley. Then he flushed deeply, and added: "But they are not really nervous, you know. They can't be merely subjective."

"You think they can't be?" said Thorndyke.

"No, I am sure they are not." He flushed again like a girl, and looked earnestly at Thorndyke with his big, dreamy eyes. "But you doctors," he said, "are so dreadfully skeptical of all spiritual phenomena. You are such materialists."

"Yes," said Mr. Brodribb; "the doctors are not hot on the supernatural, and that's the fact."

---

[3] To restore one's health.

[4] The narrator is Thorndyke's friend Christopher Jervis, M.D.—hence the medical jargon.

"Supposing you tell us about your experiences," said Thorndyke persuasively. "Give us a chance to believe, if we can't explain away."

Calverley reflected for a few moments; then, looking earnestly at Thorndyke, he said:—

"Very well; if it won't bore you, I will. It is a curious story."

"I have told Dr. Thorndyke about your voyage and your trip down the Mediterranean," said Mr. Brodribb.

"Then," said Calverley, "I will begin with the events that are actually connected with these strange visitations. The first of these occurred in Marseilles. I was in a curio-shop there, looking over some Algerian and Moorish tilings, when my attention was attracted by a sort of charm or pendant that hung in a glass case. It was not particularly beautiful, but its appearance was quaint and curious, and took my fancy. It consisted of an oblong block of ebony in which was set a single pear-shaped pearl more than three-quarters of an inch long. The sides of the ebony block were lacquered—probably to conceal a joint—and bore a number of Chinese characters, and at the top was a little gold image with a hole through it, presumably for a string to suspend it by. Excepting for the pearl, the whole thing was uncommonly like one of those ornamental tablets of Chinese ink.

"Now, I had taken a fancy to the thing, and I can afford to indulge my fancies in moderation. The man wanted five pounds for it; he assured me that the pearl was a genuine one of fine quality, and obviously did not believe it himself. To me, however, it looked like a real pearl, and I determined to take the risk; so I paid the money, and he bowed me out with a smile—I may almost say a grin—of satisfaction. He would not have been so well pleased if he had followed me to a jeweler's to whom I took it for an expert opinion; for the jeweler pronounced the pearl to be undoubtedly genuine, and worth anything up to a thousand pounds.

"A day or two later, I happened to show my new purchase to some men whom I knew, who had dropped in at Marseilles in their yacht. They were highly amused at my having bought the thing, and when I told them what I had paid for it, they positively howled with derision.

" 'Why, you silly guffin,'[5] said one of them, a man named Halliwell, 'I could have had it ten days ago for half a sovereign, or probably five shillings. I wish now I had bought it; then I could have sold it to you.'

"It seemed that a sailor had been hawking the pendant round the harbor, and had been on board the yacht with it.

" 'Deuced anxious the beggar was to get rid of it, too,' said Halliwell, grinning at the recollection. 'Swore it was a genuine pearl of priceless value, and was willing to deprive himself of it for the trifling sum of half a jimmy.[6] But we'd heard that sort of thing before. However, the curio-man seems to have speculated on the chance of meeting with a greenhorn, and he seems to have pulled it off. Lucky curio-man!'

"I listened patiently to their gibes, and when they had talked themselves out I told them about the jeweler. They were most frightfully sick; and when we had taken the

[5] A stupid, clumsy person.
[6] Cockney rhyming slang; a "Jimmy O'Goblin" is a sovereign.

pendant to a dealer in gems who happened to be staying in the town, and he had offered me five hundred pounds for it, their language wasn't fit for a divinity students' debating club. Naturally the story got noised abroad, and when I left, it was the talk of the place. The general opinion was that the sailor, who was traced to a tea-ship that had put into the harbor, had stolen it from some Chinese passenger; and no less than seventeen different Chinamen came forward to claim it as their stolen property.

"Soon after this I returned to England, and, as my nerves were still in a very shaky state, I came to live with my cousin Alfred, who has a large house at Weybridge. At this time he had a friend staying with him, a certain Captain Raggerton, and the two men appeared to be on very intimate terms. I did not take to Raggerton at all. He was a good-looking man, pleasant in his manners, and remarkably plausible. But the fact is—I am speaking in strict confidence, of course—he was a bad egg. He had been in the Guards, and I don't quite know why he left; but I do know that he played bridge[7] and baccarat pretty heavily at several clubs, and that he had a reputation for being a rather uncomfortably lucky player. He did a good deal at the race-meetings, too, and was in general such an obvious undesirable that I could never understand my cousin's intimacy with him, though I must say that Alfred's habits had changed somewhat for the worse since I had left England.

"The fame of my purchase seems to have preceded me, for when, one day, I produced the pendant to show them, I found that they knew all about it. Raggerton had heard the story from a naval man, and I gathered vaguely that he had heard something that I had not, and that he did not care to tell me; for when my cousin and he talked about the pearl, which they did pretty often, certain significant looks passed between them, and certain veiled references were made which I could not fail to notice.

"One day I happened to be telling them of a curious incident that occurred on my way home. I had travelled to England on one of Holt's big China boats[8], not liking the crowd and bustle of the regular passenger-lines. Now, one afternoon, when we had been at sea a couple of days, I took a book down to my berth, intending to have a quiet read till tea-time. Soon, however, I dropped off into a doze, and must have remained asleep for over an hour. I awoke suddenly, and as I opened my eyes, I perceived that the door of the state-room was half-open, and a well-dressed Chinaman, in native costume, was looking in at me. He closed the door immediately, and I remained for a few moments paralyzed by the start that he had given me. Then I leaped from my bunk, opened the door, and looked out. But the alley-way was empty. The Chinaman had vanished as if by magic.

"This little occurrence made me quite nervous for a day or two, which was very foolish of me; but my nerves were all on edge—and I am afraid they are still."

"Yes," said Thorndyke. "There was nothing mysterious about the affair. These boats carry a Chinese crew, and the man you saw

---

[7] This was not modern contract bridge, not really invented until 1925, but more likely the game of biritch or bridge-whist, similar to whist, or possibly auction bridge, developed in 1904.

[8] Brothers Alfred and Philip Holt set up the Ocean Steamship Company in 1865; it was later known as the Alfred Holt Group. It provided a regular steamship cargo service to China.

was probably a Serang, or whatever they call the gang-captains on these vessels. Or he may have been a native passenger who had strayed into the wrong part of the ship."

"Exactly," agreed our client. "But to return to Raggerton. He listened with quite extraordinary interest as I was telling this story, and when I had finished he looked very queerly at my cousin.

"'A deuced odd thing, this, Calverley,' said he. 'Of course, it may be only a coincidence, but it really does look as if there was something, after all, in that—'

"'Shut up, Raggerton,' said my cousin. 'We don't want any of that rot.'

"'What is he talking about?" I asked.

"'Oh, it's only a rotten, silly yarn that he has picked up somewhere. You're not to tell him, Raggerton.'

"'I don't see why I am not to be told,' I said, rather sulkily. 'I'm not a baby.'

"'No,' said Alfred, 'but you're an invalid. You don't want any horrors.'

"In effect, he refused to go into the matter any further, and I was left on tenter-hooks of curiosity.

"However, the very next day I got Raggerton alone in the smoking-room, and had a little talk with him. He had just dropped a hundred pounds on a double event that hadn't come off, and I expected to find him pliable. Nor was I disappointed, for, when we had negotiated a little loan, he was entirely at my service, and willing to tell me everything, on my promising not to give him away to Alfred.

"'Now, you understand,' he said, 'that this yarn about your pearl is nothing but a damn silly fable that's been going the round in Marseilles. I don't know where it came from, or what sort of demented rotter invented it; I had it from a Johnnie in the Mediterranean Squadron, and you can have a copy of his letter if you want it.'

"I said that I did want it. Accordingly, that same evening he handed me a copy of the narrative extracted from his friend's letter, the substance of which was this:—

"About four months ago there was lying in Canton Harbor a large English barque. Her name is not mentioned, but that is not material to the story. She had got her cargo stowed and her crew signed on, and was only waiting for certain official formalities to be completed before putting to sea on her homeward voyage. Just ahead of her, at the same quay, was a Danish ship that had been in collision outside, and was now laid up pending the decision of the Admiralty Court. She had been unloaded, and her crew paid off, with the exception of one elderly man, who remained on board as ship-keeper. Now, a considerable part of the cargo of the English barque was the property of a certain wealthy mandarin, and this person had been about the vessel a good deal while she was taking in her lading.

"One day, when the mandarin was on board the barque, it happened that three of the seamen were sitting in the galley smoking and chatting with the cook—an elderly Chinaman named Wo-li—and the latter, pointing out the mandarin to the sailors, expatiated on his enormous wealth, assuring them that he was commonly believed to carry on his person articles of sufficient value to buy up the entire lading of a ship.

"Now, unfortunately for the mandarin, it chanced that these three sailors were about the greatest rascals on board; which is saying a good deal when one considers the ordinary moral standard that prevails in the forecastle of a sailing-ship. Nor was Wo-li himself an angel; in fact, he was a consummate villain, and seems to have been the actual originator of the plot which was presently devised to rob the mandarin.

"This plot was as remarkable for its simplicity as for its cold-blooded barbarity. On the evening before the barque sailed, the three seamen, Nilsson, Foucault, and Parratt, proceeded to the Danish ship with a supply of whisky, made the ship-keeper royally drunk, and locked him up in an empty berth. Meanwhile Wo-li made a secret communication to the mandarin to the effect that certain stolen property, believed to be his, had been secreted in the hold of the empty ship. Thereupon the mandarin came down hot-foot to the quayside, and was received on board by the three seamen, who had got the covers off the after-hatch in readiness. Parratt now ran down the iron ladder to show the way, and the mandarin followed; but when they reached the lower deck, and looked down the hatch into the black darkness of the lower hold, he seems to have taken fright, and begun to climb up again. Meanwhile Nilsson had made a running bowline in the end of a loose halyard that was rove[9] through a block aloft, and had been used for hoisting out the cargo. As the mandarin came up, he leaned over the coaming[10] of the hatch, dropped the noose over the Chinaman's head, jerked it tight, and then he and Foucault hove on the fall of the rope. The unfortunate Chinaman was dragged from the ladder, and, as he swung clear, the two rascals let go the rope, allowing him to drop through the hatches into the lower hold. Then they belayed[11] the rope, and went down below. Parratt had already lighted a slush-lamp,[12] by the glimmer of which they could see the mandarin swinging to and fro like a pendulum within a few feet of the ballast, and still quivering and twitching in his death-throes. They were now joined by Wo-li, who had watched the proceedings from the quay, and the four villains proceeded, without loss of time, to rifle the body as it hung. To their surprise and disgust, they found nothing of value excepting an ebony pendant set with a single large pearl; but Wo-li, though evidently disappointed at the nature of the booty, assured his comrades that this alone was well worth the hazard, pointing out the great size and exceptional beauty of the pearl. As to this, the seamen know nothing about pearls, but the thing was done, and had to be made the best of; so they made the rope fast to the lower deck-beams, cut off the remainder and unrove it from the block, and went back to their ship.

"It was twenty-four hours before the ship-keeper was sufficiently sober to break out of the berth in which he had been locked, by which time the barque was well out to sea; and it was another three days before the body of the mandarin was found. An active search was then made for the murderers, but as they were strangers to the ship-keeper, no clues to their whereabouts could be discovered.

"Meanwhile, the four murderers were a good deal exercised as to the disposal of the booty. Since it could not be divided, it was evident that it must be entrusted to the keeping of one of them. The choice in the first place fell upon Wo-li, in whose chest the pendant was deposited as soon as the party came on board, it being arranged that the China-

---

[9] Past tense of "reeve," to pass a rope through a pulley or block.
[10] A raised border around a hatch.
[11] Secured or made fast.
[12] A crude lantern that burns fat.

man should produce the jewel for inspection by his confederates whenever called upon.

"For six weeks nothing out of the common occurred; but then a very singular event befell. The four conspirators were sitting outside the galley one evening, when suddenly the cook uttered a cry of amazement and horror. The other three turned to see what it was that had so disturbed their comrade, and then they, too, were struck dumb with consternation; for, standing at the door of the companion-hatch—the barque was a flush-decked vessel—was the mandarin whom they had left for dead. He stood quietly regarding them for fully a minute, while they stared at him transfixed with terror. Then he beckoned to them, and went below.

"So petrified were they with astonishment and mortal fear that they remained for a long time motionless and dumb. At last they plucked up courage, and began to make furtive inquiries among the crew; but no one—not even the steward—knew anything of any passengers, or, indeed, of any Chinaman, on board the ship, excepting Wo-li.

"At day-break the next morning, when the cook's mate went to the galley to fill the coppers,[13] he found Wo-li hanging from a hook in the ceiling. The cook's body was stiff and cold, and had evidently been hanging several hours. The report of the tragedy quickly spread through the ship, and the three conspirators hurried off to remove the pearl from the dead man's chest before the officers should come to examine it. The cheap lock was easily picked with a bent wire, and the jewel abstracted; but now the question arose as to who should take charge of it. The eagerness to be

the actual custodian of the precious bauble, which had been at first displayed, now gave place to equally strong reluctance. But someone had to take charge of it, and after a long and angry discussion Nilsson was prevailed upon to stow it in his chest.

"A fortnight passed. The three conspirators went about their duties soberly, like men burdened with some secret anxiety, and in their leisure moments they would sit and talk with bated breath of the apparition at the companion-hatch, and the mysterious death of their late comrade.

"At last the blow fell.

"It was at the end of the second dog-watch[14] that the hands were gathered on the forecastle, preparing to make sail after a spell of bad weather. Suddenly Nilsson gave a husky shout, and rushed at Parratt, holding out the key of his chest.

" 'Here you, Parratt,' he exclaimed, 'go below and take that accursed thing out of my chest.'

" 'What for?' demanded Parratt; and then he and Foucault, who was standing close by, looked aft to see what Nilsson was staring at.

"Instantly they both turned white as ghosts, and fell trembling so that they could hardly stand; for there was the mandarin, standing calmly by the companion, returning with a steady, impassive gaze their looks of horror. And even as they looked he beckoned and went below.

" 'D'ye hear, Parratt?' gasped Nilsson; 'take my key and do what I say, or else—'

"But at this moment the order was given to go aloft and set all plain sail; the three men went off to their respective posts, Nilsson going up the fore-topmast rigging, and the other two to the main-top. Having finished their

---

[13] A cooking pot made of copper.
[14] Either 4 to 6 pm or 6 to 8 pm.

work aloft, Foucault and Parratt who were both in the port watch, came down on deck, and then, it being their watch below, they went and turned in.

"When they turned out with their watch at midnight, they looked about for Nilsson, who was in the starboard watch, but he was nowhere to be seen. Thinking he might have slipped below unobserved, they made no re-mark, though they were very uneasy about him; but when the starboard watch came on deck at four o'clock, and Nilsson did not ap-pear with his mates, the two men became alarmed, and made inquiries about him. It was now discovered that no one had seen him since eight o'clock on the previous evening, and, this being reported to the officer of the watch, the latter ordered all hands to be called. But still Nilsson did not appear. A thorough search was now instituted, both below and aloft, and as there was still no sign of the miss-ing man, it was concluded that he had fallen overboard.

"But at eight o'clock two men were sent aloft to shake out the fore-royal.[15] They reached the yard almost simultaneously, and were just stepping on to the foot-ropes when one of them gave a shout; then the pair came sliding down a backstay, with faces as white as tallow. As soon as they reached the deck, they took the officer of the watch forward, and, standing on the heel of the bowsprit, pointed aloft. Sev-eral of the hands, including Foucault and Par-ratt, had followed, and all looked up; and there they saw the body of Nilsson, hanging on the front of the fore-top gallant sail. He was dan-gling at the end of a gasket,[16] and bouncing up and down on the taut belly of the sail as the ship rose and fell to the send of the sea.

"The two survivors were now in some doubt about having anything further to do with the pearl. But the great value of the jewel, and the consideration that it was now to be divided between two instead of four, tempted them. They abstracted it from Nilsson's chest, and then, as they could not come to an agree-ment in any other way, they decided to settle who should take charge of it by tossing a coin. The coin was accordingly spun, and the pearl went to Foucault's chest.

"From this moment Foucault lived in a state of continual apprehension. When on deck, his eyes were for ever wandering to-ward the companion hatch, and during his watch below, when not asleep, he would sit moodily on his chest, lost in gloomy reflec-tion. But a fortnight passed, then three weeks, and still nothing happened. Land was sighted, the Straits of Gibraltar passed, and the end of the voyage was but a matter of days. And still the dreaded mandarin made no sign.

"At length the ship was within twenty-four hours of Marseilles, to which port a large part of the cargo was consigned. Active prepa-rations were being made for entering the port, and among other things the shore tackle was being overhauled. A share in this latter work fell to Foucault and Parratt, and about the middle of the second dog-watch—seven o'clock in the evening—they were sitting on the deck working an eye-splice in the end of a large rope. Suddenly Foucault, who was facing for-ward, saw his companion turn pale and stare aft with an expression of terror. He immedi-ately turned and looked over his shoulder to see what Parratt was staring at. It was the

---

[15] A forward sail.

[16] A cord or strap used to secure a sail to a mast or yard-arm.

mandarin, standing by the companion, gravely watching them; and as Foucault turned and met his gaze, the Chinaman beckoned and went below.

"For the rest of that day Parratt kept close to his terrified comrade, and during their watch below he endeavored to remain awake, that he might keep his friend in view. Nothing happened through the night, and the following morning, when they came on deck for the forenoon watch, their port was well in sight. The two men now separated for the first time, Parratt going aft to take his trick at the wheel, and Foucault being set to help in getting ready the ground tackle.

"Half an hour later Parratt saw the mate stand on the rail and lean outboard, holding on to the mizzen-shrouds while he stared along the ship's side. Then he jumped on to the deck and shouted angrily: 'Forward, there! What the deuce is that man up to under the starboard cat-head?'[17]

"The men on the forecastle rushed to the side and looked over; two of them leaned over the rail with the bight of a rope between them, and a third came running aft to the mate. 'It's Foucault, sir,' Parratt heard him say. 'He's hanged hisself from the cat-head.'

"As soon as he was off duty, Parratt made his way to his dead comrade's chest, and, opening it with his pick-lock, took out the pearl. It was now his sole property, and, as the ship was within an hour or two of her destination, he thought he had little to fear from its murdered owner. As soon as the vessel was alongside the wharf, he would slip ashore and get rid of the jewel, even if he sold it at a comparatively low price. The thing looked perfectly simple.

"In actual practice, however, it turned out quite otherwise. He began by accosting a well-dressed stranger and offering the pendant for fifty pounds; but the only reply that he got was a knowing smile and a shake of the head. When this experience had been repeated a dozen times or more, and he had been followed up and down the streets for nearly an hour by a suspicious gendarme, he began to grow anxious. He visited quite a number of ships and yachts in the harbor, and at each refusal the price of his treasure came down, until he was eager to sell it for a few francs. But still no one would have it. Everyone took it for granted that the pearl was a sham, and most of the persons whom he accosted assumed that it had been stolen. The position was getting desperate. Evening was approaching—the time of the dreaded dog-watches—and still the pearl was in his possession. Gladly would he now have given it away for nothing, but he dared not try, for this would lay him open to the strongest suspicion.

"At last, in a by-street, he came upon the shop of a curio-dealer. Putting on a careless and cheerful manner, he entered and offered the pendant for ten francs. The dealer looked at it, shook his head, and handed it back.

" 'What will you give me for it?' demanded Parratt, breaking out into a cold sweat at the prospect of a final refusal.

"The dealer felt in his pocket, drew out a couple of francs, and held them out.

" 'Very well,' said Parratt. He took the money as calmly as he could, and marched out of the shop, with a gasp of relief, leaving the pendant in the dealer's hand.

[17] A beam projecting outward from the prow of a ship, used to raise the anchor.

"The jewel was hung up in a glass case, and nothing more was thought about it until some ten days later, when an English tourist, who came into the shop, noticed it and took a liking to it. Thereupon the dealer offered it to him for five pounds, assuring him that it was a genuine pearl, a statement that, to his amazement, the stranger evidently believed. He was then deeply afflicted at not having asked a higher price, but the bargain had been struck, and the Englishman went off with his purchase.

"This was the story told by Captain Raggerton's friend, and I have given it to you in full detail, having read the manuscript over many times since it was given to me. No doubt you will regard it as a mere traveler's tale, and consider me a superstitious idiot for giving any credence to it."

"It certainly seems more remarkable for picturesqueness than for credibility," Thorndyke agreed. "May I ask," he continued, "whether Captain Raggerton's friend gave any explanation as to how this singular story came to his knowledge, or to that of anybody else?"

"Oh yes," replied Calverley; "I forgot to mention that the seaman, Parratt, very shortly after he had sold the pearl, fell down the hatch into the hold as the ship was unloading, and was very badly injured. He was taken to the hospital, where he died on the following day; and it was while he was lying there in a dying condition that he confessed to the murder, and gave this circumstantial account of it."

"I see," said Thorndyke; "and I understand that you accept the story as literally true?"

"Undoubtedly." Calverley flushed defiantly as he returned Thorndyke's look, and continued: "You see, I am not a man of science: therefore my beliefs are not limited to things that can be weighed and measured. There are things, Dr. Thorndyke, which are outside the range of our puny intellects; things that science, with its arrogant materialism, puts aside and ignores with close-shut eyes. I prefer to believe in things which obviously exist, even though I cannot explain them. It is the humbler and, I think, the wiser attitude."

"But, my dear Fred," protested Mr. Brodribb, "this is a rank fairy-tale."

Calverley turned upon the solicitor. "If you had seen what I have seen, you would not only believe: you would *know*."

"Tell us what you have seen, then," said Mr. Brodribb.

"I will, if you wish to hear it," said Calverley. "I will continue the strange history of the Mandarin's Pearl."

He lit a fresh cigarette and continued:

"The night I came to Beech-hurst—that is my cousin's house, you know—a rather absurd thing happened, which I mention on account of its connection with what has followed. I had gone to my room early, and sat for some time writing letters before getting ready for bed. When I had finished my letters, I started on a tour of inspection of my room. I was then, you must remember, in a very nervous state, and it had become my habit to examine the room in which I was to sleep before undressing, looking under the bed, and in any cupboards and closets that there happened to be. Now, on looking round my new room, I perceived that there was a second door, and I at once proceeded to open it to see where it led to. As soon as I opened the door, I got a terrible start. I found myself looking into a narrow closet or passage, lined with pegs, on which the servant had hung some of my clothes; at the farther end was another door, and, as I stood looking into the closet, I observed, with startled amazement, a man standing holding the door half-open, and silently regarding me. I stood for a moment staring at him, with my heart thumping and my limbs all of a tremble; then I slammed the door and ran off to look for my cousin.

"He was in the billiard-room with Rag - gerton, and the pair looked up sharply as I entered.

" 'Alfred,' I said, 'where does that passage lead to out of my room?'

" 'Lead to?' said he. 'Why, it doesn't lead anywhere. It used to open into a cross corridor, but when the house was altered, the corridor was done away with, and this passage closed up. It is only a cupboard now.'

" 'Well, there's a man in it—or there was just now.'

" 'Nonsense!' he exclaimed; 'impossible! Let us go and look at the place.'

"He and Raggerton rose, and we went together to my room. As we flung open the door of the closet and looked in, we all three burst into a laugh. There were three men now looking at us from the open door at the other end, and the mystery was solved. A large mirror had been placed at the end of the closet to cover the partition which cut it off from the cross corridor.

"This incident naturally exposed me to a good deal of chaff from my cousin and Captain Raggerton; but I often wished that the mirror had not been placed there, for it happened over and over again that, going to the cupboard hurriedly, and not thinking of the mirror, I got quite a bad shock on being confronted by a figure apparently coming straight at me through an open door. In fact, it annoyed me so much, in my nervous state, that I even thought of asking my cousin to give me a different room; but, happening to refer to the matter when talking to Raggerton, I found the Captain so scornful of my cowardice that my pride was touched, and I let the affair drop.

"And now I come to a very strange occurrence, which I shall relate quite frankly, although I know beforehand that you will set me down as a liar or a lunatic. I had been away from home for a fortnight, and as I returned rather late at night, I went straight to my room. Having partly undressed, I took my clothes in one hand and a candle in the other, and opened the cupboard door. I stood for a moment looking nervously at my double, standing, candle in hand, looking at me through the open door at the other end of the passage; then I entered, and, setting the candle on a shelf, proceeded to hang up my clothes. I had hung them up, and had just reached up for the candle, when my eye was caught by something strange in the mirror. It no longer reflected the candle in my hand, but instead of it, a large colored paper lantern. I stood petrified with astonishment, and gazed into the mirror; and then I saw that my own reflection was changed, too; that, in place of my own figure, was that of an elderly Chinaman, who stood regarding me with stony calm.

"I must have stood for near upon a minute, unable to move and scarce able to breathe, face to face with that awful figure. At length I turned to escape, and, as I turned, he turned also, and I could see him, over my shoulder, hurrying away. As I reached the door, I halted for a moment, looking back with the door in my hand, holding the candle above my head; and even so *he* halted, looking back at me, with his hand upon the door and his lantern held above his head.

"I was so much upset that I could not go

to bed for some hours, but continued to pace the room, in spite of my fatigue. Now and again I was impelled, irresistibly, to peer into the cupboard, but nothing was to be seen in the mirror save my own figure, candle in hand, peeping in at me through the half-open door. And each time that I looked into my own white, horror-stricken face, I shut the door hastily and turned away with a shudder; for the pegs, with the clothes hanging on them, seemed to call to me. I went to bed at last, and before I fell asleep I formed the resolution that, if I was spared until the next day, I would write to the British Consul at Canton, and offer to restore the pearl to the relatives of the murdered mandarin.

"On the following day I wrote and dispatched the letter, after which I felt more composed, though I was haunted continually by the recollection of that stony, impassive figure; and from time to time I felt an irresistible impulse to go and look in at the door of the closet, at the mirror and the pegs with the clothes hanging from them. I told my cousin of the visitation that I had received, but he merely laughed, and was frankly incredulous; while the Captain bluntly advised me not to be a superstitious donkey.

"For some days after this I was left in peace, and began to hope that my letter had appeased the spirit of the murdered man; but on the fifth day, about six o'clock in the evening, happening to want some papers that I had left in the pocket of a coat which was hanging in the closet, I went in to get them. I took in no candle, as it was not yet dark, but left the door wide open to light me. The coat that I wanted was near the end of the closet, not more than four paces from the mirror, and as I went toward it I watched my reflection rather nervously as it advanced to meet me. I found my coat, and as I felt for the papers, I still kept a suspicious eye on my double. And, even as I looked, a most strange phenomenon appeared: the mirror seemed for an instant to darken or cloud over, and then, as it cleared again, I saw, standing dark against the light of the open door behind him, the figure of the mandarin. After a single glance, I ran out of the closet, shaking with agitation; but as I turned to shut the door, I noticed that it was my own figure that was reflected in the glass. The Chinaman had vanished in an instant.

"It now became evident that my letter had not served its purpose, and I was plunged in despair; the more so since, on this day, I felt again the dreadful impulse to go and look at the pegs on the walls of the closet. There was no mistaking the meaning of that impulse, and each time that I went, I dragged myself away reluctantly, though shivering with horror. One circumstance, indeed, encouraged me a little; the mandarin had not, on either occasion, beckoned to me as he had done to the sailors, so that perhaps some way of escape yet lay open to me.

"During the next few days I considered very earnestly what measures I could take to avert the doom that seemed to be hanging over me. The simplest plan, that of passing the pearl on to some other person, was out of the question; it would be nothing short of murder. On the other hand, I could not wait for an answer to my letter; for even if I remained alive, I felt that my reason would have given way long before the reply reached me. But while I was debating what I should do, the mandarin appeared to me again; and then, after an interval of only two days, he came to me once more. That was last night. I remained gazing at him, fascinated, with my flesh creeping, as he stood, lantern in hand, looking steadily in my face. At last he held out his hand to me, as if asking me to give him the pearl; then the mirror darkened, and he vanished in a flash; and in the place where he had stood there was my own reflection looking at me out of the glass.

"That last visitation decided me. When I left home this morning the pearl was in my pocket, and as I came over Waterloo Bridge, I leaned over the parapet and flung the thing into the water. After that I felt quite relieved for a time; I had shaken the accursed thing off without involving anyone in the curse that it carried. But presently I began to feel fresh misgivings, and the conviction has been growing upon me all day that I have done the wrong thing. I have only placed it for ever beyond the reach of its owner, whereas I ought to have burnt it, after the Chinese fashion, so that its non-material essence could have joined the spiritual body of him to whom it had belonged when both were clothed with material substance.

"But it can't be altered now. For good or for evil, the thing is done, and God alone knows what the end of it will be."

As he concluded, Calverley uttered a deep sigh, and covered his face with his slender, delicate hands. For a space we were all silent and, I think, deeply moved; for, grotesquely unreal as the whole thing was, there was a pathos, and even a tragedy, in it that we all felt to be very real indeed.

Suddenly Mr. Brodribb started and looked at his watch.

"Good gracious, Calverley, we shall lose our train."

The young man pulled himself together and stood up. "We shall just do it if we go at once," said he. "Good-bye," he added, shaking Thorndyke's hand and mine. "You have been very patient, and I have been

rather prosy, I am afraid. Come along, Mr. Brodribb."

Thorndyke and I followed them out on to the landing, and I heard my colleague say to the solicitor in a low tone, but very earnestly: "Get him away from that house, Brodribb, and don't let him out of your sight for a moment."

I did not catch the solicitor's reply, if he made any, but when we were back in our room I noticed that Thorndyke was more agitated than I had ever seen him.

"I ought not to have let them go," he exclaimed. "Confound me! If I had had a grain of wit, I should have made them lose their train."

He lit his pipe and fell to pacing the room with long strides, his eyes bent on the floor with an expression sternly reflective. At last, finding him hopelessly taciturn, I knocked out my pipe and went to bed.

As I was dressing on the following morning, Thorndyke entered my room. His face was grave even to sternness, and he held a telegram in his hand.

"I am going to Weybridge this morning," he said shortly, holding the "flimsy" out to me. "Shall you come?"

I took the paper from him, and read:

"*Come, for God's sake! F.C. is dead. You will understand.—BRODRIBB.*"

I handed him back the telegram, too much shocked for a moment to speak. The whole dreadful tragedy summed up in that curt message rose before me in an instant, and a wave of deep pity swept over me at this miserable end to the sad, empty life.

"What an awful thing, Thorndyke!" I exclaimed at length. "To be killed by a mere grotesque delusion."

"Do you think so?" he asked dryly. "Well, we shall see; but you will come?"

"Yes," I replied; and as he retired, I proceeded hurriedly to finish dressing.

Half an hour later, as we rose from a rapid breakfast, Polton[18] came into the room, carrying a small roll-up case of tools and a bunch of skeleton keys.

"Will you have them in a bag, sir?" he asked.

"No," replied Thorndyke; "in my overcoat pocket. Oh, and here is a note, Polton, which I want you to take round to Scotland Yard. It is to the Assistant Commissioner, and you are to make sure that it is in the right hands before you leave. And here is a telegram to Mr. Brodribb."

He dropped the keys and the tool-case into his pocket, and we went down together to the waiting hansom.

At Weybridge Station we found Mr. Brodribb pacing the platform in a state of extreme dejection. He brightened up somewhat when he saw us, and wrung our hands with emotional heartiness.

"It was very good of you both to come at a moment's notice," he said warmly, "and I feel your kindness very much. You understood, of course, Thorndyke?"

"Yes," Thorndyke replied. "I suppose the mandarin beckoned to him."

Mr. Brodribb turned with a look of surprise. "How did you guess that?" he asked; and then, without waiting for a reply, he took from his pocket a note, which he handed to my colleague. "The poor old fellow left this for me," he said. "The servant found it on his dressing-table."

Thorndyke glanced through the note and passed it to me. It consisted of but a few words, hurriedly written in a tremulous hand.

"He has beckoned to me, and I must go. Good-bye, dear old friend."

"How does his cousin take the matter?" asked Thorndyke.

"He doesn't know of it yet," replied the lawyer. "Alfred and Raggerton went out after an early breakfast, to cycle over to Guildford on some business or other, and they have not returned yet. The catastrophe was discovered soon after they left. The maid went to his room with a cup of tea, and was astonished to find that his bed had not been slept in. She ran down in alarm and reported to the butler, who went up at once and searched the room; but he could find no trace of the missing one, except my note, until it occurred to him to look in the cupboard. As he opened the door he got rather a start from his own reflection in the mirror; and then he saw poor Fred hanging from one of the pegs near the end of the closet, close to the glass. It's a melancholy affair—but here is the house, and here is the butler waiting for us. Mr. Alfred is not back yet, then, Stevens?"

"No, sir." The white-faced, frightened-looking man had evidently been waiting at the gate from distaste of the house, and he now walked back with manifest relief at our arrival. When we entered the house, he ushered us without remark up on to the first-floor, and, preceding us along a corridor, halted near the end. "That's the room, sir," said he; and without another word he turned and went down the stairs.

We entered the room, and Mr. Brodribb followed on tiptoe, looking about him fearfully, and casting awe-struck glances at the shrouded form on the bed. To the latter Thorndyke advanced, and gently drew back the sheet.

---

[18] Nathaniel Polton is Thorndyke's lab assistant.

"You'd better not look, Brodribb," said he, as he bent over the corpse. He felt the limbs and examined the cord, which still remained round the neck, its raggedly-severed end testifying to the terror of the servants who had cut down the body. Then he replaced the sheet and looked at his watch. "It happened at about three o'clock in the morning," said he. "He must have struggled with the impulse for some time, poor fellow! Now let us look at the cupboard."

We went together to a door in the corner of the room, and, as we opened it, we were confronted by three figures, apparently looking in at us through an open door at the other end.

"It is really rather startling," said the lawyer, in a subdued voice, looking almost apprehensively at the three figures that advanced to meet us. "The poor lad ought never to have been here."

It was certainly an eerie place, and I could not but feel, as we walked down the dark, narrow passage, with those other three dimly-seen figures silently coming toward us, and mimicking our every gesture, that it was no place for a nervous, superstitious man like poor Fred Calverley. Close to the end of the long row of pegs was one from which hung an end of stout box-cord, and to this Mr. Brodribb pointed with an awe-struck gesture. But Thorndyke gave it only a brief glance, and then walked up to the mirror, which he proceeded to examine minutely. It was a very large glass, nearly seven feet high, extending the full width of the closet, and reaching to within a foot of the floor; and it seemed to have been let into the partition from behind, for, both above and below, the woodwork was in front of it. While I was making these observations, I watched Thorndyke with no little curiosity. First he rapped his knuckles

on the glass; then he lighted a wax match, and, holding it close to the mirror, carefully watched the reflection of the flame. Finally, laying his cheek on the glass, he held the match at arm's length, still close to the mirror, and looked at the reflection along the surface. Then he blew out the match and walked back into the room, shutting the cupboard door as we emerged.

"I think," said he, "that as we shall all undoubtedly be subpoenaed by the coroner, it would be well to put together a few notes of the facts. I see there is a writing-table by the window, and I would propose that you, Brodribb, just jot down a *précis* of the statement that you heard last night, while Jervis notes down the exact condition of the body. While you are doing this, I will take a look around."

"We might find a more cheerful place to write in," grumbled Mr. Brodribb; "however—"

Without finishing the sentence, he sat down at the table, and, having found some sermon paper,[19] dipped a pen in the ink by way of encouraging his thoughts. At this moment Thorndyke quietly slipped out of the room, and I proceeded to make a detailed examination of the body: in which occupation I was interrupted at intervals by requests from the lawyer that I should refresh his memory.

We had been occupied thus for about a quarter of an hour, when a quick step was heard outside, the door was opened abruptly, and a man burst into the room. Brodribb rose and held out his hand.

"This is a sad home-coming for you, Alfred," said he.

"Yes, my God!" the newcomer exclaimed. "It's awful."

He looked askance at the corpse on the

[19] Writing paper of foolscap, quarto size.

bed, and wiped his forehead with his hand-kerchief. Alfred Calverley was not extremely prepossessing. Like his cousin, he was obviously neurotic, but there were signs of dissipation in his face, which, just now, was pale and ghastly, and wore an expression of abject fear. Moreover, his entrance was accompanied by that of a perceptible odor of brandy.

He had walked over, without noticing me, to the writing-table, and as he stood there, talking in subdued tones with the lawyer, I suddenly found Thorndyke at my side. He had stolen in noiselessly through the door that Calverley had left open.

"Show him Brodribb's note," he whispered, "and then make him go in and look at the peg."

With this mysterious request, he slipped out of the room as silently as he had come, unperceived either by Calverley or the lawyer.

"Has Captain Raggerton returned with you?" Brodribb was inquiring.

"No, he has gone into the town," was the reply; "but he won't be long. This will be a frightful shock to him."

At this point I stepped forward. "Have you shown Mr. Calverley the extraordinary letter that the deceased left for you?" I asked.

"What letter was that?" demanded Calverley, with a start.

Mr. Brodribb drew forth the note and handed it to him. As he read it through, Calverley turned white to the lips, and the paper trembled in his hand.

" 'He has beckoned to me, and I must go,' " he read. Then, with a furtive glance at the lawyer: "Who had beckoned? What did he mean?"

Mr. Brodribb briefly explained the meaning of the allusion, adding: "I thought you knew all about it."

"Yes, yes," said Calverley, with some confusion; "I remember the matter now you mention it. But it's all so dreadful and bewildering."

At this point I again interposed. "There is a question," I said, "that may be of some importance. It refers to the cord with which the poor fellow hanged himself. Can you identify that cord, Mr. Calverley?"

"I!" he exclaimed, staring at me, and wiping the sweat from his white face; "how should I? Where is the cord?"

"Part of it is still hanging from the peg in the closet. Would you mind looking at it?"

"If you would very kindly fetch it—you know I—er—naturally—have a—"

"It must not be disturbed before the inquest," said I; "but surely you are not afraid—"

"I didn't say I was afraid," he retorted angrily. "Why should I be?"

With a strange, tremulous swagger, he strode across to the closet, flung open the door, and plunged in.

A moment later we heard a shout of horror, and he rushed out, livid and gasping.

"What is it, Calverley?" exclaimed Mr. Brodribb, starting up in alarm.

But Calverley was incapable of speech. Dropping limply into a chair, he gazed at us for a while in silent terror; then he fell back uttering a wild shriek of laughter.

Mr. Brodribb looked at him in amazement. "What is it, Calverley?" he asked again.

As no answer was forthcoming, he stepped across to the open door of the closet and entered, peering curiously before him. Then he, too, uttered a startled exclamation, and backed out hurriedly, looking pale and flurried.

"Bless my soul!" he ejaculated. "Is the place bewitched?"

He sat down heavily and stared at Calverley, who was still shaking with hysteric laughter; while I, now consumed with curiosity, walked over to the closet to discover the cause of their singular behavior. As I flung open the door, which the lawyer had closed, I must confess to being very considerably startled; for though the reflection of the open door was plain enough in the mirror, my own reflection was replaced by that of a Chinaman. After a momentary pause of astonishment, I entered the closet and walked toward the mirror; and simultaneously the figure of the Chinaman entered and walked toward me. I had advanced more than halfway down the closet when suddenly the mirror darkened; there was a whirling flash, the Chinaman vanished in an instant, and, as I reached the glass, my own reflection faced me.

I turned back into the room pretty completely enlightened, and looked at Calverley with a new-born distaste. He still sat facing the bewildered lawyer, one moment sobbing convulsively, the next yelping with hysteric laughter. He was not an agreeable spectacle, and when, a few moments later, Thorndyke entered the room, and halted by the door with a stare of disgust, I was moved to join him. But at this juncture a man pushed past Thorndyke, and, striding up to Calverley, shook him roughly by the arm.

"Stop that row!" he exclaimed furiously. "Do you hear? Stop it!"

"I can't help it, Raggerton," gasped Calverley. "He gave me such a turn—the mandarin, you know."

"What!" ejaculated Raggerton.

He dashed across to the closet, looked in, and turned upon Calverley with a snarl. Then he walked out of the room.

"Brodribb," said Thorndyke, "I should like to have a word with you and Jervis outside." Then, as we followed him out on to the landing, he continued: "I have something rather interesting to show you. It is in here."

He softly opened an adjoining door, and we looked into a small unfurnished room. A projecting closet occupied one side of it, and at the door of the closet stood Captain Raggerton, with his hand upon the key. He turned upon us fiercely, though with a look of alarm, and demanded:—

"What is the meaning of this intrusion? And who the deuce are you? Do you know that this is my private room?"

"I suspected that it was," Thorndyke replied quietly. "Those will be your properties in the closet, then?"

Raggerton turned pale, but continued to bluster. "Do I understand that you have dared to break into my private closet?" he demanded.

"I have inspected it," replied Thorndyke, "and I may remark that it is useless to wrench at that key, because I have hampered the lock."

"The devil you have!" shouted Raggerton.

"Yes; you see, I am expecting a police-officer with a search warrant, so I wished to keep everything intact."

Raggerton turned livid with mingled fear and rage. He stalked up to Thorndyke with a threatening air, but, suddenly altering his mind, exclaimed, "I must see to this!" and flung out of the room.

Thorndyke took a key from his pocket, and, having locked the door, turned to the closet. Having taken out the key to unhamper the lock with a stout wire, he reinserted it and unlocked the door. As we entered, we found ourselves in a narrow closet, similar to the one in the other room, but darker, owing to the absence of a mirror. A few clothes hung from the pegs, and when Thorndyke had lit a candle that stood on a shelf, we could see more of the details.

"Here are some of the properties," said Thorndyke. He pointed to a peg from which hung a long, blue silk gown of Chinese make, a mandarin's cap, with a pigtail attached to it, and a beautifully-made papier-mâché mask. "Observe," said Thorndyke, taking the latter down and exhibiting a label on the inside, marked *Renouard a Paris*, "no trouble has been spared."

He took off his coat, slipped on the gown, the mask, and the cap, and was, in a moment, in that dim light, transformed into the perfect semblance of a Chinaman.

"By taking a little more time," he remarked, pointing to a pair of Chinese shoes and a large paper lantern, "the make-up could be rendered more complete; but this seems to have answered for our friend Alfred."

"But," said Mr. Brodribb, as Thorndyke shed the disguise, "still, I don't understand—"

"I will make it clear to you in a moment," said Thorndyke. He walked to the end of the closet, and, tapping the right-hand wall, said: "This is the back of the mirror. You see that it is hung on massive well-oiled hinges, and is supported on this large, rubber-tired castor, which evidently has ball bearings. You observe three black cords running along the wall, and passing through those pulleys above. Now, when I pull this cord, notice what happens."

He pulled one cord firmly, and immediately the mirror swung noiselessly inwards on its great castor, until it stood diagonally across the closet, where it was stopped by a rubber buffer.

"Bless my soul!" exclaimed Mr. Brodribb. "What an extraordinary thing!"

The effect was certainly very strange, for, the mirror being now exactly diagonal to the two closets they appeared to be a single, continuous passage, with a door at either end. On going up to the mirror, we found that the opening which it had occupied was filled by a sheet of plain glass, evidently placed there as a precaution to prevent any person from walking through from one closet into the other, and so discovering the trick.

"It's all very puzzling," said Mr. Brodribb; "I don't clearly understand it now."

"Let us finish here," replied Thorndyke, "and then I will explain. Notice this black curtain. When I pull the second cord, it slides across the closet and cuts off the light. The mirror now reflects nothing into the other closet; it simply appears dark. And now I pull the third cord."

He did so, and the mirror swung noiselessly back into its place.

"There is only one other thing to observe before we go out," said Thorndyke, "and that is this other mirror standing with its face to the wall. This, of course, is the one that Fred Calverley originally saw at the end of the closet; it has since been removed, and the larger swinging glass put in its place. And now," he continued, when we came out into the room, "let me explain the mechanism in detail. It was obvious to me, when I heard poor Fred Calverley's story, that the mirror was 'faked,' and I drew a diagram of the probable arrangement, which turns out to be correct. Here it is." He took a sheet of paper from his pocket and handed it to the lawyer. "There are two sketches. Sketch 1 shows the mirror in its ordinary position, closing the end of the closet. A person standing at A, of course, sees his reflection facing him at, apparently, A-1. Sketch 2 shows the mirror swung across. Now a person standing at A does not see his own reflection at all; but if some other person is standing in the other closet at B, A sees the reflection of B apparently at B-1—that is, in the identical position that his own reflection occupied when the mirror was straight across."

"I see now," said Brodribb; "but who set up this apparatus, and why was it done?"

"Let me ask you a question," said Thorndyke. "Is Alfred Calverley the next-of-kin?"

"No; there is Fred's younger brother. But I may say that Fred has made a will quite recently very much in Alfred's favor."

"There is the explanation, then," said Thorndyke. "These two scoundrels have conspired to drive the poor fellow to suicide, and Raggerton was clearly the leading spirit. He was evidently concocting some story with which to work on poor Fred's superstitions when the mention of the Chinaman on the steamer gave him his cue. He then invented the very picturesque story of the murdered mandarin and the stolen pearl. You remember that these 'visitations' did not begin until after that story had been told, and Fred had been absent from the house on a visit. Evidently, during his absence, Raggerton took down the original mirror, and substituted this swinging arrangement; and at the same time procured the Chinaman's dress and mask from the theatrical property dealers. No doubt he reckoned on being able quietly to remove the swinging glass and other properties and replace the original mirror before the inquest."

"By God!" exclaimed Mr. Brodribb, "it's the most infamous, cowardly plot I have ever heard of. They shall go to gaol for it, the villains, as sure as I am alive."

But in this Mr. Brodribb was mistaken; for immediately on finding themselves detected, the two conspirators had left the house, and by nightfall were safely across the Channel; and the only satisfaction that the lawyer obtained was the setting aside of the will on facts disclosed at the inquest.

As to Thorndyke, he has never to this day forgiven himself for having allowed Fred Calverley to go home to his death.

William MacHarg & Edwin Balmer

WILLIAM BRIGGS MACHARG (1872-1951) was an American journalist and author who regularly contributed to many magazines. EDWIN BALMER (1883-1959), an American editor and author, collaborated with Philip Wylie on *When Worlds Collide* in 1933 and wrote other science fiction novels on his own. The work for which each is best remembered, however, is the collection of stunning detection stories called *The Achievements of Luther Trant* (1910). Ellery Queen called it, in his *Queen's Quorum*, "one of the most daring and imaginative books ever committed to print." In one tale, "The Man Higher Up," the pair introduced the lie detector in fiction.

In the following story, which first appeared in *Hampton Magazine* in January 1910, Trant, the detective, reaches important psychological conclusions about the criminal from external clues.

THE AXTON LETTERS

WILLIAM MACHARG & EDWIN BALMER

The sounds in her dressing-room had waked her just before five. Ethel Waldron could still see, when she closed her eyes, every single, sharp detail of her room as it was that instant she sprang up in bed, with the cry that had given the alarm, and switched on the electric light. Instantly the man had shut the door; but as she sat, strained, staring at it to reopen, the hands and dial of her clock standing on the mantel beside the door, had fixed themselves upon her retina like the painted dial of a jeweler's dummy.[1] It could have been barely five, therefore, when Howard Axton, after his first swift rush in her defense had found the window which had been forced open; had picked up the queer Turkish dagger which he found broken on the sill, and, crying to the girl not to call the police, as it was surely "the same man"—the same man, he meant, who had so inexplicably followed him around the world—had rushed to his room for extra car-tridges for his revolver and run out into the cold sleet of the March morning.

So it was now an hour or more since Howard had run after the man, revolver in hand; and he had not reappeared or telephoned or sent any word at all of his safety. And however much Howard's life in wild lands had accustomed him to seek redress outside the law, hers still held the city-bred impulse to appeal to the police. She turned from her nervous pacing at the window and seized the telephone from its hook; but at the sound of the operator's voice she remembered again Howard's injunction that the man, whenever he appeared, was to be left solely to him, and dropped the receiver without answering. But she resented fiercely the advantage he held over her which must oblige her, she knew, to obey him. He had told her frankly—threatened her, indeed—that if there was the slightest publicity given to his homecoming to marry her, or any further notoriety made of the

---

[1] A "fake" clock or watch used for advertising purposes, showing a fixed time.

attending circumstances, he would surely leave her.

At the rehearsal of this threat she straightened and threw the superfluous dressing gown from her shoulders with a proud, defiant gesture. She was a straight, almost tall girl, with the figure of a more youthful Diana and with features as fair and flawless as any younger Hera, and in addition a great depth of blue in very direct eyes and a crowning glory of thick, golden hair. She was barely twenty-two. And she was not used to having any man show a sense of advantage over her, much less threaten her, as Howard had done. So, in that impulse of defiance, she was reaching again for the telephone she had just dropped, when she saw through the fog outside the window the man she was waiting for—a tall, alert figure hastening toward the house.

She ran downstairs rapidly and herself opened the door to him, a fresh flush of defiance flooding over her. Whether she resented it because this man, whom she did not love but must marry, could appear more the assured and perfect gentleman without collar, or scarf, and with his clothes and boots spattered with mud and rain, than any of her other friends could ever appear; or whether it was merely the confident, insolent smile of his full lips behind his small, close-clipped mustache, she could not tell. At any rate she motioned him into the library without speaking; but when they were alone and she had closed the door, she burst upon him.

"Well, Howard? Well? Well, Howard?" breathlessly.

"Then you have not sent any word to the police, Ethel?"

"'I was about to—the moment you came.

But—I have not—yet," she had to confess.

"Or to that—" he checked the epithet that was on his lips— "your friend Caryl?"

She flushed, and shook her head.

He drew his revolver, "broke" it, ejecting the cartridges carelessly upon the table, and threw himself wearily into a chair. "I'm glad to see you understand that this has not been the sort of affair for anyone else to interfere in!"

"Has been, you mean;" the girl's face went white; "you—you caught him this time and—and killed him, Howard?"

"Killed him, Ethel?" the man laughed, but observed her more carefully. "Of course I haven't killed him—or even caught him. But I've made myself sure, at last, that he's the same fellow that's been trying to make a fool of me all this year—that's been after me, as I wrote you. And if you remember my letters, even you—I mean even a girl brought up in a city ought to see how it's a matter of honor with me now to settle with him alone!"

"If he is merely trying to 'make a fool of you,' as you say—yes, Howard," the girl returned hotly. "But from what you yourself have told me of him, you know he must be keeping after you for some serious reason! Yes; you know it! I can see it! You can't deny it!"

"Ethel— what do you mean by that?"

"I mean that, if you do not think that the man who has been following you from Calcutta to Cape Town, to Chicago, means more than a joke for you to settle for yourself; anyway, *I* know that the man who has now twice gone through the things in *my* room, is something for me to go to the police about!"

"And have the papers flaring[2] the family scandal again?" the man returned. "I admit,

[2] Used in the obsolete sense of exposed to too much light.

Ethel," he conceded, carefully calculating the sharpness of his second sting before he delivered it, "that if you or I could call in the police without setting the whole pack of papers upon us again, I'd be glad to do it, if only to please you. But I told you, before I came back, that if there was to be any more airing of the family affairs at all, I could not come; so if you want to press the point now, of course I can leave you," he gave the very slightest but most suggestive glance about the rich, luxurious furnishings of the great room, "in possession."

"You know I can't let you do that!" the girl flushed scarlet. "But neither can you prevent me from making the private inquiry I spoke of for myself!" She went to the side of the room and, in his plain hearing, took down the telephone and called a number without having to look it up.

"Mr. Caryl, please," she said. "Oh, Henry, is it you? You can take me to your—Mr. Trant, wasn't that the name—as soon as you can now.... Yes; I want you to come here. I will have my brougham. Immediately!" And still without another word or even a glance at Axton, she brushed by him and ran up the stairs to her room.

He had made no effort to prevent her telephoning; and she wondered at it, even as, in the same impetus of reckless anger, she swept up the scattered letters and papers on her writing desk, and put on her things to go out. But on her way downstairs she stopped suddenly. The curl of his cigarette smoke through the open library door showed that he was waiting just inside it. He meant to speak to her before she went out. Perhaps he was even glad to have Caryl come in order that he might speak his say in the presence of both of them. Suddenly his tobacco's sharp, distinctive odor sickened her. She turned about, ran upstairs

again and fled, almost headlong, down the rear stairs and out the servants' door to the alley.

The dull, gray fog, which was thickening as the morning advanced, veiled her and made her unrecognizable except at a very few feet; but at the end of the alley, she shrank instinctively from the glance of the men passing until she made out a hurrying form of a man taller even than Axton and much broader. She sprang toward it with a shiver of relief as she saw Henry Caryl's light hair and recognized his even, open features.

"Ethel!" he caught her, gasping his surprise. "You here? Why—"

"Don't go to the house!" She led him the opposite way. "There is a cab stand at the corner. Get one there and take me—take me to this Mr. Trant. I will tell you everything. The man came again last night. Auntie is sick in bed from it. Howard still says it is his affair and will do nothing. I had to come to you."

Caryl steadied her against a house-wall an instant; ran to the corner for a cab and, returning with it, half lifted her into it.

Forty minutes later he led her into Trant's reception-room in the First National Bank Building; and recognizing the abrupt, decisive tones of the psychologist in conversation in the inner office, Caryl went to the door and knocked sharply.

"I beg your pardon, but—can you possibly postpone what you are doing, Mr. Trant?" he questioned quickly as the door opened and he faced the sturdy and energetic form of the red-haired young psychologist who, in six months, had made himself admittedly the chief consultant in Chicago on criminal cases. "My name is Caryl. Henry Howell introduced me to you last week at the club. But I am not presuming upon that for this interruption. I and—my friend need your help badly, Mr.

Trant, and immediately. I mean, if we can not speak with you now, we may be interrupted—unpleasantly."

Caryl had moved, as he spoke, to hide the girl behind him from the sight of the man in the inner office, who, Caryl had seen, was a police officer. Trant noted this and also that Caryl had carefully refrained from mentioning the girl's name.

"I can postpone this present business, Mr. Caryl," the psychologist replied quietly. He closed the door, but reopened it almost instantly. His official visitor had left through the entrance directly into the hall; the two young clients came into the inner room.

"This is Mr. Trant, Ethel," Caryl spoke to the girl a little nervously as she took a seat. "And, Mr. Trant, this is Miss Waldron. I have brought her to tell you of a mysterious man who has been pursuing Howard Axton about the world, and who, since Axton came home to her house two weeks ago, has been threatening her."

"Axton—Axton!" the psychologist repeated the name which Caryl had spoken, as if assured that Trant must recognize it. "Ah! Of course, Howard Axton is the son!" he frankly admitted his clearing recollection and his comprehension of how the face of the girl had seemed familiar. "Then you," he addressed her directly, "are Miss Waldron, of Drexel Boulevard?"[3]

"Yes; I am that Miss Waldron, Mr. Trant," the girl replied, flushing red to her lips, but raising her head proudly and meeting his eyes directly. "The step-daughter—the daughter of the second wife of Mr. Nimrod Axton. It was my mother, Mr. Trant, who was the cause of Mrs. Anna Axton getting a di-

[3] Then a mansion-lined street in Chicago.

vorce and the complete custody of her son from Mr. Axton twenty years ago. It was my mother who, just before Mr. Nimrod Axton's death last year, required that, in the will, the son—the first Mrs. Axton was then dead—should be cut off absolutely and entirely, without a cent, and that Mr. Axton's entire estate be put in trust for her—my mother. So, since you doubtless remember the reopening of all this again six months ago when my mother, too, died, I am now the sole heir and legatee of the Axton properties of upwards of sixty millions, they tell me. Yes; I am that Miss Waldron, Mr. Trant!"

"I recall the accounts, but only vaguely—from the death of Mr. Axton and, later, of the second Mrs. Axton, your mother, Miss Waldron," Trant replied, quietly, "though I remember the comment upon the disposition of the estate both times. It was from the pictures published of you and the accompanying comment in the papers only a week or two ago that I recognized you. I mean, of course, the recent comments upon the son, Mr. Howard Axton, whom you have mentioned, who has come home at last to contest the will!"

"You do Miss Waldron an injustice—all the papers have been doing her a great injustice, Mr. Trant, Caryl corrected quickly. "Mr. Axton has not come to contest the will."

"No?"

"No. Miss Waldron has had him come home, at her own several times repeated request, so that she may turn over to him, as completely as possible, the whole of his father's estate! If you can recall, in any detail, the provisions of Mr. Axton's will, you will appreciate, I believe, why we have preferred to let the other impression go uncorrected. For the second Mrs. Axton so carefully and completely cut off all possibility of any of the property being transferred in any form to the son, that Miss Waldron, when she went to a lawyer to see how she could transfer it to Howard Axton, as soon as she had come into the estate, found that her mother's lawyers had provided against every possibility except that of the heir marrying the disinherited son. So she sent for him, offering to establish him into his estate, even at that cost."

"You mean that you offered to marry him?"

Trant questioned the girl directly again. "And he has come to gain his estate in that way?"

"Yes, Mr. Trant; but you must be fair to Mr. Axton also," the girl replied. "When I first wrote him, almost a year ago, he refused point blank to consider such an offer. In spite of my repeated letters it was not till six weeks ago, after a shipwreck in which he lost his friend who had been traveling with him for some years, that he would consent even to come home. Even now I—I remain the one urging the marriage."

The psychologist looked at the girl keenly and questioningly.

"I need scarcely say how little urging he would need, entirely apart from the property," Caryl flushed, "if he were not gentleman enough to appreciate—partly, at least—Miss Waldron's position. I—her friends, I mean, Mr. Trant—have admitted that he appeared at first well enough in every way to permit the possibility of her marrying him if she considers that her duty. But now, this mystery has come up about the man who has been following him—the man who appeared again only this morning in Miss Waldron's room and went through her papers—"

"And Mr. Axton cannot account for it?" the psychologist helped him.

"Axton won't tell her or anybody else who the man is or why he follows him. On the contrary, he has opposed in every possible way every inquiry or search made for the man, except such as he chooses to make for himself. Only this morning he made a threat against Miss Waldron if she attempted to summon the police and 'take the man out of his hands'; and it is because I am sure that he will follow us here to prevent her consulting you—when he finds that she has come here—that I asked you to see us at once."

"Leave the details of his appearance this morning to the last then," Trant requested abruptly, "and tell me where you first heard of this man following Mr. Axton, and how? How, for instance, do you know he was following him, if Mr. Axton is so reticent about the affair?"

"That is one of the strange things about it, Mr. Trant"—the girl took from her bosom the bundle of letters she had taken from her room—"he used to write to amuse me with him, as you can see here. I told you I wrote Mr. Axton about a year ago to come home and he refused to consider it. But afterward he always wrote in reply to my letters in the half-serious, friendly way you shall see. These four letters I brought you are almost entirely taken up with his adventures with the mysterious man. He wrote on typewriter, as you see"—she handed them over—"because on his travels he used to correspond regularly for some of the London syndicates."

"London?"

"Yes; the first Mrs. Axton took Howard to England with her when he was scarcely seven, immediately after she got her divorce. He grew up there and abroad. This is his first return to America. I have arranged those letters, Mr. Trant," she added as the psychologist was opening them for examination now, "in the order they came."

"I will read them that way then," Trant said, and he glanced over the contents of the first hastily; it was postmarked at Cairo, Egypt, some ten months before. He then re-read more carefully this part of it:

"But a strange and startling incident has happened since my last letter to you, Miss Waldron, which bothers me considerably. We are, as you will see by the letter paper, at Shepheard's Hotel in Cairo,[4] but could not, after our usual custom, get communicating rooms. It was after midnight, and the million noises of this babel-town had finally died into a hot and breathless stillness. I had been writing letters, and when through I put out the lights to get rid of their heat, lighted instead the small night lamp I carry with me, and still partly dressed threw myself upon the bed, without, however, any idea of going to sleep before undressing. As I lay there I heard distinctly soft footsteps come down the corridor on which my room opens and stop apparently in front of the door. They were not, I judged, the footsteps of a European, for the walker was either barefooted or wore soft sandals. I turned my head toward the door, expecting a knock, but none followed. Neither did the door open, though I had not yet locked it. I was on the point of rising to see what was wanted, when it occurred to me that it was probably not at my door that the steps had stopped but at the door directly opposite, across the corridor. Without doubt my opposite neighbor had merely returned to his room and his footsteps had ceased to reach my ears when he entered and closed his door behind him. I dozed off. But half an hour later, as nearly as I can estimate it, I awake and was thinking of the necessity for getting undressed and into bed, when a slight—a very slight rustling noise attracted my attention. I listened intently to locate the direction of the sound and determine whether it was inside the room or out of it, and then heard in connection with it a slighter and more regular sound which could be nothing else than breathing. Some living creature, Miss Waldron, was in my room. The sounds came from the direction of the table by the window. I turned my head as silently as I was able, and was aware that a man was holding a sheet of paper under the light of the lamp. He was at the table going through the papers in my writing desk. But the very slight noise I had made in turning on the bed had warned him. He rose, with a hissing intake of the breath, his feet pattered softly and swiftly across the floor, my door creaked under his hand, and he was gone before I could jump from the bed and intercept him. I ran out into the hallway, but it was empty. I listened, but could hear no movement in any of the rooms near me. I went back and examined the writing desk, but found nothing missing; and it was plain nothing had been touched except some of my letters from you. But, before finally going to bed, you may well believe, I locked my door carefully; and in the morning I reported the matter to the hotel office. The only description I could give of the intruder was that he had certainly worn a turban, and one even larger it seemed to me than ordinary. The hotel attendants had seen no one coming from or entering my corridor that night who answered this description. The turban and the absence of European shoes, of course, determined him to have been an Egyptian, Turk or Arab. But what Egyptian, Turk or Arab could have entered my room with any other object than robbery—which was certainly not the aim of my intruder, for the valuables in

---

[4] Built in 1841, Shepheard's was destroyed by fire in 1957 but was rebuilt and remains one of the top hotels in Cairo.

the writing desk were untouched. That same afternoon, it is true, I had had an altercation amounting almost to a quarrel with a Bedouin Arab on my way back from Heliopolis; but if this were he, why should he have taken revenge on my writing desk instead of on me? And what reason on earth can any follower of the Prophet have had for examining with such particular attention my letters from you? It was so decidedly a strange thing that I have taken all this space to tell it to you—one of the strangest sort of things I've had in all my knocking about; and Lawler can make no more of it than I."

"Who is this Lawler who was with Mr. Axton then?" Trant looked up interestedly from the last page of the letter.

"I only know he was a friend Howard made in London—an interesting man who had traveled a great deal, particularly in America. Howard was lonely after his mother's death; and as Mr. Lawler was about his age, they struck up a friendship and traveled together."

"An English younger son, perhaps?"

"I don't know anything else except that he had been in the English army—in the Royal Sussex regiment—but was forced to give up his commission on account of charges that he had cheated at cards. Howard always held that the charges were false; but that was why he wanted to travel."

"You know of no other trouble which this Lawler had?"

"No, none."

"Then where is he now?"

"Dead."

"Dead?" Trant's face fell.

"Yes; he was the friend I spoke of that was lost—drowned in the wreck of the *Gladstone* just before Howard started home."

Trant picked up the next letter, which was dated and postmarked at Calcutta.

"Miss Waldron, I have seen him again," he read. "Who, you ask? My Moslem friend with a taste for your correspondence. You see, I can again joke about it; but really it was only last night and I am still in a perfect funk. It was the same man—I'll swear it—shoeless and turbaned and enjoying the pleasant pursuit of going through my writing desk for your letters. Did he follow us down the Red Sea, across the Indian Ocean—over three thousand miles of ocean travel? I can imagine no other explanation—for I would take oath to his identity—the very same man I saw at Cairo, but now here in this Great Eastern Hotel at Calcutta,[5] where we have two rooms at the end of the most noisome corridor that ever caged the sounds and odors of a babbling East Indian population, and where the doors have no locks. I had the end of a trunk against my door, notwithstanding the fact that an Indian servant I have hired was sleeping in the corridor outside across the doorway, but it booted nothing; for Lawler in the next room had neglected to fasten his door in any way, trusting to *his* servant, who occupied a like strategic position outside the threshold, and the door between our two rooms was open. I had been asleep in spite of everything—in spite of the snores and stertorous breathing of a floorful of sleeping humans, for the partitions between the rooms do not come within several feet of the ceiling; in spite of the distant bellowing of a sacred bull, and the nearer howl of a very far from sacred dog, and a jingling of elephant bells which

---

[5] Opened in 1840, the hotel became known as the "Jewel of the East" and was described in Rudyard Kipling's 1891 story "City of Dreadful Night." It suffered financial reverses in the 1970s and was taken over by the Indian government; however, it was subsequently privatized and continues in business today.

were set off intermittently somewhere close at hand whenever some living thing in their neighborhood—animal or human—shifted its position. I was awakened—at least I believe it was this which awakened me—by a creaking of the floor boards in my room, and, with what seemed a causeless, but was certainly one of the most oppressive feelings of chilling terror I have ever experienced, I started upright in my bed. He was there, again at my writing desk, and rustling the papers. For an instant I remained motionless; and in that instant, alarmed by the slight sound I had made, he fled noiselessly, pattered through the door between the rooms and loudly slammed it shut, slammed Lawler's outer door behind him, and had gone. I crashed the door open, ran across the creaking floor of the other room—where Lawler, awakened by the slamming of the doors, had whisked out of bed—and opened the door into the corridor. Lawler's servant, aroused, but still dazed with sleep, blubbered that he had seen no one, though the man must have stepped over his very body. A dozen other servants, sleeping before their masters' doors in the corridor, had awakened likewise, but cried out shrilly that they had seen no one. Lawler, too, though the noise of the man's passage had brought him out of bed, had not seen him. When I examined my writing desk I found, as before at Cairo, that nothing had been taken. The literary delight of looking over your letters seems to be all that draws him—of course, I am joking; for there must be a real reason. What it is that he is searching for, why it is that he follows me, for he has never intruded on anyone else so far as I can learn, I would like to know—I would like to know—I would like to know! The native servants asked in awe-struck whispers whether I noticed if his feet were turned backward; for it seems they believe that to be one of the characteristics of a ghost. But the man was flesh and blood—I am sure of

it; and I am bound that if he comes again I will learn his object, for I sleep now with my pistol under my pillow, and next time—I shall shoot!"

Trant, as he finished the last words, looked up suddenly at Miss Waldron, as though about to ask a question or make some comment, but checked himself, and hastily laying aside this letter he picked up the next one, which bore a Cape Town date line:

"My affair with my mysterious visitor came almost to a conclusion last night, for except for a careless mistake of my own I should have bagged him. Isn't it mystifying, bewildering—yes, and a little terrifying—he made his appearance here last night in Cape Town, thousands of miles away from the two other places I had encountered him; and he seemed to have no more difficulty in entering the house of a Cape Town correspondent, Mr. Arthur Emsley, where we are guests, than he had before in entering public hotels, and when discovered he disappeared as mysteriously as ever. This time, however, he took some precautions. He had moved my night lamp so that, with his body in shadow, he could still see the contents of my desk; but I could hear his shoulders rubbing on the wall and located him exactly. I slipped my hand noiselessly for my revolver, but it was gone. The slight noise I made in searching for it alarmed him, and he ran. I rushed out into the hall after him. Mr. Emsley and Lawler, awakened by the breaking of the glass, had come out of their rooms. They had not seen him, and though we searched the house he had disappeared as inexplicably as the two other times. But I have learned one thing: It is not a turban he wears, it is his coat, which he takes off and wraps around his head to hide his face. An odd disguise; and the possession of a coat of that sort makes it probable he is a European. I know of only two Europeans who have been in Cairo, Calcutta and Cape Town at the same time we were—both travelers like ourselves; a guttural young German named Schultz, a freight agent for the Nord Deutscher Lloyd,[6] and a nasal American named Walcott, who travels for the Seric Medicine Co. of New York.[7] I shall keep an eye on both of them. For, in my mind at least, this affair has come to be a personal and bitter contest between the unknown and myself. I am determined not only to know who this man is and what is the object of his visits, but to settle with him the score which I now have against him. I shall shoot him next time he comes as mercilessly as I would a rabid dog; and I should have shot him this time except for my own careless mistake through which I had let my revolver slip to the floor, where I found it. By the bye, we sail for home—that is, England—next week on the steamer *Gladstone*, but, I am sorry to say, without my English servant, Beasley. Poor Beasley, since these mysterious occurrences, has been bitten with superstitious terror; the man is in a perfect fright, thinks I am haunted, and does not dare to embark on the same ship with me, for he believes that the *Gladstone* will never reach England in safety if I am aboard. I shall discharge him, of course, but furnish him with his transportation home and leave him to follow at his leisure if he sees fit."

"This is the first time I have heard of another man in their party who might possibly be the masquerader, Miss Waldron;" Trant swung suddenly in his revolving chair to face the girl again. "Mr. Axton speaks of him as his English servant—I suppose, from that, he left England with Mr. Axton."

"Yes, Mr. Trant."

"And therefore was present, though not mentioned, at Cairo, Calcutta and Cape Town?"

"Yes, Mr. Trant; but he was dismissed at that time by Mr. Axton and is now, and also was, at the mysterious man's next appearance, in the Charing Cross Hospital in London. He had his leg broken by a cab; and one of the doctors there wrote Mr. Axton two days ago telling him of Beasley's need of assistance. It could not have been Beasley."

"And there was no one else with Mr. Axton, except his friend Lawler who, you say, was drowned in a wreck?"

"No one else but Mr. Lawler, Mr. Trant; and Howard himself saw him dead and identified him, as you will see in that last letter."

Trant opened the envelope and took out the enclosure interestedly; but as he unfolded the first page, a printed sheet dropped out. He spread it upon his desk—a page from the London *Illustrated News* showing four portraits with the caption, "Sole survivors of the ill-fated British steamer *Gladstone*, wrecked off Cape Blanco, January 24," the first portrait bearing the name of Howard Axton and showing the determined, distinctly handsome features and the full lips and deep-set eyes of the man whom the girl had defied that morning.

"This is a good portrait?" Trant asked abruptly.

"Very good, indeed," the girl answered, "though it was taken almost immediately after the wreck for the *News*. I have the photograph from which it was made at home. I had asked him for a picture of himself in my last previous letter, as my mother had destroyed every picture, even the early pictures, of him and his mother."

---

[6] A German shipping company founded in 1857, merged with the Hamburg America Line in 1970.

[7] A fictional, or at least untraceable at this date, company.

Trant turned to the last letter.

"Wrecked, Miss Waldron. Poor Beasley's prophecy of disaster has come only too true, and I suppose he is already congratulating himself that he was 'warned' by my mysterious visitor and so escaped the fate that so many have suffered, including poor Lawler. Of course you will have seen all about it in the staring headlines of some newspaper long before this reaches you. I am glad that when found I was at once identified, though still unconscious, and my name listed first among the very few survivors, so that you were spared the anxiety of waiting for news of me. Only four of us left out of that whole shipload! I had final proof this morning of poor Lawler's death by the finding of his body.

"I was hardly out of bed when a mangy little man—a German trader—came to tell me that more bodies had been found, and, as I have been called upon in every instance to aid in identification, I set out with him down the beach at once. It was almost impossible to realize that this blue and silver ocean glimmering under the blazing sun was the same white-frothing terror that had swallowed up all my companions of three days before. The greater part of the bodies found that morning had been already carried up the beach. Among those remaining on the sand the first we came upon was that of Lawler. It lay upon its side at the entrance of a ragged sandy cove, half buried in the sand, which here was white as leprosy. His ears, the sockets of his eyes, and every interstice of his clothing were filled with this white and leprous sand by the washing of the waves; his pockets bulged and were distended with it."

"What! What!" Trant clutched the letter from the desk in excitement and stared at it with eyes flashing with interest.

"It is a horrible picture, Mr. Trant," the girl shuddered.

"Horrible—yes, certainly," the psychologist assented tensely; "but I was not thinking of the horror," he checked himself.

"Of what, then?" asked Caryl pointedly.

But the psychologist had already returned to the letter in his hand, the remainder of which he read with intent and ever-increasing interest:

"Of course I identified him at once. His face was calm and showed no evidence of his last bitter struggle, and I am glad his look was thus peaceful. Poor Lawler! If the first part of his life was not all it should have been—as indeed he frankly told me—he atoned for all in his last hour; for undoubtedly, Miss Waldron, Lawler gave his life for mine.

"I suppose the story of the wreck is already all known to you, for our one telegraph wire that binds this isolated town to the outside world has been laboring for three days under a load of messages. You know then that eighteen hours out of St. Vincent fire was discovered among the cargo, that the captain, confident at first that the fire would be got under control, kept on his course, only drawing in somewhat toward the African shore in case of emergency. But a very heavy sea rising, prevented the fire-fighters from doing efficient work among the cargo and in the storm and darkness the *Gladstone* struck several miles to the north of Cape Blanco on a hidden reef at a distance of over a mile from the shore.

"On the night it occurred I awakened with so strong a sense of something being wrong that I rose, partly dressed myself, and went out into the cabin, where I found a white-faced steward going from door to door arousing the passengers. Heavy smoke was billowing up the main companionway in the light of the cabin lamps, and the pitching and reeling of the vessel showed that the sea had greatly increased.

I returned and awoke Lawler, and we went out on deck. The sea was a smother of startling whiteness through which the *Gladstone* was staggering at the full power of her engines. No flame as yet was anywhere visible, but huge volumes of smoke were bursting from every opening in the fore part of the vessel. The passengers, in a pale and terrified group, were kept together on the after deck as far as possible from the fire. Now and then some pallid, staring man or woman would break through the guard and rush back to the cabin in search of a missing loved one or valuables. Lawler and I determined that one of us must return to the stateroom for our money, and Lawler successfully made the attempt. He returned in ten minutes with my money and papers and two life preservers. But when I tried to put on my life preserver I found it to be old and in such a condition as made it useless. Lawler then took off the preserver that he himself had on, declaring himself to be a much better swimmer than I—which I knew to be the case—and forced me to wear it. This life preserver was all that brought me safely ashore, and the lack of it was, I believe, the reason for Lawler's death. Within ten minutes afterward the flames burst through the forward deck—a red and awful banner which the fierce wind flattened into a fan-shaped sheet of fire against the night—and the *Gladstone* struck with terrific force, throwing everything and everybody flat upon the deck. The bow was raised high upon the reef, while the stem with its maddened living freight began to sink rapidly into the swirl of foaming waters. The first two boats were overfilled at once in a wild rush, and one was stove immediately against the steamer's side and sank, while the other was badly damaged and made only about fifty yards' progress before it went down also. The remaining boats all were lowered from the starboard davits, and got away in safety; but only to capsize or be stove upon the reef. Lawler and I found places in the last boat—the captain's. At the last moment, just as we were putting off, the fiery maw of the *Gladstone* vomited out the scorched and half-blinded second engineer and a single stoker, whom we took in with difficulty. There was but one woman in our boat—a fragile, illiterate Dutchwoman from the neighborhood of Johannesburg—who had in her arms a baby. How strange that of our boatload those who alone survived should be the Dutchwoman, but without her baby; the engineer and stoker, whom the fire had already partly disabled, and myself, a very indifferent swimmer—while the strongest among us all perished! Of what happened after leaving the ship I have only the most indistinct recollection. I recall the swamping of our boat, and cruel white waters that rushed out of the night to engulf us; I recall a blind and painful struggle against a power infinitely greater than my own—a struggle which seemed interminable; for, as a matter of fact, I must have been in the water fully four hours and the impact of the waves alone beat my flesh almost to a jelly; and I recall the coming of daylight, and occasional glimpses of a shore which seemed to project itself suddenly above the sea and then at once to sink away and be swallowed by it. I was found unconscious on the sands—I have not the faintest idea how I got there—and I was identified before coming to myself (it may please you to know this) by several of your letters which were found in my pocket. At present, with my three rescued companions—whose names even I probably never should have known if the *Gladstone* had reached England safely—I am a most enthralling center of interest to the white, black and parti-colored inhabitants of this region; and I am writing this letter on an antiquated typewriter belonging to the smallest, thinnest, baldest little American that ever left his own dooryard to become a missionary."

Trant tossed aside the last page and, with eyes flashing with a deep, glowing fire, he glanced across intensely to the girl watching him; and his hands clenched on the table, in the constraint of his eagerness.

"Why—what is it, Mr. Trant?" the girl cried.

"This is so taken up with the wreck and the death of Lawler," the psychologist touched the last letter, "that there is hardly any more mention of the mysterious man. But you said, since Mr. Axton has come home, he has twice appeared and in your room, Miss Waldron. Please give me the details."

"Of his first appearance—or visit, I should say, since no one really saw him, Mr. Trant," the girl replied, still watching the psychologist with wonder, "I can't tell you much, I'm afraid. When Mr. Axton first came home, I asked him about this mysterious friend; and he put me off with a laugh and merely said he hadn't seen much of him since he last wrote. But even then I could see he wasn't so easy as he seemed. And it was only two days after that— or nights, for it was about one o'clock in the morning—that I was wakened by some sound which seemed to come from my dressing-room. I turned on the light in my room and rang the servant's bell. The butler came almost at once and, as he is not a courageous man, roused Mr. Axton before opening the door to my dressing-room. They found no one there and nothing taken or even disturbed except my letters in my writing desk, Mr. Trant. My aunt, who has been taking care of me since my mother died, was aroused and came with the servants. She thought I must have imagined everything; but I discovered and showed Mr. Axton that it was *his letters to me* that had appeared to be the ones the man was searching for. I found that two of

them had been taken and every other type-written letter in my desk—and only those— had been opened in an apparent search for more of his letters. I could see that this excited him exceedingly, though he tried to conceal it from me; and immediately afterward he found that a window on the first floor had been forced, so some man had come in, as I said."

"Then last night."

"It was early this morning, Mr. Trant, but still very dark—a little before five o'clock. It was so damp, you know, that I had not opened the window in my bedroom, which is close to the bed; but had opened the windows of my dressing-room, and so left the door between open. It had been closed and locked before. So when I awoke, I could see directly into my dressing-room."

"Clearly?"

"Of course not at all clearly. But my writing-desk is directly opposite my bedroom door; and in a sort of silhouette against my shaded desk light, which he was using, I could see his figure—a very vague, monstrous looking figure, Mr. Trant. Its lower part seemed plain enough; but the upper part was a formless blotch. I confess at first that enough of my girl's fear for ghosts came to me to make me see him as a headless man, until I remembered how Howard had seen and described him— with a coat wrapped round his head. As soon as I was sure of this, I pressed the bell-button again and this time screamed, too, and switched on my light. But he slammed the door between us and escaped. He went through another window he had forced on the lower floor with a queer sort of dagger-knife which he had broken and left on the sill. And as soon as Howard saw this, he knew it was the same man, for it was then he ordered me not to interfere. He made off after him, and when he came back, he told me he was sure it was the same man."

"This time, too, the man at your desk seemed rummaging for your correspondence with Mr. Axton?"

"It seemed so, Mr. Trant."

"But his letters were all merely personal—like these letters you have given me?"

"Yes."

"Amazing!" Trant leaped to his feet, with eyes flashing now with unrestrained fire, and took two or three rapid turns up and down the office. "If I am to believe the obvious inference from these letters, Miss Waldron—coupled with what you have told me—I have not yet come across a case, an attempt at crime more careful, more cold-blooded and, withall, more surprising!"

"A crime—an attempt at crime, Mr. Trant?" cried the white and startled girl. "So there was cause for my belief that something serious underlay these mysterious appearances?"

"Cause?" Trant swung to face her. "Yes, Miss Waldron—criminal cause, a crime so skillfully carried on, so assisted by unexpected circumstance that you—that the very people against whom it is aimed have not so much as suspected its existence."

"Then you think Howard honestly believes the man still means nothing?"

"The man never meant 'nothing,' Miss Waldron; but it was only at first the plot was aimed against Howard Axton," Trant replied. "Now it is aimed solely at you!"

The girl grew paler.

"How can you say that so surely, Mr. Trant?" Caryl demanded, "without investigation?"

"These letters are quite enough evidence for what I say, Mr. Caryl," Trant returned. "Would you have come to me unless you had known that my training in the methods of psychology enabled me to see causes and motives in such a case as this which others, untrained, can not see?

"You have nothing more to tell me which might be of assistance?" he faced the girl again, but turned back at once to Caryl. "Let me tell you then, Mr. Caryl, that I am about to make a very thorough investigation of this for you. Meanwhile, I repeat: a definite, daring crime was planned first, I believe, against Howard Axton and Miss Waldron; but now—I am practically certain—it is aimed against Miss Waldron alone. But there cannot be in it the slightest danger of intentional personal hurt to her. So neither of you need be uneasy while I am taking time to obtain full proof—"

"But, Mr. Trant," the girl interrupted, "are you not going to tell me—you *must* tell me—what the criminal secret is that these letters have revealed to you?"

"You must wait, Miss Waldron," the psychologist answered kindly, with his hand on the doorknob, as though anxious for the interview to end. "What I could tell you now would only terrify you and leave you perplexed how to act while you were waiting to hear from me. No; leave the letters, if you will, and the page from the *Illustrated News*," he said suddenly, as the girl began gathering up her papers. "There is only one thing more. You said you expected an interruption here from Howard Axton, Mr. Caryl. Is there still a good chance of his coming here or—must I go to see him?"

"Miss Waldron telephoned to me, in his presence, to take her to see you. Afterward she left the house without his knowledge. As soon as he finds she has gone, he will look up your address, and I think you may expect him."

"Very good. Then I must set to work at once!" He shook hands with both of them hurriedly and almost forcing them out his door, closed it behind them, and strode back to his desk. He picked up immediately the second of the four letters which the girl had given him, read it through again, and crossed the corridor to the opposite office, which was that of a public stenographer.

"Make a careful copy of that," he directed, "and bring it to me as soon as it is finished."

A quarter of an hour later, when the copy had been brought him, he compared it carefully with the original. He put the copy in a drawer of the desk and was apparently waiting with the four originals before him when he heard a knock on his door and, opening it, found that his visitor was again young Caryl.

"Miss Waldron did not wish to return home at once; she has gone to see a friend. So I came back," he explained, "thinking you might make a fuller statement of your suspicions to me than you would in Miss Waldron's presence."

"Fuller in what respect, Mr. Caryl?"

The young man reddened.

"I must tell you—though you already may have guessed—that before Miss Waldron inherited the estate and came to believe it her duty to do as she has done, there had been an—understanding between us, Mr. Trant. She still has no friend to look to as she looks to me. So, if you mean that you have discovered through those letters—though God knows how you can have done it—anything

in Axton which shows him unfit to marry her, you must tell me!"

"As far as Axton's past goes," Trant replied, "his letters show him a man of high type—moral, if I may make a guess, above the average. There is a most pleasing frankness about him. As to making any further explanation than I have done—but good Lord! What's that?"

The door of the office had been dashed loudly open, and its still trembling frame was filled by a tall, very angry young man in automobile costume,[8] whose highly colored, aristocratic looking features Trant recognized immediately from the print in the page of the *Illustrated London News*.

"Ah, Mr. Caryl here too?—the village busybody!" the newcomer sneered, with a slight accent which showed his English education. "You are insufferably mixing yourself in my affairs," he continued, as Caryl, with an effort, controlled himself and made no answer. "Keep out of them! That is my advice—take it! Does a woman have to order you off the premises before you can understand that you are not wanted? As for you," he swung toward Trant, "you are Trant, I suppose!"

"Yes, that is my name, Mr. Axton," replied the psychologist, leaning against his desk.

The other advanced a step and raised a threatening finger. "Then that advice is meant for you, too. I want no police, no detectives, no outsider of any sort interfering in this matter. Make no mistake; it will be the worse for anyone who pushes himself in! I came here at once to take the case out of your hands, as soon as I found Miss Waldron had

---

[8] In 1910, when this story first appeared, the typical automobile driver dressed in long cloth coat, cap, and goggles as protection from the hazards of the roads (mostly dirt) as the vehicles lacked windshields and were not enclosed.

come here. This is strictly my affair—keep out of it!"

"You mean, Mr. Axton, that you prefer to investigate it personally?" the psychologist inquired.

"Exactly—investigate and punish!"

"But you cannot blame Miss Waldron for feeling great anxiety even on your account, as your personal risk in making such an investigation will be so immensely greater than anyone's else would be."

"My risk?"

"Certainly; you may be simply playing into the hand of your strange visitor, by pursuing him unaided. Any other's risk—mine, for instance, if I were to take up the matter—would be comparatively slight, beginning perhaps by questioning the nightwatchmen and stableboys in the neighborhood with a view to learning what became of the man after he left the house; and besides, such risks are a part of my business."

Axton halted. "I had not thought of it in that light," he said reflectively.

"You are too courageous—foolishly courageous, Mr. Axton."

"Do you mind if I sit down? Thank you. You think, Mr. Trant, that an investigation such as you suggest, would satisfy Miss Waldron—make her easier in her mind, I mean?"

"I think so, certainly."

"And it would not necessarily entail calling in the police? You must appreciate how I shrink from publicity—another story concerning the Axton family exploited in the daily papers!"

"I had no intention of consulting the police, or of calling them in, at least until I was ready to make the arrest."

"I must confess, Mr. Trant," said Axton easily, "that I find you a very different man from what I had expected. I imagined an uneducated, somewhat brutal, perhaps talkative fellow; but I find you, if I may say so, a gentleman. Yes, I am tempted to let you continue your investigation—on the lines you have suggested."

"I shall ask your help."

"I will help you as much as is in my power."

"Then let me begin, Mr. Axton, with a question—pardon me if I open a window, for the room is rather warm—I want to know whether you can supplement these letters, which so far are the only real evidence against the man, by any further description of him," and Trant, who had thrown open the window beside him, undisturbed by the roar that filled the office from the traffic-laden street below, took the letters from his pocket and opened them one by one, clumsily, upon the desk.

"I am afraid I cannot add anything to them, Mr. Trant."

"We must get on then with what we have here," the psychologist hitched his chair near to the window to get a better light on the paper in his hand, and his cuff knocked one of the other letters off the desk onto the windowsill. He turned, hastily but clumsily, and touched, but could not grasp it before it slipped from the sill out into the air. He sprang to his feet with an exclamation of dismay, and dashed from the room. Axton and Caryl, rushing to the window, watched the paper, driven by a strong breeze, flutter down the street until lost to sight among wagons; and a minute later saw Trant appear below them, bareheaded and excited, darting in and out among vehicles at the spot where the paper had disappeared; but it had been carried away upon some muddy wagon-wheel or reduced to tatters, for he returned after fifteen minutes' search disheartened, vexed and empty handed.

"It was the letter describing the second visit," he exclaimed disgustedly as he opened the door. "It was most essential, for it contained the most minute description of the man of all. I do not see how I can manage well, now, without it."

"Why should you?" Caryl said in surprise at the evident stupidity of the psychologist. "Surely, Mr. Axton, if he can not add any other details, can at least repeat those he had already given."

"Of course!" Trant recollected. "If you would be so good, Mr. Axton, I will have a stenographer take down the statement to give you the least trouble."

"I will gladly do that," Axton agreed; and, when the psychologist had summoned the stenographer, he dictated without hesitation the following letter:

"The second time that I saw the man was at Calcutta, in the Great Eastern Hotel. He was the same man I had seen at Cairo—shoeless and turbaned; at least I believed then that it was a turban, but I saw later, at Cape Town, that it was his short brown coat wrapped round his head and tied by the sleeves under his chin. We had at the Great Eastern two whitewashed communicating rooms opening off a narrow, dirty corridor, along whose whitewashed walls at a height of some two feet from the floor ran a greasy smudge gathered from the heads and shoulders of the dark-skinned, white-robed native servants who spent the nights sleeping or sitting in front of their masters' doors. Though Lawler and I each had a servant also outside his door, I dragged a trunk against mine after closing it—a useless precaution, as it proved, as Lawler put no trunk against his—and though I see now that I must

have been moved by some foresight of danger, I went to sleep afterward quite peacefully. I awakened somewhat later in a cold and shuddering fright, oppressed by the sense of some presence in my room—started up in bed and looked about. My trunk was still against the door as I had left it; and besides this, I saw at first only the furniture of the room, which stood as when I had gone to sleep—two rather heavy and much scratched mahogany English chairs, a mahogany dresser with swinging mirror, and the spindle-legged, four-post canopy bed on which I lay. But presently, I saw more. He was there—a dark shadow against the whitewashed wall beside the flat-topped window marked his position, as he crouched beside my writing desk and held the papers in a bar of white moonlight to look at them. For an instant, the sight held me motionless, and suddenly becoming aware that he was seen, he leaped to his feet—a short, broad-shouldered, bulky man—sped across the blue and white straw matting into Lawler's room and drove the door to behind him. I followed, forcing the door open with my shoulder, saw Lawler just leaping out of bed in his pajamas, and tore open Lawler's corridor door, through which the man had vanished. He was not in the corridor, though I inspected it carefully, and Lawler, though he had been awakened by the man's passage, had not seen him. Lawler's servant, pretty well dazed with sleep, told me in blank and open-mouthed amazement at my question, that he had not seen him pass; and the other white-draped Hindoos, gathering about me from the doors in front of which they had been asleep, made the same statement. None of these Hindoos resembled in the least the man I had seen, for I looked them over carefully one by one with this in mind. When I made a light in my room in order to examine it thoroughly, I found nothing had been touched except the writing desk, and even from that nothing had been taken, although the papers had been disturbed. The whole affair was as mysterious and inexplicable as the man's first appearance had been, or as his subsequent appearance proved; for though I carefully questioned the hotel employees in the morning I could not learn that any such man had entered or gone out from the hotel."

"That is very satisfactory indeed;" Trant's gratification was evident in his tone, as Axton finished. "It will quite take the place of the letter that was lost. There is only one thing more—so far as I know now—in which you may be of present help to me, Mr. Axton. Besides your friend Lawler, who was drowned in the wreck of the *Gladstone*, and the man Beasley—who, Miss Waldron tells me, is in a London hospital—there were only two men in Cape Town with you who had been in Cairo and Calcutta at the same time you were. You do not happen to know what has become of that German freight agent, Schultz?"

"I have not the least idea, Mr. Trant."

"Or Walcott, the American patent medicine man?"

"I know no more of him than of the other. Whether either of them is in Chicago now, is precisely what I would like to know myself, Mr. Trant; and I hope you will be able to find out for me."

"I will do my best to locate them. By the way, Mr. Axton, you have no objection to my setting a watch over your family home, provided I employ a man who has no connection with the police?"

"With that condition I think it would be a very good idea," Axton assented. He waited

to see whether Trant had anything more to ask him; then, with a look of partially veiled hostility at Caryl, he went out.

The other followed, but stopped at the door.

"We—that is, Miss Waldron—will hear from you, Mr. Trant?" he asked with sudden distrust—"I mean, you will report to her, as well as to Mr. Axton?"

"Certainly; but I hardly expect to have anything for you for two or three days."

The psychologist smiled, as he shut the door behind Caryl. He dropped into the chair at his desk and wrote rapidly a series of telegrams, which he addressed to the chiefs of police of a dozen foreign and American cities. Then, more slowly, he wrote a message to the Seric Medicine Company, of New York, and another to the Nord Deutscher Lloyd.

The first two days, of the three Trant had specified to Caryl, passed with no other event than the installing of a burly watchman at the Axton home. On the third night this watchman reported to Miss Waldron that he had seen and driven off, without being able to catch, a man who was trying to force a lower window; and the next morning—within half an hour of the arrival of the Overland Limited[9] from San Francisco—Trant called up the Axton home on the telephone with the news that he thought he had at last positive proof of the mysterious man's identity. At least, he had with him a man whom he wanted Mr. Axton to see. Axton replied that he would be very glad to see the man, if Trant would make an appointment. In three quarters of an hour at the Axton home, Trant answered; and forty minutes later, having first telephoned young

---

[9] A train on the Union Pacific Railway, it originally ran from San Francisco to Omaha; the route was later extended to Chicago.

Caryl, Trant with his watchman, escorting a stranger who was broad-shouldered, weasel-eyed, of peculiarly alert and guarded manner, reached the Axton doorstep. Caryl had so perfectly timed his arrival, under Trant's instructions, that he joined them before the bell was answered.

Trant and Caryl, leaving the stranger under guard of the watchman in the hall, found Miss Waldron and Axton in the morning-room.

"Ah! Mr. Caryl again?" said Axton sneeringly. "Caryl was certainly not the man you wanted me to see, Trant!"

"The man is outside," the psychologist replied. "But before bringing him in for identification I thought it best to prepare Miss Waldron, and perhaps even more particularly you, Mr. Axton, for the surprise he is likely to occasion."

"A surprise?" Axton scowled questioningly. "Who is the fellow?—or rather, if that is what you have come to find out from me, where did you get him, Trant?"

"That is the explanation I wish to make," Trant replied, with his hand still upon the knob of the door, which he had pushed shut behind him. "You will recall, Mr. Axton, that there were but four men whom we know to have been in Cairo, Calcutta, and Cape Town at the same time you were. These were Lawler, your servant Beasley, the German Schultz, and the American Walcott. Through the Seric Medicine Company I have positively located Walcott; he is now in Australia. The Nord Deutscher Lloyd has given me equally positive assurance regarding Schultz. Schultz is now in Bremen. Miss Waldron has accounted for Beasley, and the Charing Cross Hospital corroborates her; Beasley is in London. There remains, therefore, the inevitable conclusion

that either there was some other man following Mr. Axton—some man whom Mr. Axton did not see—or else that the man who so pried into Mr. Axton's correspondence abroad and into your letters, Miss Waldron, this last week here in Chicago, was—Lawler; and this I believe to have been the case."

"Lawler?" the girl and Caryl echoed in amazement, while Axton stared at the psychologist with increasing surprise and wonder. "Lawler?"

"Oh! I see," Axton all at once smiled contemptuously. "You believe in ghosts, Trant—you think it is Lawler's ghost that Miss Waldron saw!"

"I did not say Lawler's ghost," Trant replied, a little testily. "I said Lawler's self, in flesh and blood. I am trying to make it plain to you," Trant took from his pocket the letters the girl had given him four days before and indicated the one describing the wreck, "that I believe the man whose death you so minutely and carefully describe here in this letter as Lawler, was not Lawler at all!"

"You mean to say that I didn't know Lawler?" Axton laughed loudly—"Lawler, who had been my companion in sixteen thousand miles of travel?"

Trant turned as though to reopen the door into the hall; then paused once more and kindly faced the girl.

"I know, Miss Waldron," he said, "that you have believed that Mr. Lawler has been dead these six weeks; and it is only because I am so certain that the man who is to be identified here now will prove to be that same Lawler that I have thought best to let you know in advance."

He threw open the door, and stood back to allow the Irish watchman to enter, preceded by the weasel-faced stranger. Then he closed the door quickly behind him, locked it, put the key in his pocket, and spun swiftly to see the effect of the stranger upon Axton.

That young man's face, despite his effort to control it, flushed and paled, flushed and went white again; but neither to Caryl nor the girl did it look at all like the face of one who saw a dead friend alive again.

"I do not know him!" Axton's eyes glanced quickly, furtively about. "I have never seen him before! Why have you brought him here? This is not Lawler!"

"No; he is not Lawler," Trant agreed; and at his signal the Irishman left his place and went to stand behind Axton. "But you know him, do you not? You have seen him before! Surely I need not recall to you this special officer Burns of the San Francisco detective bureau! That is right; you had better keep hold of him, Sullivan; and now, Burns, who is this man? Do *you* know *him*? Can you tell us who he is? "

"Do I know him?" the detective laughed. "Can I tell you who he is? Well, rather! That is Lord George Albany, who got into Claude Shelton's boy in San Francisco for $30,000 in a card game; that is Mr. Arthur Wilmering, who came within a hair of turning the same trick on young Stuyvesant in New York; that—first and last—is Mr. George Lawler himself, who makes a specialty of cards and rich men's sons!"

"Lawler? George Lawler?" Caryl and the girl gasped again.

"But why, in this affair, he used his own name," the detective continued, "is more than I can see; for surely he shouldn't have minded another change."

"He met Mr. Howard Axton in London," Trant suggested, "where there was still a chance that the card cheating in the Sussex guards was not forgotten, and he might at any moment meet someone who recalled his face. It was safer to tell Axton all about it, and protest innocence."

"Howard Axton?" the girl echoed, recovering herself at the name. "Why, Mr. Trant; if this is Mr. Lawler, as this man says and you believe, then where is Mr. Axton—oh, where is Howard Axton?"

"I am afraid, Miss Waldron," the psychologist replied, "that Mr. Howard Axton was undoubtedly lost in the wreck of the *Gladstone*. It may even have been the finding of Howard Axton's body that this man described in that last letter."

"Howard Axton drowned! Then this man—"

"Mr. George Lawler's specialty being rich men's sons," said the psychologist, "I suppose he joined company with Howard Axton because he was the son of Nimrod Axton. Possibly he did not know at first that Howard had been disinherited, and he may not have found it out until the second Mrs. Axton's death, when the estate came to Miss Waldron, and she created a situation which at least promised an opportunity. It was in seeking this opportunity, Miss Waldron, among the intimate family affairs revealed in your letters to Howard Axton that Lawler was three times seen by Axton in his room, as described in the first three letters that you showed to me. That was it, was it not, Lawler?"

The prisoner—for the attitude of Sullivan and Burns left no doubt now that he was a prisoner—made no answer.

"You mean, Mr. Trant," the eyes of the horrified girl turned from Lawler as though even the sight of him shamed her, "that if Howard Axton had not been drowned, this—this man would have come anyway?"

"I cannot say what Lawler's intentions were if the wreck had not occurred," the psychologist replied. "For you remember that I told you that this attempted crime has been most wonderfully assisted by circumstances. Lawler, cast ashore from the wreck of the *Gladstone*, found himself—if the fourth of these letters is to be believed—identified as Howard Axton, even before he had regained consciousness, by your stolen letters to Howard which he had in his pocket. From that time on he did not have to lift a finger, beyond the mere identification of a body—possibly Howard Axton's—as his own. Howard had left America so young that identification here was impossible unless you had a portrait; and Lawler undoubtedly had learned from your letters that you had no picture of Howard. His own picture, published in the *News* over Howard's name, when it escaped identification as Lawler, showed him that the game was safe and prepared you to accept him as Howard without question. He had not even the necessity of counterfeiting Howard's writing, as Howard had the correspondent's habit of using a typewriter. Only two possible dangers threatened him. First, was the chance that, if brought in contact with the police, he might be recognized. You can understand, Miss Waldron, by his threats to prevent your consulting them, how anxious he was to avoid this. And second, that there might be something in Howard Axton's letters to you which, if unknown to him, might lead him to compromise and betray himself in his relations with you. His sole mistake was that, when he attempted to search your desk for these letters, he clumsily adopted once more the same disguise that had proved so perplexing to Howard Axton. For he could have done nothing that would have been more terrifying

to you. It quite nullified the effect of the window he had fixed to prove by the man's means of exit and entrance that he was not a member of the household. It sent you, in spite of his objections and threats, to consult me; and, most important of all, it connected these visits at once with the former ones described in Howard's letters, so that you brought the letters to me—when, of course, the nature of the crime, though not the identity of the criminal, was at once plain to me."

"I see it was plain; but was it merely from these letters—these typewritten letters, Mr. Trant?" cried Caryl incredulously.

"From those alone, Mr. Caryl," the psychologist smiled slightly, "through a most elementary, primer fact of psychology. Perhaps you would like to know, Lawler," Trant turned, still smiling, to the prisoner, "just wherein you failed. And, as you will probably never have another chance such as the one just past for putting the information to practical use—even if you were not, as Mr. Burns tells me, likely to retire for a number of years from active life—I am willing to tell you."

The prisoner turned on Trant his face—now grown livid—with an expression of almost superstitious questioning.

"Did you ever happen to go to a light opera with Howard Axton, Mr. Lawler," asked Trant, "and find after the performance that you remembered all the stage-settings of the piece but could not recall a tune—you know you cannot recall a tune, Lawler—while Axton, perhaps, could whistle all the tunes but could not remember a costume or a scene? Psychologists call that difference between you and Howard Axton a difference in 'memory types.' In an almost masterly manner you imitated the style, the tricks and turns of expression of Howard Axton in your letter to Miss Waldron describing the wreck—not quite so well in the statement you dictated in my office. But you could not imitate the primary difference of Howard Axton's mind from yours. That was where you failed.

"The change in the personality of the letter writer might easily have passed unnoticed, as it passed Miss Waldron, had not the letters fallen into the hands of one who, like myself, is interested in the manifestations of mind. For different minds are so constituted that inevitably their processes run more easily along certain channels than along others. Some minds have a preference, so to speak, for a particular type of impression; they remember a sight that they have seen, they forget the sound that went with it; or they remember the sound and forget the sight. There are minds which are almost wholly ear-minds or eye-minds. In minds of the visual, or eye, type, all thoughts and memories and imaginations will consist of ideas of sight; if of the auditory type, the impressions of sound predominate and obscure the others.

"The first three letters you handed me, Miss Waldron," the psychologist turned again to the girl, "were those really written by Howard Axton. As I read through them I knew that I was dealing with what psychologists call an auditory mind. When, in ordinary memory, he recalled an event he remembered best its sounds. But I had not finished the first page of the fourth letter when I came upon the description of the body lying on the sand—a visual memory so clear and so distinct, so perfect even to the pockets distended with sand, that it startled and amazed me—for it was the first distinct visual memory I had found. As I read on I became certain that the man who had written the first three letters—who described a German as guttural and remem-

bered the American as nasal—could never have written the fourth. Would that first man—the man who recalled even the sound of his midnight visitor's shoulders when they rubbed against the wall—fail to remember in his recollection of the shipwreck the roaring wind and roaring sea, the screams of men and women, the crackling of the fire? They would have been his clearest recollection. But the man who wrote the fourth letter recalled most clearly that the sea was white and frothy, the men were pallid and staring!"

"I see! I see!" Caryl and the girl cried as, at the psychologist's bidding, they scanned together the letters he spread before them.

"The subterfuge by which I destroyed the second letter of the set, after first making a copy of it—"

"You did it on purpose? What an idiot I was!" exclaimed Caryl.

"Was merely to obviate the possibility of mistake," Trant continued, without heeding the interruption. "The statement this man dictated, as it was given in terms of 'sight,' assured me that he was not Axton. When, by means of the telegraph, I had accounted for the present whereabouts of three of the four men he might possibly be, it became plain that he must be Lawler. And finding that Lawler was badly wanted in San Francisco, I asked Mr. Burns to come on and identify him.

"And the stationing of the watchman here was a blind also, as well as his report of the man who last night tried to force the window?" Caryl exclaimed.

Trant nodded. He was watching the complete dissolution of the swindler's effrontery. Trant had appreciated that Lawler had let him speak on uninterrupted as though, after the psychologist had shown his hand, he held in reserve cards to beat it. But his attempt to sneer and scoff and contemn was so weak, when the psychologist was through, that Ethel Waldron—almost as though to spare him—arose and motioned to Trant to tell her, whatever else he wished, in the next room.

Trant followed her a moment obediently; but at the door he seemed to recollect himself.

"I think there is nothing else now, Miss Waldron," he said, "except that I believe I can spare you the reopening of your family affairs here. Burns tells me there is more than enough against him in California to keep Mr. Lawler there for some good time. I will go with him, now," and he stood aside for Caryl to go, in his place, into the next room.

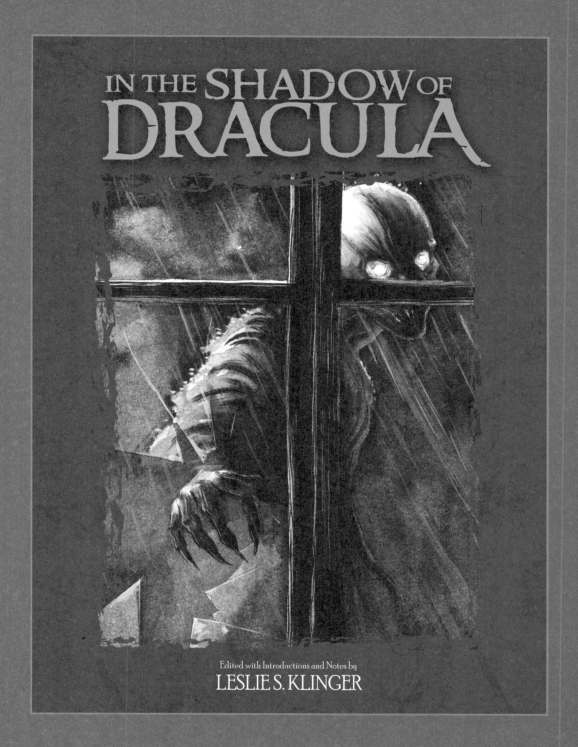

IN THE SHADOW OF DRACULA

Edited with Introductions and Notes by

LESLIE S. KLINGER

Also Available from IDW Publishing

Classic Vampyre Fiction 1819-1914